ADVOCATE

D1570973

BOOKS BY DANIEL M. FORD

THE WARDEN SERIES
The Warden
Necrobane
Advocate

ADVOCATE

DANIEL M. FORD

TOR PUBLISHING GROUP
NEW YORK

This is a work of fiction. All of the characters, organizations, and events portrayed in this novel are either products of the author's imagination or are used fictitiously.

ADVOCATE

Copyright © 2025 by Daniel M. Ford

All rights reserved.

Map by Jennifer Hanover

A Tor Book
Published by Tom Doherty Associates / Tor Publishing Group
120 Broadway
New York, NY 10271

www.torpublishinggroup.com

Tor® is a registered trademark of Macmillan Publishing Group, LLC.

The Library of Congress Cataloging-in-Publication Data is available upon request.

ISBN 978-1-250-81573-6 (trade paperback)
ISBN 978-1-250-81572-9 (ebook)

Our books may be purchased in bulk for promotional, educational, or business use. Please contact your local bookseller or the Macmillan Corporate and Premium Sales Department at 1-800-221-7945, extension 5442, or by email at MacmillanSpecialMarkets@macmillan.com.

First Edition: 2025

Printed in the United States of America

0 9 8 7 6 5 4 3 2 1

For Westley, Editor-Cat-Emeritus, 2004–2023,
who sat with me, on me, or at my feet
for uncounted hours as I worked.

I miss you so much, buddy.

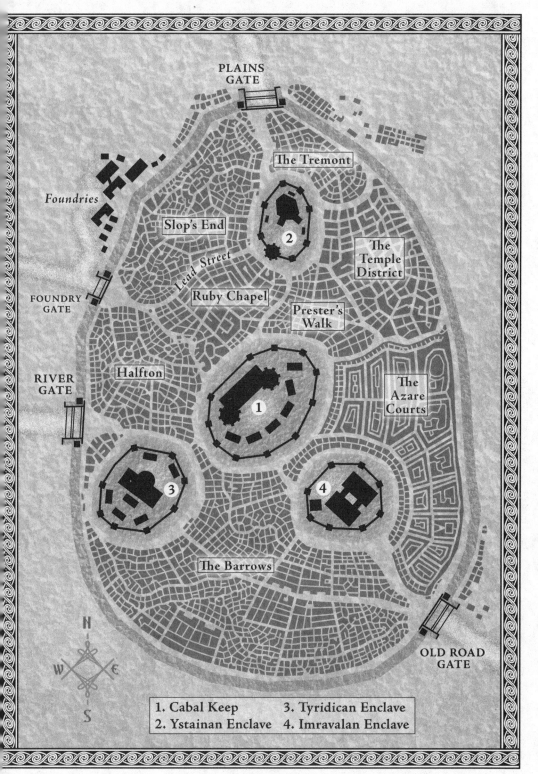

PLAINS
GATE

The Tremont

Foundries

Slop's End

2

The
Temple
District

Lead Street

FOUNDRY
GATE

Ruby Chapel

Prester's
Walk

Halfton

1

The
Azare
Courts

RIVER
GATE

3

4

The Barrows

N
W E
S

OLD ROAD
GATE

1. Cabal Keep   3. Tyridican Enclave
2. Ystainan Enclave 4. Imravalan Enclave

The City of
LASCENISE

ADVOCATE

1

REUNION

Aelis's breath caught in her throat as she rounded a turn and saw a lean, hooded figure watching her from beneath a spreading pine. She wasn't sure if she had entered the valley proper yet, as she'd last seen it in the early grip of winter, and the geography had been somewhat obscured.

But there was no mistaking the grace of the figure that watched her for a moment, then turned away and disappeared, nor the braid of deep red hair that swung down over her shoulder.

Aelis felt a fist squeeze her heart. To gather herself, she slipped from her saddle and took both her mount's and the packhorse's reins in one hand and led them forward.

Past the stand of pines, she saw the hall and the cluster of outbuildings she knew and dreaded and the tall shape she longed for leaning in the doorway.

Aelis and her two animals stopped a yard or two from the doorway, clouds of dust rising from the grass behind them.

"Been a while." The voice in the shadowed doorway creaked with disuse.

"I'm sorry," Aelis said. "But I came bearing gifts."

"Is one of them is a scroll or an amulet or some other piece of magic fuckery that can get me out of here?"

"Not yet," Aelis said. She wanted to whisper the words, murmur them in shame, but forced herself to look straight at the figure and speak to her directly. "But . . . some of it might make the time pass more pleasantly."

Maurenia took a step forward from the log wall of Rhunival's Hall—Maurenia's Hall now, Aelis supposed—and slid her hood down. Her hair was long, longer than Aelis had ever seen it, and plaited into a braid that rested over one shoulder. This new style left little doubt of her half-elven heritage, showing off the pointed tips of her ears. Aelis had known her to prefer to keep them obscured.

"There's no one here to see them." Maurenia's eyes, a pure crystal blue, bored hard into Aelis.

Can she hear my thoughts here? No. She just read my eyes, Aelis thought. She had a hard time peeling herself away from Maurenia's look, and not just for the usual reasons that she was the most beautiful woman Aelis knew and that she was badly, stupidly in love with her.

But because those blue eyes carried an accusation that Aelis, for all her abjurer's power, couldn't deflect or evade.

"Well," Maurenia said, "are you going to stand there or are you going to explain what you meant about making the time pass?"

Aelis tore herself away, went to a wicker basket strapped to the pack-horse, and untied the knot that held it shut. "A twelve of Tirravalan orange, for a start," she said, slipping a heavy glass bottle free of the basket.

When she turned around, Maurenia was a half-step behind her, not having made a sound closing the distance. Before Aelis could say another word, the half-elf slipped her arm around Aelis's waist and drew her close.

Aelis did not *quite* drop the bottle of wine, but she came closer than she ever had, sober. Maurenia filled her entire being as they kissed; her scent, the touch of her hand and her lips, the feeling of their bodies pressed together.

"I'm still angry," Maurenia said a few heated moments later. "Don't think for a moment that I'm not. I will be angry until the day you get me out of here, and for quite some time after that."

"I know," Aelis said, leaning her head on Maurenia's shoulder. "You have every right to be."

"Please tell me there's tea on that animal," Maurenia said, stepping away but keeping hold of Aelis's free hand.

"Some of Tun's herbal concoction. Which is better than tea anyway."

"Elisima's *ass*, but what you know about what is and isn't tea couldn't be pinned to a card," Maurenia sniffed. "Still, that's better than nothing. Whatever Rhunival left behind ran out and I can't figure out how to re-create it."

"Come on," Aelis said. "Let's get the packhorse unloaded, and . . ."

"*You* can get the packhorse unloaded," Maurenia said, flashing a dangerous smile. "*I'm* going to have a bath. If you hurry, the water might still be hot enough when you can join me."

✦ ✦ ✦

Maurenia had changed Rhunival's Hall in subtle ways. There was no clutter, for one; no tools or crockery sitting unused on a table. Everything was in its place. A new hearth was half constructed along the far wall, a planned replacement for the central fire pit and open ceiling. As Aelis stacked boxes, baskets, and parcels upon the empty table, she took a careful look about and realized that there was a weapon to hand within two quick steps of *anywhere* in the hall. A sharp woodaxe hanging on one wall, a too-long-for-kitchen-work knife on another, a heavy club with metal studs worked into its knob sitting handle-up right by the doorway.

"Who exactly is she expecting to fight?" Aelis muttered as she pulled more bottles free from a wicker pannier. "Or what?" The place didn't feel like Maurenia's entirely, not yet, but given another year it would be thoroughly transformed.

It will not be that long. I swear it won't. Aelis didn't dare say those words aloud, fearful that some lingering woodshade's magic might twist or bind them.

Maurenia rejoined her as she was unsaddling the horses and wondering what to do with them. Wearing only a long robe and sandals, her hair wet and dark around her neck, Maurenia went to the animals and stroked their faces. Both sets of ears turned to her, and she leaned close to them, murmuring quietly first to the one Aelis had ridden, and then to the stouter packhorse.

"Let them roam," she said, "unbridled. They won't leave m . . . the valley."

* * *

Aelis didn't *want* to mentally catalog the ways her lover had changed since her magical confinement in the wilderness had begun in early winter. But she was a necromancer, an anatomist, and observing and recording things was part of who she was. There'd be no overt physical changes, no gain in height or change of eye color or the like. Her skin had more sun in it, and her hair as well; *both were incredibly fetching on a woman whose appeal was untamed to begin with,* Aelis thought. Her scent was different; stronger and more redolent of wood, smoke, and sun. But most notably she was stronger and somehow *wilder,* a fact brought into stark relief as Aelis lay gasping on blankets spread across a bed of pine needles under the spreading shade of trees behind the hall. Maurenia was sitting up, working open the bottle of wine they'd taken outside with them as the afternoon wore on toward evening.

Aelis was not quite yet capable of sitting up, so she contemplated Maurenia's back.

And noted instantly that scars she'd seen on her lover's shoulder blades had vanished.

She sat straight up and laid her hand on Maurenia's back. Startled, the half-elf whirled around.

"I'm sorry," Aelis said. "But . . . you had scars there."

"Everyone on a ship takes a falling block or a whipping rope end at some point . . ." Maurenia grabbed at one of the blankets and tried to pull it over herself.

"*Had,* Maurenia. They're gone."

"If you go running for ink and paper to make a study of me, this is going to be a short visit."

"I'm not going to do that," Aelis said. *Not where you can see, anyway,* she thought. "We did talk about you making notes, testing limits, that kind of thing."

"We also talked about you devoting your days to figuring out how to get me out of this fucking imprisonment, but I haven't heard any plans." Maurenia stood up and stalked inside, leaving Aelis to gather the blanket and hurry after her.

"I found something," Aelis said. *And gods, but I am hoping you can read it.* She went to her baggage and pulled out a soft linen bundle wrapped with leather cordage. She unwrapped it and let the linen fall open, revealing the book the Errithsuns had brought her.

Maurenia looked at the book sharply, focusing on it immediately, her eyes sparking in the firelight inside her hall. "What is it?"

"I don't know. But . . ." Handling the cracked leaves carefully, Aelis flipped the pages one at a time, the dense, confusing characters blurring. She stopped on the illustration of the rod she had retrieved for Rhunival from the vaults beneath Mahlhewn Keep.

"We've seen that before. Now, what the fuck does any of this say?"

So much for that. Aelis felt yet another flicker of hope snuffed out like a candle after a formal dinner. "I haven't any idea."

"Don't you wizards have some way to translate any writing? That'd be the first spell I'd invent."

"It isn't that simple; a very powerful diviner can do some things with speech they're *hearing,* but if you have no frame of reference for the written language . . . and I sure as seventy-seven hells do not . . . you're just as stuck as anyone else."

"So, you have a book that's all about the bastard spirit that bound me, but you don't know what it says or, and please tell me if I'm wrong on this point, where to find anyone who can."

"Well, that last point may be about to change. That's one of the reasons I've come," Aelis said. She decided to seize the moment and pressed on. "I'm going south. To Lascenise."

"Thought your post in Lone Pine was for two years," Maurenia said. She finally worked the wine bottle open and held it out after taking a drink. Aelis grasped the cool, heavy bottle but didn't drink.

"It is. But I've been assigned as an advocate to another warden accused of serious crimes."

"So that's all it takes to get out of an assignment you hate? Get an old professor with some pull to put a word in?" Maurenia snatched the bottle and took another drink.

"He's accused of assault and murder by magic, and if I fail as his advocate, he'll likely be put to death. It's not a responsibility I asked for, but I can't refuse it."

"So you're a lawyer as well as a wizard now?"

Aelis took the bottle from Maurenia's hand and had her first sip of the orange wine, letting its bold fruit linger in her mouth, its slight coolness matching the sweat drying on her skin.

"No. He'll have a lawyer as well. An advocate is . . . well, hard to explain. Tradition of the warden service, really; a warden accused of magical crimes can have another warden act as an investigator to prove their innocence."

"That sounds an awful lot like wardens tilting Stregon's Scales for themselves," Maurenia said. "I shouldn't be surprised, but here I am."

Aelis's immediate instinct was to protest that description, but even as she opened her mouth to do so she found that the words didn't come. *It does seem that way,* she wanted to say, *but . . .* Only nothing after the "but" would come to her. She covered it up by rewrapping the delicate book in its linen and carefully tying the package closed.

"Regardless, I have to leave, and soon. But the good news, if there is any, is that I'll be a half day's ride from the Lyceum, and the man I'm defending is the most determined and resourceful warden alive. If *anyone* will have solid ideas of how to proceed in getting you out of here, he will. Not to mention the libraries and expertise of the other wizards I'll be able to draw on. Someone down there will know how to read this."

Maurenia contemplated the bottle. "How long before you have to leave?"

"As soon as I return to Lone Pine, the wardens they sent to collect me will want me to go. One will stay behind in my stead. The other is my escort."

"And how long will you be gone?"

"I can't begin to predict that. I have no idea how long the case will take or what I'll have to do in the role. It's not like I've been an advocate before."

"Why'd this warden ask for you?"

"He likely didn't. Probably a random lot."

"Who is he, anyway, this 'determined and resourceful' legend, hrm? Some broad-chested sword-swinging hero, square of jaw and sharp of eye?"

"He's thrice my age, shorter than me, and meaner than a badger in a trap." Aelis stood up. "Let's not focus on the fact that I'm leaving until I do. *Have* you made any notes I can bring with me?"

"No," Maurenia said. "But while you get dinner ready, I'll draw you a map of the valley and mark the spots where I cannot go farther."

"I'm not really much of a cook," Aelis said.

"Aelis, I have been eating mushrooms, smoked fish, oats, and eggs in varying combinations since the middle of winter. If you can put cheese and bread on a fucking plate it will seem a feast."

While Maurenia drew, Aelis did indeed arrange cheese and bread on a plate. By the time Aelis cleared her throat to signal that food was ready, Maurenia had filled a page, but she didn't stop. She worked straight through, silently, eating whatever Aelis brought to her. Her face was fierce in its concentration as her pen scratched hard across the paper. At last the map was completed, but she'd set the sheet out of Aelis's reach and was now producing line after line of small, regular handwriting. The plate held only crumbs by the time she'd finished and set two closely written sheets aside. Aelis stepped around her to reach for them but Maurenia barred her with a hand.

"No."

"But . . ."

"Aelis, if you look at that map and read those notes now, you will devil me with questions until you fall asleep, and I won't have it." Maurenia stood and snatched up the papers, folding them into a neat square. "I don't suppose you brought any wax, so put these away somewhere. Inside a saddlebag or your medical kit." She held the folded square out. "Do not let me find you looking at these until you're gone, hear me? Till you are back in Lone Pine, in your goddamn tower. If I do, I'll bar you from finding the hall again."

"You wouldn't," Aelis blurted out, but only because she sensibly stopped herself from asking, *Can you do that?*

"No," Maurenia said, the sternness melting out of her sharp features. "But I'd keep you looking for a few hours."

Aelis put the papers, as instructed, inside her medical kit, and tried, without much success, to put them from her mind.

Hours later, with the blankets thrown off inside the darkened hall, Aelis felt herself giving in to sleep but was awoken as Maurenia rolled away and stood.

"Will you not sleep?" Aelis muttered, unable to put a stop to the question.

"I can," Maurenia said, "but I'd rather not. No more questions." She bent over the bed and ran a hand through Aelis's hair and down her cheek to her neck. Aelis tried to capture Maurenia's hand but the other woman and the world both rolled away from her grasp like fog.

2

DEPARTURES

Aelis's dreams were troubled. At times there was what ought to have been a great peaceful forest, towering pines and beds of needles underfoot, but no path led her out. The trunks shifted to bar her way whatever direction she chose. Something in her sought to command them, to issue orders as a warden ought, to cut a path through them with sword and ward if she had to, but this came to nothing; wisps of shadow kept her sword in its scabbard and the will and the language to summon her wards would not come.

These dreams were broken by dreams of water, of a great flowing tide leading to a bay or a sea where no land was visible in any direction, not that she would've recognized it if it had been.

It was in one of the latter dreams that sunlight parted the clouds and Aelis thought to take her bearings by it, and by whatever moons it might reflect upon.

Aelis woke with a start. Sunlight flowed into the hall through the opening in its thatch and brought Aelis back to the solid world. She sat up and swung her feet onto the cool floor, and saw Maurenia staring at her from the table.

"Thought you were an early riser."

"By habit, not inclination," Aelis said. "How late is it?"

"No more than an hour till midday, you soft-handed city dweller." Maurenia smiled, and though brief, the sight was nearly as good to wake up to as coffee.

The fact that her very next thought was about the hours she'd lost and how she needed to leave soon sapped some of her rising energy.

"I've already called the horses back," Maurenia said. "They're saddled and wait for packing."

"Kicking me out of your bed the moment I wake, eh?"

"If it was an eider-down in a fine tavern, or even the lumpy straw in your tower, I wouldn't let you out of it. But . . . ." There were so many things that could've followed, that *but* and Aelis didn't want to face any of them.

"Maurenia, I will conclude my business as an advocate as fast as I can. And I won't come back without answers. I won't."

"You had damned well better not. Come, eat," Maurenia said. "I boiled eggs. But I'm not serving you any of the tea you brought because your effete southerner's palate won't appreciate it," she added with a sniff.

Aelis looked to where her traveling medical kit remained strapped shut, thinking not of the folded pages but the instruments and medicines inside.

After what Maurenia had said the night before, though, she decided against pressing her for an examination, and hauled it out of the hall to lash it to the packhorse's frame saddle.

Breakfast passed entirely too quickly, as did the packing. They kept brushing against each other and pausing without giving way to words, much less passion. *Don't trust myself if I started kissing her now,* Aelis thought at one such moment, as they paused hip to hip and arm to arm, leaning against each other for a brief moment as they reached for the same empty saddlebag.

Once Aelis was packed and ready to take up her animals' leads again, they came together in one last embrace.

"Aelis," Maurenia said, "just listen and do not speak, no matter how hard you of all people will find that. I fear that given a few more seasons here I may not be able to leave. I may not even *want* to. If it comes to that, understand that I am not myself anymore. I will not be Maurenia Angra then. I'll be something else, wearing my skin like a suit. I do not want to end that way. Say that you understand me. Say nothing else, because if you don't understand, then I am nothing to you."

"I understand," Aelis croaked out, through the pounding of blood and angry protest in her ears and her head. "It will not come to that." *I will lay waste to this entire fucking forest if it does.*

"Then go. Come back with answers. Or at least better fucking guesses."

Aelis mounted and took up the packhorse's lead. She walked the animal twenty yards at best before turning to look back. She could not find the opening of the clearing where the hall stood, nor a trace of Maurenia.

◆   ◆   ◆

"Haring off into the woods for days at a time is unconscionable behavior from a warden under strict orders!" Amadin's voice carried over the background noise of midday eating and drinking in Rus and Martin's inn at the crossroads in Lone Pine. "And so much the worse that you refuse to account for yourself."

"I owe you no account for seeing to business under the orders of an Archmagister of the Lyceum," Aelis said coolly, a heavy clay mug of small beer, piney and resinous, lifted halfway to her lips. *I wonder how badly I could break his nose with this,* she thought as she studied the pinched, mean face of the elf seated across the table from her. *Probably at least one of his cheeks; quite a bit of danger to the eyesocket then, though, and I can't go blinding a fellow warden.*

"I have half a mind to clap you in irons and march you straight through the village green and into the damned coach!"

Slowly, Aelis set the mug down, the temptation to bounce it off the elf's face entirely too strong.

Silence fell in the taproom. Aelis kept her eyes locked on the quivering point of the elf's nose. Benches and chairs scraped the floor as villagers stood.

None of them had gone for the row of staves, unstrung bows, and other implements that leaned on a rack by the door—yet. She should discourage them, but she found she didn't quite want to.

The door swung open and heavy footfalls made their way to her table, though Aelis knew the man making them could have been as silent as wind-blown grass if he had a mind to.

"I would keep it at *half* a mind, were I you," Tun whispered, bending to lean over Amadin's chair. Touching seven feet in height and as broad across as most any two men, Tunbridge would loom over most people whether he intended to or not.

But the way he spread his arms, with one hand on the back of Amadin's chair and the other grasping the table, left no doubt that he was, in fact, looming to the fullest. And it was not lost on the other warden.

"Now, Tun," Aelis said, "I'm sure my colleague here did not mean to use any words he'd regret. And as my business in the north is now concluded . . . well, as it is now paused pending further development," she added, for Tun's sake rather than Amadin's, "I will be ready to leave as soon as I can pack and discuss some local matters with Rhovel."

"I'm sure Rhovel has been briefed on . . ."

"Not on local conditions by someone who has been here for months and dealt with two crises in that time. We will set off at first light tomorrow, Amadin."

His mouth grew so pinched Aelis expected his cheeks to hollow out. He looked like a man who wanted to say more but decided it'd be a waste of his time, so he stomped off.

Tun slid into the seat Amadin vacated.

"You know I have a weeks-long carriage ride ahead with him," Aelis said. "I can't have him too frightened."

"Well, as I will not be in the carriage with you, he will not have anything to be frightened about, eh?" Tun smiled around the tusks that marked his half-orc heritage. "What do you think of this replacement, Rhovel?"

"Dimly remember him as a year ahead of me in the Colleges of Abjuration and Necromancy," Aelis said. She waved a hand dismissively in the air. "Part of the faceless crowd who weren't powerful enough, clever enough, or good looking enough to hold my attention."

"That . . . paints a picture of the younger Aelis," Tun said, carefully.

"The fact that he's a temporary warden, well . . ." She finally had a sip of the sour beer she'd hardly touched. "Let's say he isn't marked for great things, and I didn't miss much by not being his friend." Aelis took another sip, glanced at the remains of her midday meal and, finding that she had no stomach left for it, and stood up. Tun looked at her, then at her plate, then back to her.

"That is very unlike you," he said, before making the remains of cheese, bread, and smoked fish disappear into one of the pockets of his fringed buck-skin jacket.

"Walk with me to the Tower, Tun?"

"Of course, Aelis."

She took the plate and cup to the counter at the back of the taproom where Rus was wiping ineffectually at the watermarks on his wood, and set them down followed by a small stack of coins.

"Keep your money, Warden," Rus said. "It's only part of our contract."

"As of tomorrow morning, I won't be your warden, Rus. Call it a payment for breakfast, then."

Rus sniffed, didn't touch the money, and went back to his polishing at another end of the bar.

Outside, she and Tun fell into an easy walking pace, him shortening his stride just enough to accommodate the longest steps she could take without looking ridiculous. Once they had left the village behind, Tun broke the silence.

"How is she?"

"As well as could be expected, which is to say, not very well at all. Well, that's a simplified . . . physically, she's fine. Better than fine. Old scars are gone."

Tun grunted. "That would be a useful sort of thing to have in one's back pocket, eh? Be bound to a spot of land while the old injuries work themselves out. Once you've sorted a way to be unbound, of course."

"You and I both know you heal just fine without the help of a woodshade's curse."

"Even a werebear feels the creak of joints when the weather drops."

"Tun, Maurenia told me she's afraid that if she stays there too long, she won't want to leave."

Tun frowned and Aelis knew the soft rumble from his throat meant he was thinking carefully on his next words.

"That is not like the Maurenia who came north with us."

"No," Aelis said. "It isn't."

"Will this task of yours allow you the time to research the question?"

"I will make certain that it does," Aelis replied.

"If you had to choose between the two," Tun asked, coming to a halt so suddenly that Aelis had to dance back two steps, "if you could only save your old mentor, or Maurenia, who would it be?"

"Don't ask me that, Tun."

Her friend only stared down at her.

"I will not sell Bardun Jacques short, and I will *not* leave Maurenia cursed and confined."

"You can never be said to lack confidence."

"Tun, in the months I've been here, I've unraveled plots hatched by a male-volent spirit attached to the past-their-date mortal remains of a legendary warden commander. I've cracked barrack-crypts full of undead, matched wits with a woodshade, commanded the power of the most sought-after artifact of my primary school, and ridden atop an undead construct made entirely of *teeth*. Why shouldn't I be confident?"

"You had help," Tun said.

"I did! Able help, in all cases, but the point I'm after here is . . . I located help and did all those things out here in the forest primeval, where I knew no one and nothing!" She threw her arms out to indicate the endless pine forest and cleared pastures, the foothills to the east, the mountains just visible to the north. "Imagine what I can do once I'm back in a city!"

"A city makes that much difference?"

"By Onoma's cold tits, of course it does! Cobbles under my feet and smoke in my nose, people *everywhere*, and other people watching them. Taverns, wine-sinks, inns, dining places, private clubs, smoke dens, not to mention the *shops*, Tun. And probably best of all . . . the libraries." She plucked at her robe and held a bit of the black material between two fingers. "This is all I need to get into any of them, no questions asked, no books barred to me . . . well, except the Forbidden Books in any of the various vaults, but what's the odds I'll need one of them?"

"Are you so eager to leave us, Aelis?"

She was not prepared for the surge of conflict she suddenly felt, because on the one hand, *of course she was*, and on the other, she had to save Maurenia, and on a third and possibly fourth hand there were any number of other matters around the village she felt responsible for. The child Phillipa had some kind of latent magical talent that needed schooling and direction. There was Pips's uncle Elmo, and Rus's husband Martin, both war-haunted men whom she was determined to help. She knew better than to lie to Tun, or even attempt to equivocate with him.

"I'm a city girl, Tun. I will always be that." She laid a hand on his arm. "But even the forest primeval has yielded better friends than I imagined. Better friends than I deserved."

"Bah," Tun said, suddenly turning away and walking a few more steps. Then he turned back and looked at her. "You will come back to us, yes? You're not simply going to hide in Lascenise until the remaining year and a bit are up."

"Oh, I think in Lascenise I couldn't manage more than a few months. If they were sending me to Antraval, however, it would take a crack team of wardens led by an Archmagister of Divination to dig me out."

"Stop it."

"If it were Tirraval, I could arrange it so they wouldn't even have legal *authority* to send me back."

That brought Tun up short. He peered down at her, steepling his heavy brows. "*How?*"

"*Welll*," Aelis said, shrugging, "murdering everyone between me and the office of Countess . . . my father, all my older siblings, possibly an uncle or aunt in the bargain . . . is stretching the definition of 'arrange.' But it's *theoretically* possible."

Tun could only laugh at that, and they walked in mirthful quiet till near her tower.

"I don't think I'll come down into the village in the morning. I fear those other wardens don't like me much."

"Can I ask a favor?"

"I don't like that Amadin, Aelis, but I won't kill him for you."

By now, Aelis knew him well enough to know that no matter how deadpan and serious that statement sounded, Tun was joking, so she pressed on.

"Will you keep an eye on Maurenia?"

"She does not strike me as needing a deal of looking after."

"I know. But she might want company. And I'll bet she's a better chess player than I am."

"Fine. One eye. Occasionally." There was a moment of tension as they both waited for one or the other to say something that might allow them to part.

"I'll come back, Tun."

"See that you do," he said, before abruptly turning away and heading for the treeline. Aelis watched him go, as was her habit, and tried to pinpoint the exact moment when he disappeared into the green dimness.

"Uncanny," she muttered as she failed, and turned up the stone walk into her tower.

Before she had reached the door, she heard a clattering of hooves. Without turning to look, as she opened the door, she casually threw a ward just behind her. She felt the impact as something hit it, the magic dissipated, and she shut the door in the face of a confused goat.

Very carefully, she set her medical case down on the main worktable, and only had to shove aside a few scattered papers, one plate of stale bread, two empty wine bottles, and a few other oddments to do so. She hung her swordbelt on the back of a chair, first testing the draw of the willow-leaf blade in its scabbard.

Since the day Dalius had ambushed her in her tower, months ago, she had never set her sword out of arm's reach.

"I will unpack my rucksack and do whatever other minor chores need doing before I read her notes," Aelis said aloud, determined to follow Maurenia's instructions and to have nothing else on her mind when she did.

So she set her rucksack down on her bed, untied the laces that bound the end closed, and began to carefully draw out items from within. She got to one pair of stockings, an extra shirt, and her sword-oil, stone, and rags before turning the whole thing upside down, dumping everything else onto her bed, and flying back to unbuckle the straps of her case.

She had to fish for the packet of papers, slid as it was between surgical instruments and expensive jars of medicines, liniments, and reagents. Only the fragility and cost of the items between her and the papers stopped her from dumping them out like she had her rucksack.

Well, that and the fact that any of the knives or bone saws could easily take off a fingertip, she thought, as the papers finally came into her grasp. She unfolded them slowly, cradling them carefully like a longed-for letter, and sat down.

The map clearly laid out Rhunival's Hall and buildings, had a fair compass in the top left corner, and a notation of scale in the bottom right.

"Always the engineer," Aelis murmured. Based on the scale, Maurenia couldn't go much farther than a mile in any direction, though it seemed closer to a mile and a half to the east.

Aelis got out a clean sheet of paper, pen, and ink, and noted that fact first. "I wish I'd taken Urizen's elective on Curses, the Making and Breaking Thereof," she said as she set the pen down, making sure not to let the nib rest against the page. "Oh, that'll never come up," she added, in a mocking singsong. "Curses are so passé, no one uses them anymore."

Still, she reasoned that any information could be useful. Maurenia's notes were direct and straightforward, no style, no editorial voice. Mostly a list of facts.

Days spent, and her changing perceptions of the flora and fauna around her. She had immediately been able to sense the number of animals of any given type within the little vale, as well as the kinds, numbers, and nature of the trees and mushrooms.

Now she was able to distinguish *individuals*, however, and had given some of them straightforward names *only to differentiate them for my own purposes,* she had written, *not out of attachment.* Given that the names were things like black-spots-tail for a doe and fourteen-point for a stag, and gray, brown, and red squirrels numbers one through fifteen each, Aelis was willing to believe that much.

The notes on the second page were rather more personal.

I no longer need to sleep, the second page began, *more than once every three days. I can, if I choose, but I don't unless I have to because who would choose sleep over activity, and because of the dreams I have. In them, trees keep me captive. I know that you will read this, Aelis, and say that my mind is simply translating the circumstances of my days. It is not. The trees are malevolent jailers, I am their prisoner, and when I sleep I have no defense against the way they claw at my mind.*

I am changing, and I know it. In my early days here I thought I would find hunting easy. I dreamed all the winter about taking deer, eating the liver fresh and hot, the dishes I would make with the choicest bits, how I would not waste even the offal, because I do not believe in waste. I even planned to make tools with the antlers if I took a buck.

I went hunting as soon as the weather allowed. First, I found the sport much diminished given that I could know where every animal was at any time.

Then I found that I could call an animal to me and compel *it to come. I did. I was ready to slit the throat of an old buck. And I could not do it. Not because it felt unsporting, though it did. But because the thought of shedding blood repulsed me. The idea of eating that flesh was abhorrent.*

I can manage eggs, and fish present no problem, nor do I have any influence over them. I think it is creatures of the woods that I cannot bring myself to touch. There are worse fates than never eating venison again, but it should be my choice to do so or not, and it does not feel like I can choose.

When you get me off this land, Aelis, if I never see another tree again, I will count it no loss. I long to go back to sea, where I spent some of my younger years, where the only wood is the good creaking timbers of a ship. I cling to my memories of the sea. Someday, and I hope it is not soon, the green dreams will take even that from me, and I will no longer be Maurenia Angra.

Here Maurenia's pen trailed off.

"I will ride back up there with a lumbering crew, clear cut in every direction for three miles, and burn the stumps out," Aelis said aloud. She lowered her head and curled her hand into so tight a fist her nails dug red lines into the palm.

The spirit of the place is not the trees, she thought. *Occupying the trees, perhaps. Speaking through them. But it is not the trees themselves, which are blameless.*

Aelis finished writing her own accounts and summations about Maurenia's state, her supposition that Rhunival had been a woodshade summoned and bound, probably by Dalius, as some kind of stratagem during the war. She took out that linen-wrapped stack of pages again and unwrapped them.

No matter how hard Aelis looked at the characters that covered those pages, they remained incomprehensible; they didn't even resemble any of the lettering systems she'd ever seen. If the pile of ragged leaves held any key for deciphering its own code, she couldn't find it.

The one thing this stack of loosely connected pages had was that drawing of the rod. Aelis felt she had a key, but no idea what door it opened. She looked at her own writing again. *Woodshade, bound by Dalius during the war as a weapon or tool of some kind.*

She'd never voiced the last part of that aloud, but it stood to reason. The magical rod that had bound him had been stored in the vault of Mahlhewn Keep, along with Aldayim's Matrix. There was also the fact that Rhunival had responded angrily to any suggestion that he was allied with Dalius.

"If Dalius hadn't bound him," Aelis continued, tapping the end of her pen against her writing desk, "Rhunival at least *knew* the name. Dalius must have been complicit in keeping him there."

Was Maurenia's imprisonment a trade for his escape? Revenge because Aelis had slighted him somehow?

"Well, I did threaten to destroy the rod he'd made me agree to find for him, after he'd made it possible to find it in the first place," she mused. "It was a stressful day, and I didn't have an excess of time."

Stop making excuses. The voice of a teacher, of many of them, cracked in her head like a whip. *Take responsibility.* It might've been Bardun Jacques, or Urizen. Probably both, if she was being honest.

She carefully collected Maurenia's notes, the book, and her own scribbles, wrapped them back in the linen, then wrapped that in some canvas she had for her official letters, sealed that with black wax, and set it aside.

She watched the wax cool and harden, then took a deep breath.

"Right," she said. "Rhovel's instructions."

+ + +

She had just about finished writing them out carefully when there was a polite knock at her door.

"Early for dinner," she murmured as she went to answer, only to find her replacement warden himself standing at her threshold.

Rhovel was only a couple of years older than her, with the unfortunate thick-cheeked, hangdog sort of face that would always look older than it was, and a hairline in hasty retreat. He wore blue robes, slashed with black, almost a counter to her own, and the sword at his side was shorter and broader than hers.

"Warden," he said, "as I understand I am to take up duties tomorrow, I thought we should finally talk."

"We should. I was just writing up some instructions." She waved him inside, pretending she didn't see the way he grimaced when she said "instructions."

"Have a seat," she said as she walked back into the workspace ahead of him, making sure to snatch up the folded notes from earlier and stuff the packet into her sleeve.

Rhovel's steps were hesitant and unsure. Then something caught his eye, and he dashed off to the far side of the room, near the hearth.

"A full-sized calcination oven? How on earth was one brought out here, to the end of civilization?" Then he laughed stiffly. "Well, I suppose when one's father is a count . . ."

Aelis had been fetching a bottle of wine, but she set it down and stared hard at him.

"Finish your thought, Warden," she said coldly.

"I'm sorry, it's just . . . it must have been enormously expensive."

"It was here when I arrived, though not in working order," Aelis said. "Took the help of the Lone Pine folk to put it right. It also might do you well to remember, Warden, that this was once the *middle* of civilization, and is still that, though it is not the one we are used to."

"Onoma's icy milk, tell me that *Aelis de Lenti* hasn't turned farmer on us," Rhovel said.

"Not for any money," Aelis said, smiling just a little. "I don't think it's a secret, even to these folk, that I would've preferred a post in Antraval. But it does us no good to always think out of step with the people we serve."

"The people we guard, you mean," Rhovel said.

"I know what I meant." Aelis decided she was going to have to open a bottle of wine whether she wanted to share it with him or not. She held out the bottle and said, "Care to do the honors?"

Whatever his faults, Rhovel didn't shrink from the small challenge. He took the bottle from her with one hand, drew his sword with the other, and swept the cork off in one confident motion. She took the bottle back and poured.

"What do you know of Dalius Enthal de Morgantis un Mahlgren?"

"Sounds like a name I ought to know. Famous warden? Had a chapter in *Lives of the Wardens* before he'd even died."

"Aye, well," she said, "I think he lived rather longer than anyone knew."

"What do you mean?"

"I mean that since I came here, I've killed him . . . or, to be more precise, something wearing his likeness . . . twice."

Rhovel paused with the glass halfway to his mouth, then sipped anyway before going on.

"If this is some sort of joke initiation, Aelis, I don't care for it."

"Rhovel, I am as serious as Lavanalla at sword drill right now. If you encounter anyone who claims to be Dalius, kill it as fast and as thoroughly as you can. I've detailed my encounters with him in the papers I'm leaving with you. I have very little wish to speak of them aloud."

She thought of her tower door thrown open, a blast of force tossing her away from her sword, a shard of glass shoved into her stomach and twisted up into her ribs. She winced and caught her breath.

"I think he's dead, for sure this time."

"Put a number on 'think,' if you would be so kind."

Aelis thought a moment. "Call it ninety percent." She declined to mention the spirit-trap inside the hastily built null-cage in a chest under her worktable that held whatever it was she'd pulled out of him just a few months ago. *I'm too afraid to examine it and find out what it is, and I'm not taking the trap out of the cage until it's inside a containment room and there's at least one other wizard I trust standing next to me.*

"The remaining ten percent is not nothing, Aelis."

"Which is why I'm warning you," she said. "As I said, there's more details in my report. There are a few other matters I've named; a couple of local veterans who're war-haunted. I've recommended the occasional enchantment to them. Well . . . one I've had to enforce it. The other has declined. The first, Elmo . . . he has been violent, under the influence of malign magic."

"Midarra's Mirrors, this is a busy posting, isn't it? And we all thought you were off to the end of the world to rot away for two years."

"We? All?"

"You know what gossip-shops the Colleges are," Rhovel said, waving a hand vaguely in the air. "A number of people were, well . . . let's call it amused to see someone so unhappy with their post."

Aelis had been able to keep a hold of her tongue and her anger until he added that, and she shot back, "Well, could've been worse. I could've started my career with no post at all, just cooling my heels in a barracks somewhere waiting to be thrown scraps."

Rhovel covered a flush in his cheeks by sipping his wine, staring at Aelis over the rim of the cup. She thought for a moment he was going to hold that stare long enough to demand an answer for her open insult.

His color subsided and the moment passed. Aelis picked up the packet she'd written out for him. "Now unless you have any questions, I need to pack . . ."

"Well, I need to familiarize myself with my tower and instruments," Rhovel protested. "Surely both can be done . . ."

"With your *temporary* tower and *borrowed* instruments," Aelis said. "And you do not occupy this tower until I say you do."

Once again Rhovel sought out her eyes, and Aelis was ready to keep and hold his stare and see if he decided to demand a test. But he turned away first and she held out the packet of papers.

"The people here will be slow to trust," she said, as he took them. "They only took to me because I sought out ways to make myself useful to their daily lives. If they don't trust you in the smaller things, they won't come to you for the larger. Get to know the innkeepers, Rus and Martin, and the wise woman Emilie . . ."

"Wise woman," Rhovel said, brows raised. "She trouble?"

"No," Aelis said. "Just be polite to her. She knows some of the basics of medicine and can be a great help, provided you stop her from bleeding or purging someone to balance their humors."

Rhovel nodded, swallowed the last of his wine, and didn't protest as Aelis ushered him out, papers in hand. With him gone and her door shut, bolted, and warded, she turned toward the two chests under her worktable, and thought about the most important things she had to pack.

◆   ◆   ◆

Aelis wouldn't let anyone else place her trunks on the roof of the carriage that was preparing to depart the village green the next morning. She climbed up on the fender and atop the box with each on her shoulder, surprising some of those in the crowd who were watching, but not many who'd come to know her well.

In truth, one trunk was quite light. But she didn't need anyone knowing what it held. Amadin was in such a hurry to leave, it was barely light by the time he'd harangued her all the way to the green. Still, there was a crowd to see her off, and Elmo and Otto had pushed to the front to hand up the rest of her baggage and see to stowing it themselves.

"Just a moment, Warden," she said to Amadin, who'd taken a seat on the board, reins in hand, and she climbed nimbly down before he could protest.

Aelis went straight to the smallest figure that stood apart from the rest of the crowd, the only child come to see her off.

"Pips," she said, reaching inside the voluminous sleeve of her traveling robe, where she'd stored a small packet. "Everything I need to say to you is written here. And the exercises in reading and writing that you need to keep up with."

"What if I can't read it all yet?" The girl reached up for the packet hesitantly. "I'm still learnin'."

"Then all the more reason to pay attention to the lessons. And don't forget the cyphering. That's just as important."

"But it's so *boring*," the girl whined.

Aelis squatted on one leg to put herself at eye level with the girl. "It is," she agreed. *No sense arguing with plain fact.* "Math is as boring as anything. But you *have* to know it, Pips. You have to have a grounding in it for a school to even consider you, and if you want to see if you can someday attend the Lyceum."

"My uncles say there's no coin to send me to any school anyway . . ."

"I couldn't pin down what your uncles know about schooling in general, and the Lyceum in particular, with my sharpest, finest needle," Aelis said. To Pips's laughter, she added, "Don't tell them I said that. But *do* tell them that if it comes to distant schooling, they shouldn't worry themselves about fees." Aelis had done so already, of course, but they clearly hadn't believed her on that score.

The mirth drained from Pips's face then, and she looked somberly up at Aelis.

"You're never going to come back, are you?"

"Of course I am," Aelis said, wounded but trying not to show it. *Why does everyone think I hate it so much here?*

Probably because I clearly hate it here? The answering thought was quickly dismissed.

"I will be gone for some months. But I'll have to come back here and finish my term. Nothing can release me from that."

"What if you get the chance, though, to go on and stay in one of the cities you love so much?"

"I won't," Aelis said. "I will come back. If nothing else, I'm leaving most of my clothes and my books and my orrery here. Attend to your lessons, mind the new warden, and write me letters."

"Can't afford to post 'em."

"Give them to Rus, and tell him I'll make good on the coin when I come back."

"Uncle Otto won't like that, says it comes to no good to owe anyone anything."

"He won't," Aelis agreed, resisting the urge to roll her eyes. *Now is not the time to tell her that a great deal of her uncle's problems comes from thinking like that.* "Now if I don't go, Warden Amadin may well throw some lightning at me."

"Can he do that?" Pips's eyes shot up. "I want to see . . ."

"I'd rather not get into a wizards' duel here in Lone Pine," Aelis said, standing up and giving the girl an awkward hug with one arm. Pips returned it in force, throwing her arms as tight as she could around Aelis's middle. Aelis groaned and gently eased away.

When she got to the wagon, Rus was holding up a wrapped packet and Amadin was refusing to listen to him.

"We're not a *post wagon*." The scorn in the voice would've been clear to anyone who could hear him, whether they shared a common tongue or not. "We're on warden business . . ."

Aelis took the packet from Rus. "I'll take it as a personal favor, Amadin. Rus and Martin more or less kept me alive with food in my first days here, and on no shortage of days since."

To Rus, she grinned. "Just a down payment on everything I owe." She climbed into the carriage before he could protest and banged on the roof with her hand, twice, if for no other reason than she knew it would infuriate Amadin to be treated like a coachman.

"Two hours only," he called, "then it'll be your turn."

The coach lurched into motion and Aelis was thrown back into the cushions of the seat for a moment. They were in fine shape, though; nothing less for a warden coach.

Once they were off the green and onto the road, more of a rutted track really, she felt the magic in it engage and the way became a great deal smoother. Not without a lurch here or there, given the state of the road, but soon enough the passage was so eased that she did the only thing she could imagine to pass the time.

She fell asleep.

+ + +

Aelis woke to a loud rapping on the side of the coach door and was less than thrilled to see Amadin grinning at her from the step.

"Have the country folk worn you so very ragged?"

Aelis snorted and shook the sleep from her head. Without an immediate crisis to hand she was having a hard time fighting herself awake, but she'd get there eventually.

"Believe it or not, even on this road a warden coach feels like the kind of luxury I'd forgotten all about."

Amadin snorted. "Well, by all means do go enjoy the luxury of powering the damn thing." He opened the door and gestured with mock gallantry for her to climb out.

Staring at him, Aelis opened the door on the other side and hopped down. She felt the coach lurch as he slid in.

She climbed up the fender and settled on the board, picking up the reins with one hand, and two silver-linked cords with the other.

"We shouldn't need the heat in the fenders," Amadin called from within. "So just the stabilizers will do."

Aelis followed the path of the two silver-leafed chains by running the links through her hands. Both disappeared inside the wood of the coach beneath her, into separate holes; one was marked with a carving of a flame, the other a shield. She dropped the cord that led to the flame and took a deep, centering breath.

She summoned a first order ward and trickled it into the chain in her hand. Immediately she felt the coach straighten up, take weight and pressure off the axles, the wheels, the greased mechanisms that typical vehicles of the kind depended on.

Then there was a loud thumping beneath and Amadin's muted voice. "You know it's not an automaton, yes? You have to make the horses move the old-fashioned way."

Snorting, she flicked the reins lightly, just so that the team would know she was there, and *tsked* them into moving. They began at a light step but soon enough she had them moving at a reasonable trot, the kind they could maintain for a long while.

Since she'd never been responsible for the sole operation of a warden coach before, she held herself very still and paid at least as much attention to the chain in her hand and the feel of the vehicle beneath her as she did to the road. Perhaps too much, waiting for the slightest hint that her order was wearing out, that she had to brake rather more sharply than she would've liked to guide the team into a gentle turn instead of tearing off straight across country.

She needn't have worried so much. The magical parts of a warden coach were sturdily built, for endurance and not for fine control; when the magic wore off it did so all at once and without warning. She quickly piped another ward into the cord and resigned herself to trying to time it.

It seemed one might last a quarter hour or so. *Good thing I've had to summon so many damned wards in the last year*, she thought. Before she'd taken up her post, that many wards in a two-hour shift would've exhausted her quickly.

When the end of this first shift did come and she slowed the wagon to a halt, she stood up and stretched, feeling only the slight fatigue of exercise or study. Amadin emerged.

"The first leg will take a good deal of our time and energy," he said. "We won't likely see a post-house for a couple of days. Once we can change horses regularly, of course, we can really let the trap fly."

"Right." Aelis was determined not to let the idea of a few days of this kind of work distress her, or at least to not let it show on her face, and she climbed back into the coach.

She was about to bang the roof again but thought about how long she was going to be spending with Amadin and decided that antagonizing him further was likely to be counterproductive. Sleep eluded her this time, and she cursed the fact that the books she'd brought were all in a trunk lashed to the roof.

She did have a small sheaf of parchment held together with a brass pin, and a small pen case, so she fished them out and thought to make notes.

Instead, she found herself sketching.

Before her talent for necromancy asserted itself, Aelis's favorite tutors had been the artists. While a career as an artist would've been improper for a count's daughter, it was accounted a useful skill that would show well on the family if she proved a talented amateur.

It wasn't a skill she'd indulged much in Lone Pine, without the time and with materials too precious to waste, but it was quick to come back. She started sketching folk. Rus and Martin, Elmo and Otto, Emilie. These were quick ink impressions, nothing too detailed, and she was about to get started on Tun when her turn came again.

3

AMBUSH

They went on for three days like that, trading shifts. At times they shared the board rather than retreating to the interior, just to exchange a word or two. Aelis desperately wanted to ask Amadin if he knew any details of the accusations against Bardun Jacques, but he might well be forbidden from speaking of it or friendly with the accuser, and besides, she felt that best practice was to wait to hear it from direct sources.

Still, the curiosity was distracting her, and she responded by covering the leaves of her pad with sketches. The people of Lone Pine, her tower, her orrery, even the various forms she'd seen Dalius in. She struggled the most with the last version of him she'd fought, a misshapen assemblage of out-of-place bones with his skin grotesquely stretched across it.

"What is *that?*" Amadin asked, glancing over her shoulder as she worked on detailing it.

"Just a potential kind of spirit-animated bone chimera," she said quickly, closing the pad and probably smearing some of her work.

"Gods, but necromancy is an ugly art. Have you people got no sense of harmony? No unifying aesthetic?"

"Death is only pretty in the distant and the abstract," Aelis said, "after the poets and the minstrels have had their go of it. Never up close." For just a moment she thought of Dalius's apparent apprentice, the hedge-enchanter Nathalie, her throat's vital artery opened wide by a knife in Aelis's hand, dying before her eyes. She pushed that thought firmly away.

"Listen to you, veteran warden, come home from the great and terrible wars," Amadin chided. "I know it's no fault of your own that you were too young to join the fight against the orc bands. Let me tell you, when you catch a string of enemies unaware in a perfect line for a Djagenmar's Fire-Drake, or run them straight into an ambush with a mere puff of Invoker's Spark, it is a beautiful thing indeed."

"Well, if you were a fighting warden during the war, you must've seen some units of animations before they were outlawed."

"I wouldn't have it." Amadin spat over the side of the wagon. "Some things are too unnatural for an elf to countenance." He looked down at her from his high seat on the wagon and seemed about to say more. Instead, they lapsed into an uncomfortable silence.

"How much farther till we start making post-houses?" Aelis had never been able to let awkward silences linger.

"Tomorrow," Amadin answered, "I think around midday. Fresh horses and the first decent food I've had since arriving at that shithole of a village."

Aelis felt honor-bound to speak in defense of Lone Pine, but something else drew her attention. The horses were tossing their heads, shying. Amadin snapped the reins harder, but the left-hand horse was having none of it, and the wagon began to slew. Amadin pulled up, set the brake, and hopped down.

Aelis did not know what she saw, or felt, or smelled. A rustle in the grass, or the horse's reaction, or abjurer's training, or possibly just the experiences she'd had of ambushing and being ambushed. Something was *wrong*.

She acted without thinking whether she'd look foolish or not . She leapt from the seat, tackling Amadin to the ground, and threw her longest ward across them.

Two crossbow bolts tore through the space they'd just occupied. One sank into the wagon, but the other took the horse in the flank.

"Ambush!" she screamed into Amadin's ear. "Under the coach!" She rolled herself away from him and scrambled under the wheels. Amadin soon threw himself beside her as two more bolts spattered mud from the road.

Aelis wrapped her hand around her sword's hilt and held a ward ready to summon.

"Make for the other side of the road. Keep the coach between you and their fire. I need my staff," Amadin said, then gave her a shove out the other side. She rolled with it, came to her feet and drew her sword in the same motion, and ran as hard as she could for the far side of the road. There was cover just a few steps away, down the embankment. She held as big a ward as she could manage behind her back as she went.

She risked a glance back only once she was a step away from throwing herself behind a fold in the ground for cover.

The far side of the coach was a *wall* of smoke. She didn't know precisely what Amadin had used, but it should do to hide his position. She heard the hiss of crossbow bolts regardless. They arced over the coach and landed several yards behind her.

That their attackers had even that good an idea of her position was troubling. *Move move move*, her mind blared, but she needed to see Amadin emerge from the coach and the smoke with his staff.

Which he did, the smoke dissipating around him and his staff, a rod of ebony topped by a white crystal that blazed with energy, a ball of white-blue power growing around it.

He grabbed the side of the coach to gain height and lifted the staff. Aelis threw a ward around him, flat and broad, angling it downward. A crossbow bolt deflected from it and fell harmlessly to the ground.

She shut her eyes just in time; the ball of white-blue had snapped out as a long streak of crackling lightning, burned a smoking path through the foliage, and ended in a short, wet scream.

Then another bolt whizzed in and sliced across Amadin's arm as he swung off the edge of the wagon. Aelis summoned wards to the hilt of her drawn sword and ran forward to his side, sparing a sorry glance for the wounded horse. She made it around the carriage and almost crashed into Amadin, who had clapped a hand over his wounded arm. Aelis got her shoulder under his and ran to the far side of the road, dragging him along.

She set him down along the ditch and pried his hand off his wound to assess it. "Can you summon that smoke again, give us some cover?"

"Certainly." Amadin's voice was slurred, rather than gritted through pain-clenched teeth, as Aelis expected. He lifted his staff and breathlessly muttered a few words; nothing happened.

She bent to sniff at his wound. A sharp, resinous scent came to her, with undertones of herbal sweetness.

Witsend and something else, something to strengthen and hasten it. Why would common road agents have that? They wouldn't. Solve that problem later.

"Amadin, I'm sorry for how much this is about to hurt," she said, setting down her sword and gripping her dagger. Trying not to worry about another crossbow bolt arcing down on her, she cast Aldayim's Blood Purge directly over his wound.

Amadin screamed raggedly as the spell made blood gush from the wound, spilling out what poison it could, burning away what it couldn't. Then his eyes refocused and he gathered himself.

"Left and right," he said, lifting his staff and spilling smoke from its end; it drifted into the road and lay thickly over the coach and the slope they clung to.

"We want him alive," Aelis said. He made no answer but stood, smoke billowing out around him, and went to the right-hand side of the carriage.

Aelis slipped to the left, ramming her dagger back home in her belt and crouching low, her sword in a two-handed grip, ready to spring into a guard or an attack. She crossed the road through the smoke, holding in a cough so as not to give herself away, dashed into and over the ditch on the other side.

The second crossbowman had gone to ground; no bolts had come. *Gone to ground, or waiting for a clear shot? He has no reason to believe Amadin isn't out of the fight.*

Aelis slid back down into the ditch and clutched her dagger, reached into her will for a Second Order Necromantic pulse; Isring's Life-Finder. She cast a new sense, not her ears or eyes or skin, spread out over twelve-to-fifteen yards. Two pulses, two breathing beacons of life that were vague, green-tinged outlines in her field of vision. They converged rapidly. She sprinted toward them, drawing her wand, calling a Somnolence to mind.

She burst through overgrown, bristly dry grass into a small clearing in time to see Amadin release a bolt of purple energy from the end of his staff into a fleeing man. She had only a brief impression of their attacker, in faded brown and green, crossbow bouncing on his back and quiver on his hip, when the bolt struck him.

He stopped dead in his tracks and fell to the ground, twitching, arms and legs splaying out.

"That's handy," Aelis said as she took a step forward to disarm him while he was incapacitated. Amadin suddenly thrust his staff in front of her, blocking her progress.

"Don't touch him," the elf said coldly.

And that is when the smell of cooking flesh reached her.

The twitching became convulsions and smoke leaked from his ears, then began to pour from cracks in his skin. Within moments, before she could even gather herself to react, his skin was seared red, his body had curled up as tendons and muscles burned, and the smell in her nostrils was sickening.

Aelis turned on Amadin, anger blazing in her eyes. "We needed him alive," she spat.

"Attacking a warden is a death sentence," he replied coldly.

"Do you think they were common bandits? Carrying bolts treated with alchemically enhanced witsend, waiting to attack a warden coach?"

Amadin sniffed and poked at the corpse with the end of his staff. "Such things can be had for coin from any half-trained alchemist, and we are targets anywhere just outside the range of civilization. Brigands are desperate men, and careless. I'll go find the other body. He was in one of those trees over there." He waved a hand vaguely and turned on his heel.

Aelis squatted by the body in front of her and turned it over.

Almost immediately, she wished she hadn't.

The bandit's face was a ruined mass of cooked flesh. His eyes had exploded, leaving melted trails of glistening, steaming jelly down his cheeks.

Aelis was a surgeon. The things that could happen to, or inside, a body were not a mystery to her.

But this is a vicious, awful way to die, she thought as she began stripping the man. She set his crossbow aside, then unhooked the sheaf of bolts from his belt. Half were gray, half were black. She pulled one of each; the gray-fletched one was coated with the same resinous-smelling concoction she'd smelled from Amadin's wound.

She rubbed the bolt into the grass and dirt, trying to wipe it clean, but the stuff was too thickly applied to wipe easily away.

"This is professional work," she muttered.

The man had two knives on his belt, one with a longer and thicker blade. Both had bone handles lacquered and then worn to a smooth, dull brown. She pulled the longer one free and was startled to see that it had been carefully blacked. The blade was sharp and well cared for; Aelis found no maker's mark. Not on the bottom of the hilt, not on the tang just before the hilt started, not anywhere on the blade.

"So is this," she muttered. *Or, rather, a professional tool.*

She made a quick search of the rest of him; no more weapons, no papers, no coins, no oddments, trinkets, or mementos on him. She gathered up the bow; a small model, no use for hunting, not military issue, made of dark wood and steel blacked similarly to the knife.

She slid a ward beneath the body, grabbed an ankle, and hauled him to the road with his weapons upon his chest.

She found Amadin emerging from the roadside, rubbing his hands.

"What are you bringing the body for?" he muttered.

"Was going to load him into the coach and take him to the post-house. I can learn something from it, given time."

"What's to learn? As I said; brigands. Desperate men."

She dropped the body and went to the wounded horse, patting its trembling neck. "There was nothing desperate about these men. These were professional killers, and they weren't woodsmen."

"On what evidence do you base this great insight?"

She bent down and picked up one of the knives. "No maker's mark. Blacked steel. A carefully sharpened edge. Well oiled, and soft leather scabbards. An assassin's tool, not cheap, not common." She tucked the knife into her own belt and picked up the crossbow. It felt light and deadly in her hands; she could easily aim and fire it with one hand.

"This is no hunter's tool, nor a mustered-out soldier's friend. This is made to do one thing: kill people, quietly, swiftly, at a distance, preferably with poison."

Amadin eyed her in silence. "There may be something in what you say," he admitted at last. "But there is no loading him on the coach." He pointed to the fletching bristling from the wounded horse's flank. "This horse is not hauling anything to the nearest post-house. Best we simply put it down now."

Aelis sighed and approached the animal again, wrapping her hand around her dagger. She put her hand to its neck and delved its systems. "No," she said after a moment. "The wound isn't deep and hasn't damaged anything vital. The muscle will knit provided I get it out safely. Come on," she said, waving Amadin to her, "let's get them out of harness."

4

A LONG WALK

Aelis was able to cut the bolt from the horse's rear hip, soothing it all the while with the most powerful enchantments she could muster and her anatomist's blade guiding her. The animal would live, but Amadin had been right when he said it couldn't pull the coach, so they set off the next day with as much of their baggage lashed to the healthy animal as they could.

Aelis had been forced to leave a trunk behind, and when the choice was clothes or her *second* trunk, that decision had been easy. She transferred some of her spare clothes, the books she'd packed, and her medical kit to a rucksack, making it heavier than when she'd carried it into the wilderness. And she was only carrying that because Amadin had insisted on burning the coach and the baggage left behind. She had wanted to argue, but there'd been no point.

"Standard warden doctrine," Amadin had said, the instant she'd opened her mouth.

"Leave no magical equipment behind," she'd said, in a flat voice. "Destroy that which cannot be carried. I know. Just let me shift some baggage."

Soon after she'd walked off a few dozen yards with the horses, she'd felt the heat of the immolation. She turned to watch and saw the sparks rise into the air, those from plain wood and metal, and those rather more colorful; blue vapors, bright red sparks, a flash that she felt rather than saw. The magical components of the coach rendered useless.

And now here I am, footsore and sweating on the king's road, hurting my back by hauling this fucking pack, and hoping the post-house shows itself soon.

Amadin hadn't nearly the load she did. His clothes and effects had been minimal and stowed easily on the healthy draft horse in a handy grip. He walked with his staff in hand—apparently it could be lengthened or shortened by some means, whether magical or mechanical Aelis couldn't tell—and his sword swinging on his right hip.

Gods, I hate him, she thought, recognizing even as she did how unfair it was. He was a messenger and owed her nothing, not even an offer to carry her pack for a while.

Aelis felt disgust at herself. *If I can keep up with Tunbridge in the gods-damned Old Ystainian wilderness, I can keep up with one elf on the road.*

They saw little traffic and didn't spend any time in communication with those they did see. Most folk, seeing two wardens along the road, fled as fast as decency allowed for fear of getting their cart or horse commandeered.

The first night they camped, Amadin tried to make some talk, gesturing toward the heavy trunk she kept locked and bound.

"Nothing in there you couldn't leave behind?"

"No."

"They sell clothes and books in Lascenise, you know."

It was an ill-considered jest, if not ill meant. Aelis had briefly envisioned herself breaking his nose with a sharp punch. but instead she tried to guide the conversation elsewhere.

"Let's talk about those assassins."

"Brigands," he insisted.

"Really? Custom weapons without maker's marks, the features of which point to a trade in murder. Alchemically empowered witsend."

"Say I agree on these two points. What do they add up to?"

"Those men were prepared to kill wizards."

"Prepared to and intending to are worlds apart in motive, Aelis. We may have been a target of opportunity. For all they knew the coach was hauling magical artifacts, gold, treasures recovered from Old Ystain."

"We should've tracked them to their point of origin," she said. "At the very least I would've liked a better look at their clothing." *Onoma, I wish I could've necropsied at least one of them.*

"The world and many in it may well mean us harm," Amadin said. "But that does not mean you ought to give in to paranoia and assume that everyone means harm to *you* specifically."

"That . . . sounds familiar."

"More crudely put, it is a sentiment often preached by Warden Emeritus Bardun Jacques."

"Ah." Aelis found herself at a loss, and in the darkness she couldn't make out much of Amadin's face. Occasionally his eyes gleamed in the sliver of Midarra's yellow moon that was the only visible satellite that night, revealing them as green, then blue, despite Aelis knowing full well they were brown.

Aelis wasn't quite ready to give up, so she tried a different tack.

"Where are you bound once we reach Lascenise?"

"Wherever the commander sends me."

"Messenger warden, then? Do you enjoy that duty?"

"I don't like being too settled, and it looks good in the file, flitting about three kingdoms or beyond, dangerous orders sometimes . . ."

Ahh, Aelis thought, *a climber.*

"How will the loss of a warden coach look in your file?"

That brought Amadin up short. He sat up straight, shaking off the weariness that had been creeping into his features. "I expect there will be some inquiries. Of both of us, mind."

"But you're the messenger, and the senior. The coach was yours."

"What are you driving at, de Lenti?"

"Only that we should be in agreement about what happened on the road. That was an ambush targeting *wizards*. Not necessarily one of us, but wizards, of a certainty."

"Go on. Convince me."

"Besides what I've already said about their weapons, those men had nothing on them to identify them. No papers, no letters, no coinage, no mementos, nothing personal but the tools of a grisly trade. And who, anywhere the wardens serve, doesn't know what the arms on that coach meant? No one attacks wardens traveling openly in a warden coach unless certain conditions are met."

"What conditions?"

"One is that they are out to kill a warden, likely a specific one. Two, that they are told the wardens are transporting something of value. Three, they are trying to prevent a warden from reaching a destination. No one who values his life . . . no *professional* . . . is going to take a warden coach as a target of opportunity."

"Desperate men will take chances."

"Desperate men are not well fed, well clad, well shod, and well armed, generally," Aelis countered. "Had they been carrying old army bows, or rusted farm tools, had they been underfed, maybe I'd agree with you. But even your lesser sort of road agent is after gold, not blood."

"Easier to take the gold when blood's already been spilled."

"It doesn't add up, and you know it doesn't. If we'd had the time to track them back to a camp, to investigate more . . ."

"We didn't, and we're not heading back. My orders say bring you to Lascenise as soon as can be arranged, and those are the orders to carry out. What you do once you get there is your business."

"If there is an inquiry on the coach, I will tell them everything I am saying now, and I will puzzle over your unwillingness to investigate, or even to entertain the possibility."

Amadin's stare became colder, harder. Midarra's moon played no tricks on his eyes now. *Nothing can frost over like elvish eyes*, Aelis thought, but she knew she had him.

"I've been stared at harder, by better," she said flatly, holding his eyes. "Agree with me or don't; I am only telling you what my behavior will be, not trying to dictate yours."

"If our stories differ, an inquiry will be harder."

"You don't say."

Amadin sighed. "Fine. We will write up our accounts and square them. I'm not saying I agree with you, mind. Only that I don't need Cabal command trying to recoup the cost of a warden coach from me. Not all of us who enter the wardens are blessed with personal fortune."

"Happy to come to an arrangement." She worked hard to keep the smile off her face as Amadin sat back against his bedroll with a yawn. She popped to her feet and resigned herself to a slow walk between their small camp and the picket line of the horses.

Something was pricking at her mind, and she wasn't sure what. Amadin was too calm about what had happened. Too calm by half. *Or he's just arrogant.* Those men had been set there to attack them, or her, or him. She wished she'd at least looked more closely at the dead man's boots, or his clothing. Anything.

But she had his knives, and his crossbow, and in Lascenise she could learn a great deal about them. The long walk between here and there daunted her a little less as she thought on it.

5

LASCENISE

The night before arriving in Lascenise, when they'd seen the twinkle of the city's lights and trails of its smoke as they trotted over a rise, Aelis thought she'd been able to smell it. It had been a fanciful notion then, miles away, the city only visible because of how it stood out against the dark.

But now, still a few miles out from the Great Crossroad where the city had been built purposefully, she *knew* she could smell it. In fact, she reined up her post-horse, the fourth she'd taken since they'd started reaching post-houses and by far her favorite, to have a deep breath.

"What are you doing, de Lenti?"

"Do you not smell that, Amadin?"

"What? The earth before the sun bakes it? I'm no farmer."

"No, no. The smell of the city. The rivers! The people! The money and the noise and the clangor and *life*, Amadin."

"I might grant, if I were being generous, that you could smell the river and the city's drainage from here. But the rest of the things you've mentioned don't even have a scent, much less one that can be detected from this distance."

"Those are the words of one who has not spent almost a year mired in the inescapable scent of sheep shit."

Amadin laughed and nudged his horse back into a trot. Aelis joined him. They came upon the city just before noon and there was a great throng of wagons, carts, and hand-pulled barrows queueing up outside the Plains Gate, the busiest entry point, given that it faced so much of Ystain's most fertile land.

They shared a look, nodded simultaneously, nudged their horses over the edge of the road, and began making for the gate.

"WARDENS!" they shouted in unison. "Make way for WARDEN BUSINESS."

Undoubtedly there was grumbling among the gathered folk who were going to have to wait just that much longer to let two wardens bypass the queue. But none of it was loud enough to reach their ears.

Amadin reined up first and slid from his saddle. His long red invoker's coat had turned nearly brown from the mud and dust of their ride, but there was no mistaking it, nor the warrant he pulled from an interior pocket.

"Thank you, Warden Mauntell," the bored, tired gate-guard said, taking only the merest glance at the papers.

Aelis held hers out, ignored the way the guard's eyes widened at the sight of her black jacket with the blue and green slashes on the sleeves. *Even here, some will gawk at a necromancer,* she thought.

"Thank you, Warden de Lenti." The guard handed her warrant back and waved them through. A farm family sat their wagon impatiently behind them. Or at least, Aelis suspected they were impatient; she would've been. But their passive faces offered no sign.

And then they were through the gate, leading their horses, and she marveled at feeling *cobblestones* under her feet again. Sure, the footing was uncertain and she was used to grass, packed dirt, or maybe boards, but this felt like *home.*

"Onward to Cabal Keep," Amadin said. Aelis needed no directing, and the crowd more or less parted around them, used to seeing wizards in their midst and skilled at noting the difference between wizard and warden; if someone in Lyceum robes or colors was wearing a sword or carrying a staff, they did not have to work hard to get through the press of bodies.

All Aelis wanted to do was stop and appreciate it, to follow the cry of hawkers, whatever they were selling, to let her nose lead her to a stand selling fried things covered in sugar or skewers of meat, or let her feet lead her to a favorite wineshop.

But she knew that Amadin was right; the need to report outweighed all other considerations. And she, of course, needed to see Bardun Jacques, find out the name of his lawyer, and begin to pick at the nature of the job she'd been handed.

The Plains Gate and the central districts its wide avenues led to were the planned parts of a city. Lascenise had grown up out of border-fort towns where the three nations came closest against one another, Imraval's river-bound border with Tyridice just a narrow strip of plain away from Ystain's southern reaches. Thus the main roads were easily navigable, carefully tended, and regularly spaced.

Soon the streets narrowed and sank beneath their feet, and low hitching posts that had once been for canal boats began popping up irregularly at knee-height. The tang of river water, confined underground, seeped out of the cobbles, though, and mud squelched around their feet as they walked. The smoke of dozens of fires scented the air and darkened the afternoon sun.

Aelis could still not have been happier.

"Ah, the Tremont," she muttered. "Every student's favorite neighborhood."

"Until they get robbed," Amadin pointed out.

"Only idiots and problem drunks manage to get mugged here. It's not Slop's End or the Barrows."

"The Tremont was rather rougher in my student days," Amadin said. "Wineshops trying to sell you sugared vinegar, and every bawdy house bearing three toughs ready to cut a throat."

Aelis laughed and tried not to roll her eyes. "Of course," she agreed. "The older generation always had it worse."

Amadin sniffed and quickened his pace. They followed Old River Road on its somewhat winding path deeper into the city. Here, even warden colors didn't earn you wide passage. No one jostled them and whatever pickpockets might be about likely knew better than to try wardens traveling in tandem, but they had to go single file and mind their horses. Food vendors lurked in the doorways of shops rather than in freestanding stalls. Aelis had to remind herself they'd be fed at Cabal Keep when the scents of frying fish and pickled vegetables reached her.

Eventually they turned off Old River Road onto Southern Fort Street. Hard gray walls of the city's inner keep reared above the rooftops, and no lines wended toward the open portcullis.

A guard, not a warden or wizard, waved them past without a glance at their papers. Once inside they were met by a team of grooms, and a Cabal servant in livery striped with the colors of each college came out to meet them.

"Welcome, wardens," the servant—a woman, tall for a gnome, with a heavy silver chain around her neck—said. "I am Tower-Keeper Myra. We will have rooms prepared and food is available in the refectory . . ."

"I will take refreshment with Warden Emeritus Bardun Jacques," Aelis said firmly. "I'm here to act on his behalf in a legal matter. Where can I find him?"

"I'm afraid you'll need to speak to the warden of the watch," Myra said haltingly. "I cannot give you those directions nor provide you those permissions."

"Then where do I find the warden of the watch?"

Myra swallowed once. "In the first level below the far tower."

"You could just say 'at the entrance to the dungeon,'" Aelis said.

The gnome woman winced. "I do hate that word, Warden. Please—"

"We have to present ourselves to the Cabal commander first," Amadin interrupted. "Where might we find him?"

"The private study," Myra said. "He has a full day today, he will not . . ."

"He'll want to read our report," Amadin said. At that, their horses were led to nearby stables; Myra made comforting noises about seeing to their baggage, and Aelis followed Amadin into the keep's central block of a tower.

She'd been at Cabal Keep before, during parts of her Warden training, but she'd never met her putative commander or been inside the towers that could house every warden on the northern station. Thankfully Amadin knew precisely where to lead her: up the first flight of stairs they found, to the left, up the second flight of stairs, and then another left, to an unguarded door.

Unguarded but not *unlocked* or even unwarded. Aelis could feel the abjuration that radiated from the black-painted, iron-banded oak. There were no signs or marks of rank on the door.

"Commander Mazadar is fair but likes to bark," Amadin murmured a few steps from the door. "Do not show him weakness, or even deference, unless he's *truly* angry."

"How will I know if he's truly angry?"

"Trust me," Amadin said. "You'll know."

He made one sharp knock on the door with the back of his hand.

The wood of the door suddenly grew a gnarled, bearded face, its eyes swiveling from one of them to the other.

"Well?" The door's voice was hard, dusty.

"Wardens Mauntell and de Lenti reporting," Amadin said.

The face on the door furled and screwed up in thought.

"Anything of consequence?"

"Loss of a warden coach," Amadin said through gritted teeth.

The door swung open with a grunt.

Aelis followed Amadin into a long, narrow room. At the far end there was a heavy desk of dark wood, and behind it sat a dwarf, his face recognizable from the door she'd just seen it in. If anything, in the flesh it looked harder, meaner, and more prone to violence than the wooden simulacrum had.

Warden Commander Mazadar did not stand as they entered. Nor did he gesture them to take a seat. The office was lined on the sides by glass-fronted cases full of leather folders bound in many colors of ribbon. There were no visible latches or hinges; Aelis imagined there was a Blood Catalogue hidden in the wood of the cases that would allow anyone with proper authorization to reach through the glass.

Behind his desk, Mazadar was flanked by two full suits of gleaming plate armor. He drummed one hand, knuckles as thick as walnuts, on his desk. He wore a gambeson of rich conjurer's brown, trimmed with gold on the collar, shoulders, and cuffs, and a ceremonial breastplate on a chain around his neck.

"Loss of a coach."

Aelis was not sure if this was a question or a statement, so she stayed quiet, silently thanking Stregon that Amadin was the senior warden.

"Yes, Commander," Amadin muttered, pulling the written statement they'd crafted together. "The details are here." He placed the folded sheets on the desk. Mazadar did not reach for them, instead looking steadily at the elf.

"Summarize."

"We were set upon by brigands who were prepared to fight wizards. We . . ."

"Prepared how?"

"Alchemically enhanced witsend poison on their crossbow bolts. No identifying marks on the bodies anywhere."

"How did brigands, even those with alchemical weapons, destroy a coach?"

"They wounded one of our horses so it could not pull, Commander. The coach was destroyed in accordance with warden procedure . . ."

Mazadar extended one hand and slid the paper toward himself slowly, muttering under his breath. Aelis thought she caught "harness yourself to it next time," but bit down on her tongue to stifle a laugh.

"Now." The dwarf's attention settled on her; it was like a weight pulling on her neck. "I thought you were somewhere in the godsforsaken hinterlands, de Lenti."

"I was recalled to serve as advocate for Warden Emeritus Bardun Jacques. I understand I'll need permission to see him from the warden of the watch."

Mazadar let out a heavy breath through his broad, previously broken nose. "Yes. Let me get you the file." He sat back in his chair and gestured.

The suit of armor on his right hand suddenly stood straight and then stepped forward with a clank and a whisper of air.

Aelis was unsettled for a moment, but she had to admit it was one of the more impressive displays of conjuring she'd seen. Air, she supposed, and possibly earth, given all the ore that had gone into making the armor in the first place.

With the clanking of plate against plate it came to one of the glass-fronted cases; the glass opened around the gauntlet as it retrieved a folder. In two more steps, it held the folder out to her.

She took it delicately and tucked it under her arm. "If I may, Commander, I'm eager to speak to Warden Emeritus Jacques."

"Go, then," Mazadar said, flicking a finger at the door.

"And permission from the warden of the watch?"

"Get it from her," the dwarf said. "I haven't got time to write orders for every minor function in a station this size."

Aelis had no wish to put herself under the thumb of some other bureaucratic sort, but she had even less wish to push the commander further. She bowed and left as quickly as decency would allow.

6

CATCHING UP

Aelis only had to stop to ask for directions twice. When she knew she was nearing the correct place in the correct tower, she stopped to compose herself. She smoothed her jacket and riding skirt, kicked some of the worst mud off her boots in an alcove, and pulled out a handkerchief to wipe at her face.

You're a warden, called to serve as an advocate. You have the right to be here, the right to ask questions, and if it comes to it, the authority to make many kinds of demands.

She gave her belt a final adjustment and stepped back into the stone hallway, bootheels echoing confidently.

She pushed open the door with WARDEN OF THE WATCH painted on its boards. There was a desk, behind a cage of metal bars another door, and rows of shelves and racks beyond. The chair behind the desk sat empty, a closed ledger before it, but she could hear someone rattling around in the shelves.

"Warden of the watch! I'm here to see Warden Emeritus Bardun Jacques."

"Well," a distracted voice called back, "he's under strictest lockdown. Censors outside his cell at all times. You'd need to show authorization . . ." The voice slowly grew closer as the woman speaking returned to her desk. She was looking down at a leather folder as she walked, but as soon as Aelis saw the mass of dark curls atop her head and the way her diviner's white robes clung to her, Aelis knew her.

"*Miralla?*"

Hearing her name, Miralla looked up from her folder and nearly dropped it. "*Aelis?* I thought you were gone past the edge of civilization for two years!"

They each took a quick step toward each other, then halted at the bars that separated them. Miralla smiled, brilliantly, Aelis thought, and tapped a key that hung from a ring on her wide belt.

Miralla unlocked the door and stepped out. They shared an awkward hug and then stepped back.

"You look wonderful," Aelis said, because it was the truth.

"And you look . . . *awful*," Miralla teased, brushing something off Aelis's shoulder.

"You try making a five-post-house ride with one change of clothes and let me know how you look."

"As if I would ever find myself in that circumstance," Miralla shot back. "At least you could have bathed before coming to see me." Aelis was surprised to find herself flushing as Miralla's brown eyes caught hers.

"In truth, I'm not here to see you. As I said . . . I'm here to see Bardun Jacques."

"I'm wounded that you'd come all the way here on leave to see an imprisoned old man rather than me," Miralla sniffed.

"I'm here to be his advocate," Aelis said. "Which is why I'm here to see him fresh off the road."

Miralla sighed and slipped the folder she carried back between the bars and onto her desk. "Who assigned you? Mazadar?"

"My orders merely told me to report to function as advocate," Aelis said. "The letters are in my trunk."

"I'm not sure I can let you in without them."

"Miralla, why would I lie about it? You said he's under constant censor guard so even if I was part of some political plot, what could I do to him?"

"Fine. On one condition."

"And that is?"

"Dinner. Tonight. Tausner's."

"The clothes I've got won't get me past the door there," Aelis said.

"If only you were in a city equipped with any number of fine tailors."

"If I have the time to find better clothes, I will. But you might wind up sharing a table with a warden in second-best duty robes for coach travel."

"I'll make sure it's a table where no one can see us." Miralla winked, slipped back behind her partitioned desk, and locked the door behind her. She took a blank sheet of paper from a drawer, quickly wrote something and stamped a wax seal on it, then slid it toward Aelis.

Aelis reached down to get it and Miralla made sure to brush her hand as she passed it over.

"See you tonight; three hours after the end of first watch."

"If they don't refuse my poor country self at the door," Aelis agreed. She found herself more flustered than she would've expected. Miralla *had* looked good. And smelled good, wearing the same expensive, sweet-but-not-cloying scent she'd worn in their Lyceum days. Aelis forced those thoughts away as she descended two levels down a spiral stone staircase. The temperature grew noticeably cooler; the daylight disappeared, though it was replaced with the even blue glow of conjurer's lights, set at even intervals along the walls.

Miralla's written orders let her through the first iron gate, manned by ordinary guards in plain leather jerkins, heavy cudgels on their belts. When she told them she was there to see Bardun Jacques, they pointed down a hall.

She assumed his was the only door with a pair of tall censors standing before it. Wearing abjurer blue and heavy helms that left only an inscrutable sliver of eye, nose, and mouth visible, they were a frightening enough sight to any wizard, but the fact that their flamberges—two-handed, with five feet of sinuous blade—were naked in their hands, points resting on the floor, was doubly unsettling.

When Aelis was a sword-length away from them, she suddenly felt odd.

Colder. Closer to the physicality of the world, vulnerable to it in a way she couldn't describe. Her breathing was interrupted, her vision swam, and she suddenly felt an absence in her chest, the snuffing of a flame she had carried so steadily for so long that she did not quite know how to perceive the world in its absence.

She knew that were she to attempt to reach for a spell then, she would not find it.

"Warden." One of the censors spoke, their voice muffled by the helm, disguised by its magic. "What business have you here?"

"I am to be Warden Emeritus Bardun Jacques's advocate," Aelis said. "And I am here to meet with him." She held out the paper with Miralla's seal.

A hand, gloved, took it delicately and held it up to the eyeslits of the helm.

"You must surrender your implements," the other censor said, "before you may enter the cell." The censor lifted one hand from the crosspiece of the sword they held and pointed to a small table next to them.

Aelis dropped her wand into her hand and set it down first. Then she drew her sword, which felt more like a lump of metal than it ever had, wrong in her hand, the hilt's wrapping dry and coarse, the balance all wrong. Then she drew her dagger.

She felt a blazing cold emptiness in her chest when she held it and had to force herself to set it carefully down and step back.

"We trust you carry no other weapons, Warden," the first censor said. "If you are found to do so, you will be barred from further meetings. If you attempt to bring the prisoner anything without authorization, you will be barred from further meetings. If you should attempt to work a spell while meeting with the prisoner, we will know, and you will be immediately arrested . . ."

"I know all that," Aelis snapped. "Now let me in."

"As you say, Warden," the censor answered, before turning and unlocking the door. It did not open immediately into a cell but into a small walled tunnel perhaps five paces long, with another door at the end.

"When the outer door is locked, we will use a pull to open the inner." With that, the censor shut the door behind her.

The steady conjurer's lights that had lit the rest of the dungeon had given way to the flickering of torches, and Aelis's eyes took a moment to adjust. The door behind her slammed shut. She heard a key turning in it, then a loud grating as the heavy door before her slid upward into the ceiling.

She hurried through. She was first hit with the powerful smell of unwashed bodies, straw, and mildew. The cell was barren, cold, and unfurnished but for cutouts in the walls, one table with a wooden pitcher and basin set on it, and a bucket in the corner from which worse smells emanated.

Lying on a sack full of straw on one of the cutouts was an old man with a bald head mapped with scars. A stick cut into a crude crutch lay at an angle next to him, and he swung up into a seated position at the edge, slowly, as Aelis came deeper into the room.

The left leg of his rough trousers lay half empty as he sat up with the aid of his stick. He sniffed once, eyed her closely.

Pity and outrage built up in Aelis's chest. Her mentor, widely agreed to be the greatest warden of his generation, one of the most powerful and feared wizards the Lyceum had ever made, reduced to *this?*

Those feelings melted away when she heard his voice, as deep and powerful as if he were standing at a Lyceum lectern in an Archmagister's most formal robes.

"Took you fucking long enough, de Lenti."

"Archmagister, why in seventy hells are they keeping you in here?" Aelis was too incensed by the conditions she'd found him in to respond to his half jest.

Bardun Jacques blinked. His left eye did so more slowly than his right, and didn't fully open, either.

"Well, because I'm accused of quite a number of crimes . . ."

"This kind of cell is for the already guilty. It's inappropriate to your station, and I won't have it."

He gave a little laugh and swung himself upward with his rough crutch. "You know that's not the kind of advocacy your job implies."

"Doesn't mean I can't also demand that they give you better treatment."

"You may spend your breath on it if you wish, Aelis." He took a few steps, swinging his crutch in place of his missing left leg, then turned around and took the same few steps, his soft sandal and the hard tip of his crutch making alternating tap-slap-tap-slap sounds.

"And I will. In fact, that ought to be our first priority . . ."

"I'll tell you what the first priority is," Bardun Jacques rasped. "And that is discussing my case."

"Right." Aelis produced her pin-bound sheaf of loose leaves and a piece of writing charcoal held in an elegant silver-chased wooden stick. "If I remember correctly, it's, what . . . assault by magic, murder by magic?"

"Murder of another *wizard* by magic."

"Right, right. I suppose you have a lawyer to defend you in the legal sense."

"I do. Gnomish woman. Book smart, but young, and stupid in every way that matters. Completely in over her head. But now that she's got you to help her, I'm sure we can delay the date of my execution by weeks. Months, even."

"You're innocent," Aelis said, "and we're going to prove that. Now, let's go over the details I need to do so."

With that, Bardun Jacques stopped his pacing and took a couple of hopping steps toward her.

"One thing you need to understand right now, de Lenti." He leaned closer and Aelis found his eyes intense and hard to meet beneath his wrinkled, beetled brows. "I did *everything* they're accusing me of."

7

ADVOCATING

Aelis stood in shock for a moment as the force of Bardun Jacques's admission rolled over her. He didn't move, didn't blink, just stared at her.

"You . . . murdered another wizard? By magic?"

"I might quibble over 'murder,' but yes, I killed the bastard."

"Why? Why even ask for an advocate if you know you're guilty?"

Bardun Jacques retreated to his stone bed and sat hard upon it. "You think about that first question and tell me why you think I killed another wizard."

Aelis ran her stunned mind through years' worth of lectures, harangues, advisory sessions, all the foul and wise and profane and useful and mysterious pronouncements she'd heard this man make, and landed on an answer somehow.

"If you killed someone . . . he probably wanted killing," she said haltingly, deciding to trust in her instinct and her mentor, at least for a few more moments, though she felt adrift.

"Oh, he did," Bardun Jacques agreed. "I'd like to think I never killed anyone who didn't. Now, let's hold off on moving to the more *specific* why and to your second question. Why would I want an advocate?"

"To prove something," Aelis said. "That it wasn't murder. That it had cause that gave it some . . . official sanction."

Bardun Jacques's face creased in what might have been a smile or a grimace; Aelis couldn't tell. "Now let's move to the specific. And here I don't expect you to have enough information to guess." He took a deep breath, then settled both hands on the top of his crutch. His voice dropped to a hoarse whisper.

"Wizards . . . powerful wizards, maybe some wardens . . . are smuggling magical artifacts into Lascenise. Maybe to other places. But definitely *from* here *into* the Lyceum. What use they're putting them to, where they're storing them . . . I can't guess. I was only pulling on this end of the thread. They were using some local thieves in town, working out of Slop's End down in the river tunnels, for the smuggling."

"Under the noses of Cabal Command? How?"

"That's a great question," Bardun Jacques said, and here he was interrupted by a small cough, but one that quickly grew to a coughing fit that caused him to double over. Aelis rushed to his side and was on the verge of reaching for a Necromantic Delve to see if it was some small infection or a larger, more chronic problem when she felt that omnipresent suppression, like a lead-lined cloak draped over her inner self. She handed him a clean handkerchief and poured him some water from the chipped pitcher. She eyed the water with suspicion, then smelled it. *At least they could let me kill anything in the water with a simple Prahnis's Purgative.*

By the time she'd turned back to him his cough had subsided, but the handkerchief had disappeared. He took the offered water and drank it sloppily.

"Where was I?"

"I'd asked a great question."

Bardun Jacques snorted. "Right. And it's one you should set about *answering.*"

"How they're smuggling these artifacts past the dozens of wardens who are stationed here at any given time."

"Exactly. As I said, I was tugging on these thieves . . . trying to capture one alive was a tall fucking order, believe me . . ."

"Should've brought a good enchanter," Aelis said.

"Do you know one?"

She laughed, deciding to play it off as a joke rather than an insult. "This thieves guild have a name?"

"Hmm . . . the Hidden Skulls? The Silent Skulls? Something like that. Not much imagination on this kind of scum. Let me tell you something: they're professional. Good smugglers. Fast, clean, don't litter the place with bodies if they can avoid it. Fight like dogs when cornered, though."

"Where did the wizard come into it?"

"He was somebody's bagman. Arstan Nicholaz, invoker of little consequence and diviner of even less, based on the color of his robes. *He* was in command of a group of throat-cutters come to, um, discourage my investigation."

"Another wizard challenged you openly to cease your investigation?"

"No, he was with the assassins that came after me."

"And what became of them?"

Bardun Jacques stared straight at her. "I blew them to seven kinds of hell. What do *you* do to people who're trying to kill you?"

"I haven't had as much experience there as you, Archmagister. But usually I try to . . . disable them. I am an enchanter, you know."

Bardun Jacques harrumphed. "Hasn't always worked though, has it?"

Should've known he'd see right through me, Aelis thought, then shook her head.

Bardun Jacques nodded slowly. "We'll talk about it later, under better circumstances. After you've gotten me out of this mess. Which you should start by going after these Hidden-Silent Skulls. Whoever they are, well, their assassins might come out to play, and we'll find out what you do to people who are trying to kill you."

"Right." Aelis made a flurry of notes. After a moment, the Archmagister cleared his throat. She looked up at him.

"You might not want to write too much of this down. Somebody looks through your notes and sees what I'm telling you in black and white . . ."

"I'm making a list. Priorities. Responsibilities. First thing first is still getting you out of this Onoma-cursed cell and somewhere I can investigate that cough."

"Still on that, eh?"

"I will be until they move you."

"And that, de Lenti, is why I didn't ask for just an advocate and get one by the luck of roster-shuffling and bureaucratic grudges."

That gave Aelis pause. "You asked for me, specifically?"

"I did. And do you know why?"

"Because I was your favorite student?"

"Because you're a pain in the ass," Bardun Jacques said. "You were a never-ending annoyance in the lecture hall. Hand always up first: *Pick me, Magister, I'm so very smart, I need the rest of these assholes to know I'm better than them*," he muttered, raising his hand in imitation of an overeager student. "Always first to attempt *anything* at exercises or in the laboratory, face-first like a *true* daughter of Stregon. Anaerion's fiery spunk, de Lenti, do you have *any* idea how tired a teacher grows of that kind of student?"

"I do now," Aelis said, chastened, feeling five years of things she apparently should've been embarrassed about all piling on her shoulders at once. It was an effort not to visibly sag.

Bardun Jacques lifted a crooked finger at her. "And that is why I knew you'd be a warden. There might have been students who were stronger, or faster, or smarter, or all three. But *nobody* needed the world to know who they were like you did. And at the bottom of it all, no matter how much power in the staff, how strong the sword-arm, or how keen the mind . . . what a warden needs most is to be a pain in the ass when everyone around them would prefer they weren't. Do you understand me?"

"I do, Archmagister," Aelis said, feeling the shame that had collected suddenly warring with a hot surge of pride based on what, on balance, was the greatest compliment she'd ever heard Bardun Jacques give anyone.

"Good. Now go be a pain in the ass to the people who need it most, then come back here and tell me all about it."

"I will, Archmagister. And the next time I see you it'll be to help you move to better quarters." Aelis stuffed her notes back into the pouch on her belt and hurried to the door, wiping the back of her hand at the corners of her eyes, though she would've lied about it under any oath.

✦ ✦ ✦

Moments later she was pounding on the door of Mazadar's private office again, her face set in an angry mask. *Do not show deference*, she remembered Amadin telling her, and by Onoma she had no intention of showing anything of the kind.

The door's wooden face reappeared, looking angrier than before.

"What now?"

"We need to talk about Warden Emeritus Bardun Jacques."

Mazadar's face in the door frowned so hard the wood creaked. "Your task as his advocate is your own, and . . ."

"The conditions of his imprisonment are unacceptable."

"He is a dangerous invoker. Perhaps the most dangerous alive. He cannot be—"

"I am not talking about the censors." Aelis dug her nails into her palms to keep from shouting. "Commander, do we need to have this discussion in a hallway?"

The face dissolved and the door swung open. Aelis marched past the cases of folders and stopped a respectful sword-length from the desk, where Mazadar sat like a scowling thundercloud.

"Now, Warden," he began, his voice like gravel tossed over rocks, "whatever special treatment you think Jacques is entitled to . . ."

"His title is Archmagister, Warden Emeritus, and Aldayim Chair of Magical Practice at the Lyceum, Commander," Aelis interjected. "And even if you think *that* doesn't deserve better treatment than would be given a common thief or murderer," she quickly added, seeing that she'd chosen a wrong tack from the way Mazadar stood up out of his chair and flattened his hands on his desk, "I come to you as an anatomist and surgeon. His imprisonment is going to *kill* him."

"Why do you say that?" His white-knuckled hands relaxed a bit.

"I was not able to examine him in any meaningful way under the influence of his censor guards," Aelis replied, "but he may have an advancing lung disease."

"Could you treat it, given free access to your magic?"

"I could," Aelis said, "but the fact is that given his age and the many wounds that have accrued during his decades of warden service, the conditions of that imprisonment are entirely unsuitable. He needs clean, dry air, better food, better water, and better clothing."

"And I suppose you want him put up in your family's townhouse, then? A comfortable spot he can easily escape from?"

"Are you accusing me of plotting an escape, Commander?" Aelis slipped her notebook out of her belt pouch. "That is a very serious charge. Do I need to hire a lawyer?" She smiled very faintly. "Please let me know so I can stop at an Urdimonte branch to arrange retainers." *If you're going to bring my family into it, I'll remind you of what that* fucking *means.*

"I make no accusations, Warden," Mazadar said, waving a hand. "I meant no offense. Still and all, he is a dangerous man and that must be accounted for."

"By all means keep him in Cabal Command," Aelis said, "but do it in a tower above ground, with fresh air and sunlight, give him what is served in the refectory, all the water he can drink, and allow me, free of the censor's field, to examine him and to call in other necromancers if I decide it is necessary."

"You take the title of advocate rather too literally, I think."

"Maybe. But I do know that if he is too ill to stand trial or, Onoma forfend, he dies before the trial is convened, that will reflect very poorly on his custodians and everyone connected to them."

The dwarf's eyebrows knit tightly together and Aelis decided to risk her point.

"In fact, given the accusations against him, there may be connections who fervently wish that to be the case. The wardens cannot be seen as a political tool willing to dispose of one of their own once he proves inconvenient."

"Fine," Mazadar said. "I will have Jacques moved to a less isolated . . . but still secure . . . room in the south tower."

"Thank you, Commander. This decision does you credit," Aelis replied.

"You may go now, Warden."

"Not till I have the orders moving him in my hand to deliver to the warden of the watch."

Mazadar's glare was strong enough to break glass. Aelis only smiled at him until he seized a pen and a sheet of paper and began scribbling orders.

8

OLD FRIENDS

Aelis felt at least moderately accomplished when she left the keep that after-noon. Miralla had been off duty by the time she'd made it down to the warden of the watch's station, replaced by a thin middle-aged man in shabby illusion-ist's yellow who had seemed uninterested in the orders until Aelis demanded to oversee the process or take the matter to Commander Mazadar.

She made the trip back down with him to the censors and a shocked Bar-dun Jacques. The move up to his new quarters in the south tower had been slow and laborious, but they arrived to find liveried servants cleaning out the room, laying a fire in the small hearth, and setting out fresh clothing.

Mazadar runs an efficient command, she thought. *Useful knowledge.*

Her old mentor had been too taxed by the sudden change in surround-ings to talk much, and while Aelis had been afraid that parading through the keep in his dirty prisoner's robe, escorted by censors, might have wounded his pride, no other wizard had crossed their path.

Likely enough they can feel the censors and are avoiding them. She didn't like being inside their sphere any better for the second time in as many hours, but there was nothing for it.

"Well, de Lenti," Bardun Jacques said, once the censors were back outside his door, "I can't say you don't get results. Now go and get more important things done."

"Yes, Archmagister," she murmured. The fact that there'd been no insult or mockery attached to his tired words drove home how weary he must have been, and she left without further fuss, promising to check in again in the morning; he'd only grunted in answer.

Now she was on her way out of the keep entirely, dressed in her only clean clothing: the slightly more formal but still sturdy robes she'd worn when they'd first set out on the coach some weeks ago. She hadn't spent as much time as she would've liked in Lascenise while she was at the Lyceum, but she knew her way to the Ruby Chapel district as well as she knew the garden paths of her father's summer palace.

She had to cut through several short streets to hit Iziod's Way, a main east-west thoroughfare, and then it was a long walk under the afternoon sun. The buildings got taller and grander, the clothing richer, the smells more en-ticing than the sewer-scented tang of the harder, grimmer parts of the city left behind.

The farther west she went, the more it smelled like *money*.

She saw houses she knew, houses where she'd attended parties both grand and tedious, houses with coats of arms above the doors, with coachways lined with gravel and armed guards at their gates. The guards were for show; nobody in their right mind robbed houses or businesses in Ruby Chapel.

Should've hired a coach, she thought, though her legs weren't tired and her feet were unbothered by the city streets. She found them a relief, in fact, after so much grass and loose dirt and stubbled fields and snowy hills. But she should've hired a coach just because she *could have*.

It wasn't long before she arrived at her destination: a collection of the finest clothiers, haberdashers, outfitters, bookbinders, tailors, jewelers, and leatherworkers to be found for hundreds of miles in any direction. There were no stalls set out here, only brightly lit, glass-fronted shops with silk awnings or cloth banners stuck on poles outside their door to signal that they were open.

She saw the bright gold-edged green silk flag she was looking for, with a script *M* gracefully embroidered upon it.

Aelis brushed hopelessly at her robes as she entered the shop, There was a little vestibule lit with hanging conjurer's lights and a long iron boot-scraper, the angled bar held up by wrought-iron dogs

"Welcome to Manxam's Outfitters," called a voice as Aelis gave the bottom of her boots a cursory scrape. Aelis thought she recognized the voice, braced herself, then pushed aside the curtain that led into the shop itself.

The narrow entryway opened onto widely spaced shelves and mannequins bearing all manner of robes, jackets, dresses, skirts, trousers, blouses, belts, hats, and boots in every Lyceum color and combination.

Aelis gravitated toward a row of predominantly black clothing, naturally, from practical jackets and riding skirts to heavily brocaded formal robes with silver thread around the collar and cuffs. She was leaning close to take in the details, rows of grinning death's heads picked delicately out in the finest gray thread, when a gasp brought her up short.

She turned to see a dwarf who came out from behind the raised counter. He wore a four-pocket silk waistcoat that looked black at first glance, then gray, then purple, then deep blue, gray trousers, fine spectacles with faceted crystal lenses, and no beard, just carefully trimmed sideburns that came to points along his chin.

"*Lady de Lenti*," he breathed, "what have you *done* to those robes? And why are you walking around Ruby Chapel in them? People will know they are my work . . ."

"Good to see you too, Drewic," she muttered. "And these robes being the best clothes I have to hand at the moment is really the reason I'm here."

"The *best* clothes? I may demand satisfaction for that insult," Drewic said indignantly as he hurried over to her side, picking at a stray thread here, a stain there. "Were you chasing pigs in this? Rustling cattle?"

"Fighting brigands, in point of fact," Aelis said. "I made it to Lascenise with but two sets of clothes; these robes, and a jacket and riding skirts. Those are fine for what they are, but, of course, not fit to wear here in the Ruby."

"Fighting brigands in perfectly serviceable function robes? How dare you!" The dwarf looked up at her, smiling. "The good news, of course, is that this means we get to dress you all over again. Come, come in, to the back rooms. Coffee? Wine?"

"Aren't we nearing your closing hour?"

Drewic turned back toward her and lifted one eyebrow over the rim of his silver spectacles. "To address this horror you have wrought, Lady de Lenti, my staff and are I prepared to work overtime." When he said "staff," he reached into a pocket and produced a tiny crystal bell, which he rang twice.

From no doors that Aelis could spot, four people appeared, dressed in similar but less grand versions of Drewic's vest, trousers, and gartered shirt, his white, theirs gray or green. All of them stood a respectful distance away, hands behind their back. One dwarf, one gnome, and two humans; the dwarf was likely enough a relation, a son or nephew, but she knew enough about the reputation of Manxam's to know that nepotism would only go so far as to get a family member in the door.

Aelis was slightly unnerved at the speed and efficiency and to some extent the *extravagance* of this service. She'd grown up with it, of course, but a year around folk who in the main did not know of her family or title had put all this in a different light. She decided to lean into the luxury, if only for the night.

"I . . . couldn't say no to coffee, Drewic. I am afraid, however, that I only have time tonight to fit one piece . . ."

"You wound me, Lady de Lenti. To come into my shop promising a complete fitting out, and then . . ."

"I am meeting a friend for dinner at Tausner's," Aelis said. "In two hours. But I am likely to be in the city and possibly the Lyceum for some time. Perhaps as long as a month."

Drewic took a deep breath, then his eyes narrowed as he fixed them on her, immediately seizing on the problem before him. He pointed to one of the employees and said, "Coffee." To a second, "Get Lady de Lenti's file." Then to the third, "Draw a bath in the finest private chamber." To the fourth, the gnome, he waved to come with him.

"Follow if you please, Lady de Lenti," Drewic said, and led her to the back of the shop. A door opened to admit the three of them into a round chamber with mirrors against one section of wall, a small step in its center, a lacquer screen against the far side of the wall for privacy, and several chairs.

"Now, this dinner; how friendly?"

"We have a history."

"Are you planning to continue it? Are we looking for seductive? Cold and forbidding as a true daughter of Onoma?"

"Why don't we walk a middle ground. And remember, it's dinner at a fine eating house, not a Duke's ball."

"I do not tell you what to do with corpses, Lady de Lenti. Have a seat. It'll be a moment."

By the time she'd sunk gratefully into a seat, a silver coffee cup and saucer were being presented to her by one of the apprentices. Steam wafted up to her as she studied the engraving, the Manxam name over the symbols of all the schools: sword, staff, dagger, wand, diadem, orb, and mirror. She sipped the coffee, which had already been mixed with cream and sugar almost precisely to her taste.

They do know what they're about here, she thought.

While she sat and sipped, Drewic conversed quietly with the gnome and sent him off on some errand. Aelis was too pleased with her coffee to eavesdrop.

The dwarf returned with the file, a wooden board with several sheets of paper clipped to it. Drewic flipped through the pages, considering them as he went.

"If you would take your boots off and stand up, Lady de Lenti," he said, with a shallow bow, "we should confirm some measurements."

"This is the finest coffee I have had since I left for the north," she said, setting the half-full cup down and tugging her boots free. "I don't suppose you'll tell me your supplier."

"We must seize every advantage in our trade. If free coffee with every garment is one of them . . ." He shrugged, reached into a pocket, and produced a black measuring tape and a piece of chalk.

Aelis began to work at the hooks of her robe.

A few moments later, with measurements discreetly taken on the black tape with the bright chalk, Drewic was muttering to himself in Dwarfish.

"Seen it many times down the years. Life in a hard post agrees with you, Lady de Lenti."

Aelis had been somewhat surprised to see the extra muscle definition on her legs, arms, and shoulders in the mirror as well.

"Now. Tonight's dress. It will be warm enough to go without a shawl, but perhaps a sheer scarf in enchanter's green. And I presume you simply must have black, *and* to carry your implements."

"I'm a warden, Drewic. I have to carry at least one of them."

"Someday a warden will let me make a simple, well-fitted dress or jacket that does not have to accommodate a sword belt or a wand or a pocket for a mirror . . ."

He rang his little crystal bell again and the junior dwarf came in, pulling a wheeled rack with three dresses hanging on it.

"Are you sure I can't convince you to wear something primarily in blue? It isn't that black doesn't suit you, Lady, it's just that blue . . ."

"I am a necromancer first and always," Aelis said.

"Of course, of course. Perish the thought. Instead of the traditional slashes on the arms, a green scarf, as I suggested . . ."

"Drewic, I will be guided by all your suggestions, but . . ."

"Yes, yes, time is of the essence. So Marvech will lead you to a private bathing chamber. We will have you dressed, summon a coach, and deposit you at Tausner's doorstep at precisely the right moment. Do I need to send for jewels?"

"No," Aelis said. "It's just dinner, Drewic, not a ball. And I've lost the habit anyway." Aelis had delighted in jewels as much as any child of a noble family when she was young, but such obvious markers of wealth were frowned upon at the Lyceum and in warden service.

"Fine. Off you go then while I make some final adjustments." From yet another vest pocket he produced a small leather case, opening it to reveal a selection of needles in different sizes, already threaded in many colors.

◆ ◆ ◆

Aelis's bath had included a small snifter of brandy, so by the time she was bundled into her coach she was feeling the warm pangs of happy appetites. Her dress had none of the stiffness or discomfort she so often associated with new clothes; it was wonderfully light and free, but she still felt like a warden, sword and dagger on her belt. The first thing she did once she had it all on was to try the quick release of the wand sheath; her slim length of wood fell right into her hand.

"Right in front of me?" Drewic's features were aggrieved in the way only an artist whose work has been questioned could be.

"I have to know, Drewic." She slipped the wand back into place. "If it helps, these sleeve-sheaths have literally saved my life, and the lives of friends." Even as she said that, though, she thought with a pang of the tiny portrait locket the wild enchanter Nathalie had worn, and how it lay in her trunk with two other items of rather more magical import. *Another thing to add to my list while in civilization,* she thought.

"Of course it did. Had you shopped at Litch & Noravious you'd be dead now. May we put that in a testimonial?"

"Perhaps not in that language," Aelis said, stifling a laugh as it seemed the dwarf was deadly serious. "But come, Master Manxam; I would *never* shop anywhere else."

The dwarf sniffed, as if he took that statement as simply a matter of course. "Now, where can a courier find you in the morning? I'll have a list drawn up that you can select from."

"Cabal Keep," Aelis said. "And if I may make one request, Drewic, it is so much colder in Lone Pine than I ever could have believed. To simply walk to the village from my tower in deepest winter means wearing two or three robes, every scarf I own, a hat over a stocking cap . . ."

"Warm. Understood, Lady de Lenti."

"I do have one other question, Drewic, if you do not mind."

"Of course."

"Do you know of the Dobrusz brothers?"

Drewic slipped his spectacles off and began polishing them with a tiny square of cloth he retrieved from a vest pocket. "I know of a Dobrusz family. Distant relations of the Manxams. Very disreputable folk, Lady de Lenti. Moneylenders, caravaners." Drewic's voice slipped to a low, disapproving whisper.

"Those would be the Dobruszes I have in mind," Aelis said. "Know where I could find them in town?"

"They have a trade office in the seedier part of Halfton and likely a yard or a stable or a corral or wherever one keeps horses near a gate," Drewic said. "Easy enough to find if you wanted to ruin your reputation. May I ask why?"

"The Dobrusz brothers are friends of mine, so I'm afraid it is already quite ruined, Drewic," Aelis said, "but I appreciate your concern."

"Well, Lady de Lenti, unless you wish me to find you a tavern brawler or leg-breaker . . . your coach?"

It was hard for Aelis to keep from laughing as the proprietor led her to the front door, where a four-horse team stood at the head of an elegant coach. Aelis strode up into it before the coachman could step down to help her up, one of the assistants told him the destination, and she was off.

Almost immediately she began to feel a little guilty. Why wasn't she working the case yet? *Well, maybe I am. Miralla being in a position here in the city could make her a valuable source of information.* There was no need to engage in profligate luxury like new dresses and hired teams. *Where did that even come from? Even a warden needs clothes, and I haven't got nearly enough with me.*

"Spending all this time in Lone Pine is rubbing off on me," she murmured aloud. *And I already achieved one goal today in getting Bardun Jacques better treatment.*

She resolved to enjoy dinner just as the coach pulled to a stop in front of Tausner's, an unassuming building with a gray brick front and a small stairway leading to frosted glass doors. Aelis could read the strength of the wards written upon them with the barest glance. What they told her, she already knew; Tausner's was the sort of private place where the wealthy and powerful went when they wanted to meet in comfort, without fear of scrying or interruption. As the doors were opened for her by a red-jacketed porter, she felt herself pass through the barrier the abjurations formed, and knew the weapons she carried had been identified and that information relayed to whoever maintained the wards.

"Good evening, Warden Lady de Lenti," a red-jacketed elf said with a slight bow and the faintest ghost of a smile that showed he was not going to stint on the titles of anyone who walked through his door. And it was likely his, Aelis reflected; probably a younger member of the owning family learning the trade from the ground up.

She nodded, and before she could get any words out, he added, "The other member of your party is already seated in the Vesper Room. Shall I guide you there?"

"Please do." The elf turned without a sound and ghosted his way down a corridor, Aelis feeling ungainly and loud in his wake.

The Vesper was one of the smaller dining rooms; Tausner's comprised many distinct rooms, and Aelis would've been hopelessly lost without the guide. She wasn't entirely sure magic wasn't used to obscure the passage—illusions to make corridors seem longer or hide entrances, light enchantments to guide the eye past doors one was not intended to see, abjurations that allowed only authorized people past doors to kitchens and staff areas.

It was only a few moments, though, when she entered a cool, dimly lit room that held only one table. There were also three plinths or obelisks on the walls that didn't feature a door; one of smooth red stone, one of clear crystal, and one of blue-and-silver-veined rock; each emitted wafts of vapor that formed into a shape before disappearing: a pair of dueling knights in armor, a flock of birds, nude figures intertwined. With each half-formed shape there was the merest suggestion of the kind of sounds they would have made: the clash of steel, the trill of birdsong, the moaning of lovers.

Aelis had been in the room before, but this sort of magical art installation had made the place famous, and it was never less than impressive after some time away.

None of it, though, was *quite* as striking as Miralla waiting at the table for her. Her dress was more silver than diviner's white and gleamed around the dark of her exposed neck and shoulders. There were dark abjurer's blue slashes across the bodice; like Aelis, she'd forgone any significant jewelry.

"Do not hesitate to call upon us for anything," the elf said before backing out of the room and disappearing for good. Aelis felt a flush creeping up her cheeks as the full effect of Miralla's dress settled over her, so she quickly pressed forward and unbuckled her swordbelt.

Miralla's own belt hung from a hook on a stand next to the table. Aelis carefully set hers next to it.

"Don't you feel ridiculous wearing a swordbelt to a fine dinner?" Miralla smiled, holding a nearly full glass of white wine near her chin, as she watched Aelis fumble slightly as she set her belt down.

"Fine dinners in this sort of place are in rather short supply at my post," Aelis said. "And I generally don't take my swordbelt off there till the day's work is done." *And sometimes not even then, really*, she thought, recalling the times in the wilderness when she'd slept cold and hard, a hand on her sword through the night.

"Sit. Have a glass." Miralla took up the bottle and poured. Aelis eyed the label.

"Indaran Glacial? My, my." Aelis accepted the glass and considered the pale, nearly colorless wine. "What exactly is the occasion?"

"Can't we just decide to make it one?" They clinked glasses and sipped. The wine was as cold and clear and dry and herbal as she'd hoped. Some part of Aelis's mind wondered how much the private room and rare wine were going to cost Miralla. In their student days, Aelis had never worried about those kinds of costs; a count's daughter generally didn't. Miralla had family wealth, to be sure, but not the ancient kind that Aelis had, and warden pay was taken from military traditions, where a young officer's pay could hardly be expected to meet his expenses. As Aelis considered the cost, the presentation, and the way Miralla leaned over the table, the flush in her cheeks deepened, and she had a realization.

She and Miralla had been friends and lovers, though always with more emphasis on the former. But this sort of display was not something Miralla would put on for a friend she was simply happy to see again.

Do I want to be seduced? Well, of course I do, Aelis thought, covering her brief moment of fluster with a second sip of wine.

But it felt wrong, like a temptation she should not, for once, give in to. In her mind's eye she pictured Maurenia, trapped in the wilderness, gripped by strange magic, and alone. And though no words of dedication had passed between them—and might never—she felt like even reviving an old dalliance was a kind of betrayal. Maurenia had no such choices before her, and they could have this conversation when she did. But until then, Aelis thought, perhaps she owed Maurenia this.

She was opening her mouth to say something when a gold-jacketed server slipped into the room. On the tray the elf balanced lightly on one hand sat a bowl of crushed ice, and atop the ice a glass plate with twelve half-shell oysters, plump and glistening. The server placed it on the center of the table and immediately vanished through the side door she'd materialized in.

"I remember your taste for shellfish," Miralla said. "And I doubt you've seen any since you went so far north . . ."

"Most of the fish I've had has been either smoked or salted," Aelis said, feeling her mouth water.

"Wild-harvested this morning," Miralla said. "There's also fresh squid on the catch list this evening."

"Miralla, before this dinner goes any further, there's something I have to . . ."

The other woman's smile changed. "Don't tell me you met some stout shepherd lad up there in the frozen wastes."

"Not exactly," Aelis said. "But there is someone. I don't know exactly what words to put to it, but . . ." She forced herself to make eye contact before she finished. "I can't."

Miralla reached across the table and took Aelis's wrist. "As long as I haven't lost you to that fumbling idiot Humphrey . . ."

"Not at all," Aelis said with a laugh, and squeezed Miralla's hand as she felt the tension she'd been imagining start to melt away. "He's away in An-traval, the lucky prat. And honestly, fumbling idiot is . . . unkind, isn't it?"

"Fine. Well-meaning fumbler then," Miralla said, and they both paused to sip their wine again.

They shared the oysters, then squid fried just lightly enough that it lost none of its briny tang, then cold melon soup with cream and toasted nuts, then more fish, herb crusted and served in a butter and white wine and lemon sauce that Aelis could've cried over, all with more bottles of white wine as suggested by their various red-and gold-jacketed servers. Their talk became easier, more friendly and calm. Aelis recounted some of her adventures into the wilderness outside Lone Pine, though she left out certain facts. That Tun was a werebear was his secret to divulge, never hers; that she had killed and trapped the spirit of Dalius Enthal de Morgantis un Mahlgren seemed like a note best kept close, so she simply described his actions as a malevolent spirit, origin unknown. She had told the story of Nathalie, though, in all its pity. She didn't spare her own feelings or hesitate when she described how she'd cut the woman's throat. That was the only part where Miralla inter-rupted, laying a hand across the table and onto Aelis's wrist.

"There was nothing else you could have done."

"I could have figured out a way not to be in that moment," Aelis said. "I should never have let it come to that."

"We both know that becoming a warden meant the possibility of taking life, Aelis. All that sword practice isn't just for show."

Aelis eyed her friend across the table and almost said, *Get back to me when you've done it,* but instead she smiled gently and encouraged Miralla to tell of her own first posting.

Miralla's posting in Lascenise had come with more creature comforts than Aelis's but not without action. Local crime had sometimes drawn the ire of the wardens, including an attempt to kill the leader of the Imravalan delegation, which governed the southernmost section of the city, by fanatical Ystainian separatists.

"Dealt with any thieves' guilds?" Aelis asked as Miralla described some of her investigations and confrontations.

"Not directly. Why?"

"Well," Aelis lingered on the word, "it may intersect with my case."

"Aelis, you know that any help I am allowed to provide you by Cabal Com-mand, I will. But before we discuss that, let me say this, friend to friend." She leaned over the table and lowered her voice. "You've been handed a bag of shit, and you'd do well to get rid of it before it starts spreading on you."

"What do you mean?"

"I mean powerful forces in the wardens and the Lyceum are arrayed against Bardun Jacques, and that he is almost *certainly* guilty, and I have no idea what an advocate is going to turn up that can change any of that."

"I think you might be surprised."

"Aelis, I know enough not to underestimate *you*. But this is a bad case. This is the kind of thing that derails a career. He killed a wizard, and he did it horribly and painfully."

"What do you know about it?"

Miralla was silent a moment, looking down and tugging on the table-cloth. "I was on the team that arrested him. I'd seen the remains of the dead wizard, what there was left. Looked like half of him had been stuck into a roaring oven and forgotten."

"Was the arrest peaceful?"

"It was," Miralla said, "but I think only because Bardun Jacques *let* it be. I felt some of what he could have called down with that Anaerion's Eye in his staff. It was terrifying. Stronger than anything I've felt before. That man is dangerous, and I think he's lost his mind."

"He was plenty lucid when I spoke with him. And bag of shit or no bag of shit, I'm here to do a job, and I won't leave it undone," Aelis said.

"You don't change, do you?"

"I've probably changed more than you'd think this past year."

"Oh, your arms and your shoulders told me *that*," Miralla said. "Plenty of physical work to do up there, I see, and lots of sword practice. But in other ways, you probably haven't."

"So his arrest was entirely peaceful?"

Miralla smirked at this blatant attempt at redirecting the conversation, but she nodded. "All the excitement was a couple of warden students near pissing themselves over the legend they thought they were going up against."

"I don't blame them."

"I didn't say I did, but no legend bears scrutiny when you see it up close."

"Maybe. But I've read the same *Lives of the Wardens* you have, Mira, and spoken with the same veterans. However embellished the legend may be by now, Bardun Jacques has done in more villains than any handful of other living wardens you'd care to name."

"If I had the accolades he did, I'd be locked up in a tower full of books and lovers, not poking my nose around in thieves' guilds."

"So, you know what he was poking around at?"

Miralla suddenly avoided eye contact and Aelis knew she'd found something.

"Lucky guess," her friend said lamely. "Just a supposition based on where he was and what he tried to claim . . ."

"Mira, the last place I want to be is on the opposite side of a fight with you."

"Do you think I feel any differently?"

"Then don't lie to me."

"Is this an interrogation now? Is it formal?"

"Of course not." *Not if I can get you to admit to things without it coming to that.* "But you do know something, or you wouldn't have said that."

"Word is the thieves he was investigating—Saltmen of the Tunnels— were stepping too far out of acceptable lines."

"He thought they were called the Hidden Skulls or some such nonsense."

"*They* aren't thieves. They're hired killers. Worlds apart."

"There's a known guild of assassins under the nose of northern Cabal Command and they haven't been rooted out?"

"You say that like it's easy."

"It is. You find one and you kill him, and when more show up you kill them, and so on. Eventually you run out of assassins to kill, and you crack a good bottle to celebrate a job well done."

"Two questions," Miralla said, sitting up straighter, her brown eyes narrowing. "First: Are you *trying* to sound like Bardun Jacques? Because you're doing a damn good impression. Second: Do you really think all non-wizards are that stupid? Professional assassins are not easily seen, much less caught. They've killed wizards. Wardens, even."

Aelis had a sudden cold stab in her gut that had nothing at all to do with the exquisite meal she'd just eaten, followed by an intense desire to get back to her rooms in the keep and examine some of the things she'd lugged down the king's road.

"Miralla, I . . . have to go. It'll be an early start and a great deal of work tomorrow."

"But we've got a half bottle of Orvalyn Berrydrop still to drink with the cakes . . ."

"I am afraid even another half bottle is going to do me in," Aelis said. The thought of missing out on that rich dessert wine and Tausner's legendary cake cart tugged at Aelis's heart for a moment. But her intuition had spoken, and she needed to get back to her rooms to find out what it meant.

"The Aelis de Lenti I knew would've dragged me out to her favorite winesinks in the Tremont after we finished here, stayed out till two hours past midnight, and kept me *awake* till the sun came up."

"And if I had no responsibilities or attachments, then I'd do all of that again," Aelis said, with not a little regret. She stood up and slipped her swordbelt back on. Miralla came to her, and they hugged tightly. Miralla smelled like spice and wine and rosewater, and felt good in Aelis's arms.

Would Maurenia really object?

Sensing a shift in Aelis's body language, Miralla brought her face up, shifting their embrace to something more intimate and less friendlike, running her hand across Aelis's shoulder.

"Are you sure . . . ?"

Past a throat thick with desire and regret, Aelis said, "I am." She stepped out of Miralla's arms, squeezed her wrist with her hand. "We'll see each other while I'm here, won't we? Lunch, dinner again?"

"Of course."

"Good night, and thank you for dinner. There is . . . nothing like this where

I've been." Saying it felt like a betrayal of Rus and Martin's honest little inn, and especially Martin's cooking. But there was no lie to it.

"Next dinner is on you," Miralla said, smiling again. "The next two, in fact."

"Deal." Then Aelis was making for the door and a red-jacketed elf appeared at her elbow.

"Will the Warden Lady require a coach?"

"I think yes," Aelis said. As much as she wanted to do some more walking about the city, a coach would get her back where she needed to be much faster.

9

HIDDEN SKULLS

The night air was cool and the ride bracing, Aelis having pressed the window open as they went, and it seemed to drive most of the slowness imparted by her rich, wine-heavy dinner out of her head. A guard barred the coach's way at the gate, but Aelis stuck her head out and changed that quickly, and a yawning keep servant conveyed her to her quarters.

There was a smoored fire in the hearth and no tapers lit; Aelis kept the fire as it was but lit three candles and dug in her trunk for her alchemy lamp. She got it blazing a focused white light on her bed, and then pulled forth a wrapped and tied bundle from the same trunk.

She set it down and undid the knots, then took out one of the dead assassins' cloaks wrapped about his knife and his compact yet deadly crossbow.

"I wish Maurenia were here," Aelis murmured. "Or the Dobruszes. They'd have these things apart in a moment."

When it came to weapon maintenance, she had nothing but rags, oil, and stones. An abjurer's sword was not meant to be prised apart and inspected by anyone short of a conjurer-smith, and an anatomist's blade *couldn't* be taken apart without damaging its magical components.

She certainly couldn't use them as tools, either, and risk chipping or dulling the blades. So, she settled on her medical kit and pulled out lancets, needles, knives, and a few vials of reagents that might prove useful.

It took some testing to find the edge of a tool, a small bone saw, in fact, that was the right size and strength to begin levering a pin out of the crossbow's assembly. Then it was a matter of carefully breaking it down till each part, most of which she couldn't name, lay spread out atop the blanket on her bed. She wasn't sure what she was looking for, but she held each piece up to her alchemy lamp and looked over them carefully.

Nothing. Not one single maker's mark, nor any identifying bit that might confirm that sudden suspicion riding strong in her gut. She swept the pieces onto her small table in a jumble and turned to the blade. She spread a few drops of solvent around the solid pommel of the dagger and schooled herself to patience.

Count to one hundred, she thought, but abandoned it by twenty-five and began prying at the thing with her bare hands, eventually wresting it off at the cost of skinned knuckles and raw fingers. She gave the freed parts of the blade the same intent examination she'd given the crossbow, searching every newly exposed piece for a mark of any kind. She saw none, and turned and sat on her bed in exasperation.

She tightened her fist around the tang of the knife and was surprised to feel a different texture along one side; something, however slight, that projected. She held it up to the light and saw only a slight discoloration.

Biting her lip, she rifled through a handful of vials till she found the one she wanted; a weak acid.

She was still careful with it, though, setting the blade down on the table, uncorking the vial with care, and dribbling just a drop or three onto the metal. She corked it and secured it back in the case and then turned to the knife blade with a rag, rubbing the acid carefully into the metal, feeling bits of it crumble away like corrosion.

When she lifted it to the light, she saw the faintest outline of a skull traced on the metal.

"Hidden fucking Skulls," she muttered. "Aren't you so very goddamned clever?"

She carefully wrapped all the pieces of both weapons back up in the dead assassin's cloak, carefully hung up her perfect new dress, and fell into a restless sleep.

◆ ◆ ◆

Aelis was up slightly after dawn, bleary-eyed and slow from wine and rich food she was no longer used to. Fortunately, the keep kitchen turned out coffee by the cauldron and a pot and a half set her on her feet before she went to visit Bardun Jacques.

Again she made that peculiar passage into a world devoid of magic, bound by purely mundane physical laws once she came within range of the censors. The handle of her medical kit became rougher against her skin; the smell of the leather became less clear to her, and blood pounded in her head.

She had no idea if they were the same pair she'd seen before; part of the effect intended by their helms, identical swords, and long cloaks. One of them stepped forward to bar her way.

"You cannot bring that in with you unless it has been cleared by the commander . . ."

"It was as the prisoner's physician that I argued for him to be moved here," Aelis said. "And I need to examine him to be sure that he will survive long enough to even stand trial. To do that I *must* maintain at least some connection to my own power."

"Then we will have to accompany you into his cell."

"Absolutely not. Communication between an accused warden and their advocate must be undertaken in complete confidential privacy. You know this."

The censor snarled behind her helm. Aelis felt a stab of fear in her gut; any wizard did when under the effect of a censor's power.

"Fine. I will allow you a *trickle*, but no more. Nothing more than a First Order Necromantic Pulse. If I feel the slightest tang of invocation coming from inside that room, we will come in swinging."

"Understood." Aelis swept in through the door and was surprised to find Bardun Jacques leaning against the far wall, his face pushed as far into the narrow slit of a window as he could. He was wearing a plain brown robe; certainly nothing befitting his rank, but better than the rags he'd been wearing down in the dungeon, though he still held onto that roughly carved crutch.

"Morning, de Lenti," he drawled. "Given the rate at which you accomplished this yesterday, I assume you've come to tell me I'm free to go."

"Not quite, Archmagister," she said. "They fed you better this morning?"

"They did indeed. All the water I can drink, a mug of weak tea, bread that doesn't test an old man's teeth, even a couple boiled eggs. Paradise."

"Good. Now sit on your bed, please. They're going to allow me enough necromancy to examine your health."

"I'm healthy as an ox," he protested.

"I'm the only one here qualified to make those comparisons. Sit, please."

With an inarticulate grumble he took up his crutch, tapped his slow way to the bed and sat down.

Aelis could feel her power again, lurking largely beyond her reach. Without her dagger it was a genuine struggle to reach out and grasp enough of it to use a First Order Diagnostic.

The resulting swell of information nearly overwhelmed her. First and foremost, she realized quickly that Bardun Jacques was in a great deal of constant pain; the muscles of his leg, his back, and his hands sent steady pulses of red through the spread of colors that represented his many organ systems.

How is he standing upright?

She ignored these for the moment and reached into her bag for a small silver cone so she could focus on his lungs. She placed the wide end against his chest and the smaller to her ear and listened, all the while examining the color her power showed her.

Healthy lungs were a blue so pale it was nearly white; his were darker, with the occasional floating specks of black.

Her ears, too, told her the story; a constant gurgling wetness in every breath he took.

"What is it, de Lenti?" he rumbled, the words coming like a distant roar through her listening cone. She straightened up and set the cone down.

"It isn't good, Archmagister."

"Did they manage to kill me in that cell?"

"Not quite. There's plenty I can do about it." She put the cone back in her bag. "I'll need to write some orders on the keep's apothecary to make up the medicaments I plan to administer, and if the censors would let me draw enough for some second and third order pulses I can do even more."

"Does sound like plenty. Doesn't sound like a cure, though."

"The kind of treatment I can offer will give you years," Aelis said. "If you follow my instructions closely."

"So I'm a lunger?"

"I don't like that term. No patient can be reduced to one part of their body, no matter how damaged it might be."

"You aren't saying no."

"In every way that matters," Aelis said, "I'm right. But if you want to use that term, I can't stop you."

Bardun Jacques grunted. "Fine. Midarra has given me enough close escapes for any two lifetimes. Let's just see if She doesn't come up with another one before all is said and done, eh?"

"Let's also talk about pain management . . ."

"Like poppy brandy? No."

"Archmagister, the pain I could detect must be debilitating. I don't know how you're walking and talking with it."

"Hasn't stopped me yet," he replied, shrugging. "And I can't afford to have this slowed down any." He tapped the side of his head. "I haven't got the reflexes or the power I had when I was merely twice your age. So I have to be smarter to see the bastards coming. They get close enough, I'm already dead."

"Fine. But there are less intrusive therapies. Willow-bark tea should answer at least a little."

"That tastes like boiled dirt."

"Take it anyway. Now, Archmagister . . ." Aelis looked at the stump of his leg. "What happened? When I last saw you, you had a limp, but . . ."

"I had a limp because I wore a Wychwood leg. They took it away when I was imprisoned."

"What? Took it away?"

"Didn't belong to me. It belonged to the service, to the Lyceum, whoever owns those sorts of things, so it was revoked. Along with my staff."

"I can't get you the staff back, but I could at *least* get you a new prosthesis. A mundane one."

"For my trial, maybe."

Aelis decided to take the small victory and nodded, putting her kit back in order, then slipping something out of it into her hand.

"I may have an update on something related to your case. You mentioned the Hidden Skulls as the name of a thieves' guild. Well, they aren't that . . . they're *assassins*, and I'm told they operate out of Lascenise, that they've killed wizards."

He grunted. "That's what I get for assuming the thieves and the hired killers were the same."

"I was attacked by them on the road to Lascenise. We killed two of them, armed with alchemically enhanced witsend bolts. I had to burn some of that poison out of the warden I traveled with. This was hundreds of miles from Lascenise."

"Well," Bardun Jacques said, turning to face her. "Sounds like someone didn't fucking want you to get here, doesn't it?"

"It certainly raises a number of questions."

"Were I you, I'd go talk to the warden I rode down with."

"I was already thinking I needed to," Aelis said. "He ought to be angry that someone laid a trap for us that deliberately."

"Or . . ."

"Or he was in on it. I can't see it, though . . ." Aelis thought back to the ambush, and Amadin's reaction. "Son of a *bitch*," she suddenly spat.

"My mother's been dead long enough I no longer feel a son's reflexive impulse to defend her honor," Bardun Jacques said, "but you might explain lest I take offense anyway, out of sheer boredom."

"When we took the assassins on the road, I told him we should keep one alive. And I was about to; an enchantment would've seen to it. He did *something* that cooked the poor bastard alive from the inside."

"Ahh." Bardun Jacques nodded slowly. "Probably the Tingler. It can disable. It can also get away from the weak willed and, well . . . do what you just said. Doesn't prove anything."

"No, but it makes me trust him a good deal less."

"Well, there's an important lesson for you in all this regardless. The only wizard you can trust right now is yourself."

"Why do you say that?"

"Did I not tell you yesterday, de Lenti? Wizards are smuggling artifacts. *Powerful* wizards. They can get other wizards on side just by offering them plums—promotion, better posts, academic sinecures, political appointments. We're an ambitious and grasping lot."

"How do you know that wizards are smuggling artifacts? We didn't really cover that part."

"Stumbled on to a crate of the things bound for the Lyceum. I *knew* that smugglers were moving something important . . . too much bribe money was changing hands, they were hiring goddamned wagons instead of walking the shit through a gate in one nondescript pocket. So I stopped one of their wagons. Manifest said they were carrying plates to the Lyceum. Dishes and crockery. And they were . . . but I could feel the magic in them. So, I cracked one open and dug around."

"What . . . were the men on the wagon doing?"

"Chasing an illusion I wove. Pretty woman. Works often. When it doesn't, a pretty man usually does," he said, shrugging. "Inside that crate I did find some plates, alright. And one of them was a Silver Plate of Staranoviz. In another I found a Tremallon's Visor; see *straight* through the best illusion an Archmagister can build with one of those. A good, well-organized band of smugglers and thieves might come across one of those in a career-making job. Two of them? In one shipment, and going *to* the Lyceum? Didn't add up. That's when I started leaning on them."

"Why were you watching them in the first place? You're an Emeritus Warden and you have an endowed chair at the Lyceum. You . . ."

"You're trying to say I'm old, and I shouldn't be out running down villains anymore, aren't you? Well, I can't stand more than one term at the Colleges at a time, and I sure as seven hells don't intend to retire."

"Okay . . . I need more information. Who was supposed to take receipt of that shipment of goods?"

"I don't remember." Bardun Jacques sighed. "I knew they were running these wagons fairly regularly. Some servant or functionary at one of the Colleges, undoubtedly." He rubbed at his eyes, and suddenly looked every day of his battered age. "I'm sorry, de Lenti. I used to remember everything. Age, I'm afraid."

That's the kind of detail I really could've used, Aelis thought but didn't say. Instead, she said, "If I can find another one of these wagons, I can follow it and see who takes responsibility for it."

"Or shake down this guild of thieves till they give up their source."

"Or both," Aelis said. "Definitely both. Give me a moment to make one of my lists."

"You shouldn't write down things that just anyone can read. Put it in a cipher if you must."

"I haven't got the head for those things," Aelis muttered, as she dug out her paper and writing stick.

1. *Apothecary*
2. *Lawyer*
3. *Wagons/slums*
4. *Lyceum/libraries?*
5. *Talk to Am.*

Aelis surprised herself slightly with that last item, but she felt she needed to at least touch base with him. She noted Bardun Jacques's eyes closing and stood up quietly.

"Get some rest. Eat all the food and drink, all the water they'll bring you," she murmured. "Your body needs it after your confinement."

"Don't suppose you can talk them into sending up some spirits. Whiskey, for preference. Brandy if need be. Anaerion help me, even rum would do."

"I doubt it," Aelis said. "Spirits will not help. Maybe I could arrange some light wine."

Bardun Jacques grumbled but pushed himself back onto his bed and lay down. "Some physician you are. A stiff glass of good dwarfish whiskey would make a fine tonic to take down whatever poisons you're going to have the apothecary whip up for me."

Aelis ignored this, finished packing her kit, and slipped out the door, pondering the list in her pocket as she made her way to the keep's apothecary.

✦ ✦ ✦

Bardun Jacques's file listed his lawyer as one Khorais Angleton, of Rue's Inn Court, Halfton. That was a long walk to the far southwestern corner of the city, so she hailed a coach and watched the scenery change as she rode from the blocky military trappings around Cabal Keep, around the glittering commercial edges of Ruby Chapel, and eventually into the less dense, more elegant houses of Halfton, where a number of Lascenise's gnomish and dwarvish citizens and businesses congregated.

Rue's Inn Court proved to be a curving street end surrounded by an absolute *warren* of law offices, bookbinders, copyists, printshops, stationers, ink merchants, and stalls selling pens, quills, quill-sharpeners, inkpots, tree-gum, dyes, pigments, and glues of every description.

She wasn't long on the street with a puzzled look on her face before a gnomish child, barely higher than her knee and moving so fast he was hard to get a good look at, was tugging at her jacket.

"Can guide you anywhere, ma'am, just give me the name, I'll have you there, no charge if I'm wrong, just trust in me and don't forget if I lead you right . . ."

"Khorais Angleton," she said. "Lawyer."

"Ahh, young Angleton," the child squeaked. "With Pyriot and Gleese, very good firm, very old, well regarded, follow me, follow me."

The gnome wrapped both hands around one of Aelis's and started dragging her onward. It was easy enough for her to see over the bustling crowd, as most of it were gnomish and dwarfish folk, but she would've certainly lost her guide if not for the strong grip on her hand, as the child was mostly just a bobbing head amid the throng.

Aelis was forced to brush off two pen-sellers on their way, though one particularly dedicated wax merchant stuck half a black cylinder into her hand yelling, "Sample, Warden, sample, wise Warden, you'll know where to come back and get the best, Jebble and Daughters Limited, best wax in Halfton!"

She was still gripping it when the gnome pointed her to a staircase on the side of a building and held out her hand. Aelis stuck two small pieces of silver in it and the child vanished directly.

The entire stairway shook as she set foot on it. *No staircase ought to even be here*, she thought. It looked as if it had just been wandering by and decided to lean up against the building to catch its breath. But she got to the top, to a small, beautifully painted sign with impeccable lettering that read PYRIOT AND GLEESE, ATTORNEYS. Beneath that, in smaller letters, CONTRACTS, WILLS, SUITS, DISPUTES, COUNTERSUITS, FAMILY MATTERS, COUNTRY COMPLAINTS, WAR BENEFITS, and beneath that, in letters she had to squint to read, CRIMINAL DEFENSE.

There was a cord she assumed to be a bellpull dangling to one side, so she gave it a tug. She heard nothing, so she pulled it twice more. Still nothing. She was about to pull it a fourth time when the door opened, and a gnome in a long green jacket with lace peeking out from the cuffs glared up at her.

"No need to ring the bell off the hook," he growled. "Stupid big clods, always hanging on it."

"I'm sorry, good gnome," Aelis said, gathering what little patience she had, "but I didn't hear anything when I rang."

"And you didn't *need* to, did you?" He tapped his dangling earlobe. "Gnomes hear plenty of things you don't. Ring it and wait! Is that so hard?"

Waiting was getting harder by the moment, but Aelis reasoned that giving this gnome a box on his large ears wasn't the way to open her relationship with the firm.

"I apologize, good gnome," she said, through teeth that were just this side of clenched. "I need to speak with one Khorais Angleton. I am told they work at this firm."

"Maybe she does and maybe she doesn't," the gnome said, narrowing his eyes. "Have you an appointment?"

"No."

"Then why would you need to see Ms. Angleton?"

"Because we are, technically, meant to work together. She is defending a warden against criminal charges, and I am that warden's advocate."

"Damn stupid system, assigning an accused *two* people to work on their behalf. You'd never have that kind of chaos in a gnome-ordered system, no ma'am. Only wizards could come up with such self-serving nonsense. I'd have a word with . . ."

"Please," Aelis said, raising a hand, "we can debate the equity of internal warden justice another time. Please take me to Ms. Angleton."

"I'll have to see if she's in," the gnome said, moving to shut the door. Aelis closed her eyes and started counting, which soon got derailed with a lovingly rendered daydream of kicking the door in front of her wide open and giving that gnome a good shaking. She had just about convinced herself to pull the bell again when the door opened.

"Come in, please," the green-coated gnome said, now all stiff manners. She had to bend down a bit to fit through the door; they had made some effort to anticipate taller clients, but in general Halfton just wasn't built for people her height, and moving about in it was a constant reminder of that fact.

Aelis was led past a sitting room and into a room with a table and four chairs, two of which were sized for her, two smaller. Greencoat disappeared as soon as she'd entered.

After a few moments of solitude both the door she'd entered and one on the far wall opened; Greencoat came in with a silver coffee service on a tray, and Aelis's opinion of him positively soared. The other entrant was a young gnome with sleek dark hair cut short against her head, dressed in a dark red coat and trousers that seemed, to Aelis's eye, just a couple of seasons out of date. This new gnome had a thick leather folder bound in black ribbons under her arm, a magnifying glass on a loop around her neck, and a harried, sleepless expression that Aelis knew from her own mirror in her student days.

"Thank you, Kavan," the gnome woman said, "we can pour for ourselves."

The gnome steward bowed and retreated but not without a stream of murmured protestations. "Pour their own coffee, not in the founders' day, mark my words, isn't *done*, an associate needs a steward's hand to do anything right . . ."

Aelis knew that if she could hear it, so could the gnome, and as their eyes met, they both stifled their laughter.

"When you get hired by Pyriot and Gleese, they give you a set of keys, an outfitting allowance that will buy one new or two used court robes, and Kavan," Khorais said. "He means well, but nothing is up to his standards."

"I am absolutely sure he and my father's chief butler would get on famously," Aelis said.

"Khorais Angleton, newest and only criminal defense associate, Pyriot and Gleese." The gnome extended a hand.

Aelis took it carefully. "Warden Aelis de Lenti. Advocate for Bardun Jacques. Pleased to meet you, Ms. Angleton."

"Call me Khorais, Warden."

"Then by all means, call me Aelis."

"Fine. With that out of the way," Khorais said as she dropped her heavy leather file to the table with a resounding thump, "let us have some of that coffee and see if we can't get your mentor out of the trouble he's gotten into."

Aelis already had a pot on board, but she needed to make up for lost time, so she mixed her regular cup, two spoons of sugar and a splash of milk, and sipped, while Khorais took hers black.

"How much do you know about the charges?" the lawyer asked as they both set their cups down.

"Assault by magic, murder by magic."

"Let's not forget Malfeasance and Misuse of Power," Khorais added. "Though since those don't carry a death sentence, it's easier to lose sight of them. What about the circumstances?"

"I know what he told *me*," Aelis said. "I don't know the official account."

"The official account, condensed, is that he was interfering in a warden investigation of local crime, and using his power to intimidate people of interest, as well as witnesses, hence the Malfeasance and Misuse of Power. Then a wizard was tasked to intervene, one—" Khorais checked her notes. "Arstan Nicholaz."

"I note you said wizard and not *warden*."

"I did. He isn't noted as a warden in any of my notes or any of the official documents."

"If Bardun Jacques was interfering with a warden operation, why wasn't a *warden* sent to back him down?"

"I feel like you are better qualified to answer that than I am, Aelis."

"There's any number of possible answers. Perhaps he wasn't commissioned but working with local wardens; it happens. But," she added after a moment's consideration, "I doubt that was the case."

Khorais only raised a thin eyebrow at her.

"I think he was representing someone outside the warden service. Someone at the Lyceum."

"How do you people keep your power structures straight? Confuses seventeen kinds of devil out of me."

"As a warden, I'm obligated to take orders that originate from Cabal Command; Mazadar, here in Lascenise, and anyone he appoints to convey orders to me; and I have to at least consider the word of wardens of longer service. As a *wizard*, well . . . it becomes more complicated."

"Doesn't it always?"

Aelis decided she liked Khorais at that moment. "The very first rule at the heart of all wizard politics is very much the same as in every other kind of politics: shit rolls downhill." Khorais echoed her last three words as soon as Aelis began to say them, and they chuckled. "There is a constant, ongoing game of figuring out who is above, below, and roughly parallel to you on said hill. One never-changing rule is that if someone's full name begins with *Arch*, you had damn well better do as they say."

"So, an Archmagister can order a warden off a case if it is in their interest?"

"Let's say, they can strongly suggest it, and make a warden's life very difficult if they choose not to."

"And does the fact that Bardun Jacques is both an Archmagister and, what is it . . . Warden Emeritus . . . not mean that everyone needs to get out of his way?"

"Building bridges has never been one of the Archmagister's strong suits," Aelis said. "He's more likely to burn the bridge, everyone on it, and the towns on either side. Burn the river too, if he thinks the river deserves it."

"Assuming you aren't being literal, you mean he is not good at backroom politics and manipulation?"

"I believe he thinks those are beneath his notice," Aelis said.

"How'd he become an Archmagister, then?"

"You can play as many political tricks as you like, but at the root of it, promotion and position are born of arcane power. If there is a living invoker who can match him, I haven't met them and I wouldn't much want to."

"That doesn't clarify everything, but it paints a bit of a picture," Khorais said. "How do you know which wizard is more powerful?"

"Well, aside from duels to the death, now quite outlawed, if it's a wizard of your same Colleges and years at the Lyceum . . . you know. If you aren't, well . . . there are ways. They aren't always pleasant, and they generally aren't talked about."

Khorais sipped her coffee. "You people could stand to be about forty percent less mysterious, and at least that much less full of yourselves."

Aelis laughed, unable to help it. "I think you're right. What kind of defense were you hoping to mount, if I may ask?"

Khorais poured the last of her coffee down her throat, set the cup down, adjusted it, tugged at the fall of the reading glass on her chest, aligned the folder with the bottom of the table, and finally said, "I don't know. On the face of it, he appears guilty, but all the direction he's given me has been that he will absolutely not throw himself upon the mercy of the court."

"How much has he told you about it, from his side?"

"Not enough. We've only been able to have a few short meetings, as the censors always usher me out . . ."

Aelis felt the anger that had flared in her when she'd seen his conditions the day before roar again. "*That* will be cleared up. He's been moved to safer, healthier confinement on my authority. If you are given any further trouble as far as meeting with him, you bring it to me, and I'll fix it." She spread her hands on the cool tabletop and took a deep breath.

"As far his defense goes," Khorais said, "I do think he should at least consider the chance that he should accept guilt, and . . ."

"He won't," Aelis said. "And nothing will convince him to do so."

Khorais rubbed her temples with one hand. "Did he do it?"

"I'm not sure I can answer that. But I will say this: I'm going to pick up the investigation he had interrupted, immediately. I expect to uncover evidence that should change the lay of the case."

"That means he did it."

"Not my words."

"No," Khorais said, shuffling some papers around in the file. "But you wouldn't be looking to *change the lay* if he hadn't done it, would you? Please, Aelis. You have to be honest with me. And we need to be ready to appear in court."

"When?"

"Thirteen days."

"Can we delay that?"

"It was already delayed for your arrival."

"Maybe I can delay it further on medical grounds. Claim he's not healthy enough to begin proceedings just yet."

"Is he ill?"

"He isn't as well as I would like," Aelis said. "I'm working on that, too."

"Every prisoner should be so lucky to have someone like you seeing to their needs," Khorais said. "Now, where are you going to get this, ah, exculpatory evidence you're promising me?"

"Probably best you don't know that."

"A policy of direct and unvarnished honesty would suit me best, Aelis. Hiding things from each other will not help us, and it will not help Bardun Jacques."

"Fine. I'm going down to Slop's End to poke at this thieves' guild."

Khorais sat in silence for a while, composing her face. "And how, exactly, are you going to do that? Just walk around the district asking people if they are thieves?"

"I'm not really a *planner*," Aelis said. "More likely I'll just stick my thumb in someone's eye and see how they react."

"Is that a euphemism?"

"To be honest, Khorais, I'm never sure. Might take me a while to figure out whose eye to poke, and exactly how. But I am good at making things happen, and I'm even better at reacting to them."

"I might be able to help. I know someone down there, and he knows plenty of people."

"This sounds like it's going to cost me money," Aelis said.

"It is hard to get him to focus unless there's silver in it," Khorais admitted. "But I find that's true of many of us."

Aelis didn't have a perspective on that, so she didn't offer one, just waited Khorais out.

"It's my cousin. Name's Mihil Angleton. He is sort of a, well . . ."

"Is he a thief?"

"Nothing like that. It wouldn't surprise me if he was *arrested*, but he's sort of a freelance thief-taker and finder of lost things."

Aelis tried not to groan. "I don't need an amateur hanging around . . ."

"He's not an amateur. He's made his living doing this sort of thing since the war ended."

"What did he do while the war was on?"

"He was in the Tyridician Naval Infantry."

"There's *one* brigade of Naval Infantry," Aelis said, carefully. "And I would imagine you could bring it up to double its full strength just by people *in* Lascenise right now who claim to have been in it."

"I know how it sounds," Khorais said. "But I think he could help. *At least* let me give you an introduction. He knows the lay of things down there, and he can point you in the right direction."

"Fine," Aelis said. An introduction to someone who knew his way around couldn't hurt. *And the kind of person she's describing probably knows all about the criminal underworld in the city, because likely enough he's a part of it.*

"You can probably find him at the Fallow Sow," Khorais said. "Tanner's Edge."

Aelis tried not wince as she imagined what the place must smell like. Meanwhile, the gnome sitting at the table with her scribbled a note, folded it, and rang a bell she took from a pocket.

Everyone in this city carries a bell in their pocket, Aelis thought. *Maybe I ought to get one just to see who comes running when I ring it.*

Predictably it was Kavan who glided into the room, his eyes already fixed on Khorais.

"Wax and a candle, if you please."

Kavan half bowed, half nodded, and swept back out, returning moments later with a tray on which a candle and a stick of green wax sat, bearing it directly to the lawyer's elbow. She heated the wax over the candle flame, pressed it down on the letter, then removed a seal on a chain from inside the pocket of her coat and pressed it into the wax.

"Mihil is not likely to be up and awake just yet, but I'm confident if you go to the Sow, you'll find him, or someone who knows where to find him." She held out the note and Aelis pocketed it. "I'll want to stay in touch," Khorais said. "How do I get word to you?"

"Send it to Cabal Keep. Do you have a preferred courier for return?"

"The firm has messengers."

Aelis stood to leave when Bardun Jacques's words ran through her head. *The only wizard you can trust right now is yourself.*

"One more thing, Khorais. If you send a note to Cabal Keep, tell your messenger not to hand it to anyone but me. Even if they have to wait all day, if they have to leave and return. Put it in *my* hand. No one else's."

Khorais sighed and looked down at the table before her. "I knew this case was a loser."

"We'll figure it out," Aelis said, trying for a conviction she didn't truly feel.

◆　◆　◆

Kavan led her back out of the warren-like offices and she once more assayed the stairway. With no guide through the surging, darting crowd of folk half her size, she had to take her time getting clear to the street. She thought of her list; she'd seen to the medicaments and visited the lawyer. Item three was *wagons/slums*, and right now Khorais's cousin was her only somewhat solid lead, so she called the first empty coach she saw.

The driver, a dwarf, pulled his team up for her and she hopped in.

"Tanner's Edge, please," she said, "a pub called the Fallow Sow."

"Apologies, Warden," the coachman said, looking back through the window, "but I won't go that far into Slop's End. I'll go as far as Lead Street, but no farther."

"You'd be riding with a warden, gooddwarf," Aelis said.

"But I wouldn't be riding *out* with one," he countered.

"Well, it's not too long a walk," she said, and the dwarf slapped his team into motion.

Aelis pondered the dwarf's reluctance. Slop's End *was* a dangerous district to be sure, but not daylight-coach-robbery dangerous.

Might need to recalibrate what dangerous *means, I suppose.* Anyone in the city would know she was a warden, and attacking a warden in a city full of them may not be quite like pulling a dragon's tail, but it would only be done by the desperate or the very well prepared.

While she thought about what danger meant for a Lyceum-trained abjurer as opposed to a non-magical citizen of Lascenise, the city around her got steadily less opulent. The road became crowded, hemmed in on both sides and shaded by precariously built structures that overhung it. There were fewer closed coaches like the one she rode in, more open ones, and no individually ridden horses at all.

And then there was the smell. If Ruby Chapel smelled like money to her, then this place smelled like the agricultural input needed to feed a city this size turned into waste products and left to molder. Underneath it was the smell of hot metal and fetid water. The former had to do with the foundries beyond the city walls where half the residents of Slop's End earned their beer and bread, and the latter with the resurgence of the river that was buried in tunnels and sluice gates and locks beneath other, wealthier sections of the city, and opened into canals and slag pools here.

She hadn't seen much of it before the coach pulled up to an abrupt stop.

"Lead Street, Warden," the coachman called. She hopped down, paying his fare and tip, and watched as he expertly turned his team using the mouth of an alley and drove off. She kept watching the wagon until it rode out of sight, feeling responsible for dragging the reluctant dwarf out here.

When she turned around, three boys were standing not four yards behind her, openly sizing her up.

Aelis sighed.

"Don't hold with wardens here," one of them, said.

I do not have time for this, Aelis thought.

"You know what black robes mean, boys? Want me to have your skeletons shed your bodies like cheap cloaks and dance around in the streets?"

Two of them backed away. Aelis dropped her wand into her hand and let the tip glow green—among the first tricks any enchanter learned—and the backing away turned into a run.

The third took half a step back and she decided to try to make him useful.

"Two silver pieces if you tell me how to get to the Fallow Sow."

"What's a warden want with a place like that?"

"Warden business. Want the silver or not?"

The local tough shrugged and spat out some turns, and a few moments later Aelis found herself turning down what she imagined was a blind alley till she saw a sign hanging over a door that sagged on its hinges, depicting a sleeping pig.

While the tough darted off, coins jingling in his palm, Aelis centered herself in the alley and concentrated on the Fallow Sow and wondered at the complete absence of a crowd moving around the alley or headed to the pub. True, it was still early in the day and those who'd gone to work in the morning were not after their evening drinks yet, but the alley was deserted.

She opened the door slowly because she genuinely feared it might fall off if she as much as nudged it. It inspired a brief pang of nostalgia for the door of her tower back in Lone Pine. Inside the Sow was no more crowded than out. There was a barman, gray fringe around a bald pate, dirty apron over a dirty brown shirt, leaning on his elbows on the bar. Nobody stood near it. There were booths on the far side and along it, just enough room for two people to pass by if they didn't mind rubbing elbows. The windows were greasy enough to stop too much light from getting in and none of the lamps or rushlights were lit, so the place was darker than it ought to have been.

Aelis sighed and dropped her hand on the bar, not too loud or too forceful, but the barman jumped up, blinking gummy eyes at her.

She could identify the moment when his vision cut through the gloom and realized who, or really what, he was looking at, because he suddenly stood straight up and knuckled his forehead.

"Warden," he croaked out. "Don't often see your kind here in the Sow. What'll you drink? Our buy, of course . . ."

"Nothing, barman. Looking for someone. Mihil Angleton. Know where to find him?"

The barman cleared his throat, coughed, and yelled, "Mihil? You back there?"

"No," came a weak voice from the booth in the corner farthest from the entrance.

The barman lifted a thumb and pointed over his shoulder. "You may want to stay nimble on your feet, you get too near his booth, Warden," he rasped. "Mihil don't wake up pretty."

"He got a typical eye-opener?"

The barman nodded.

"Start making it."

He seized a mug from under the bar, opened a tap on a barrel behind his shoulder, and filled it about halfway up.

There was a jar of boiled peeled eggs floating in brine at one end of the bar. Aelis watched just long enough to see the barman catch up one egg with the ladle chained to the jar and mash it against the side of the mug, then follow it with half a ladle of brine before deciding she didn't need the rest of the recipe.

She rounded the corner and made the short walk to the last booth. There was no one sitting at it, but she could hear someone breathing under it.

"Mihil?"

"Go away."

"Your cousin sent me."

"Got a lot of cousins. Hope this one doesn't want money back."

"No," Aelis said, "she wanted me to hire you."

There was some shuffling under the booth's table and a gnomish hand extended from it, holding up one finger, asking her to wait.

Slowly, painfully, the rest of the gnome followed; first a greasy, matted beard, then a graying head with a long double-clubbed sailor's queue. He wore a sky-blue jacket, and she could read the worn spots on the shoulders where armor straps had once been affixed, and the darker spots where rank and unit patches had been ripped free.

The coat's right, she thought, *but that alone doesn't mean anything.*

Finally Mihil dragged himself up into a sitting position. Aelis thought she could *hear* the crust flaking off his red-rimmed, yellowish eyes as he blinked at her.

"Hmm," he grunted. "Warden. Was the cousin bit a ruse?"

"No. She really did." She dug into a pouch and pulled out the note Khorais had given her, handed it over. "Here."

Mihil waved it away. "Too bright in here to focus on reading."

Aelis looked questioningly around at the almost impenetrable dimness of the barroom. It was then that the barman arrived with Mihil's morning draft.

He set it down and Mihil said, "You're always a gentleman to me, Arris, no matter what they say about you."

"It's still going on your tab," Arris said as he stumped back to his bar.

"A moment, Warden." Mihil picked up the mug and sniffed at it, recoiled sharply, then tipped it back and drank all the contents down without stopping, not even when foam and ale and bits of crushed egg, brine, and less identifiable liquors ran down the corners of his mouth and onto his collar.

He set it down, belched thunderously, then winced at the sound.

"Okay," he said, "let me see that note now, please."

She handed it over and he slipped a knife out of one sleeve to unseal it, and read it quickly.

He turned one unhealthy-looking eye at her. "Dear Khorais says there'd be silver in it."

"There would be, if you or your information prove useful."

"Nothing motivates me to swift utility like the gleam of argent coin."

"If I hand over silver now, you're just going to drink yourself right back under that table."

"One," he said, "it'd probably take gold to clear my bill. Two, now that I've had my tea and porridge, Arris won't serve me till night falls. Three," he finished, shrugging, "I only sleep here two, three nights a week. At most."

"How good to know," Aelis said. "So, what can you do for me?" She decided to risk sliding into the booth opposite him. Mihil watched her, unblinking.

"Depends on what you're asking." He waved the paper. "Khorais's note said you were planning to come down here to stick your thumb in someone's eye. I could probably point out whose eye you want to avoid."

"Oh?"

"I know everyone in Slop's End. And they know me. The thieves, the smugglers, the flesh-peddlers, the tanners, the slug-workers, the heavies, everyone. If I can't find a person or a thing down here, it doesn't exist."

"Big claims considering I'm not sure you can walk straight."

"Just give me a moment to, ah, warm to the morning."

"It's well past noon."

"To the day, then." He shut his eyes and let his head drift to the tabletop for a moment. "Don't suppose you can magic up a way to get rid of a hangover."

"I can ease pain, though that's more easily done with medicine than magic. I can diagnose the underlying problems and the basic treatment: sleep, adequate food, lots of water, and staying away from drink."

"No would've been easier." He sat up, took a deep breath, and looked longingly into his mug. "Let's go take the air and you tell me who you're looking for, why, and I'll tell you how much it'll cost."

Mihil worked his way free of the booth and nearly fell down, clutching the table for a moment. Aelis felt her doubts growing rapidly.

Follow him outside, see what he has to say, and then cut him loose if he's as useless as he looks.

He waved a hand for her to follow, and instead of going out the front entrance past the bar, he pushed open a back door Aelis had missed behind a stack of empty quarter casks. Sighing, she slapped a silver down on the table and made her way outside.

The stink in the alleyway was a fresh hell to her, but Mihil was breathing deep.

"Gods love it," he said, after bending back to fill his lungs, "the last real piece of this city left. Proper air."

Then he turned his head and vomited thunderously against the side of the building, in enough volume to force Aelis to dance several steps away.

On the bright side, the air of Slop's End already smelled so foul that Mihil couldn't really add to it.

After a few final heaves, he stood up, wiped his mouth with a rag he pulled from a pocket, sniffed it and stuffed it back into his pocket, then turned to her.

"Right," he said, and she found him surprisingly clear-eyed and steady on his feet, if pale. "What are you looking for?"

Aelis looked up and down the alley and saw no one close and no one who appeared to want to get close.

"Thieves," she muttered. "Smugglers. Assassins."

Before she could elaborate, Mihil snorted. "Midarra's moon, you could just throw a stone at any crowd in a pub . . . not this one, mind you," he said, jerking a thumb to the wall of the Fallow Sow, "and have at least one in three odds of hitting a thief. But . . . assassins? We haven't got those down here."

"Never heard of the Hidden Skulls?"

"You try to use a name like that down here you'll just get laughed at," Mihil said. "No . . . we don't have those. So, this has been a waste of everyone's time," he concluded, and turned back to the door of the tavern.

"Wait. Let's focus on smugglers."

Mihil turned back to her and nodded, then winced and held his head for a moment.

"There are smugglers bringing *significant* cargo into Lascenise, and then packing it up and shipping it out to the Lyceum, apparently spreading the important pieces among regular goods that flow into the Colleges all the time."

Mihil kept his hand shading his eyes and said, "So they're smuggling some kind of magical nonsense, then?"

Aelis shrugged. "Something like that."

"Right. So, are we interested in how it's getting here, where from, how it's getting out, or where it's going?"

"All," Aelis said, "but mostly the last two."

"Hrm." He took a deep breath and paled still further. "I can help."

"What's it cost?"

"My rates are on a sliding scale, and you look like money. So, it'll be one gold tree a day, plus expenses."

"One silver vine a day, one extra each time you do something useful, and I make that headache go away immediately."

"Oh gods, yes," Mihil moaned.

Aelis extended her hand, and they shook. His hand was clammy and trembled slightly.

Then she placed her hand on his head and called for a Third Order Tranzid's Refreshment. There were reasons necromancers, as a rule, preferred to treat pain with drugs rather than with direct magical intervention. Pain could be held at bay with enchantments, true, but if she was going to get anything useful out of Mihil she didn't need him Compelled. But for necromancy to deal with pain it either required a great deal of energy and the patient to immediately recuperate with food and bed rest, useful in the case of major surgery but not so much for a hangover, or the pain had to be *transferred*.

She didn't want to give herself a horrifying hangover headache, but at least she had some discretionary power over exactly what the pain became.

Gritting her teeth, she drew it out of him and let it spread throughout her body. When the spell was complete, she felt like she'd had a bad day of sparring after a number of long walks, but nothing that would keep her out of commission.

Mihil's eyes cleared and he stared at her with something near reverence.

"And you could do this *every* day?"

"Could," Aelis said, rubbing at her suddenly aching lower back. "Won't."

"Could make a mint just setting up business outside a foundry in the morning."

"Can we focus?"

"Sure. Now, do you have a name for these smugglers?"

"I heard the name Saltmen. But I also heard they were assassins. Someone thought they might be the Saltmen."

Mihil grunted and shook his head. "Saltmen are real enough. Watermen families put out of their business as the city bricked over their canals and buried the rivers under stone. They're not killers, though. I mean, they'll dust up with other gangs if they have to, but they're not *hired* killers. Just people trying to make a living."

"How do we find them?" Aelis decided to ignore the assassin half of the equation for the moment.

"Tunnels. They move around in 'em, though, and those aren't always safe with or without the Saltmen in 'em. We can go bumbling around and maybe run into them. Put enough time into it, we're bound to find some."

"This is time sensitive."

"They're clannish sorts. Organized around family trees, don't like to talk to outsiders about *anything*, and you won't beat business secrets out of them."

Aelis tapped the green stripe on the sleeve of her jacket. "Usually don't need to beat anyone."

"You'd still have to snatch them, and that can turn bloody. But I think I can find out what you need. Who's moving the cargo, when it goes, where it leaves from." He sniffed and looked up at her.

"And you can talk them into smuggling something for me?"

"Well, now . . . that's a problem," Mihil said. "Everyone in Slop's End knows me, and to know me is to love me. But . . . they're not going to accept me as a wizard's bagman, and they know I haven't got the money to hire them myself. Give me two days to take some soundings. You use that time to put together the package you want smuggled, then we slip it on to their next wagon."

"Done." *Looks like I'm changing my mind about jewels. Drewic will be thrilled.*

"Well," Mihil said, grinning lopsidedly, "that's at least two days of work, and two days worth of expenses, so . . ."

"I didn't agree to expenses," Aelis said. "I said one silver a day, and one every time you do something useful. So two days." She took two silver out of her purse and held them out. Mihil made them disappear faster than she would've credited had they not been in her hand one moment and gone the next. She produced a third. "And you presented a useful idea."

That third silver was whisked out of her hand at a blur. "There are going to be expenses on this job, you know. Going to have to cross some palms, buy some drinks . . ." At Aelis's raised eyebrow, he said, "Mainly for other people, but around here there's no faster way to raise suspicion than buy drinks without you drinking yourself."

"Fine," Aelis said, "but I will pay no expenses *in advance*. Submit to me an itemized list of costs, in a fair hand, and I will pay what seems fair."

"Done," Mihil said. He sniffed. "Now, Warden . . . fair chance this is all gonna lead to some rough people. You, ah, ready for that?"

"You just said they weren't killers."

"Well, they're not *assassins*, but they'll mix it up if they have to."

"Doesn't matter. I'm a warden."

Mihil shrugged. "That's no proof against violent people with violent intent."

Aelis tapped the deep blue stripe on her sleeve. "The properly prepared and ever vigilant abjurer is the antithesis of danger."

"Fine. Do I contact you through Khorais?"

"No. I'll tell her anything she needs to know about what we're doing. Come to Cabal Keep and ask for me. Do I send word for you to the Fallow Sow?"

"I don't always sleep on the floor there," Mihil began, wounded, but under Aelis's stare he finally shrugged. "Yeah, they'll know how to lay hands on me, one way or another."

"Good. Let's meet again in two days, unless developments demand it sooner."

"Fine. Two days, lunchtime. Leave word at the Sow and with Khorais, one of them'll get it to me."

"That'll do. And Mihil . . . I won't cure a hangover for you again."

"To be honest, Warden, I don't feel right unless I'm a *little* drink-sick."

"One who feels that way all the time is on a quick ride to Onoma's Embrace, Mihil."

All mirth disappeared from the gnome's face, and Aelis suddenly saw that he was old beyond his years. Old, tired, gone gray in the beard and hair, and blotched red and white beneath it.

"And?" His challenging look, haggard and without pretense, chilled her a little.

"Just . . . a note from a physician and surgeon, that's all."

"Two days hence. I'm on the job. Go back through the Sow and don't look for me." He knuckled his forehead with his left hand, somewhat exaggerating the motion, and Aelis glimpsed a flicker of steel around his wrist. Then he turned and sauntered out of the alley.

Aelis waited till he cleared the mouth of the alley and left her view, then shouldered her way back through the door and into the sad little pub. She knocked on the bar and Arris, sleeping on his hand again, jolted awake.

"Arris. You own the place or just run it?"

"Run it."

"Who owns it?"

"Ship's purser. Saved his pay and his hazard-money and actually did the thing every hand says they will."

Aelis raised a brow. "So, were you Tyridician Naval Infantry? Don't try and puff up your record on my account."

Arris shook his head. "Nah. I was just a common sailor off the riverboats, but fresh and salt ain't too different to a hand, and Stregon knows the orcs had boats on both."

"And Mihil? The coat's right, but a lot of folk brag about the war."

"He don't," Arris said, "and the coat's right 'cause it's his."

"The genuine article, then? You don't generally see a lot of gnomefolk in boarding actions and the like."

"You do in the rigging, sharpshooting," Arris said. "Or I suppose . . . you don't, more's the point."

"Rigging Sharpshooter, eh? Well, if he comes in here trying to spend my Imravalan vines on ruining his health any more than he already has, you don't take it. Understand me? I'm buying his work, not his ale."

"He'll stay sober enough to do whatever you hired him for," Arris said, defiant. "Not everyone down here in Slop's End is full of piss and sawdust, no more than everyone up in the keep is made of iron and honor."

"Alright," Aelis said. "I'll take your word for it." She dropped a heavy silver coin on the bar. "Have one on me, Arris."

The sleepy old man eyed her suspiciously for a moment, but he dropped his hand over her coin all the same. "Thanks, Warden," he said grudgingly.

Aelis nodded and headed out to the street. She had a long walk to the edge of the district before she could hail a coach to take her back to the better-smelling parts of town, and then walk to a coach station near a gate.

A day, she thought. *To the Lyceum and back.*

10

A LIBRARY VISIT

Aelis kept her head down over her notes as the carriage rattled down the familiar road from Lascenise to the Lyceum. She was put in mind of her student days, which suddenly seemed to be both *just yesterday* and ancient history at the same time, when this carriage would've been full of her friends. Certainly it never would've been so quiet that she could hear the words of the driver to his team or the jingle and slap of harnesses.

Miralla, Humphrey, and Engel would've filled both the space and her attention. So would the others who came in and out of their circle, or who fell in or out of love with one or more of them. They'd have been arguing about the origins of magic, the role of the moons, the superiority of their primary schools, the proper sword and ward forms. She laughed as she pictured Engel's face reddening as he argued that an axe was every bit as efficient an abjurer's weapon as a sword.

Where is he now? She realized she hadn't thought of him since graduation. Nor, to be honest, of Humphrey. As much as she didn't like to admit it, she'd been so bitter at his posting to Antraval she hadn't even *wanted* to talk to him.

If I had to run into just one of them, I'm glad it was Mira. She laughed to herself, a bit ruefully, as she thought of what was important to her in those days. The next exam. The next sword-form test or Necromantic Practical. At the time they had meant the world and all its moons.

None of that mattered now. Their weight would've felt like a silk scarf across her neck compared to the lives she carried now. Maurenia. Bardun Jacques. Phillipa's future.

Nathalie. She thought of that poor woman, certainly within a handful of years of her own age, her throat cut and bleeding, savaged beyond her ability to heal on her best day.

By her own hand.

Aelis pushed aside the notes she wasn't reading and dug into her small bag for the worn locket. She unsnapped it, looked closely at the poorly rendered miniature. Two adults in tradesmen's clothing, its details too vague to show what sort of trade. They had city-pale skin—*if* this was a genuine representation of them and not just paint faded with time. The woman had dark hair and dark eyes, like Nathalie's. The man, a blond beard and receding hair. Not much to go on.

I'll find them for you, Nath. And tell them what became of you. She wrapped the miniature back up and stuffed it into her bag, then went back to the notes she'd gotten from Khorais.

She had the details of Bardun Jacques's arrest and all the circumstances, all of it quite dry, with the Archmagister surrendering peacefully to a team of guards and wardens as soon as they'd come for him. Apparently three wardens, two censors, and a dozen Lascenise watchmen had been detailed.

"Probably half of them shitting their pants," she muttered as she rifled the papers. She stopped on the description of the deceased, one Arstan Nicholaz, wizard. The notes hadn't much to say about him. Human, abjurer and conjurer, graduated the Lyceum seven years ago. But later on the page there was a discrepancy, saying he'd graduated eight years before. Clerical errors of that kind were common enough. He wasn't a warden, and the notes had no clear indicator of who he worked for or in what capacity. Nicholaz wasn't a name she recognized, and if he'd been from an Estates House family, her mentor would likely have been put to death already. He might have money from trade, but then he'd have some kind of occupation listed. Families didn't let wizards sit idle if they were blood relations.

Someone's bagman, Bardun Jacques had called him. And that seemed likely enough. A hanger-on at the Lyceum, where it wasn't unusual for a wizard to appear to be at leisure, waiting around for someone more powerful—magical or institutional—to give them something to do.

The rattling of the coach had the same effect it always had if there was no one for Aelis to talk with and distract herself, and she found herself drifting off. She packed up the folder of notes, wrapped the green ribbon around it and stuffed it back into her writing case, and that into her bag, and let her head fall against the cushioned seat.

◆ ◆ ◆

Aelis woke the instant the coach drew to a stop. She was pulled from another dream of trees and mist and glad enough of it. *Why do I have such boring dreams?*

She paid the coachman, including a generous tip in gold, and let her feet find the familiar paths of the Lyceum. Students passed by in their gray robes, corded in the colors of their primary schools, and many stole glances at her, the warden in their midst. Professors in their colored robes—none of them with the warden badge, or the slashes of color on the sleeves—ignored her, and she them. There was long enmity between these branches of wizardry, the warden and the academic, and by Onoma she was going to uphold her own side of it.

It was two or three hours past midday, and lovely outside. The sun was warm without being oppressive, and the air stirred with a faint breeze that brushed her cheeks and hair. The kind of day meant for sitting out of doors drinking wine and thinking of nothing much.

Aelis's steps did not lead to any outdoor cafe or wineshop, though a few had sprung up around the edges of the Lyceum itself. No, she headed straight to a long, thick-walled building, with only small high windows, and huge bronze doors stamped with pens and quills. Her hand wrapped around a wrought-iron handle; it always took a satisfying effort to open the doors of the Cradle of Learning, called by students the Crèche or the Nursery for how much of their time the newest students spent there.

Just inside the door stooped a massive construction of gleaming brass shaped like a man in ancient muscle-sculpted armor—or at least with the requisite number of arms and legs—its joints flywheel-and-cog contraptions that allowed the arms and legs to rotate in any direction. Mounted on a similarly constructed neck was a face with an elaborately sculpted brass beard and two spinning-wheel eyes.

Aelis smiled and paused a moment to listen, then said, "Hello, Bob."

"Hello, Warden." The stooped-over construct rotated some of its joints and extended a long-fingered brass hand. "May I take your sword?"

She looked at the wide leather belt slung over Brass Bob's shoulder, with double rows of hooks running all along its length. It held three other swords, belts wrapped around the scabbards, one of a similar pattern to hers and two of the longer and straight variety. Dangling from a ring anchored to the Porter's hip was an axe.

Aelis didn't like giving up her weapons, but if one of the Lyceum Porters was asking for it, she didn't have many options. With a sigh, she began unbuckling her swordbelt.

"Is it really necessary, Bob?"

"Only if you wish to enter the Grand Library, Warden." She was never sure how the Porters generated their voices; this one had a certain vibrating, dual-toned quality to it, and she suspected the vibration of taut wires, not entirely unlike a harpsichord. Brass Bob's fingers clicked closed around the belt and the scabbards as she laid it in his hand, then carefully positioned it so that it dangled by the hilt from two of the hooks on his belt.

"Thank you, Warden. I will return it to no hand but your own. I will guard it with all my power."

Aelis nodded her approval and passed by the Porter through a second set of smaller, wooden doors, breathing in the scent of books. She had no real words to describe that scent, nothing to compare it to. Some would've called it musty, she supposed. She, who could hold forth at some length over the nose of a wine, would only say that books smelled like themselves, and nothing else.

She glided to the large circular desk in the front, staffed by gray-robed students overseen by one white-robed diviner.

"Good afternoon, Warden." One of the students—a gnome woman, young, with a gray cap pinned over curly blond hair and a green cord wrapped thrice about her waist—stood to address her. "How may we help you?"

"I'll need a quiet room, and probably some assistance carrying books once I've got a pile of them."

"Pens? Ink? Paper?"

Aelis tapped the bag slung over her shoulder. "Have my own."

"A lamp?"

Before the words were out of the gnome's mouth, Aelis had slipped her alchemy lamp from her bag and almost dropped it as she tried to clip it to the swordbelt she was no longer wearing. She only just saved her dignity, but a ghost of a smile did creep over the gnome's face.

"Very good, Warden. Can I ask if you'll be searching by yourself, or did you want assistance?"

"Some of the books I can find myself . . . but I do have a cross-reference search."

The gnome turned to the diviner, who sat on a high stool at the center of the desk. The diviner, a man of middle years, had a face that promised infinite patience for whatever nonsense was about to be asked of him.

"How many words, Warden?" His voice was soft, a carrying whisper.

"Three," she said. The gnome, meanwhile, ducked behind the desk and came up with a wax tablet and a metal stylus.

Meanwhile, Aelis dug into her belt pouch and fished out a golden coin and placed it carefully on the desk.

"For your trouble, colleague," she said, then followed with a silver, and a nod to the gnome. Both coins disappeared so fast she couldn't rule out the involvement of illusion. The diviner slipped a diadem onto his balding crown and pulled a tiny model building from a shelf behind the desk. The gnome also placed a key with 4–15 graven onto its wide body, which Aelis took up in one hand.

"Your words, Warden?" The diviner's eyes lit with a faint white light, answered by the small crystal set in the center of the diadem.

"Woodshade. Shaper. Binding."

"In any combination?"

"Where the third word refers to either of the first two," Aelis said.

The diviner's eyes brightened and he ran his fingers over the model—the library itself, in miniature—and began speaking words to the gnome, who started recording them with quick flicks of the stylus.

"Third floor. Second alcove. Fourteenth shelf . . ."

Aelis left them to it, and, key in hand, set off for the stacks.

✦ ✦ ✦

She made it to her quiet room—the fifteenth room on the fourth floor—before any assistant with books could beat her there. Aelis had with her three of the most basic texts on summoning, binding, and curses she could find. She piled them onto a desk, configured her alchemy lamp for ambient rather than focused light, and lowered herself into a library chair.

It was as hard and rickety as every single one of them she'd ever sat in during her five years of toiling away in a room like this one. No matter how she tried to adjust, one leg was always off the floor.

"Carpenters should study this," she said as she considered jamming some paper or some other object beneath the leg to try to balance it. "Tun would be appalled." *So would Maurenia*, a little voice said, and she immediately put it from her mind and hunched over the desk, opening the first book.

One thing Aelis knew how to do was skim a book till she found the important part. How she knew *what* the important part was, she couldn't have articulated. But she let her eyes drift over chapter titles and headings until they were arrested in their flight by pins-and-stitches details of summoning and deals and the kinds of spirits that *could* be summoned.

Spirit was a bit of a stumbling block. Aelis knew from ghosts, haunts, haints, specters, phantasms, revenants, wraiths, and shades. But the key thing those all shared is they had once been *alive*, in the flesh, walking upon the Worldsoul as a human or an elf or a dwarf or something else.

But woodspirits? Woodshades? Earth, fire, air, and water spirits? Whatever Rhunival had been? Were Shapers—the inherent spirits of the world he claimed had lost a kind of war with the gods—real or just some malevolent Other Thing's fancy? She hadn't the faintest idea.

Aelis copied down some basic notes; there were some basic formulas of how big an area a summoned natural spirit could be confined in based on how strong it was that she thought might be applicable. She was reaching into her bag for Maurenia's notes on the distances she could travel in any direction when the door opened. Aelis stood to help the gnome who tottered in, burdened with a stack of heavy books, some of which even had locks across the boards.

"Thank you very much," Aelis was saying as she took two and set them on her worktable. It was only when the other four were set down that she realized that, first, the books had been hovering just above the gnome's hands, and second, the gnome was not wearing the gray robe of a student but rather a splendid green teacher's robe open over an immaculate brown coat and trousers crossed by the gold chains and fobs of various academic honors and societies.

Magister Urizen, Dean of the College of Enchantment, and her academic adviser at the Lyceum, stared at her expectantly.

"Magister!" she burst out, taking his hands in her own, and then running her eyes over his over-robe again and noting the wide cut of the sleeves, the gold edging on the collar, and the cord worn loosely over his neck.

"My apologies," she said. "Archmagister! Congratulations!"

"Why thank you, Miss de Lenti," he said with a warm smile, taking his hands from hers and pulling a chair free from the table with a gesture of his hand, then stepping up on it to seat himself on the table, where he could meet her gaze more easily. "It's a very recent promotion and I can't quite bring myself to take off the robe or the honor cord, you know. What brings our intrepid warden of the north marches back to the cradle of learning?"

Aelis leaned against the table and let out a slight sigh. She caught the Archmagister's face and noticed a kind of tightness around his eyes that quickly vanished.

"I'm here working as an advocate. May I ask what the honor cord is for?"

"Oh, just some minor technical points regarding the synergies of alchemy and enchantment. Not very useful stuff," Urizen said. "An advocate? Unusual duty for one of your experience, insofar as I understand the warden service. Random and unlucky draw?"

Aelis shook her head. "Apparently not. I was directly requested."

"It's Jacques, isn't it?" Urizen shook his head. "So much potential there. So much power . . . but he's only ever understood the one kind."

"He is the most decorated warden alive, Archmagister," Aelis said respectfully.

"Indeed," Urizen said, nodding in agreement. "And he has always been convinced that the only way he could affect the world is by running about it flinging fire and lightning. Had he taken an interest in the future of the university that *taught* him that power, how much more could he have done? Hrm?" He sighed and lifted a hand to forestall Aelis's retort.

"Somehow I doubt that these books you've asked for have aught to do with his case . . ."

"They don't," Aelis agreed. "How did you . . . ?"

"I was going over one of these texts when Janine came looking for it. She's one of my sponsored students, so we caught up and she let slip she was picking out books for a *warden*, a *three-schools graduate*, a necromancer . . . so I had to come and check, as I don't know too many people who meet all those descriptors."

Aelis felt a blush rise in her cheeks and squashed it as she'd long ago learned to do. "I'm afraid what I'm after here is a bit of a . . . personal project. Unrelated to the Archmagister's case. I had a few free hours, so I thought I'd pop over to the library."

Urizen fixed her with a wry smile. "I remember quite the opposite in your undergraduate days, Miss de Lenti. When you had a few free hours, you were off to Lascenise in a coach to hit the wineshops of the Tremont, and came back to morning lectures with the whiff of smoke and the canals on you."

"But I was *at* the morning lectures, Archmagister."

"Fair point." Urizen tapped a finger against the locked book. "You're after some . . . exotic words here, Miss de Lenti."

Lady, Aelis thought, followed by *warden*, but she said nothing. Urizen had always made a point of calling her Miss, which had rankled at first. But over time he'd been one of the few professors, one of two, to be precise, who never made any criticism of her about her title, family, or wealth. Calling her Miss had been a way of acknowledging that her place in the Lyceum was earned, not bought. And she was surprised at how much she enjoyed hearing it just then.

Urizen was waiting for her to reply, and said, "Woodshades? These are not generally within your area of expertise."

"No," Aelis said, "certainly not. And I still don't know if that's what I found." She slipped a leaf of her note paper into the book she'd been reading to mark her page and shut it. "I don't wish to bother you with my troubles, Archmagister . . ."

"Oh, nonsense. I love a good puzzle, and besides, if you'll recall, the summoning and binding of various magical entities, and the curses on offer from same, are one of my academic specialties."

"I do find myself wishing I'd been able to take your course . . ."

"The Logic, Rhetoric, and Semantics of Curses, Bargains, and Bindings? It was more for conjurers than enchanters, but it does seem as though it might have come in handy."

"I was packing in as many Warden Practicals as I could."

"Yes," Urizen said, settling down on the tabletop and crossing his legs with poise. "Why learn careful wording when you can play with a sword or an axe? Why spend your time with the collected wisdom of generations when you could go for endless marches along the graveled squares of Abjurer's College?" He adjusted the flow of his over-robe and said, "Why don't you tell me about this woodshade?"

"Well, I . . . might have made a bargain with one."

"Then I hope your affairs are in order, or you know a very competent invoker. One who *isn't* imprisoned under censor guard and likely to never leave it."

"I did not make the deal, or at least, I am not the one suffering the consequences."

"If I am going to help in any way, Aelis, you must cease speaking around the point and come directly at it. What did you do, and to whom?"

Aelis launched into as concise a tale of her dealings with Rhunival as she could, leaving out Maurenia's name but explaining that she'd been imprisoned, that a drop of her blood had apparently touched the dirt of Rhunival's home.

"If this was a woodshade, it was bound *very* tightly, under strict rules. And by whom? It makes very little sense," Urizen said when she described the time they had spent with Rhunival, eating of his food and drinking of his wine in exchange for stories. "Woodshades do not care for our tales; they see us as so much walking mulch, so far as I understand them."

He went on at some length about the finer points of woodshades—where they originated, who'd had dealings with them, books the encounters were recorded in—but Aelis had let herself think of Maurenia, and she heard none of it. The thought of her—fierce, proud, owing no one, trapped through Aelis's own negligence—gripped Aelis's heart and mind with talons of self-loathing and fear. She pushed them away and drew in a sharp breath.

"Are you quite well, Miss de Lenti?"

"Sorry, Archmagister," she said, giving her head a shake.

"You looked like you were seeing a woodshade here in the room. You visibly paled."

"I was . . . thinking of the person who was trapped. Cursed, I suppose. I do not wish for their imprisonment to last one second longer than it already has."

"Well, I can write out a few texts for you to find. Accounts of woodshades, that kind of thing. Cutterleaf wrote a monograph about his dealings with one . . . it's half fiction but the other half is informative enough. I think there's at least one antiquarian bookshop in Lascenise that'll have it."

"It's not here in the library?"

"I shouldn't think so—it's not written by a wizard and thus not considered a credible source, but I can have Janine look for it if you like."

"What about breaking curses?"

"Well." Urizen peered at the stack of books she had. "You've got the standard texts by Urquhardt and Barston, those are good enough starts. But this is second-year Lyceum training material. You need an advanced course, and you need it immediately."

Urizen tapped the locked book he'd brought Aelis. "This is . . . a controlled-access book. Obviously. Why did you ask for it?"

"I didn't ask for any specific titles, of course. Just woodshades, binding, and . . ."

"Shapers?"

"Have you ever heard the term, Archmagister?"

Urizen was silent for a long moment while he considered the question. He took his spectacles, small crystal lenses connected with thin silver wires, from the end of his nose and polished them with a cloth he produced from a sleeve. Aelis knew this was one of his classroom tricks for pausing to compose a complicated answer.

"If I had . . . and I am not saying I have . . . but if I had, that would be some very privileged knowledge indeed, Miss de Lenti. It is . . . you see, there are, within the Lyceum, various societies and sodalities . . ."

"The Sodality of the Plaited Wand?"

He stopped his polishing and squinted down his nose at her. "Where did you hear those words, Miss de Lenti?"

"From you, Archmagister. Some years ago. I don't remember when exactly, but I'd come to you during office hours and our talk went a bit long and you rushed out, muttering you were late for a meeting."

"I see. So, you know nothing more about it?"

"Not a thing, Archmagister."

"Good."

Aelis had an impulsive thought, and wished she'd brought the loose collection of pages she'd been given by the Errithsuns with her, but remembered that it was safely wrapped in a trunk in her rooms.

"Archmagister, if you could let me know any other books or monographs or pamphlets I should be looking for, I'd be greatly indebted to you. And I'm sure I'll be back here at some point. There's a book I came into possession of that I should very much like for you to look at."

"Where did you hear this term, *shapers?*"

"From Rhunival himself. Itself. A story it told . . ."

"If I am going to be able to help you, I'd like to know everything he said about them."

Aelis looked at the pile of books before her, then back to Urizen.

"Not now, Miss de Lenti. Write it up as a report, if you would be so kind. Have it sent by courier, and I will think on it. My suspicion is that what you have heard lies somewhere in the middle of a scale that starts with 'fanciful lie' and ends in 'rank heresy,' but if I can help, I should like to."

Why? Aelis wanted to ask, then decided she'd simply accept the gift being offered to her.

"Of course, Archmagister. I'll do that. For now, I have this basic research to do, and I'm sure you're very busy."

"I am," Urizen said. "But if you'll give me a scrap of paper, I'll list off the chapters you need to look at in these books to rule out a woodshade and perhaps figure out what you need. I'll also list a few of those other titles I mentioned that you might need to scour the bookshops for." Aelis slid her sheaf of paper and pen and ink over toward him; the pen rose in the air at a gesture and dipped itself in the inkwell, then began to write.

✦ ✦ ✦

Some hours later, her hand cramping, and all but one of the books piled on the table in front of her, Aelis had grown increasingly uncertain whether Rhunival was a woodshade.

But she was no closer to understanding what he *was.*

She had no idea what time it was; there were no windows or distractions in her study room, but she had a sense that if she didn't hurry, she was going to be waiting for the first morning coach back to Lascenise. She turned to the last book, the one with a lock.

A lock with no key fitted to it.

Slowly, she stood up and began systematically searching her worktable. She shuffled aside papers, lifted each book and set them down at the far end, and found nothing. Then she knelt, alchemy lamp in hand, and searched the carpet, under the chairs, everywhere.

No key.

She sat back in her chair and sighed. "If I walk out of here and take this book back to the reference desk, they're going to reshelve it, because if there's one thing I know about the librarians here, it's that they *will* follow the rules, to the very letter . . ."

Aelis took up the book and tugged at the lock. It was not the sturdiest of locks, but she strongly suspected it was warded, as a brief push of her senses toward it confirmed. If she broke it off, she'd be dealing with a Porter before she could possibly take any useful notes.

She made a note of the title: *Primal Forces of Magic, Their Expressions, Manifestations, and Explications; A Theory Based upon the Early Divination Trance Poems of Naugalmir the Lidless Eye.*

"Sounds boring," Aelis muttered, turning the heavy book over in her hands. If the locked cover was *just* a cover, she could maybe slip the leaves out of it.

But that examination revealed the tiny sigils stamped into the spine of the binding. There were significant wards, not just on the lock but on the chains that held it closed.

She jotted down the title. "Naugalmir the Lidless Eye," she muttered. "Never heard of him."

She stacked all the texts up, putting *Primal Forces* at the top, and slipped out of her private room, alchemy lamp clipped her jacket

The library was strangely empty. It never technically closed, but overnight hours were strictly the province of the first-year student worker, with no diviner on duty. She set the books on the nearest cart for reshelving, all except for *Primal Forces*, which she carried with her down several flights to the reference desk.

They weren't quite into overnight hours, but there were only gray-robed students at the desk. As she approached, one of them had to look up from what he was reading by the feeble rays of a conjured light that floated over his shoulder.

"Can I help you?"

"This book was brought to me without a key."

The young man, a boy really, licked his lips, nonplussed. "I, ah . . . I don't have access to the keys. I'm only a minor clerk."

"Who does?"

He looked about him for help, but the other student clerks had melted away. None of them wanted to tell her the obvious truth, and none wanted to be the target of a warden's anger.

"Uh, no one who is on duty at the moment, Warden. You'd have to wait till . . ."

"I know. Till the morning. But I can't."

She held out the book and he took it, gingerly. "I, uh, apologize, Warden . . ."

"You didn't do anything wrong, lad." She felt ridiculous saying that. He was probably no more than four years her junior.

Feeling defeated by the chance and incompetence of bureaucracy, but with some potentially useful notes and leads, Aelis beat a hasty path to the coach station. She sprinkled enough silver about the place to get an express and left the library less than ten minutes later.

11

JEWELS

Aelis slept most of the way back to Lascenise. The habit of sleeping in a carriage came back to her quickly, though she had often been able to sleep when the carriage went in the other direction, with Miralla or Humphrey to cushion her. Eventually her body remembered the trick of bracing her feet so she didn't slide dramatically from side to side, and she got a solid few hours as the carriage rattled down the road in the night.

She was back in the city as it was lurching into the morning. She made one stop, for coffee and rolls with butter, which she ate as she walked.

"Sorry, Martin," she murmured, savoring the last crumb and trying to discreetly lick a greasy spot on her thumb. "But they do not ship finest sea-salt-flake butter to Lone Pine."

Lascenise woke up in waves. With the sun only just up, there was hardly any foot traffic, so she made good time to Cabal Keep, had a quick change of clothes—several parcels from Manxam's awaited inside her rooms—and called on her mentor, patient, and defendant.

✦ ✦ ✦

The censors made the same tedious speech as before and relieved her of sword and wand. Bardun Jacques was awake, reading, scratching at a piece of paper with a writing stick. He looked up as she came in but made no pretense of standing.

"De Lenti. Am I free to go yet?"

"Afraid not, Archmagister."

"I thought maybe you'd work a second miracle in as many days." He hrmphed and set down the stick, a simple wooden frame holding the thin writing coal in it. "I hate these fucking things. Nothing like a proper nib on a pen. No flair in it, no style. Just scratching across the page."

"They won't give you pens and ink?" Aelis set her kit down and leaned on it.

"Claim it can be used as a weapon."

"A pen?"

"Well," Bardun Jacques allowed, "I did gouge a hedge wizard's eye out with one once. Bastard was using conjuring to play tricks with water and wind in a little circuit of villages, just extorting the people, and fucking up the weather for miles. Could've started a real crisis, given time."

"Sounds like a lot of power for a hedge wizard."

He cocked an eyebrow at her. "Not surprising. They often are. Have one trick, but . . ."

"Wield it like a hammer. I ran into one like that up in Old Ystain. Enchanter. Most power in it I've felt, more than Urizen."

"But it's not about power—" Bardun Jacques began.

"It's about control," Aelis finished. "What about quills?"

"Need a quill-knife, and *that* the bastards are right not to let me have."

"Fine. Let me examine you." Aelis got out her dagger. "Been taking the medicines I sent up?"

Jacques pointed to the mantelpiece, where three corked bottles and several plain wooden pill-cases stood arranged.

"Good." She pressed the dagger against his wrist, no need to prick his skin, and examined his various systems. Things were superficially better, and nothing was in imminent danger. But it would take a great deal more power than she had to make his lungs *better* at this point. Holding the line was the best she could do, and the best she would wager any necromancer short of Aldayim himself could do.

Of course, I could always ask him, she thought, given the wrought-iron candelabra sitting wrapped in sacking in the trunk in her room. *Do I have a secret to trade?*

"So, I met with your lawyer. I like her," she said as she went to the bottles and pillcases and began preparing a before-dinner dose. "She . . . does think that you should ask for the mercy . . ."

"I haven't asked anyone for mercy in my too-long life, and I don't intend to start now."

"I know," Aelis said, selecting pills from two of the cases and bringing them to him, then taking some measuring spoons and a mixing cup from her medical kit. "And I am working on making sure that you won't need to."

"How?"

"Probably best that I don't go too far into detail," she murmured, "but I expect to be doing some underground sightseeing in the next day, two at the most. I have a freelancer looking into things down in the slops."

"Good, good," he muttered, as she presented him a foul-smelling dose in a small silver cup.

"Archmagister, if I may ask . . . did you ever encounter a woodshade?"

"A what now?" He tipped the cup back and grimaced dramatically. "Gods, I'd rather drink from a cuspidor than that again."

Aelis ignored the comment and took the silver cup back, briefly casting a Purgative on it to clean it of any pestilence; silver was particularly receptive to such a spell. "Well, I'm not . . . entirely convinced it was a woodshade, but it was something like it. A spirit of a forest coalesced into a form and bound in one place. Not a spirit summoned from death, so a bit out of my expertise, but . . ."

"You encountered this creature?"

"I did," Aelis said.

"How'd you kill it?"

"I . . . didn't. I bargained with it."

Bardun Jacques looked sharply up at her. "*Never* bargain with any kind of shade, specter, haunt, ghost. . . ."

"There were some other pressing matters, Archmagister."

"Came out worse in the bargain, didn't you?"

"We did, yes."

"Why are you asking me?"

"Looking for guidance. There are libraries here, book traders, resources I don't have access to in Lone Pine."

"So, it's an ongoing bargain. But not for you."

"No, Archmagister. Not for me."

He took a deep breath. "You'll want Hughinn, *Deals with Devils and Their Ilk* if you can find it. Won't be in a library. The standard reference texts might have some cross-references for place-haunts, woodshades. Barston and Urquhardt, that sort of thing . . ."

"And curses, I think," Aelis admitted, quietly. "Are book-traders in Lascenise likely to have it?"

"None of the too-dear shops in Ruby Chapel will. It's too good for them. There's a good old fellow out in Prester's Walk, in the shadow of that monstrous cathedral they're building, if the priests haven't taken it away from him yet in Stregon's name. Shop doesn't have a name, just Books bought, Occasionally Sold on a sign. If Rax doesn't have it, he'll know someone who does."

"Thank you, Archmagister. I'll get out there tomorrow . . ."

"Send someone. Preferably someone the keep can't connect to you."

"You don't think that's overdoing it?"

"De Lenti, a group of our own wizards tried to have me killed just for investigating something I didn't know they were connected to. If you're doing research into curses and bargains with spirits, and *you're* free and walking around, then someone else must have taken the shit end of whatever bargain you foolishly made, and you're rushing around trying to free them. How'm I doing?"

"Pretty well, Archmagister."

"So, you feel obligated to this person, whoever they are. You care for them?"

Aelis closed her eyes and sighed. "Very much, Archmagister."

He let out a hard sigh. "That's a mistake."

"Maybe," Aelis said. "Felt worth it."

"It's not about you, de Lenti. It's about them, whoever they are. If the people who are after *me* think they can get to *you* through this person . . ."

"She's eight hundred miles away. And I don't think they can find her if she doesn't want them to."

"Explain."

As quickly as she could, Aelis related the story; Rhunival, the rod she'd given, Maurenia's blood, how Maurenia was trapped.

"If this thing was a woodshade, it was damn well shackled with as fine a piece of conjuring as I've ever heard. They're not sociable spirits, generally," Bardun Jacques said when she finished. "Got any more information on it? Anything at all?"

Aelis thought of the bundle of old pages the Errithsuns had given her, and of her conversation with Urizen.

"Well, I already have a book I can't read . . . I'll copy some of the characters to show you later. But here . . ." She took up one of the charcoal writing-sticks and a slip of paper, and quickly sketched out the rod that Rhunival had wanted, and that was depicted in the pages of the book, from memory.

Bardun Jacques leaned forward and concentrated on it as she drew. "That," he rumbled quietly, "is a very dangerous thing, if your drawing is correct."

"How dangerous?"

"There are secret societies among wizards devoted to creating or finding one of those. You had it in your hands and gave it away?" He shook his head.

"*More* secret societies among wizards? Is this the sodality-of-the-plaited-wand nonsense I once heard from Magister Urizen?"

"Might be, though I don't know that I've heard of that one. Was good that you talked to him, though. Up on his theory, that one, lots of research on curses and bargains and the like. I'd take that book to him. If you trust him."

Aelis weighed that. "You just told me not to trust any other wizard while I'm here."

"So I did. But don't go thinking I know everything, de Lenti. Urizen's a smart gnome. Never did any fieldwork, though, which is the real work, as we both know."

"Fine, I'll bring it to him as soon as I can get back to the Lyceum, see what he makes of it."

"Good. And I'll search my memories. Maybe something will turn up. You get me out of this mess, and I'll see if I can't help you out of that one."

"I don't expect anything in repayment for helping you, Archmagister," Aelis said.

Bardun Jacques looked sharply up at her, his gaze having drifted to the table. He looked quickly away. "Nonsense. I made you throw over your post and whatever life you'd settled into to pull my old ass out of the fire. I'll owe you."

Aelis came from a family who observed stiff manners at all times. She didn't doubt that her parents and her older siblings had some regard for her, were proud of her becoming a warden, all that.

It was simply that demonstrating those sorts of emotions was done with stiff handclasps and polite nods of the head. So while on some level she knew she wanted to communicate some of the regard she felt for Bardun Jacques, and the pride that welled within her from knowing that he asked for her personally, she really lacked the vocabulary for it.

But she tried anyway.

"Archmagister," she began, drawing herself up straight and fixing on a point on the stone wall just above her. "I had many teachers at the Lyceum I have . . . great regard for." She swallowed hard. "But none of them . . ."

"Don't embarrass us both, de Lenti," Bardun Jacques said. "I made mistakes in my life. You don't have to make them, too. I'll help free this person you care for. But I need to be free of this mess first."

Aelis swallowed whatever she'd been about to say. She had no clear idea how she was going to finish; somewhere between *but none of them had as much impact on the warden I am as you* and *I would've walked here barefoot over crushed glass to help you.* She hoped her flush didn't show too much in her cheeks.

"Right. Off with you then. I feel sleep coming on me before they bring dinner." He coughed lightly and said, "I don't suppose you could talk them into allowing me a pipe . . ."

"Out of the question, Archmagister. All forms of smoking are lost to you, I'm afraid." Her voice was sharper than she'd intended it to be, but then, she'd answered as an anatomist. "None of it would do your lungs any good at all."

"I thought you'd say that."

"Till the morning, then." She bowed lightly, she wasn't entirely sure why, and backed quickly out of the chamber.

12

BOOK HUNTING

The next morning, Aelis found herself in a cafe on Khorais's recommendation. and was sitting over her second cup of coffee with a small map of Lascenise open on the table.

She was also sitting on the floor, because—as she should've guessed—a cafe in Halfton that Khorais would recommend was built for gnomes. It was hardly uncomfortable. The floor was clean enough to eat off, the table was just right for looking at the map, the coffee was quite good, the cups large enough for humans or dwarves, and with her back up against the wall she was almost snug.

She had taken enough precaution, at least, not to sit with her back to the door, so some sense warned her that someone was approaching—months spent expecting Tun to sneak up on her at any moment, probably—and the scuff of a loose bootheel told her who it was.

"Morning, Mihil."

"Morning, boss," he said, sliding onto a chair opposite her on the floor and peering down at the map. "Still need another day on the business we discussed."

"I know. But Khorais said you could spare the time."

"I can if you're paying and if I can get back to work on it tonight."

Aelis set some coins on the table, next to the map. Mihil made them disappear.

"What are we up to today?"

Aelis smiled at him. "We're book-shopping."

"Book-shopping?"

"Indeed. I've got a list of some titles from two professors of great esteem, and we're going to hit Ruby Chapel, the Tremont, Prester's Walk, and Temple Street."

"Posh, regular, posh-trying-to-be-regular, and full of god-botherers," Mihil said, commenting on the districts she'd named. "And none of them any too close to one another."

"Oh, nonsense. The Tremont and Ruby Chapel are close enough, and Prester's Walk abuts Temple Street."

"Aye, but the far west end of it, we come at it from the Chapel, we're at the east end, and it's one of the longest straight roads in the city."

"Then eat well. And fast. Lots of walking in our future."

"Can't we just hire a coach?"

"No."

"Come on, boss. I know you've got the money . . ."

"I do," Aelis admitted. "It's not about that. Mainly it's that a cab waiting for us everywhere we go for a day is going to draw attention to us."

"You worried over a tail?"

"Let's just say that if anyone is following me, I want them to work for it." *And if someone does take a shot, I can make* certain *to keep one alive this time.*

By then the aproned waiter had come along, looking askance at Mihil's tattered coat and pale, blotchy features. He retreated gratefully when Mihil waved him away.

"It would be better for you to eat something," Aelis said.

"I'm sure it would, but I've never got an appetite before noon."

"Not even coffee?"

He waved her off, and the physician in Aelis couldn't help but notice the trembling in his fingers. She filed it away, tossed back her own coffee, paid the bill, and came to her feet.

"Come on then. We're off to Ruby Chapel."

♦   ♦   ♦

The first store was a complete bust. Aelis felt it in her bones as soon as they walked in. It was full of sets of richly dyed leather-bound books with gilt titles that would look good on the shelves of a library or an office without ever inconveniencing anyone by being *read*. But she dutifully handed over her list of titles anyway, and the bored clerk barely set down the cheap historical romance he was reading to glance over it.

"Never heard of any of these," he said, sliding the paper back over. Aelis was about to turn away when she pointed at the book he was reading.

"Is that anything like *The Ballads of Gavelden?*"

"A *bit*, though there's less focus on all the glorious combat and more on the politics . . ."

"If there's a standard six- or twelve-volume set of that kind of thing, I'll take it."

That got the clerk's attention. He left his book where it was and immediately began chattering about romances, lays, songs, ballads, and so on, until Aelis shoved some gold at him and told him to deliver the dozen newest, best of "that kind of thing" to the keep, under her name.

"Didn't take you for the kind to go for chivalric romances," Mihil said on their way out the door.

"Oh, it's not for me. It's for the man who's been feeding me since I got to Lone Pine last year," Aelis said.

"You're a sentimentalist at heart. I knew it."

"Hardly," Aelis said. She set a swift pace, but Mihil managed to keep up. "I just feel like I owe him more than his husband will let me pay. This'll go a little way toward clearing that debt."

The next two stores in Ruby Chapel were also failures, with nothing of any interest about them. The fourth had a shelf labeled "Magical Theory," but they were mostly introductory-level textbooks. Aelis assumed they'd been pawned off by Lyceum washouts. Her list produced a raised eyebrow from the aging dwarf proprietor, but nothing else.

There was a long walk to the next shop, and Aelis's eye was caught by a sign that pulled her to a stop so sudden that Mihil trod on the back of her foot.

**LIKENESSES PAINTED, ENGRAVED, CUT, ETC.
PRICES REASONABLE. ANY SIZE.**

Her mind flashed to the little portrait locket in her pouch, and she changed course, swerving through the crowd toward that tiny storefront, Mihil sputtering questions behind her.

"Books, boss. Thought we were looking for *books*."

"Bear with me, Mihil," Aelis said. Her hand found the handle of the door. It took some force to open, and the bell that rang as the door pushed against it sounded, if anything, surprised.

There was a counter, crowded with various dusty portraits, starting with a rack as small as the one she carried and others in full-size, if cheap, wooden frames that occupied the wall behind. From a doorway behind the counter came several startled sounds, objects toppling over, grunted curses, the *thunk* of a head or a boot hitting something it didn't expect, and then a stooped old human man came out.

"How can Master Lucretius help you, gentlefolk?" the man said, rubbing his forehead and not looking up at them. When he finally did, his manner chilled.

"Warden. Is this some kind of official visit?"

"I don't wish to disturb you from your craft, Master Lucretius," Aelis said, putting on her best count's-daughter face and walking smoothly to the edge of the counter. "And I'm happy to pay you for your lost time."

Eyeing the work on the counter, she wasn't entirely sure the painter had ever earned the title master; it was journeyman's work at best. But then, so was the locket she carried.

"Proceed then, Warden," the man said, still stiff and cold.

Aelis removed the rolled-up bundle, and pulled out the tarnished locket. She opened it up and set it on the counter.

Lucretius produced a small glass and fitted it to his eye. "Would you like me to touch this up, Warden? I can restore some of the color, I suspect, and . . ."

"I was hoping you might have any insight into its construction or making or . . ."

"Well, the locket is a standard piece you can get from any job-lot jeweler in Lascenise. Or Mizanta, or Antraval, or . . . any place that has job-lot jewelers, I expect. The painting is . . . well, it's quick work, I'll say that."

Aelis felt like a weak candle someone had just dumped a flagon of water on.

"So there's no . . . identifying mark? No artist's signature?"

Lucretius looked up from the locket and removed the glass from his eye, squinted at her.

"Are you . . . familiar with painting, Warden?"

"I had a fair amount of training as an artist in my youth . . ."

"But, if I were to guess, that would be from studio painters. Maestros. The kind who have noble patronage?"

"They were that," Aelis said.

"Well, that's what we all start out dreaming of, Warden. But most of us are, at best, jobbers like me. I don't sign these . . . why would I? I paint them in a day. I paint three or four of them in a day if I can. It's good, honest craft, and it makes the customer happy, but it's never hanging in a Count's palace."

"I see," Aelis said. And she did, though she didn't want to admit it. "So, there are probably no identifying details?"

"I can pry it apart easily enough and look. Shall I?"

She nodded and he removed some small tools from a belt pouch, and quickly had the locket apart, the tiny wooden panels that made up the painting loose. He fitted the lens back to his eye and moved the pieces with his little chisel and tweezers.

"Nothing, Warden. These are the most common materials, the most common work. Shall I put it back together?"

"Please do."

As quickly as he'd taken it apart, Lucretius had the locket back together. He slid it toward her.

"Sorry I can't be of help, Warden."

Aelis swept the locket up and left a couple of silver pieces in its place. "Thank you for your time, Master."

Mihil had watched the entire exchange without a word, but barely waited till they were out the door before spilling over with questions.

"What was that about? Why that locket? If I had to guess, I'd say every one of your forefathers and mothers has a portrait the size of a gnomish-house door in gilded frames hanging on marble walls. So why that—"

"Ask me another time, when I haven't got much else to do, Mihil."

"I'll hold you to that."

Nathalie. Bardun Jacques. Maurenia. The conspiracy of wizards. Assassins. Smugglers. I will handle every fucking one of these problems.

✦ ✦ ✦

What she couldn't handle was their complete failure not only in Ruby Chapel but also in the Tremont. Two bookshop clerks had regarded her list with the same bewildered expression. One had graciously asked for her patience, retrieved a heavy leather-bound ledger, and paged through it for nearly a quarter of an hour, checking her list every so often, before handing it back.

"I'm sorry, Warden," he said, shaking his head. "I . . . one of these titles tickles my memory but I cannot recall why."

The other had looked at her list like a dog looking at something it couldn't identify and handed it back with a shake of the head.

One bookshop had been closed, and none of the others had returned any useful information. By the time they stopped for lunch, at a cart selling sliced meat on rolls, she was seething so hot she barely tasted the food and resisted all Mihil's attempts to draw her out.

Temple Street, where she held out hope, proved no good. Everything was religious literature, and not even real theology or scholarship. At one shop near Onoma's Chapel—the only Temple Aelis might even consider visiting was in the Lyceum, not here—the staff got so excited over her appearance that she had to turn down several offers of coffee, wine, or dinner.

The sun was low, her stomach was grumbling, and even Mihil had stopped trying to talk to her by the time they turned down Prester's Walk and she saw a simply chalked sign reading BOOKS BOUGHT, OCCASIONALLY SOLD.

Aelis hurried to the door, just in time to see the owner—a thick gray beard his most prominent feature—come toward the door to lock it.

She tried the doorknob, but he gave his head a firm shake.

Two impulses warred in her, authority versus bribery. She had no real authority, as a warden, to force a private citizen who had done nothing wrong to open his door, so she decided that gold might be the better option.

The flash of it in the window caught his eye, but she could see he wasn't moved. So she did the only thing she could think of, something she'd never done in all her Lyceum days, something that had never occurred to her at Lone Pine, something she probably hadn't done since she was less than half her current age.

Aelis *pouted*. She made her eyes as large as she could, put a quiver in her lip, and crinkled the skin of her face.

The elderly man behind the glass sighed, said something that was probably a curse, and swung the door open for her.

"Fine. But I'll be taking that gold piece you showed me, too."

Aelis placed it gratefully in his hand and slipped through the open door, Mihil at her heels.

"Would you be Master Rax?"

The man, not as old as she'd thought, perhaps just gone gray early, snorted. "Not master of anything," he said. "Just Rax."

A slight chill settled in her stomach. The wand in her left sleeve felt heavy; her hand itched for the heft of her sword-hilt.

Rax eyed her strangely, a glint in his dark green eyes that hadn't been there before. The moment hung there, tense, feeling like the moment before swords were drawn.

Mihil stepped in, a hand on her right wrist, between her and the bookstore owner.

"Rax, we've got silver, even gold, to spend, and been frustrated in every stop along the way. My associate here has a short list of titles she's looking for, and we've been told you're the one man who can help."

Something about the gnome's tone, his chatty confidence, pricked a hole in the moment through which the tension escaped. Rax's beard quivered as his face drew up in a smile. There was still something a bit predatory in his eyes, something that reminded Aelis far too much of someone else. But she uncurled her hand—just a twitch away from dropping her wand into it—and took the now well-worn list from her pouch.

He took it in fingers with ink stains worked deep into their calloused tips and held it scant inches from his eyes.

Rax grunted. "Hughinn, I've got. Take me two cock-shakes to find it, and at my age that's a long time. Have a seat." He gestured vaguely with his other hand, and Aelis and Mihil looked around for the indicated seats.

Aelis didn't see any. Mihil went to a greasy window that wouldn't have been big enough for her and managed to perch himself on the inside ledge. "Benefits of a world made for larger folk," he said, smiling. Then, dropping his voice, he muttered, "Why'd you look so ready to do . . ."

"Shh!" Aelis even lifted her forefinger over her mouth to quiet him and Mihil shrugged, then leaned his head against the window, and, to all appearances, immediately dropped off to sleep.

Aelis began looking around the store. As far as she could tell there was simply no order to it. Novels and histories lay piled next to one another on the shelves. She saw a book of music theory next to a Gnomish Grammar next to a book on the geography of Lascenise. That, she plucked from the shelf, wiped free of dust, and opened.

She was almost immediately lost in it, poring over the old maps of when Lascenise was a neutral meeting point right at the border of three occasionally hostile nations. Maps carried the narrative, really, showing how embassies and forts had grown together into a multinational city and, in many ways, created the Tri-Crowns and then the Estates House. She'd never been much interested in politics—too many siblings between her and ever having to worry about sitting in it—but this kind of political history was gripping in its own way. Her time in Lone Pine had, she thought, given her a better window into how land shaped character than she'd understood in her privileged childhood of palaces, manicured gardens, and lovingly tended vineyards.

She heard the shuffle of slippered feet against wood and set the book down. Mihil popped to his feet, and she couldn't have truly guessed whether he'd been asleep against the window or not, but either way he looked fully awake.

Rax had her list sitting atop one small book bound in black cloth.

"I don't have the Cutterleaf," Rax growled. "You after information about Woodshades, I take it?"

"Why do you ask?"

He shrugged. "Just surprising, is all. Someone else was in asking for the same monograph."

"Who? When?"

"I buy books, and I sometimes sell them. What I don't do is sell information about my clients."

"That's a rather large coincidence . . ."

"Look, Warden. I'll sell you this book and then be after my dinner and my pint of brandy. I don't want to have any further conversation about it."

"If it was warden business . . ."

"Then you could come back here with a writ, and I'll have a lawyer meet you. Buying the book or not? Last chance."

"Yes," Aelis said. She paid the price he asked without haggling, which seemed to please him, and he was less than half a step behind them to lock the door and pull down a curtain as they left.

Two steps away from the small, cluttered shop, Mihil turned on her.

"What in the seven hells, boss? Why'd you come so close to stabbing that man?"

"He reminded me of someone. Uncannily."

"Seemed like an old man to me."

"Come on" Aelis said. Let's find a cab and take it back to the keep and get some dinner."

"No keep for me, boss. Not unless you're ordering it. I like you—I think you're trying to help someone, and I think you're the decent sort of warden— but things have to get a lot worse before I willingly walk into Cabal Keep."

"What are you afraid of there, Mihil?"

"What *isn't* to be afraid of? The best-case scenario of an interaction with a wizard, much less a warden, is they slip you something round and shiny to do what they're too lazy or too incompetent or too dignified to do for themselves. Literally everything else that can happen is worse."

"Is that how the people of Lascenise see us?"

"Lazy and powerful and scary, but easy to soak for some gold? 'Fraid so, boss. Sorry to be the one to tell you."

"You don't *sound* sorry."

"It was meant to be a comforting little white lie to make the truth easier to swallow." Mihil sighed. "You *are* young, aren't you?"

Aelis felt suddenly affronted, more so than when he'd insulted wizards in general and wardens in particular. "Well, I'll still pay for a cab," she said, muted, trying and failing not to sound defensive. "If you can bear to share it with me," she added, wishing she could stuff the words back in her mouth even as she said them.

"I'll always share a cab on a wizard's dime. Oh, don't pout at *me*, boss." He patted her wrist. "I think you're trying to be a good one."

Aelis didn't bother to ask what that meant, and Mihil stopped trying to tell her. She found a cab stand, hired one, and paid the driver to take Mihil as far as he asked, paid the gnome for the days of work he'd already done, and avoided his few conversational gambits.

13

ASSASSINS, DEAD AND OTHERWISE

Cabal Keep may have been very much a military installation, neat and precisely run. But wizards were given to their creature comforts, and wardens were no different.

Which is to say that dinner in the refectory of a Warden Cabal castle was not warm beer, dry bread, and unidentifiable stew.

There *was* bread, of course. A profusion of it. Soft white loaves, hearty brown rounds, knotted crusty rolls, buckets of butter. And there was soup. A soup course, in fact, shellfish in a light tomato broth. Then the meat-carving stations were set up, and all the while decanters moved around the tables, often so quickly that Aelis was pouring from one while passing another. She didn't eat too much, though the temptation was there, and she restricted herself to only enough wine so as not to stand out. Nothing was quite as fine as the memory of Tausner's so recent to her palate, but it was much better than most folk in Lascenise outside Ruby Chapel or the Azare Courts were eating.

What she *wanted* was to find Amadin, but there was no sign of the lanky elf invoker anywhere. She did catch up with Miralla and they traded gossip as they ate, nothing of consequence, just her friend pointing out who was sleeping with who and who didn't know that their sometimes bedmate was also someone else's.

"Any idea where Amadin is?" Aelis asked, her tone casual.

"Keeps to himself, that one. Takes most of his meals in his rooms, I think, if he even eats. Who can tell with elves? Half of them won't eat meat." Miralla folded a thin slice of roast beef and tore half of it away with one bite. "Unnatural," she said a few moments later.

"Just need to talk to him about the events of our trip down from Lone Pine."

"He can't be as interesting as me. And you've hardly told me a *thing* about whoever you met up there . . ."

Aelis sighed. "Why do you need to know?"

"Just tell me one thing about her," Miralla said. "Not that she's beautiful. I already know your taste is impeccable."

Aelis thought a moment. "She's . . . free. Free in a way neither of us has ever been."

"What do you mean?"

"I mean she does as she thinks best, as she likes, with no apologies, and nothing left owing to anyone. She's a wanderer, an adventurer . . ."

"Wardens live adventurous lives, Aelis."

"At someone else's orders, Mira. I only know pieces of her life before I met her. I think she's had enough taking orders, and no desire to give them."

"I think I see the picture," Miralla said, then focused on her food. Aelis took the opportunity to excuse herself and wound her way through the warren of Cabal Keep to Amadin's rooms.

There was no light coming from under his door. She thought about waiting for the morning, then raised her hand to knock.

And the door swung silently open. The room was dark, but the light from the hallway illuminated something stretched out on the bed, and Aelis's anatomist training told her it was the right size and shape for a body.

"Amadin?" Aelis dropped her hand to her sword, though she did not draw it as she swept in.

She felt just the smallest rush of air behind her, heard the barest whisper of a soft-soled boot on stone.

Then there was the tang of metal in the air. If it was a blade, it was small, thin, and sinister. She summoned one of the more single-purpose, specialized wards she knew; the Gorget.

The wafer-thin ring of force that surrounded her neck saved her from the garrote that someone slipped around her neck. The would-be strangler fought for purchase against the ward but had been so focused on making his strategy work that Aelis had time to react. She stomped on the inside of his foot, drawing a muffled scream, then threw her elbow into his midsection even as she was bending down to flip the assailant over her back. He hit the floor hard, a tangle of limbs wheezing for air.

She threw herself atop him, punching down at his face once, twice, then held her dagger over his already swelling eye. A coruscating line of black energy radiated along the edge; Iriphet's Bloody Rupture, ready to do awful things with all the blood pooling so close to the surface of his skin. She couldn't cut living flesh with that blade, but she could certainly do interesting things through it. Only then did she look down at her assailant.

It was Amadin.

Aelis scrambled to her feet and slid her wand into her hand, hit Amadin with the most powerful Catnap she could summon while breathing hard. She shut the door and barred it, using the glowing tip of her wand to provide just enough light to see in the darkened chamber. Once she had some tapers lit, she surveyed the scene.

There was a body in Amadin's bed. There was no mistaking that. A nondescript man in common clothes. She saw a neat stab wound through the throat, and the blankets on the bed soaked with sticky, drying blood. She flicked her eyes about the room. Amadin's sword was sheathed and wrapped in his belt, leaning in the corner of the room with his staff.

The owner of said sword was already groaning and stirring on the floor.

"Gods-damned Elisima-favored elves," she muttered. She knew another

Catnap would do nothing but drain her, so she cast about for options. A glint of metal caught her eye and she found the garrote Amadin had tried to slip around her neck. She tried to grab it by the wire, a twisted braid of three strands of metal, felt it cut into a part of her she couldn't have named, something deeper and more important than her skin. She recoiled as if she'd been scalded.

"Where the fuck did you get this, Amadin?" Delicately, she took it by the handles. He resisted, feebly, as she wound the cord around his wrists, careful not to touch the wire, and propped him up against his bed.

She took the only chair in the room, pushed under a desk against the far wall and its tiny, fortified window, set its back against the door, and sat down. Then, for good measure, she drew her sword and pressed the point under Amadin's chin, lifting it up slowly.

His eyes fluttered and his mouth opened. Despite the scream he tried to utter, no sound passed his lips.

"You're an abjurer too, Amadin. Did you really think you'd get a scream out when another one has her sword against your throat?" Aelis hoped he interpreted her gritted teeth as anger, not the tight concentration she needed to keep the ward she'd called clapped around his mouth. "Now. I can suffocate you. Or we can talk, like comrades, which I *thought* we were."

Amadin's throat worked soundlessly and his eyes opened wide and plaintive, his head bobbing up and down in assent.

"Understand that if you scream when I drop this ward, or you try to rush at me, I will cut your throat first and figure out a way to dodge the shit that will rain down on me later. If you know anything about me, you'll know that acting on impulse and worrying about consequences later is something of a house specialty. Am I clear?"

Amadin nodded, a frantic edge to the gesture, his eyes wide and bulging, and Aelis let her ward drop. She sat up a little straighter but did not allow herself the deep breath she wanted to take.

"Stregon's balls," Amadin gasped, his voice scratched and rasping, as if he'd been screaming for the last several hours. "You really are a student of Jacques, aren't you?"

"Complimenting me doesn't get you out of trouble. Now," Aelis said, her mind racing, "I wasn't supposed to survive the ride to Lascenise, was I? And once I did, neither of the hired assassins could, either."

"You're slow, but you get there," Amadin said. His wide eyes lost some of their shine and he sagged back against the bed. "Once you smelled the ambush, it threw everything off."

"It was a clumsy fucking ambush," Aelis said. Anger started to rise in her like smoke off a fire. "You want to kill me, Amadin, you better work a little *fucking* harder. Who's behind it?"

"You don't want to know. You can still get out of all this, with your life and your career. Just . . . let the whole thing rest. Let them put Jacques out of the way. They won't execute him. Just stick him in a hole under censor guard until Onoma does the job for them. Won't be long."

Aelis rocketed out of her seat and punched Amadin straight over the eye socket, a short blow with a loose fist. She didn't truly step into it and twist her hips, but it was fast enough that even elven reflexes didn't allow him to turn away from it.

He recoiled and held his bound hands up to his eye.

"I pulled the punch, so I didn't break any bones. You're lucky I'm an anatomist, but reasonably soon you might become *unlucky* that I'm an anatomist," she snarled. When he looked up from behind his wired wrists, his eye already swollen shut, her anger turned inward. *Striking a beaten enemy, even one who tried to kill me, is beneath me*, she thought. *Well, I'll deal with the shame of that later.*

"Let's try a different question." She jerked her chin toward the body on his bed. "Who in seventy hells is *that?*"

"Hired killer. Probably from the same guild that were supposed to take you on the road. They have special rates for wizards. Higher for wardens."

"The Hidden Skulls," she said, and Amadin nodded. If he was surprised that she'd produced the name, he didn't show it. "I don't even want to know where they got enough cold iron, silver, and manganese wire for *that*," she said, pointing to the garrote twisted around his wrists.

"Neither do I. But he was waiting for me with it."

"Somehow, though, you got the drop on him. Took him right through the throat."

"Damn right I did, put him right on the bed too, so as not to soak blood through the floor."

"Considerate," Aelis muttered. "So he was coming to do what, put you down for failing to get me killed?"

"I expect." He looked at her, his one open eye wide with fear, his nostrils flaring as he breathed. "The Shadow Congress does not like loose ends."

"The *what?*"

"The Shadow Congress," Amadin repeated. He licked his lips. "I'm a dead elf anyway, so I might as well tell you."

"Let me hazard a guess: a secret coven of wizards, power brokers. They're behind the movement of magical artifacts through Lascenise to the Lyceum."

"You're quicker than I thought."

"I am, after all, a student of Bardun Jacques."

"That wasn't meant as a compliment. He finally picked a fight he is not going to win."

"Maybe not on his own, but he's got . . ."

"Got who . . . you? A child, barely out of the Colleges, pulled from a posting on the *frontier?* You're going to stand against a group of the oldest and most powerful wizards alive?"

"Well, Amadin," Aelis said, "I walked, unprepared, into an ambush where *you* had a fucking wizard-killer in your hands. All you had to do was get it against my skin." She laid the tip of her sword against his neck again. "And yet . . . here I am, with a sword to your throat. Who's on the Shadow Congress?"

"Do you think I know? Merely knowing that they exist, merely speaking the word aloud, could make me the target of better, more expensive assassins than this one. Of spells, of accidents, of curses."

"Yet you're perfectly willing to be their dogsbody, aren't you? To lead a fellow warden to her death and send the most celebrated warden of the age to his."

"He deserves it," Amadin said bluntly. "You're . . ." He shrugged. "An acceptable loss."

"You're going to write out a confession," Aelis said.

"It won't matter. They'll kill me, and you'll have no proof. Jacques dies, you go back to your frozen shithole, and they'll find some other way to kill you."

"We bring you to the censors, keep you under guard . . ."

"You do not understand what you're dealing with. Listen to me." He leaned forward and Aelis had to move her sword to keep from cutting him. "There is no facet of our existence as wizards they cannot control. This is . . ."

"Why don't we just assume you aren't going to talk me out of doing my job?" Aelis said. "Let's make that the bedrock of whatever our working relationship is going to be. So save your breath, and think of reasons I shouldn't turn you in."

"You have no proof. Your word against mine, and there aren't a half-dozen wardens in this keep who don't want to see this mess with Jacques go away. They'll side with me."

"What I'm hearing is that I need to find a way to make my success indispensable to you." Aelis sat back and lowered her sword. "I can't keep that wire wrapped around your wrists forever."

"By morning they'd be asking questions," Amadin sneered.

"Amadin, if I left that on overnight, you'd lose your hands. As it is, the lack of blood flow is doing damage to them. In fact . . . just an hour or two longer and the finer gestures of your fingers are going to be a problem." Aelis blew out a long breath. "If I had my medical kit here, I'd make you swallow a poison that needed regular antidotes, or at least make you *think* I did. Too many failure points though; you could go straight to the keep apothecary and sort that out." She looked at his face; a smirk crept over his features, despite the beating he'd taken and his swollen-shut eye. "I don't want to just kill you, however satisfying it may be." *I do not want to say these next words.*

Aelis gathered herself, blew out a deep breath, and stared hard at the bound and defenseless warden before her.

"I can think of only one way to keep you on my side and invested in my survival."

Amadin suddenly struggled against the bed, tried to stand up; Aelis kicked his legs out from under him and leaned forward.

"I will compose a death curse, Warden Amadin," she whispered. "I will do it before I leave this room and name you my sole target. And I will not discharge it until my time as advocate for Bardun Jacques is successfully concluded. Do you understand me?"

"What if you fail?" he half moaned. "What if the assassins succeed?"

"You had better see to it that they don't."

Amadin struggled against his bonds, but Aelis knew he'd just dig them in deeper, so she drew her dagger, laid both it and her sword on her lap, one in each hand, gathered her will and her power, and began composing in the stillness of her mind.

What she composed did not begin in words as much as it was imagined gestures, intent, the drawing of power through the implements in her hands. In her mind's eye they were strong bars of visible energy, one a coruscating black, the other a vibrant blue. She wrapped them together, vaguely aware that her hands were moving. Someone in the room with her was letting out a low moan but she ignored them. She may have been sitting in a physical space in a castle, near a panicked elf wizard and a corpse, but her true self existed only in the realm of her own power.

And it was more than she had imagined it was, more than she had expected, and she had to be judicious in its use.

If I die before dissipating what I have made, let this curse pass to Amadin, wizard and warden, she formulated, her lips moving and making a faint murmur in the physical world while in her head her voice resounded like a giant's. *May his blood thicken and his organs shrivel. May his spells rebound upon his hands. May these afflictions baffle all who seek to undo them.*

There were more things she might have added, but Aelis stopped there. When she was done, she felt the thing she had made—the curse—solidify in her mind. She opened her eyes and returned to more awareness of her physical self. Sweat ran down her forehead and her back. Amadin stared hard at her, and she glanced at his pale, bruising hands.

Aelis stood up, and the effort it took drew a heavy grunt from her. She felt like she'd walked sixty miles with a pack on since her last rest; it was a tremendous effort to lift her sword and sheath it. She didn't want Amadin to see her arm tremble as she slid the blade home.

"It is done, Amadin," she said, her voice a hoarse rasp. "I will not tell you the words I formed." Inside her mind, the curse throbbed, distracting her for a moment. "But it will be in your best interest to see that I live through whatever comes. Do you understand?"

"Just take this fucking thing off," Amadin hissed, holding up his hands.

Aelis realized that her hand was still curled tightly around her dagger. It took enormous effort to move her fingers from the grip and more to find the sheath at the back of her belt. Then, careful to touch only the handles, she unwound the garrote from Amadin's wrists.

"As the blood flows back into your hands, it is going to hurt. I will go get my kit, come back, and do what I can." She stared hard at the body on his bed. "And we need to decide what we're going to do about that."

✦ ✦ ✦

Neither Aelis nor Amadin got very much sleep that night. After she'd treated his wounds, they called on the warden of the watch to report the dead assassin.

The word *assassin* had sent select parts of the keep into a flurry of activity. Mazadar had to be summoned from his habitual early rest to question them both, together and then separately.

The lie they'd settled on was based on the truth, which generally made for the best kind of lie. The assassin had gotten into the keep, targeting Amadin, and Aelis had happened by at precisely the right time to assist.

Aelis hated handing over the garrote only slightly more than she hated having it near her skin. A garrote was the weapon of a coward and a skulker, to begin with. But a garrote that was a *wizard-killer*, cutting off the access to magic through its physical and alchemical construction, was offensive to her very nature.

And yet, she thought to herself as she waited outside Mazadar's study, *I found an immediate use for it. And I am very afraid I would continue finding uses for it.*

When she was brought in to speak to Mazadar alone, she felt a tiny spark of fear that Amadin might have spilled the entire truth, but the battered and weary elf didn't look at her or speak to her as he walked out. *Unless Mazadar is part of this* Shadow Congress, *I ought to be safe. And even then, a Death Curse is a seven-horned devil of a thing to unwind.*

She repeated her rehearsed story; she'd called on Amadin after eating in the refectory because she hadn't seen him there. Heard a struggle, immediately entered his room, found him with the assassin, intervened.

"Why didn't you attempt to take him alive?" Mazadar drummed his thick, blunt fingers on his desktop. He was wearing only a nightshirt, lacking time to put on proper robes.

"With all due respect, Commander," Aelis said, "it became quickly apparent he was waving a wizard-killing weapon around. Drastic measures were called for."

"I'm given to understand that you are a uniquely gifted necromancer and anatomist, Warden de Lenti. You could not bind his soul or tend his wounds?"

"A sword wound through the throat is beyond my power to heal, Commander."

Mazadar let out a grunt. "I do not like that an assassin got into my keep, Warden."

"I'm not any happier about it, Commander."

"We will need to conduct a thorough security review," Mazadar said. His expression suggested he would rather eat a rock, and he looked at Aelis speculatively.

"Commander, I would not have the time to devote to it given my duties as advocate to Archmagister Bardun Jacques . . ."

"Warden de Lenti, I would not appoint someone with your experience to review the security of my privy chamber, much less a space the size and significance of Cabal Keep."

Aelis's first thought was, *Wait, why in seventeen hells am I not good enough?* but that was quickly replaced with relief that something else wasn't about to be added to her burdens.

Mazadar eyed her sharply, one of his tapping hands curling into a fist. "I do not take well to being interrupted by junior wardens in my private study at two hours past the change of day."

Aelis refused to lower her eyes, and let the dwarf lay the full force of his gaze on her. Her voice, however, was a bit more demure.

"I apologize, Commander. It has been a very long day, and tomorrow promises to be no shorter."

"Fine. Get out. Be where I can find you." Mazadar sank back into his chair as Aelis strode quickly out of his office. She didn't allow herself to feel tired until she'd stripped off her clothes and sank into her bed. It should have felt as good as any eider-down, but for at least a while she tossed and turned, unable to grasp sleep for reasons that slowly became clear.

In the back of her mind, the Death Curse pulsed, drawing her attention, tugging at her will. When her eyes finally closed, light was touching the corners of her narrow window.

* * *

Aelis woke much later than she had hoped to, hurried through a very late breakfast, then went to see Bardun Jacques. She hadn't formulated much of a plan based on the events of the previous night, but she knew she needed to inform him immediately, and cursed her waste of the morning yet again.

Once again the censors took her sword and wand, and performed a cursory search of her medical kit and other possessions. She found the Archmagister eating his lunch early; cold sausage, pickles, day-old bread, some faintly musty smelling cheese.

"What have you been about this morning? I wondered if you'd already been out of the keep and . . ."

"Oh, nothing," Aelis said brightly. Even as she set her medical kit down, though, she pointed to the book he'd been filling in with his writing stick yesterday and gestured for him to hand it over. He did, eyes narrow, while chewing the end of a sausage.

Quickly, she wrote, *Amadin tried to kill me. Assassin tried to kill him. Was supposed to die on road. I've ensured his compliance. Shadow Congress?*

When she slid the book back to him, he took only a moment to read the words and began writing his response. She opened her medical kit and began to go through the motions of examining him. "Have to make it seem like a normal visit," she murmured as she placed an ear against his chest to listen to his lungs.

"Of course," he replied.

To any eavesdroppers, it was a normal visit. She checked his various systems with her dagger, compounded and dosed his medicaments for the day. But all the while they kept pausing to write in his book as fast as they could while still making a legible hand.

Shadow Congress a long rumor. Must be the smugglers. How'd assassin get in? How armed?

To which Aelis wrote, *Don't know, Cmdr furious. With a wizard-killer garrote.*

How'd you ensure compliance?

Aelis saw no way around answering that but was reluctant to put the words on paper, so grabbing his attention, she mouthed the words "Death Curse," with exaggerated movement but no sound audible from a foot away.

She wasn't sure if she feared Bardun Jacques's judgment on that point. He seemed to mull it over a moment and then shrugged and nodded his head simultaneously. She took that as assent to her plan.

Got to get close, identify one of the SC, he wrote after a moment.

Working via the smuggling side, she wrote. *Arstan Nicholaz?*

That'd be clumsy, but powerful wizards don't always operate smart. And your book?

Found it.

To that, Bardun Jacques nodded, then carefully ripped out the page they'd scrawled on, took up his crutch to make his way to the fireplace, and laid it on his small fire.

"Thank you, de Lenti," he said. "Now get out there and be a pain in someone's ass, eh?"

14

THE URDIMONTE

Aelis went out to face the day with the full intention of becoming *someone's* pain in the ass. She was mostly able to keep a lid on whatever it was she was feeling about the night before.

Assassination attempts are all a part of becoming involved in wizardly politics, I suppose, she thought. Yet she was hardly out of the gate when a messenger in a bright green jacket with silver buttons burnished to mirror perfection pulled up near her on a horse.

"Lady de Lenti?" The messenger, a woman about her own age, was an excellent rider, navigating the crowd without getting near enough to frighten anyone, and the horse responded to her subtle commands instantly. Aelis thought for a moment about ignoring her and continuing on her way, but she knew a brilliant rider when she saw one; she'd have no chance of getting away on the broad avenues around Cabal Keep.

She looked up to the rider and saw, stamped on those brilliant silver buttons, a scale weighing a fish on one plate and a pile of coins on the other.

"Have you a moment, Lady?"

"I always have a moment for the Urdimonte," Aelis responded. "Though I note that my proper term of address is *Warden* de Lenti."

"My apologies, Warden," the messenger said, bowing in the saddle *and* drawing out a beautiful scrollcase with one smooth movement. It was teak, Aelis thought, with silver caps and ivory handles. "The honor of a reply is requested."

Aelis sighed and opened the case. The quality of the paper inside it—not parchment, not vellum, paper—almost made her moan. The ink was bright green, the calligraphy impeccable, and most of the message bullshit. Wishing her well, faithful servants of her family, no irregularities, would just like a meeting, earliest convenience, today would really be best and so on. Signed Carlassa Urdimonte.

While Aelis wasn't up-to-date on the Urdimonte family tree, someone using the name of the banking family itself as their surname was *probably* too high in their hierarchy to be ignored.

"What time would Lady Urdimonte prefer to meet?"

"Soonest is best, Warden."

"Fine," Aelis said. "Lead on." She handed the scrollcase back; the messenger slid it back into the leather bag slung from her pommel and whistled softly.

Another horse, matched in bay coloring and height to the one the messenger rode, trotted out from an alley and pulled docilely up next to them.

"I hate being a foregone conclusion," Aelis muttered as she climbed into the green tooled saddle and rode behind the messenger. It was an easy ride to the Ruby Quarter, and Aelis began to fume on the way.

Whatever this is about, I do not need the distraction, she thought. *Mihil might have already made the arrangements, I need to see Drewic about the jewelry, and possibly dodge assassins the entire way.*

The Urdimonte branch in Lascenise looked like a small fortress, because it was. There were no grand windows, no great gravel-strewn drive for coaches to approach the doors, only a ten-foot-high wall, with spikes, patrolling guards carrying loaded crossbows, and arrow-slits regularly spaced along it where undoubtedly more crossbow-wielding guards waited unseen. The gates were stout wood, banded on either side with steel, and not wide enough for more than two to ride abreast. Guards in similar dress to the messenger, their steel cuirasses polished till they *looked* like silver, shouldered halberds at either side.

The messenger peeled off at the gate, and a minor banker of some kind came out of the gate of the inner keep to meet Aelis. Her robe was of a more muted green, but of fine cut and immaculately clean, with one silver chain across the breast.

"Lady de Lenti," she began, and Aelis seized the mistake.

"*Warden* de Lenti," she said through gritted teeth. *Onoma's frigid tits, give me the title I earned, not the one I was born into.*

"Most sincere apologies, Warden de Lenti," the banker said, bowing deeply from the waist. "I am sorry to have given offense, I . . ."

"Don't worry about it," Aelis said, immediately regretting the harshness of her tone. "Just promise me I'm not going to be left in an anteroom to knock my boots against the marble for half an hour."

"Oh, I very much doubt it. This meeting is *very* important to the Fiduciatrix. I am to take you directly to her private meeting room."

The way the banker uttered those last three words made it sound like a holy place, forbidden to most, especially outsiders. The hair on the back of Aelis's neck pricked up. She seized the hilt of her sword and half drew on a ward, surprised at the fact that she had to push through some resistance provided by the Death Curse that lingered in her mind, oscillating strangely between her and her power.

If the Shadow Congress can buy the Urdimonte to stage an assassination, then I was dead the moment I walked in here, Aelis thought. That possibility seemed remote as she followed the banker in, her boots loud against the beautiful light green marble floor. Inside, the Urdimonte bank worked hard to hide the fact that one was in fact inside a small fortress. There were conjured lights set on the walls, alchemy lamps resting on desks, and chandeliers full of beeswax candles to be lit as whatever natural light was let in faded. Everything gleamed; Aelis was certain that even her home palace's housekeeper could find nothing wrong with the floors, the woodwork, the columns, or any surface. Guards lurked like statues in corners left intentionally dim.

Aelis was ushered past the cage, its bars running from floor to ceiling, where tellers dealt with ordinary clients, past rows of desks that became larger and more privately spaced, and through a door in the back that the banker only had to press her hand against to unlock.

Even an advanced Blood Catalogue for their door locks, she thought. Past that door the security was a bit more mundane, but she still saw guards patrolling beyond it, on rich though undecorated carpets laid over hardwood floors.

Eventually, they reached a door Aelis's guide could not unlock, neither with the press of her hand nor the keys on the ring attached to her belt with a chain.

Here, she discreetly knocked, then stepped aside, bowing to Aelis and holding one hand toward the door.

Aelis kept the ward at the ready and tugged on the front of her jacket, following the instinct to appear presentable before a powerful person.

The door opened. Another woman, taller, a few years Aelis's senior, with ash-blond hair cut short and a robe similar to what the minor functionary who'd just disappeared down the corridor wore, only *obviously* finer, with silk embroidery on the cuffs and collar, and four chains—copper, silver, gold, and platinum—dangling over the front.

"Warden Lady de Lenti," the woman said. "So glad you could come."

"Always time for the Urdimonte," Aelis said. "Fiduciatrix Carlassa, I take it?" She extended a hand, and the woman nodded, accepted her grip, and led her into the room. A long table, a sideboard, several wooden chairs with the Urdimonte arms, silver coffee service, water pitcher, glasses, bowls of dainties on the table. Aelis saw someone was sitting at the far end but assumed that the woman openly wearing so very much money was the important one in the room. And besides, the other presence had their attention buried in a folder. "To what do I owe the pleasure? I hope I have not caused you any trouble."

"Oh, of course not," Carlassa said. "I'm afraid this meeting is at the request of our other guest."

Aelis turned toward the far end of the table, seizing her sword and half drawing it, every instinct telling her this was a setup. *Seize control of the banker and . . .*

This line of thinking broke off as the figure at the far end of the long table cleared his throat and stood. He was a few inches taller than her, but had similar features and the same dark hair, only slightly shot with gray. Aelis took it in quickly: the blue coat, generously cut to hide a slight paunch, the heavy silver chain of office draped over his shoulders, the simple cap set beside the papers, the heavy ring on the middle finger of his right hand, dark blue gem sparkling with whatever light it caught.

A count's signet ring.

Her *father's* signet ring.

Aelis slid her sword back home and caught her breath. Before she could get any words out, he spoke.

"I know it must be a surprise to see me, daughter." Count Guillame's voice was rich, but reserved, like fine dessert wine poured into a plain glass. "But I would not expect a drawn sword."

Abashed and *completely* thrown off, Aelis walked quickly to the far end of the table and bent low over his outstretched hand to press her lips to the signet ring he offered. She did it mechanically, the result of long training in protocol.

In his turn, her father took her hands between his and pressed them to his chest, then released them. "Please, Aelis. Sit."

She did, but only after he had taken his seat.

Carlassa, meanwhile, had stealthily advanced up the side of the table. "Will you be needing anything else, my lord?"

"Perhaps a fresh pot of coffee," he said, with a sidelong glance at Aelis, who nodded gratefully.

"I will have it sent. You have the room for as long as you need it, my lord." Carlassa bowed—shallow, but enough for the form of the thing—and disappeared through a side door.

"Why are you in Lascenise, my lord?" Aelis had to focus to get the words out carefully; her heart thrummed in her chest.

"Pursuant to some family business. I was given to understand that you were in the city."

"My lord, I must ask . . ."

"No need to be so formal, Aelis," the Count said.

"Father," Aelis said, "it may be important to my work to know *how* you learned I was in Lascenise."

"Oh, it's nothing sinister," the Count said. "I came to the Urdimonte yesterday to review some accounts. Those accounts showed a recent note of hand for Manxam's Outfitters here in town, with local delivery rather than post. By simple logic, either you were in Lascenise, or someone was trading on your name. I asked the bank to find you."

Aelis let out a breath she'd been holding, one that she hoped was small enough for her father not to notice. Before she could reply, he went on.

"Now I must confess to questions about that note, as well as the one drawn in your name by some . . . freight concern in Lascenise a few months ago." He quickly sorted through papers, the subdued but immaculate cabochon sapphire on his signet ring flashing. "Ahh, here it is. Dobrusz and Dash; a considerable sum." He slid the paper toward Aelis. "And the outfitters, barely a year since your outfitting for the warden service?"

"The first was connected to warden business. While I do have some discretionary funds associated with my post, it was nowhere near enough to compensate the—" She almost said "adventurers" but stopped herself cold. "The tradespeople in question. It forestalled the possibility of violence, and it gained me valuable allies in my work. Friends, even."

"Hrm." Her father could imbue that tiny sound with so very many meanings, Aelis despaired of untangling them all. Disappointment? Perhaps. Disbelief? Certainly. Questioning her competence? That she didn't find very likely; her family *expected* competence of their blood. It was just that her particular abilities were quite a bit outside the de Lenti traditions of horsemanship, moneymaking, administration, and battlefield command.

"As for the outfitters," she went on, seeing that he expected more, "on the road to Lascenise, we were ambushed, and had to leave the coach behind. I had to choose between clothes and equipment, so I chose the latter. Landed in the city with two nearly ruined outfits, one of them completely unsuited to difficult work."

"Ambushed? By common brigands?"

She weighed how much to say, and settled on, "Not exactly. I should not say more."

"You certainly should. Assault upon a daughter of an Estates House family . . ."

"Father," Aelis said, ignoring the way his face darkened at being interrupted, "while I am in warden service, I am *not* a Count's daughter in any legal sense." *There have been two attempts on my life, by assassins specially equipped for the purpose. If I told you that, your response would ensure that everything would get worse.*

"Well, legal fictions are all well and good, but . . ." Guillame was waving his hand vaguely in the air, unsure exactly how to follow that up.

"Father, my job is based on upholding those 'legal fictions.' And at the moment it is best that you do not ask me any further questions about what I'm doing in Lascenise, or how I'm doing it."

"At the very least you will surely dine in the townhouse with me tonight. It's a small dinner . . ."

"I am afraid I cannot. Work must supersede any social obligations right now."

"Before I leave next week, there will be a more formal dinner," Guillame said. "With important guests, *including* the Fiduciatrix. We always make time for the Urdimonte, Aelis. They may not sit in the Estates House but there are any number of votes within it that they control outright, much *less* the number they can influence."

"I understand, but—"

"Aelis." When her father's voice was firm, he didn't crack it like a whip the way many of her teachers would. Instead, it was like the solid outer walls of a great keep; ancient, implacable, unassailable. "You will attend this dinner. Taking on new obligations as a warden does *not* absolve you of obligations to your family, and you *will* meet them." Then, seeing the cast of her face and probably mistaking her anger for petulance, he said, "I will lay places for, let's say, two guests. They need not even be of noble family, though, of course, it may be awkward for them if they are not."

"Very well," Aelis said, through nearly clenched teeth. "But I cannot make it a very late night. Dinner and no more."

"Oh, we'll see what you say after the cellars have been thrown open."

Aelis suppressed a sigh; one didn't sigh in front of the Count unless one wanted an impromptu lecture on the necessity of appearing implacable and unbothered at all times. She hated knowing that, on the one hand, he was right; she wouldn't want to say no to the parade of decanters and the loose discussion that followed them, but she also couldn't see doing more than the bare minimum in this case, given the responsibilities and threats she was facing.

She was on the verge of asking for his leave to depart when he gathered up the papers he'd spread out and put them carefully back in the folder. "One more thing, daughter. Your mother *would* like a letter now and then. I daresay your sisters might, as well."

They could write to me too, she thought, but his words still stung because they were true. "I don't know that Mother would credit the conditions of my service," she said, "but . . . I will carve out some time to compose some notes." *In between investigating a conspiracy of some of the most powerful wizards alive, trying to keep my mentor from being swallowed up by it, and dodging professional assassins, I'll scribble some letters.*

"Very good." Her father stood, and she did as well. He gathered up the portfolio and took her hands again. "You do the family credit in the warden service, Aelis," he said, in the same indifferent voice he would've used to explain something about estates or grazing land or vineyards. "Do not think we do not recognize that."

As Aelis left the bank, she wasn't sure whether she was angry at her father's demands on her time or at her own reaction to his stilted, wooden compliment, which had been a flush of pride in her chest.

✦ ✦ ✦

With a late and now interrupted start to the day, Aelis felt, if not panic, then at least some sense of failure and waste beginning to rise within her as she departed the fortress-like bank, strong enough that she had to pause just outside the gate to lean against the wall.

These distractions will not deter me. I will go meet with Khorais and Mihil and discuss plans with both. For just a moment, the pressures of what she was tasked with and currently *not* accomplishing fell down on her shoulders like the blow of a staff. Maurenia, losing touch with herself and becoming part of a landscape she hated. Bardun Jacques, slowly dying in prison. Assassins after her. A warden on their side and only temporarily turned to hers, at best. A secret group of powerful wizards, bending and breaking the law as they schemed, with no concern for what they did to others, whether her, Bardun Jacques, or likely enough, even the thieves and assassins they were willing to work with.

The first is my fault, she told herself. *The rest is just my* responsibility. And with that thought Aelis found a surprising well of anger erupting inside her, a dull roar in her ears. *Wizards are supposed to be* better *than this*, she thought, and she felt her lip curl. Then, out loud in a murmur, as she realized she'd stalked away from the bank's outer wall, her footsteps loud and determined on the cobblestones of the street, "We are *obligated* to be better than this." She gritted her teeth in a fury that had no immediate outlet as she stalked on.

"You cannot be given this much," she hissed, "this much power, and the status it confers, and decide you'll only use that to get *more*." She didn't know to what ultimate purpose the Shadow Congress might be smuggling magical artifacts. Certainly it would keep the Crowns and the Estates House out of the whole business; technically magical artifacts were the property of the Crowns. But in most cases they were simply turned over to the Lyceum— which meant the Archmagisters—to do with as they saw fit within the law. "They must be doing something else." She filed that away and walked on in anger, finding herself halfway to Ruby Chapel. She thought of hailing a coach but decided to simply walk on. Covering that much ground on foot, by herself, she reasoned, would probably make her a tempting target.

Good, she thought. *Let someone else have a try.*

As it turned out, no one did, and she burned away some of that rage on the long walk. What was left, though not the roaring furnace it had been, was a nice even heat, a simmering calcination oven ready to turn her thoughts, her skills, her power, into whatever tool was needed at the moment. Whether that was violence, or investigation, or a bit of magical skullduggery, Aelis was ready for anything.

She arrived outside Manxam's and took a moment to compose herself; if she went into that shop angry enough and yelled at an apprentice who didn't deserve it, there was every chance Drewic would just dismiss the poor soul.

"I have no reason to be angry at anyone in this building," she murmured before she went in. She was met almost immediately by a two-pocket apprentice, a young dwarf.

"Warden Lady de Lenti," she said, bowing. "I am journeyworker Magda. Master Drewic is in a private meeting. However, the jewels he discussed with you are available for viewing and fitting, if you'd like to come with me."

What followed would've been a pleasant hour of being fitted for and choosing various jewels cut to reflect certain phases of the moon had she not been focused on her litany of worries. Ultimately she selected a black schorl for her smallest finger and various blue-and-green pieces, had them wrapped, and went on her way.

15

DIVINATION

Aelis got back to Cabal Keep just a half hour or so before the resident wizards would be gathering for dinner. She checked with the warden of the watch and got directions to Miralla's rooms. She had a good spot, with a fair view of the city from the outside of one of the south-facing towers. Aelis knocked gently on the door, then dropped her hand to her sword, remembering what had happened the last time she'd knocked on the door to a wizard's rooms.

"A moment." Miralla's voice from within, sounding normal, if distracted. She heard the door being unbarred and then Miralla's curvy, white-and-blue-robed form leaning against the doorjamb filled most of her senses.

"Aelis." A cocked eyebrow and a tilt of the head. "To what do I owe the visit?"

"A favor to ask. May I come in?"

Miralla pushed the door open and gestured past her. "Always." She didn't move as Aelis entered, though, which meant brushing past her in the crowded doorway. Miralla shut the door and leaned against it, smiling, as Aelis went to a desk at the far wall and set the jewelry case down on it.

"Brought me gifts? That's a good start."

"Not exactly," Aelis said. "I . . . am going to be handing this case off to someone. I need to know where it's going."

"This all seems very secret and dangerous."

"Well, yes. It is both of those things."

"This is related to the Jacques case, isn't it? I tried to tell you, Aelis . . . this is a loser. It's a career breaker. It . . ."

"It's *Bardun Jacques*, Mira. He's the warden of the age. He taught both of us what it means to do this work."

"So did Vosghez. So did Lavanalla. Neither of them burned a fellow wizard to death."

"Mira," Aelis said, a thought swirling in her head, "do you trust me or not?"

"Of course. Always."

"Then I need this help. Please. And I need to know that I can trust *you*."

"Same answer," Miralla replied. She straightened up, shedding most of the sultry pose she'd adopted since she'd opened the door and coming to a few paces away. "You're . . . you're scared of something, aren't you?"

"Yes," Aelis said, forcing the word out against every instinctive drive she had to *never* admit a weakness. "Some things have come to light recently. Things you *don't* want to know . . ."

"Something about that intruder killed in Amadin's rooms, then?"

Onoma's mercy, she is too clever. "Mira, will you help me track these? You're the best diviner I know."

"Am I the only diviner you know?"

"Of course not," Aelis said, which was half a lie, since the other diviners she knew were teachers or Archmagisters. "But you are maybe the only person in this keep right now besides Bardun Jacques that I want to trust. With my life, if I have to. Can I do that or not? If it's a choice between me, and something career making . . . between me and powerful, influential wizards . . . will you stay on my side? If you say you can't be sure, I'll understand . . ."

"Aelis," Miralla said. "Your friendship may not be the *only* thing I'd like to have from you, but if you think I'd cast it aside for *politics* . . ."

"Then you'll do it?"

Miralla smiled again. "Not until you tell me that *something* is in it for me."

"At the end of the week, my father is giving a grand dinner at our townhouse. He told me I can bring two guests. You're the first person on my list."

"The Count is in town? How'd you . . ." Miralla must've read the exhaustion on Aelis's face because she immediately dropped that line of questioning. "Do you really have the time to be attending dinners?"

"He didn't leave any room to argue," Aelis said.

"He's not Cabal Command or the Lyceum, Aelis . . ."

"As he pointed out, choosing new obligations does not absolve me from the older kind."

"Fine. Dinner. And at Count un Tirraval's townhouse? My mother will have the letter I write about it cast in bronze." She looked at the case for a moment. "How formal will it be?"

"I imagine the invitation will say." Then, after just a bit of revenge on her father, she added, "If it turns out you need something new to wear for it, I'll pay."

"This deal gets better," Miralla muttered. "You think you know roughly where this case is going? That'll make my job easier."

"I do."

"Well, then I'll need a map. And," she added, "we should eat. I don't intend to cast Lewyd's Distance Beacon *and* tie it to a map *and* lay Murkhaz's Countersign into the bargain on an empty stomach."

"That seems like . . . a lot."

"Do you want the theoretical explanation you won't understand, or will you just assume I know what I'm doing?"

"The latter," Aelis said. "You know I always found it boring."

"Yes," Miralla said as they headed for the door, "why waste your theurgic energy on seeing the warp and weft of the future, on unraveling the very fabric of the world and the seven energies in order to see straight to what you want or need, when instead you could be rooting around inside a dead or dying body?"

"Exactly," Aelis said, and the two of them went off to dinner, laughing.

◆   ◆   ◆

A bit over an hour later they returned to Miralla's rooms, with a map they'd picked up from Cabal Keep's quartermaster, a surly dwarf in a soiled diviner's robe who had not been happy at having his nap disturbed.

"Get some light in this room while I fetch my tools," Miralla said. Dutifully Aelis lit a taper from the fireplace and began lighting candles, of which there were a great number, many of which had trails of hardened wax dripping over their holders.

"I can go to my room and get my alchemy lamp," she offered.

"We don't need that much light. But you *do* owe me a decent bottle of wine," Miralla said as she removed various oddments from her desk—a dry ink bottle, a book that was open with its pages facing down, a mug—so she could set the map down. She immediately hunted those objects out again to hold the corners of her map flat. "Can't have more than a glass if I'm to be doing complex divination, and if a dinner *anywhere* needed more than one glass it was that overdone pork."

"The mustard sauce made it tolerable," Aelis said as she watched Miralla's haphazard preparations. "And for this favor I owe you at least two bottles of wine. Better than decent." Aelis was not a perfect model of neatness, as Maurenia often reminded her. Compared to Miralla, though, she lived a life of precision and simplicity that a monk of Peyron would find hard. Clothes, books, bottles, and detritus were scattered everywhere. The moment Miralla walked back into her room she set her sword-belt aside, next to the door; Aelis picked up the belt and hung it on a peg where it faced less danger of falling over or being lost in a rush.

"Now where did I put that diadem?" Aelis suspected she wasn't meant to hear that, as Miralla had muttered it to herself as she went rummaging near her bed, one hand quickly emerging from under a silk pillow and holding the needed implement triumphantly aloft, the simple silver band with an inset white crystal catching the light. Miralla absently put it on her forehead, pushing back her cloud of dark curls in a maddeningly fetching way.

Aelis bit the inside of her cheek and thought of Maurenia, alone and isolated.

Miralla got the map smoothed out and held down to her satisfaction and took a box from a drawer. She opened it to reveal a jumble of pins and tacks, all of them gleaming silver.

"Bring me the box," she said. Aelis had left it on a side table and now dutifully brought it to her, setting it down.

Miralla opened it and carefully pulled out one of the rings within, holding it up to what light Aelis had kindled.

"Ah, the new young wizard style, eh? Would think you above trends."

"I needed something of high value for the smugglers to move."

"And I'm sure you never plan to wear anything like this."

"I . . . might've ordered a fourth one. In black. For my smallest finger."

Miralla smiled. "Understated and appropriate. Now." She selected the smallest size of silver tack she had and set it on her desk, then a twin to it. "One of these inside the box and the other twinned to it . . ."

She picked up the tacks and settled them in the palm of one hand. She began to mutter words Aelis opted not to focus on, just as she'd decided not to focus on them in dry, boring divination lectures her second year at the Lyceum. Miralla's eyes took on a solid off-white color, not as if they'd rolled back in her head but as they simply *changed* and began to drink in some of the candlelight around her. There was an answering flicker in the diadem she wore crookedly against her hair.

As soon as she began, she stopped, then slipped one of the tacks inside the box, hiding it beneath the velvet that held the rings in place.

The second one, she stuck into her map, roughly in the center of Las-cenise. Her eyes went pale again; this time the crystal in the center of the diadem flared brightly.

"What if the smugglers ditch the case?" Aelis said, as soon as Miralla looked up at her.

"What did we say about just *assuming* I know more about divination and how we'd save time? Do you think that if I were going to do this on behalf of my dear friend, I would not do it *right*?"

"I apologize most profusely," Aelis said, bowing slightly.

"Good. Lewyd's Distance Beacon is certainly the easiest and most all-purpose long-distance, object-based divination. But it's hardly the *only* one. Now, of these three rings, which do you think is the most valuable?"

"Probably the black one, the schorl . . . I'm told that while the stone is not rare, the quality is."

"Will common smugglers know that? Will they have a jeweler on staff?"

"In that case, the sapphire."

"Good," Miralla said. "I really can't afford to do this three times in one go, as it's a Fourth Order. So let's bet on the highest apparent worth."

"Three bottles of wine, then," Aelis said.

"Right." Miralla wet her lips. "I may have to do something I hate to do." To Aelis's raised eyebrow, she lifted a longer silver needle and placed it against the inside of the ring's band, gouging a small line into the metal. Aelis winced, and Miralla shrugged apologetically. Then she held the needle she'd used up to her eyes. "A few grains of the silver itself will suffice for Dahja's Hound." She took a small pouch out of the box of pins and tacks and squeezed it to be sure that it was empty, then stuck the needle with the curl of metal on it inside. "Now for the Countersign."

She set the marked ring back inside the case and lifted it off the desk.

She went to one of her windows, genuine glass, unlike Aelis's arrow-slits, and opened it wide. "Lucky for us Peyron's Eye is open."

Aelis took a few steps closer to the window, enough to see the faint crescent of the white moon hanging over the night sky, looking indeed like an opening eye.

Holding the case up, Miralla took a deep breath and spoke again, long, low, fast syllables that poured out of her quickly until her arms shook and her knees trembled. Aelis was halfway to her side when she whirled around, the faint white glow of power on her fingertips, her eyes, and crowning her diadem like fire on a horizon as she held the box out.

"There," she said, her voice distant and weak. "There are diviners who *will* beat this sign; tracking is not my particular skill. But it should hold for common smugglers."

Good thing I'm not sending this to a secretive group of wizards, then, Aelis thought.

"Thank you, Mira," she said as she took it. "I cannot tell you what it is to have at least one warden I know I can trust."

"Always, Aelis," Miralla said.

Aelis nodded and tucked the box under her arm, turned awkwardly for the door.

"Three bottles," Miralla called after her, a chuckle in her voice. "Tirravalan!"

"Of course," Aelis called back as she left, carrying the box gingerly under her arm like a favored small pet.

16

A GOOD BREAKFAST FOR A GOOD DAY'S WORK

Aelis's dreams that night were troubled. She and Maurenia were on ships sailing in opposite directions; sometimes Miralla was on one or the other ship.

She dreamed of Lone Pine; of Tun; of Rus and Martin; of Elmo, Otto, and Pips; of the other people of the village; of goats and sheep. She even woke up imagining she smelled a faint whiff of sheep shit.

"Stregon's balls," Aelis swore as she sat up in the bed, rubbing her nose. "I do not miss that. Why would my mind decide I did?"

At least it was helpful in waking up. Unlike the prior day she hadn't slept in late, and her room was not suffused with daylight. She dressed in her newest set of working clothes from Manxam's, an arming jacket and divided riding skirts, all in the colors of her schools, though more subtly than the usual arm or chest slashes; piping on the collar and the vents showed green and blue against the black.

The jacket had pockets and tabs where armor plates could be inserted, or mail attached if she chose to seek it out; Manxam's would've provided it, if she'd wanted it. Generally she didn't, though it had been common to abjurers just a generation or two older than her. Lavanalla in particular would sometimes go on training runs in a chain hauberk that rippled in patterns of bronze and silver links that looked like light filtering through autumn leaves.

"All Archmagisters are show-offs, one way or another," Aelis muttered. She decided to steal down to the refectory and have an early solitary breakfast. She was not quite the first to arrive, though, as she saw Amadin sitting in a distant corner, hunched over toast and tea. His head whipped up as she walked in, and he waved her over.

A kitchen servant beat her to the table with a cup, saucer, and coffeepot, poured for her while Aelis sat down.

"What will you take, Warden? We have lovely mushrooms this morning."

"Four eggs, fried very hard, over those mushrooms on toast, then," she said. "And thank you."

Amadin watched the servant disappear and set down the piece of buttered toast he'd been nibbling on.

"You're in danger," he said, in a quiet but casual voice.

"I know," Aelis replied in the same tone, taking his hint; whispering was more likely to draw attention than two colleagues simply talking. She smiled as brightly as she could manage so early in the morning.

"I mean that further attempts are going to be made on your life," he said, picking up a knife and aimlessly spreading the soft yellow smear of butter to the corners of his bread. "And possibly on your father's."

"I'm just a warden, but assassinating the Count un Tirraval would, I imagine, bring the kind of political consequences that competent assassins, and even their wizard paymasters, would like to avoid." Aelis felt a flare of fury but she swallowed it with her coffee.

"Unless," he said, "it is made to look like some idiotic robbery attempt, at a gathering of the rich and foolish . . ."

"Ah," Aelis said, "you mean they're going to try something at my father's dinner next week. How do you know this?"

"If I suddenly break off all contact with no explanation, they'll kill me," Amadin said. "They use a dread drop, illusion on the paper, keyed to my touch. No one else can read it, and it melts away after I do."

"They have you in a blood catalogue?" Aelis had difficulty swallowing her surprise at that. "Foolish of you."

"De Lenti, do you think there is any wizard they do *not* have in a blood catalogue?"

Their talk paused and they both offered smiles as the servant appeared and set Aelis's plate down. "Anything else, Warden?"

"Nothing at all," Aelis said, and once again they both watched the servant depart.

Amadin read the question in her face and answered before she could ask it. "They put drops of blood in your sword and your dagger, didn't they?"

"*And* my wand," Aelis said. Amadin grimaced at the reminder that she commanded three magics to his two, then pressed on.

"And do you think each implement needs as much as they take? Or do you think a few of those drops find their way into one of the Lyceum's storied vaults? Hrm? Filed away should the need arise. Oh, not many have access, and they don't use them rashly. But once they decide to make you a tool, they'll find it."

Aelis felt the bite of fried egg, mushroom, and toast she'd just put in her mouth suddenly drain of their savor. She chewed, swallowed, then set her fork down.

"All of us?"

"Every one," Amadin said. "But as I told you . . . they'll do nothing with it unless it becomes the *only* way. Dip into that well too often, and too many wizards might realize they exist."

Aelis looked down at her plate. The threat posed by her blood being in the hands of the skilled and powerful wizards who must've made up this Shadow Congress was not a small one, and it set a cold fear against that furnace of anger in her stomach.

But, on the other hand, the eggs in front of her were fried exactly as she'd asked, barely a hint of yolk leaking into the finely chopped mushrooms with their nutty, woodsy scent, and the bread was crisp and tasted faintly of the good oil it had been fried in.

No distant threat, however powerful, could stand up against a good breakfast. She dug back in.

"So," she said, only just mindful of her manners as she swallowed, "this threat against my father's dinner. Hired blades in force, I take it."

"That would seem likely," Amadin said. "And many to die in the attempt. Maybe they'll play a political angle; the nobles of southern Imraval do have their detractors."

"Nobles everywhere have their detractors. It's a good thing, then, that my father told me I can bring two guests." She cut another bite, carefully pushing mushrooms onto her fork with the edge of her knife, smiling at Amadin, whose face slowly creased and eyes widened as he took her meaning.

"Oh no, no, I . . ."

"Oh yes," she said. "After all, you have a vested interest in seeing to my continued life." In her head, a tiny prick of pain, the throb of the curse lingering, waiting to be dispelled or unleashed.

"Anaerion help me, I might just throw myself on some gutter rat's knife," he said, "if I have to sit through a dinner party."

"There'll be three abjurers there, Amadin; you, me, and Warden Miralla Despatia."

"Isn't she more diviner than abjurer?"

"Have you ever sparred against someone who specializes in combat divination?"

Amadin snorted. "Those are rarer than all-around conjurers."

"She is one."

"I don't trust her, or you," Amadin said. "But I have no choice but to keep you alive. To that end, tell me where you're going today, so I don't have to try to follow you."

"You couldn't . . ."

"Yesterday you slept in, spent a considerable amount of time at the Urdimonte, went back to your overpriced tailor's . . . need I go on?"

Aelis felt immense embarrassment flood her cheeks and shook her head.

"Good," Amadin said. "As long as I have a general idea, it's easier to shadow you. *And* if anyone is shadowing me, it looks as though I'm just waiting for the opportune moment or working on your habits and routines."

Aelis set her fork and knife down on her clean plate. A cold, angry question cut through her embarrassment.

"Amadin," she said, working very hard to keep her tone conversational, "this makes it sound very much as though you've killed on behalf of the . . . of them before. Have you?"

In response, the elf took a last sip of his tea and stood, adjusting the fall of his swordbelt as he left.

•   •   •

Checking in on Bardun Jacques had taken a while, as the censors seemed determined to slow her down and bar her way as much as they could, searching everything, taking their time. It was largely a medical trip, as she wrested with whether to tell him about the upcoming attack. She opted not to until she sorted out exactly how she felt about it, and tried to make out the features of the censor who, on her way back out, dithered over returning her sword and wand. By the time that was all dealt with, she had a message brought by a courier from Khorais, telling her that Mihil wanted a meeting. It didn't say *where*, but Aelis had a solid guess. She only had time to return to her rooms and grab the jewelry case, tucking it awkwardly into a belt pouch before she left.

Dwelling on these problems is not going to solve them, Aelis mused as she rode a coach as near to Slop's End as its driver would go. She had thought through and discarded several scenarios regarding the apparent threat to her father's dinner. It would be difficult to convince him to cancel it, but not impossible. However, doing so would immediately alert these enemies she knew almost nothing about that she was, in fact, on to them, losing her only possible advantage. It would also likely cause them to abandon the relatively subtle option of a robbery or political assassination gone wrong and move to simple main force.

When an abjurer knew *main force* was coming, there were seven hells worth of things she could do about it. *But,* Aelis told herself, *that depends a great deal on how much, where it's coming from, and in what form. Right now I have a better idea of those things for this end of week dinner than I do if I throw that over.*

She was confident in her first impulse; meet it head on with Amadin and Miralla by her side.

"Will three wardens be enough, though?" she muttered as the coach slowly rocked over uneven streets, a sure sign that they were approaching worse parts of town. "Well," she decided, "I can always hire the Dobrusz brothers as coachmen; putting them in the back of the house while expecting an attack couldn't hurt."

She took out her pocket sheaf to make a note of it when the coach pulled to a stop and the driver rapped on the box. She hopped out, tossed some vines to the driver, and stepped into the street, settling her hands on her belt and hunching her shoulders, walking with purpose.

This time, no one accosted her. Frankly, no one should've the first time; Slop's End may have been the tougher quarter of the city, but an abjurer's sword was usually enough to keep street operators away.

She remembered the way to the Fallow Sow easily enough; she'd never been the sort to forget her way to a tavern. There was a small crowd at the bar this time; shabbily dressed, most leaning on the short length of coat-polished wood like they'd fall over if they didn't, and Arris presiding over it all with a half sneer and a deliberately languid response time. When she walked in, though, the bartender straightened up a bit. The half-dozen denizens holding up or being held up by the bar turned to look at the intrusion of light from the street, or perhaps at Arris's reaction.

Talk quieted. She felt all the eyes on her and decided to ignore them.

"Mihil?" She looked at Arris, and he jerked his chin toward the back corner. She nodded her thanks and threaded the narrow passage between the wall and the bar. No one said a word, but she could feel their eyes boring into her. There wasn't a threat in it, she didn't think. She certainly didn't feel one. It was more curiosity, perhaps a disbelief that a warden existed, much less moved among them.

By the time she got to Mihil's booth, where he was snoozing lightly on a pool of drool, she realized something all the crowd had in common; they were wearing old military jackets.

And more than one of them had a pinned-up, empty sleeve. Several lacked the full complement of fingers.

She pushed those thoughts away and shook Mihil's shoulder. He started awake, lifting his head from the table, a long string of drool trailing from the corner of his mouth to the wet wood.

"Wha? Boarders away! To the tops!" She could barely understand the words as his slack jaw made them sound more like "borshers ava, tozheto." In response she shook him until his eyes opened all the way and focused on her. Mihil wrenched himself free of her grasp and sat straight up in his booth.

"Warden," he said, summoning as much dignity as he could, which wasn't much. He slipped a handkerchief that had once been white from a pocket and wiped at his mouth. "Got my note?"

"I got a note saying to meet you," Aelis said as she slid into the booth, trying not to think of what the contact with the furniture might be doing to her new clothes. "I took *at this shithole tavern* as read."

"Fair enough." The same mug Aelis had seen him drink from before sat at his elbow. He lifted it, and gave it a shake; it sloshed, but mournfully. He looked up at her, hopefully. She shook her head.

Mihil's grin dissolved into a sigh.

"I've listened at enough doors and bought enough drinks in enough places to learn that they've got a wagon leaving *tonight*, and I know where from. So if you can skulk a bit, we slip your piece on said wagon, you can still track it where you want it to go . . . I assume . . . and all is still well."

"When do we go? Tonight, I presume?"

"Oh no," Mihil said. "Soonest is best. Wagon probably rolls well before moonrise. A smart smuggler doesn't try to move anything at *night*. That's when everyone suspects. We ought to go now."

"Fine," Aelis said. *I'm not sure I trust you to stand, much less to lead me anywhere useful or, Stregon help us, fight anything more dangerous than a bottle of corked wine.*

She stood and gestured for him to follow.

With a shaking hand, Mihil took up his tankard and finished whatever was in it, then slid out of the booth, pulled his jacket up around his neck, and headed for the nearest door. Aelis followed him out into the alley, looking at him askance and staying a few steps back.

He turned, caught her glance, and shrugged, though he had the decency to look at least a bit embarrassed.

"Look. The eye-opener has that effect. I haven't had one of those this morning. You can stay close without fearing for your boots."

"If you say so," Aelis muttered.

"Word down here is you're trying to help Bardun Jacques beat a case," Mihil said as they passed the mouth of the alley, walked just a few paces on the main thoroughfare, and then veered off to a side street.

"Is it? Where would that word come from?"

"People down here do hear things, you know. We pay attention. We have to," Mihil said. "Because if we don't see the boulder rolling down the hill, *we're* the ones who'll get crushed." They were silent a moment, boots tapping the pavement in a counterbeat. "So, is it true?"

"How do you know the name Bardun Jacques?"

"Plenty of us served in that last war know that name," Mihil said. "Some saw him in action. I didn't, mind, but the tales ran through the Tyridician Fleet. Sailed as the battle-witch on the *Wyvern's Sting*, the flagship, didn't he? Well, I was never near any flagships, but I had shipmates who were, or who said they were. Some of 'em wouldn't be up and about today without he was at their engagements and actions. Some of 'em aren't regardless."

"Mihil," Aelis said, "while I would, under other circumstances, love to swap stories about the Archmagister, Aldayim Endowed Chair in Magical Practice, and Warden Emeritus Bardun Jacques, let me make certain you understand something. There is nothing you or anyone else can say that will make me any *more* determined to clear his name than I already am. He is—" she paused here—"my mentor." She cut herself off before she might say anything that might be embarrassing or shameful. "Just . . . understand that."

"Very well, Warden."

They walked to the very edge of the city, the walls growing in their vision. The scent of the tanners' fields grew ever more powerful, with an undercurrent of sewage meeting freshwater in a war the sewage was winning.

Buildings grew less stable and more haphazard, the leaning tenements giving way to shacks, lean-tos, and even tents. Laws dictated that the city walls needed a hundred yards' clearance before permanent structures could be built, though in Aelis's experience that hundred yards could be interpreted as something closer to fifty feet, and nowhere was that more true than in Slop's End, with buildings creeping to the walls' very edges. The city's southernmost entry and exit point, one of the River Gate, was wide open, with a team of guards offering the most cursory checks of wagons leaving and folk entering. The streets beneath their feet grew softer, wetter, as if the old buried rivers were trying to rise up and claim what had once been theirs. Nearby, they emerged as canals, disgorging the city's filth through the walls into the surrounding rivers and marshy forests. It was to one of these canals that Mihil led Aelis, pointing toward a rusted ladder leaning treacherously against the slick stones of the retaining wall.

"I am not swimming in that," Aelis said.

"If we do this right you won't have to," Mihil said. "And, for what it's worth, I *can't* swim, so I'm not like to lead you somewhere you'd have to, am I?"

"You were Naval Infantry, but you can't swim?"

"Be surprised how common that is in a navy," Mihil said, then hoisted himself over the ladder and slid down it, his feet braced against either side, never touching the steps. Aelis looked down and saw a walkway, just a foot or two above the fetid water. She did not attempt to emulate Mihil's casual slide; the slick steps and shaking ladder were challenging enough.

There was just a narrow walkway along the side of the canal, intended, Aelis supposed, for maintenance or sewage workers to make their way into the canal tunnels. The rushing water stunk, and was the color of rusting iron.

They followed along the walkway, Mihil walking casually, Aelis pressed up against the slick stonework as the boards creaked menacingly under her boots.

"Not far now," Mihil said, pointing ahead of them, where the canal disappeared into a narrow slit in the stone. Inset in the wall was a wooden door, with a heavy lock hanging through the latch. Before Aelis had even reached the door, Mihil had slipped a wire and an iron rod from a pocket and went to work. By the time Aelis was close behind him, the lock had clicked open. He slipped it off the door and tossed it casually over one shoulder into the rushing canal. It sank with a tiny splash.

Aelis gave him a questioning look as he held the door open for her.

"Don't want some too-efficient worker to walk by, see it unlocked, and lock us in now, do we?"

"If the same worker sees the lock is gone, isn't he likely to come investigate?"

"Or just put it in a report, send it to his inspector or corporal or bosun or . . . whatever it is public works laborers have," Mihil said, "and they'll spend at least three days finding funds to buy a new lock, then someone will steal the funds, then . . ."

Aelis cut him off by brushing past him into the tunnel.

Mihil pulled the door closed behind them; or as closed as it could, at any rate, as the wood had swollen and wouldn't sit flush against the stone.

"Now, I can see well in the dark," Mihil began. "Perhaps you can do something magical about . . ."

Aelis was already bringing her alchemy lamp to life, adjusting the dials so that it cast a wide-angle white light. She clipped it to her swordbelt and gestured into the light it cast. "After you."

"Is that magical?" Mihil asked, with a certain hesitancy.

"Alchemical, which is close enough."

"Because open flames have been known to set people alight down here, all of a sudden like, or so they say."

"This will not explode unless I specifically make it do so," Aelis said. "And open flames will do that because at times the miasma coming off the water is likely flammable."

"Miasma," Mihil muttered. "Thought those were only in graveyards. Well, look . . . just follow me. There are spots where the tunnels lead up to street level, or even outside the walls. Meant for midden-wagons and such, and the Saltmen use them the same way. If you hear anyone coming, or I say to douse that light, you do it, aye?"

"I won't be effective in any kind of fight if I have to do that," Aelis said.

"Won't come to that. We sneak in, we sneak out, they never know your thing is on their wagon. Then you find it at the other end. Piece of piss. Give me whatever's going on the wagon, while we're at it."

Aelis had put enough trust in Mihil to this point that backing out would be pointless. If he was lying or had sold her out the plan would be blown and the smuggled jewels wouldn't matter anyway, so she handed him the case. He opened the hinged lid for a peek and in the light of her alchemy lamp she saw his eyes widen.

"Not messing about, are you, Warden?"

"I usually don't."

He slipped the case into one of the capacious pockets on the side of his long, dingy blue coat, and walked on. She could only just make him out as an outline at the edge of her light, but she could not *hear* him at all. No footfalls, no bootheels on stone, no coughing, not even his breathing, not even if she concentrated.

I can understand a gnome who can do that, she said to herself, conscious of how loud her own footsteps sounded to her, echoing over the noisome water that gurgled and oozed its way through the middle of the tunnel. *But how does Tun do it?* She did find herself, at that moment, wishing that her friend were there, undertaking these dangers with her. *Always handy to have a wer-ebear on your side*, she thought. It was more than that, of course. There was the absolute solidity of his presence, the sharpness of his mind, the *certainty* she had that if there were anything Tun could do for her in a tight spot, it would be done. All she had in Lascenise were alliances she felt uneasy about. Mihil, she was paying. She feared that Miralla was being led on by promises Aelis wasn't going to make good on, and Amadin she'd simply threatened into something like compliance. There were the Dobruszes, too, and she couldn't count them out. Against thieves and assassins she had no doubt of their prowess. But against a secret group of wizards like the Shadow Congress appeared to be, she just wasn't sure.

She shook herself out of this reverie and focused on the here and now.

The awful stench in her nostrils, the stone under her feet, the shadow of the gnome bobbing before her. They'd been walking for some time, Mihil making sharp turns and choosing between various sections of tunnel with unerring certainty, never a pause or hesitation.

"Are you certain you know where . . ."

"Yes," Mihil hissed. "But we're getting close to their territory now, so quiet down a bit and keep eyes and ears sharp."

With that, he began walking a little more slowly, closer to her, keeping near the slime-encrusted stone wall.

Aelis had to slow herself to keep from stumbling into him. She reached to the back of her belt and loosened her dagger, did the same with the sword at her side.

She turned all her senses outward. She considered using her dagger to send a small pulse to detect life, but she wasn't sure that it wouldn't also detect anyone walking just a few feet above them along the streets of Slop's End or Delmaigne or the Foundries; she hadn't kept her bearings as to where they were under the city.

Aelis didn't need magical senses, though, to hear a voice echoing down the tunnel. She did not know what direction it came from, so she grabbed Mihil by the back of his collar with one hand and killed the light of her lamp with the other.

The gnome didn't struggle; he seemed to understand exactly what she'd done and why. He did gently disentangle his collar from her grasp and crouch low beside her. She weighed drawing her sword, thought the sound of the blade scraping against the scabbard might be too great a risk. She did drop her wand into her left hand; the smooth length of wood reassured her, gave her something with which to shape what might come next.

In truth, what came next was a small band of shabbily dressed men and women who wouldn't have been out of place in any of the city's laboring districts. They wore the clothes of foundry workers or canal-boaters, and cheap wooden-soled shoes that smacked against the stones. One had a lantern that creaked as she walked, three guttering candles shedding dim light behind thick, poorly made glass.

The group walked straight past them, on the other side of the burbling mess that Aelis hesitated to call water, the light of their lantern and the sounds of their discussion steadily diminishing. She hadn't been able to get an accurate count, too many shadows, their voices blending together as they discussed that night's run or this morning's work. The echoes made it mostly unintelligible as the shadows obscured their number, but she made it at least eight of them.

Once she could no longer hear or see them, she began to count to fifty. She got to thirty when Mihil touched her hand. "Safe to risk the light again. We're close," he whispered.

She did dial the lantern back to life then, on its dimmest and tightest setting, just enough to make out Mihil lifting a leather flask, which he wore around his neck on a bit of cordage, to his lips.

Aelis lifted her lantern so that he would see her glare. It was a fine glare, even in the dark. She'd worked on it in the long winter stuck in her tower in Lone Pine.

Mihil saw it but shrugged it away. "Just got to steady the hand, Warden," he said, though it took him two tries to slip the flask back under his dingy shirt. "That's probably the crew who're taking the wagon tonight, and a few extra about other errands. Let's see if we can't follow them. Probably some tracks in the mud on the other side."

"How do we get across the . . ." Aelis swallowed hard. "Water."

"I'm afraid it involves getting dirty, 'less we find a crossing . . . there was one about eighty yards back."

"No," Aelis said. "I've walked on water once; I can do it again. This may be undignified." She slid her wand back into its pocket, drew her sword, and grabbed Mihil by the collar again before he could object. She took two steps and leaped over the wide, foul runoff, and used her sword to plant wards beneath her feet, wards that needed to exist for just long enough for her to push off them, which she did, jumping from one to the other like a child finding stones to take them across a brook. Once on the other side, she set Mihil down.

"I thought wizards could just fly."

"A really excellent conjurer of air could probably make it look like they were," Aelis admitted. "I'm not any kind of conjurer. That's just a little trick; not really what wards were meant for, but if they can deflect the hardest blow a weapon can deliver, they can serve as a stepping stone for a moment."

"Great. Now, for'ard at best speed, and lower that lantern when I ask," Mihil said. They forged ahead, not too fast, but picking up some of their previous speed. Every so often the gnome would gesture as he knelt low over the ground and Aelis would hold the lantern low. Even she could discern the bootprints, wooden slatted and hobnailed, that were made in the mud and filth. They pressed on; Aelis thought she caught distant snatches of conversation. They came to a great intersection, where six wide tunnels converged, the one they exited being on the far left; small footbridges led across each one.

Mihil pointed to the one exactly opposite them.

"I think it's that one," he said. "But it could be that," he added, pointing to the one headed straight on. "Come." He hurried across the footbridges and began looking for something on the stonework of the two tunnels he'd pointed out. "Here it is," he said, beckoning the lantern over. Symbols were carved into the stone at eye-height for Aelis; a waving line, a straight line, and a pair of four-legged creatures she thought were meant to be horses.

"This tunnel leads out under the walls, to a wagon loading spot," he said. "See? The river, the walls, horses . . ."

"Clever," Aelis admitted, and they hurried along it.

"Douse the light," Mihil suddenly hissed, throwing himself against the wall.

Aelis did as he asked and saw why; a sentry, carrying a small, shuttered lantern in one hand and, from the hasty impression she had, a weapon in the other, making his way down the tunnel, directly toward them.

"Can kill 'im easy," Mihil murmured.

"No," Aelis replied. "Best we don't."

They waited, motionless, watching his swinging point of light come closer and closer. The weapon in his hand was some kind of cudgel, she guessed, given the way it swung heavily in his hand and its general shape. He got closer, closer, till she could hear his breathing and the creaking sound of the lantern's handle as he walked.

She flexed her wrist, raising her hand even as her grip settled around her wand. The tip flared green, bright and startling in the darkness, and he fell to the ground with a heavy thud. Aelis ran forward to grab his lantern and stopped his cudgel from rolling loudly along the stone with a foot. She stayed in that posture for several moments before finally, carefully straightening up. She kept her foot on the weapon and relit her alchemy lamp before dousing the lantern.

"That's handy," Mihil said, appearing out of the shadows behind her. "Don't imagine you can do that to a whole lot of 'em."

"Best I could do to a large group is make them yawn," she said. She bent to pick up his weapon and found it was not just a crude club but a heavy mace with a rounded, rust-flecked iron head. "You got any cordage on you?"

"Not enough to tie him up, if that's what you mean," Mihil said.

"Well. Then we just hope he sleeps a long while. Keep his head from hitting the stones, will you? I don't want to crack his skull." She grabbed the guard's ankles and Mihil supported his neck as she dragged him to an alcove along the wall. She set his lantern next to his hand, but the mace she gently slipped into the water, grimacing as, despite her care, some of it splashed onto her hand.

"Let's go," she muttered, wishing she'd brought rope or at least some clean rags from her medical kit to make a gag.

Mihil led her forward and before too long it became evident that light—natural light—was entering the tunnels from somewhere up ahead as the stones beneath their feet sloped upward.

Mihil held out a hand to stop her. "Count a hundred, slowly. If I'm not back by then, count another. If I'm not back by *then*, give my best to Arris back at the Sow." Then he padded off on his preternaturally silent feet. Aelis dimmed her lamp till it was the barest point of light and started to lean back against the stones till she realized just what she'd be leaning on. Mihil had disappeared so completely it astonished her, then she focused on what he'd suggested, counting slowly. Sounds came to her then, distant and echoing; voices, a general clatter, maybe a hoof stamping on stone. She couldn't make any sense of it, though her brain tried. She imagined the gnome, wily and small and slippery, darting into a makeshift smugglers' camp, hiding behind wagons, crates, or folds of earth as he stole up to reconnoiter.

Simultaneously, part of her imagined him being found, putting up a brave but futile fight, and the operation being blown.

Or immediately taking a handful of gold and telling a team of Hidden Skulls assassins, equipped with witsend poison, precisely where to find her.

She quieted herself then, centering her emotions by gripping her sword, nearly drawing it. She thought she felt someone close by in the darkness. Thought of the fights she'd been in when it mattered, against the leftover animated soldiers of Mahlgren, against Dalius twice, and prepared for something like it.

Then a soft voice came out of the darkness, just as she was starting the second hundred.

"Warden? It's done."

"That was fast," Aelis said.

"Told you, a piece of piss," Mihil said. "Now let's get the fuck out of here and wrap ourselves around some drinks before Arris realizes you're not going to pay off my notes."

"Let's do the first, anyway," Aelis said, turning up her lantern more brightly and once again falling in behind Mihil. "Once we're out I'll need to see . . ." She had been about to say *the diviner who is tracking that shipment for me* but decided there was no reason for the gnome to know that much. He'd done his part and would be paid for it, and that was enough.

They started forward, Aelis following him, when suddenly two unmistakable points of light emerged from the tunnel ahead of them. Aelis doused her lantern and they flattened themselves, but a voice came out of the darkness.

"Mihil," it called, echoing his name down the tunnels. "You little fucking meddler! We know you've been seen with a warden *and* asking around after the Saltmen. We can't have that. We know you're down here! Give us that wizard and you won't leave here through a sluice gate!"

Many thoughts intruded on Aelis in that moment; that this was what you got for trusting a sloppy drunk; that she should've found another way to do this; that Mihil was almost certainly about to sell her out; that she definitely didn't want to hurt or kill a bunch of citizens of Lascenise, thieves or otherwise, but that they weren't going to give her a choice.

She could only act on one of them immediately; she grabbed the gnome and drew her sword, holding it level with where she expected his eyes were.

"Say a word, gnome," she breathed, "and I'll make sure you die first."

"I'm a lot of things, Warden," he hissed, "most of 'em bad . . . but none of 'em are *that*. Now let me go, and let's run."

"Running's not really an option," Aelis muttered.

"MIHIL!" The drifting sound of the speaker's voice made the gnome's name into a taunt. "We're not gonna give you much more time. Don't make us come hunt you out."

"Why not?" the gnome said, smoothing his collar where Aelis had grabbed it.

"We make a getaway, they probably have time to tell the crew above we were here; as it is there's still a chance our shipment goes through and I get the information I need. We run, there's no chance of that."

"Are you . . ."

Aelis ignored him and reached for her alchemy lamp, turning it on to its highest, brightest settings and setting it on her belt.

"*Fuck*," Mihil whispered.

"I'm the warden here," Aelis called out. "I declare this an unlawful assembly and order you to disperse immediately." She drew her sword and called a ward to the very edge of her mind, the Targe, a midsized shield she could fold most of her body behind if need be. She dropped her wand into her other hand; she couldn't Catnap a large group, but she liked to have options.

"Order us to disperse?" said the spokesman, still ten yards away. "On what authority?"

"The Tri-Crowns, the Estates House, and if those are too distant for you to care, the sword in my hand." She snapped the blade up into a guard, spreading her feet, flexing her knees, the ward that would spring into being centered on her left hand, throbbing on the very edge of her mind.

There was a brief pause. A ripple of uncertainty. Then the leader, now close enough in the light of her alchemy lamp for her to make out his features, cracked a broken-toothed smile.

"Looks like your meddlin' little friend has fucked off. Needed a drink, no doubt." He pulled a long knife from his belt, the kind that could pass for a laborer's tool, if the laborer had to do a lot of cutting weeds or chopping hay.

Aelis didn't think there was much call for that kind of work here in the sewers of Lascenise.

"You don't actually think I'm about to turn around and look, do you?"

The leader laughed gutturally, and around him there was a general drawing of weapons—knives, blunt instruments, the clink of a chain.

"Doesn't matter to me if you see it comin' or not," the man said, "can't have wardens stickin' their fingers in our business." He pointed at Aelis's sword with his knife. "Bet that'll fetch a pretty pile o'silver . . ."

He didn't finish his sentence, because Aelis had been judging how many more steps he needed to take to get within springing distance, and he had just taken the last two. She called her ward and lunged. She made herself small behind the Targe, the shimmering disc of force glowing where her lamp's light met the solid darkness of the tunnel.

She had her intended effect. He was wrong-footed, and his weapon was in no place to do anything about her plan, and he had no idea how much force a Lyceum-trained abjurer could put behind a ward with her lowered shoulder.

Aelis knocked the speaker clear off his feet. His knife went spiraling into the darkness and he hit the shit-slick stones of the tunnel with a thud. She danced away from his flailing hands and drove the heel of her boot into his forehead with a crack that echoed shockingly loud in the quiet of the tunnel.

The others exploded into motion around her. One leaped at her with a cudgel over his head in a two-handed grip.

Aelis reacted in exactly the way she'd been trained. She lunged in perfect form, her sword parallel with the ground, felt the tip meet the too-thin resistance of flesh and slide cleanly into the vitals. She drew it back out and slipped around the now-stunned attacker, who pressed his hands to his stomach and sagged against the wall.

Then everything around her was chaos, as the attackers, maybe eight or ten of them, converged on her all at once. Training and instincts took over; she summoned wards, parried blows, thrust and cut with her sword. A curved knife looked to tear out her guts; Aelis took the hand holding it off above the wrist on a quick downswing. She distinctly saw the look of triumph on the face of the woman who'd been about to gut her turn to shock and pain as she fell backward, clutching the stump.

Aelis was, by any measure, a skilled swordswoman. Her wards gave her a decided advantage, and she hoped that seeing their leader downed and two more dealt wounds that would quickly be fatal if not addressed quickly might cause them to stand down. No matter what fury and early victories she scored, one against ten was a losing proposition.

To her dismay, it seemed they realized that, too. And then she heard a strange whisper in the air and felt a heavy blow land against her right arm, then something wrapped around it and tugged her off her footing. She nearly slipped, threw up the smallest ward she could against a cudgel that would have at least concussed her, if not fractured her skull.

She was just regaining her feet when *two* of her attackers seized the chain wrapped around her arm and pulled hard.

Aelis hit the ground and her sword spun out of her hands.

"Take her hand first, for mine!" This weak yell came from the woman clutching her bleeding stump against the wall. It was met with a general roar of approval; the chain around her arm pulled taut and another thief stomped on the inside of her calf to hold her in place and lifted a knife long enough to masquerade as a short sword. He held it where she could see it, grinning. Aelis knew that gloating was imminent. She slid her wand into her left hand and lifted her arm.

The man's words died in his mouth, and for the briefest of moments Aelis was stunned, because she hadn't gotten her Compulsion out.

Then she realized that a small, feathered bolt had suddenly sprouted in the man's eye, and he fell backward, profoundly dead.

The chain on her arm slackened and Aelis whipped to her feet to see Mihil, standing some feet away, with a small crossbow held in his right hand, in a perfect shooting stance, his left wrist under his right arm for balance.

He'd already reloaded, and loosed another bolt into the man who'd wrapped the chain around Aelis's arm. Then she saw him twist his right hand and drag the bow across his left wrist; when he brought it back up it was loaded and cocked, and he loosed again, at the second smuggler on the chain.

Their wounds weren't fatal, but they hurt, with one in the meat of a hand and the other in a calf.

With more than half their numbers depleted, the rest broke and ran, the wounded calf and missing hand lagging behind. Remaining behind were the dead man with the bolt in his eye, the unconscious leader, and the belly wound, who sat pale and unmoving, his hands pressed to his stomach.

Aelis saw Mihil make that same odd twisting motion with his hands and realized that, having shed his long Naval Infantryman's coat, he wore a long leather cuff on his left forearm.

It bristled with the small gray-fletched bolts for his crossbow, and part of it looped over his thumb; that part had a spur that jutted up when he curled the digit. By brushing the weapon over a bolt and then that spur, he loaded and cocked it faster than she'd imagined possible.

By the time she'd put that together, he'd loosed another bolt after the fleeing Saltmen and loaded again, his face set in grim concentration, lips curled back over his teeth.

"Mihil! They're beaten!"

Hearing his name broke him halfway out of whatever trance he was in; for a moment he swung the loaded bow at her, but he was already lowering it. He sagged, hands on his knees, and trembled as if he might be sick.

Aelis decided to go check on the three men who were left behind. *After* she picked up her sword.

She walked right past the man with the bolt in his eye, letting her lanternlight fall on the badly wounded man huddled against the wall.

"Save . . . save my brother," he said, teeth chattering, pointing with his chin toward the dead man.

"He is beyond anything I can do," Aelis said, "unless you want to see his corpse stand up and walk. But *you*," she went on, "you don't have to die today."

"This . . . this is a stomach wound. I'll smell my guts in a minute, and then it's a long and slow death. Better you just slit my throat."

"He isn't wrong," Mihil said, suddenly appearing at her side.

"You are bound by the laws of Lascenise, the Three Crowns, and the Estates

House," Aelis said to the man, touching his shoulder with the tip of her sword. "And if you swear to lead us to the quickest exit, I should be able to save your life."

Aelis thought of the minimal medical supplies she had on her: just a pair of threaded needles, a scalpel, and two small vials, one of astringent, one of a pain-reducer, in a waxed canvas packet inside a belt pouch. Even so, those plus her anatomist's blade would keep him alive until she could properly save him.

"And why would you . . ."

"Because it's what I do," Aelis said. "Don't move."

She looked over the dead man; there wasn't a scrap of what she'd consider clean cloth on him. The unconscious spokesman was somewhat better, as he wore a thick vest over a shirt that wasn't truly clean but might just be clean *enough*. She cut some off with her dagger, then wadded it up; the man stirred only slightly.

"Here," she said, handing it to the wounded man, "hold it over the wound, apply light pressure. Do *not* press it in too hard or I'll have Onoma's work picking it out of you to prevent rot and inflammation."

She looked down at the barely stirring man. "You know this one, Mihil?"

"I do," he said. "Steppan."

"How big of a bastard is he?"

"To be honest, I wouldn't have thought him the kind to attack a warden. But . . . the right odds, the right money to be made, he'd give it a shot, I suppose. Always an eye on the chance."

"So if we leave him here to wake up on his own, he's not likely to die, but he's also not likely to raise a war party and assault Cabal Keep."

"I don't think the Worldsoul and five hundred good lads could move *that* man to assault a wall," Mihil said. "He's your basic street tough, which means he's a coward if you scratch him."

"Good." Aelis looked around for his knife, found it, and threw it into the rushing stream of filth. Then she bent down over his face, resisted the urge to slap him awake, and summoned a simple First Order Awakening with her wand. His eyes flew open and she bent even lower, holding her sword point at his eye.

"My name," she said, "is *Warden* Aelis de Lenti. If you ever see me on the street, cross to the other side and pray I don't see you. You hear someone speak my name, you leave the fucking room and hope I'm not on my way there. Because if I *ever* see you again, I will carve out that bloodshot eye, and you do not want to know what I will do with it but I *promise* you'll be alive to see it. Do you understand?"

"Y-Yes," he stammered.

"Yes *what*?" she hissed, letting the tip of her sword graze his cheek.

"Yes, Warden."

She let him go, sheathed her sword, and said to the wounded man, "Come on. I'll help you up and deal with that wound. But know this; if you try to lead us anywhere but the nearest exit, I'll leave you to die in agony."

She wouldn't. But the wounded man probably didn't know that.

17

LUXURIES

The captured thief led them quickly up and out of the tunnels. They had really left the residential parts of Slop's End behind and found themselves in the shadow of the Foundries that lay at the very distant outskirts of the city. Aelis was able to stabilize the man's wounds and then, with Mihil's help and a handful of silver, convinced a teamster leaving in a freight wagon to take them as close to the city's center as he was going; there they flagged a coach. By the time she placed him in custody at Cabal Keep he was too drained to undergo an interrogation, but she had no worries about him living through the night once she'd seen to his wound.

The wound she'd dealt him was clean and professional and ghastly, and it *would* have killed him without her intervention. But the day she couldn't deal with a simple stomach wound was the day she'd give up her anatomist's blade, and the keep's facilities made it far easier than when she'd pulled a wickedly jagged knife out of Otto's stomach on the dirt floor of his crumbling shack in the dark of night.

She had attempted to dismiss Mihil with a handful of gold and silver once her prisoner and patient was stable and asleep.

"We'll check in tomorrow," she said.

Mihil nodded. She saw his hand start to shake before he shoved it into the pocket of his reclaimed blue coat. Beneath his stubble his cheeks were gray, and his eyes were red-rimmed.

"If I didn't have yet more business to do today, I'd bring you inside and get a couple bottles of wine and we could lie to each other about how great we feel," Aelis said.

Mihil looked up at her then. "I don't feel anything, Warden."

"That's a lie, but you saved my life, so I'll let it go. That was a timely shot."

"To tell the truth, Aelis . . . can I call you Aelis?" She nodded. "By all the seas of the Worldsoul . . . I was aiming for his knife hand."

Aelis didn't know whether to laugh or call him a liar, but his face was as serious as his oath.

"Mihil," she said instead. "At least promise you'll eat a good meal before you go back to the Sow and get swill-sick."

"Seems like a waste of food."

Aelis sighed. *Do not chase lost causes.* She was sure it was Bardun Jacques's voice she heard say that. "You saved my life, Mihil. That levies an obligation on me."

"I'll let you out of it."

"Not up to you. Now, am I going to put you in a cab under trust that you'll take it to a good eating house, or bring you into Cabal Keep and take you to the wardens' mess?"

"Never been comfortable in restaurants."

"Alright then. With me."

She waved the guards away as Mihil came with her and marched him straight to the wardens' refectory. Only a very few wardens were eating, as it was not yet their usual dinner time. Aelis sat Mihil down at a table by himself, and intercepted the servant who made a beeline for him.

"That gnome is my guest. Feed him absolutely anything he wants and as much of it as he asks for but bring him no wine, no beer, no spirits. Tell him we don't have them."

"But, Warden, the head butler has just opened two twelves of finest de Tarnis cuvee, and . . ."

"Lie to him. Then when I have collected him and I see that he has eaten but not wet his throat, there'll be gold in it for you."

"Yes, Warden," the woman said, slightly awed, and slipped around Aelis, holding a hand over her nose and mouth. Aelis thought nothing of that, and was back out into the courtyard and heading for the duty station of the warden of the watch when she ran into Miralla.

"Aelis!" As her friend drew closer, the smile that had graced her features vanished into a gag. "Anaerion's Cock, you smell like *shit*. And I mean *shit*."

"Right . . . suppose I don't notice it after a while. Look, Mira . . ." Aelis tried to grab her elbow, but Miralla dodged away from her. "Mira, the package is on the move."

"Well, the Distance Beacon won't be any less active in the hour it'll take you to wash and have those clothes sent to the laundry."

"Miralla, it's . . ."

"Aelis, I am not spending one minute in a room with you right now. Not even if you stripped naked and gave me *that* look."

"What look?"

"The one where your eyes narrowed and your lips curled and I knew I was in for a night of it. Go! Bathe! Launder! Now!"

With that, Miralla skipped away from her and continued on her way, presumably to the mess. Aelis assumed her nose had stopped telling her just how awful she smelled, and wondered how Mihil was faring.

Is there an anatomist's approach to someone trying to drink himself to death? Should I even try and find one?

The baths of Cabal Keep were in the deep sublevels, where the conquered subterranean rivers were allowed to rise once again into numerous stone-lined pools. The work of conjurers and invokers kept them in a range from too hot for Aelis to stand all the way to too cold for her to stand for long. By the time she had scrubbed herself clean, toweled off, and then gone from hottest to coldest pool, spending as long as she could stand in the extremes, her clothes had already been laundered and were waiting for her. Her boots had been shined, and her swordbelt and its pouches and scabbards had been carefully waxed.

"Ah, the luxuries of a keep full of wizards," she sighed contentedly. Briefly, she thought about the time and effort that went into such things in a place like Lone Pine. To even have hot water for washing clothes meant hard work felling trees, hauling, splitting, and stacking wood, or having enough surplus to trade with the charcoal-burner, and then difficult work by hand to scrub, wring, and dry everything. *What would Maurenia think of it here? Well . . . she probably wouldn't waste time thinking about the places where she couldn't enjoy luxury, that's for sure.*

"And here I am having my clothes handed back to me less an hour after shedding them," she murmured. She pushed the thoughts from her mind and went directly to the mess. She found Mihil, alone at a table, head down, sleeping soundly, surrounded by half-empty plates no one had yet gathered up, and no sign of Miralla.

She flagged down a servant and pointed to Mihil. "That gnome is my guest," she murmured as the man neared her. "Please guide him to the baths, have his clothes cleaned, and see him to a guest room." From her purse she produced a thick oval of gold. The servant made a very slight bow, the coin disappeared, and he glided silently to Mihil's table. Aelis thought she saw the man take a deep breath and then hold it before getting close.

That done, she found a cook and asked for bread, cheese, and a bottle of cuvee to be sent to her rooms, before marching off to find Miralla.

"Come in, Aelis," Miralla called, before Aelis had even put her hand to the door. *Ought to expect that from a diviner.*

Her friend had not been idle while Aelis bathed and ordered dinner. She had several other maps spread haphazardly on her desk and was clutching a silver pin in her hand. Aelis knew better than to interrupt her while in a Diviner's Trance.

At her desk, Miralla shuffled a map to the floor. As carefully as she could, Aelis made her way over and bent down to examine it. It appeared to be a map of Lascenise and its surroundings. She peered over Miralla's shoulder and saw her looking at a map of the Lyceum.

"I cannot find it on either map," she said, her voice distant. "But the spell responds at the edges of either, and it is traveling in the direction of the Lyceum."

"Good," Aelis said. "That's what we expected."

"And what do you plan to do when it's there?"

"Find out who retrieved it."

"And then?"

"And then . . . make myself a pain in their ass until I figure out who is running this nonsense."

Miralla sighed. "You might be doing your career in, you know."

"One thing at a time," Aelis said. "Besides, proving the innocence of an Archmagister and Warden Emeritus would have to be a bright spot in my brief." Then, more seriously, she said, "Miralla . . . the dinner at my father's townhouse. I'm given to understand that there may be an attempt on my life there. Probably in force."

"And?"

"And I still want you to come. My second guest will be another warden. I hope that the three of us together can master the situation."

"Why not just cancel the dinner, Aelis? Or refuse to go?"

"Then I give away that I know it's coming and reveal an important source of information."

"Are you going to give your father warning?"

"I'm going to place some . . . security experts with the servants."

"Doesn't seem like a good idea to me."

"My *ideas* never are. But my execution is flawless."

Miralla laughed, then waved to the chair on the other side of her bed. Aelis only had to move a dress, a pillow, two books, and a half-empty bottle of wine to sit in it. *Sitting* felt good. Probably too good.

"Why do you care so much, Aelis?"

"About Archmagister Bardun Jacques? He's a legend, he's my mentor, he's . . ."

"About *any* of it," Miralla said. "With your family name, your money, and your power, you could be living the easiest life any wizard ever had. Some minor banneret or margrave would've taken you on as court wizard simply upon seeing your last name. In ten years you'd be sitting next to a grand duchess. Honors, wealth, power, your pick of the prettiest knights and courtiers . . ."

"I never wanted to live on being a *de Lenti*," Aelis said.

"I've known you for six years, so I know you don't want to live on it, but you don't mind trading on it now and then. But why? Why does it stop at walking this hardest road?"

"What about you, Mira? Your family has comfortable money. Your mother is one of the sharpest trading minds in the three kingdoms. What could she do with a diviner of your gifts sitting next to her?"

"Deflecting the question isn't fair, but since you asked . . . because even if my mother never laid a wrong bet, and every investment, every caravan, every trading cog and caravel paid off with no loss, in three generations we *might* be sitting on the outer benches of the Estates House. But a warden in the family? Maybe I cut that to two with the right contacts, the right career path. One, if I make a chapter in *Lives of the Wardens*."

"So you're doing it for family."

"That, and I like a challenge."

"Well, so do I. Question answered."

"It's more than that, Aelis. Answer me really, honestly: why?"

Aelis took a deep breath and thought of Bardun Jacques's words to her of a few days before. *Nobody needed the world to know who they were like you did.*

"Because I need everyone to know that *this*, of all things, wasn't given to me. That I earned it. That it belongs to me. Not to my father, not to my family name, not to our wealth."

"Something is given to all of us, the spark that makes magic possible."

"I know, and I know an awful lot of ink has been spilled and a lot of sheep skinned to write down any number of Archmagisterial theories about how and why that happens. Bloodlines, conjunctions of the moons, the timing of the Worldsoul's change, but you and I both know that the merest First Orders didn't come to us naturally. It takes study. Discipline. Will. A graduate of even one college has achieved something that can't be credited to anyone else. The Archmagisters may be a backstabbing and grasping lot but say this for them: as long as there has been a Lyceum, no one who could not honestly pass a college's test could truly call themselves a wizard."

"You don't think Archmagisters take pity on favored students?"

"Mira, Lavanalla liked you, and she *broke your nose* during your Abjurer's Test."

Miralla self-consciously lifted a hand to her face. Aelis smiled. "Do you think anyone can tell," she said, "after my handiwork?"

"You are the only anatomist I'd trust with my looks," Miralla said, her eyes narrowing, her tongue-tip peeking out between her lips in a look that Aelis recognized.

"Mira," she said, as she thought she saw the other woman start to leave her chair. "Don't. Please."

"Are you truly so taken with whoever you met up in shepherd country?"

"Miralla, I love her," Aelis said, her voice a harsh whisper. "I think. I don't know that she loves me; Onoma knows she has enough reasons not to. She is cursed, and imprisoned, and it is my fault, and if I do not fix it, then . . ."

As it happened, Miralla did rise from her chair then, but there was no seduction in her walk, no smolder in her eyes when she knelt next to the chair where Aelis sat and caught her hand.

Aelis had not realized that she had clasped her hands together in her lap, or how hard, or that they were shaking until Miralla reached for her.

"Aelis, you cannot take everything that happens around you onto your own shoulders. What would Bardun Jacques say to a warden who did that?"

"That they weren't fit for the service, that they were no better than a hedge wizard, that they were losing a war to their own stupidity . . ."

"Probably with more fucks thrown in," Miralla offered.

Aelis laughed, and with it dashed the sudden, unexpected tears that had gathered at the corners of her eyes. "I'm sorry, Mira, for getting emotional," she said as she felt her eyes dry and her color return. "It has been a trying day." *A dozen or so thieves tried to kill me; I gut-stuck one, cut the hand off another, dealt wounds to four or five more, almost died. Usual warden stuff, why in seventeen hells would I cry about this day? Wardens don't cry, neither do de Lentis.*

"Aelis, I have never known anyone less likely to give in to a trying day than you, so whatever it is . . . do you want to, you know . . . tell me about it?"

"Not really."

"Then tell me about this woman up north, and her curse. I'm a warden too, you know. I might have an insight."

Aelis squeezed Miralla's hand and felt something settle between them then, some pendulum that had been swinging first one way and then the other finally catch and stay. When Miralla had resumed her seat, there was no longer any tension in the air. Aelis knew very well how beautiful her friend was, and how wonderful sharing her bed could be, but there was nothing pressing on her any longer. Saying aloud, to another person and not just to a construct of a mind trapped inside a magical object, that she loved Maurenia had tilted the entire world and settled something inside her.

"Her name is Maurenia, and she is beautiful and deadly as . . . as a sword," Aelis said, settling on a simile they would both understand. She didn't tell Miralla everything; that she was an elfling, yes, but not what Maurenia had told her of her mother's marriage being destroyed by it; that she had joined Aelis on her expedition to ruined Mahlgren; that she had been trapped by the woodshade Rhunival; that her body and her mind were changing during her confinement.

Miralla made her pause, and back up, and speak more about Rhunival, pressing her for details. Eventually, she posed a question.

"And you said this being was a woodshade?"

"That's what I thought," Aelis said. "Now I'm . . . not so sure. I'm not terribly familiar with terrestrial spirits; Kiaw didn't cover them in great detail but . . ."

"But nothing," Miralla said. "You haven't read Djeppe, who covers terrestrial spirits in detail. He sounds like a gestalt spirit to me."

Aelis sat forward. "A what?"

"A gestalt spirit; like someone, perhaps clumsy but with a great deal of power to call on, gathered all the woodshades, rock-spirits, naiads, leaf-sprites, and shadows of a forest that he could bind, and pressed them into one being."

Aelis's mind raced. "If Rhunival had been that powerful, how could he have been confined so closely?"

"Well, I never met and spoke to this creature, but if I am being asked to speculate . . ."

Aelis stared at her flatly; Miralla's smile was small and expectant. Finally, Aelis said, "Please speculate."

"I would suggest that perhaps the wizard in question summoned this gestalt into being, found that he could not control it in quite the way he wished, and at the last minute he bound it in place to keep it from overwhelming him, or from discorporating itself back into its constituent parts."

"That . . . is a neat theory. Did I tell you of the rod it wanted? Its summoning key?"

"No."

Aelis described it in detail; the living branch that did not seem cut, so much as carefully extracted from a tree, without being damaged in any appreciable way. How, despite years locked inside an airless, lightless vault, its bark and leaves were still live to the touch. "Back in my rooms, among my baggage I have a book I can't read, with a picture of this very rod carefully drawn in it."

"But it did not harm you, even when you gave it this rod back?"

"No, but it . . . he . . . had made a bargain."

"Woodshades, as a rule, do not like us. Not elf, dwarf, human, or gnome. They see us as mulch. If there had been a mote of wiggle room in the bargain you'd struck, it would have attacked you."

"When did you become an authority on terrestrial spirits?"

"I have briefly entertained the notion of trying to enroll at the College of Conjurers," Miralla admitted, folding her arms and looking casually away. "When my post here is done. I have been doing a bit of studying."

"But you didn't take any conjuring in first year, did you?"

"I don't know, Aelis," Miralla said with a sudden shrug. "I'm not satisfied with two Colleges. I want that third."

"No power in this world could make me go back for another."

"Well, you've already done three. It would be something to be the first warden in centuries to command four. If you had an inkling that you could do that, you *would*, because you're . . . you."

Aelis thought guiltily of the divination classes she had intentionally weeded herself out of. Her incomplete exam papers; the insights she had not shared; the dream portent journals she had left unfinished.

"Well, there is that," she said casually, well aware of how foolish she'd sound and how, even if she could make Miralla believe her, it would wound the other woman's pride. The moment of quiet had her sagging in her chair, and the day's doings caught up with her. She suddenly felt very weary, ready to sleep, and fully aware that whatever sleep she did get wouldn't be enough.

"Go on," Miralla said, picking up on Aelis's slump immediately. "To bed with you."

Aelis stood, slowly, feeling an ache that started in her feet and went up through her shoulders, to her neck and down into her hands.

Miralla stood with her and came to her side once again and took her hand.

"Aelis," she said, "you're going to free this Maurenia. And you're going to do it because I'll be damned if I won't clap eyes on the woman who can win you that completely. And if you're stumped about curses and whatever that being was, you're a half day's hard ride from the greatest collection of arcane knowledge in the three kingdoms. Maybe take advantage of it."

Aelis smiled, and they embraced, arms around each other's necks, and Aelis left Miralla's room knowing that one door had closed forever, but that another, different, deeper, perhaps more honest, had opened.

18

COFFEE AND OATHS

By the time Aelis got to her room, her bottle of wine had warmed considerably, but she still drank half a glass before she even noticed the large, green-wrapped parcel in the middle of her bed.

She tossed her glass aside and had her sword half-drawn before she realized that the paper was the green and gold of Manxam's, sealed with several wax wafers. A last-second ward—about as much magic as she could possibly muster then—kept the glass from shattering on the floor, but most of the wine spilled.

It took her several moments and a repetition of her Abjurer's Litany before she calmed down enough to examine it. She took out each garment—a jacket, a dress, a robe—and sundry accessories and put them carefully away either in the wardrobe or the chest. The simple ritual of it, the care and precision, calmed her, and made her think of Maurenia. She doubted Maurenia ever, at any given time, owned as many clothes as Aelis had already purchased this week, and wondered again if it wasn't that freedom, that rootlessness, that attracted her so strongly to Maurenia in the first place.

Aelis sat down, too worked up to sleep, too tired to do much useful work. As she let her eyes wander the room, they settled on another parcel—the single book she'd managed to buy in her long day of shopping with Mihil.

It was a much slimmer volume than she'd expected when she'd gone looking for it. Bound in purple cloth faded to blue, the boards sagging and wrinkled, the book only had the author's name stamped on it in silver ink; *Hughinn.* Aelis flipped it open and read *Deals with Devils and Their Ilk* stamped on the frontspiece, over the author's name again, along with Magister, College of Conjuring, and some other boring things like dates that she didn't bother to look at.

"I am bone tired, far too given to emotions, and have not eaten," Aelis said aloud. She set the book down and walked back to the tray that sat on her table. She removed the silver-lined wooden top that sealed it, felt the simple abjurer's mark that had kept the contents fresh, and ate a half loaf of bread and a wheel of white cheese quickly and mechanically, tasting none of it. She did taste the wine, and drank rather more of it faster than she should have.

Then, with half a glass of wine left, she retrieved Hughinn's book. She flipped past the introduction and looked at the chapter headings. There were only three.

I. How to Deal with Devils and Their Ilk
II. How to Salvage the Deal You Have Made
III. How to Break a Contract

Aelis's first impulse was to flip to that third chapter, but she assumed it might reference parts of the preceding chapters and anyway, it wasn't a very long book. The day she couldn't make quick work of a book of less than two hundred pages was the day she'd hang up her robes.

There was an author's note that she glossed over; something about *requisite understanding of the basic texts of the Conjurer's trade, knowing Barston's* Basic Terrestrial Summonings *and Urquhardt's* Laws of Conjuring. Aelis had only just encountered those texts at the library on her day trip to the Lyceum, and could hardly be said to have a master's knowledge of them, but she pressed on.

She flipped the cover page of chapter 1, or perhaps part 1, and saw a single word taking up a quarter of the leaf.

DON'T

There was a space after and a serif, to set off this sage advice from the rest of it, which began, *But if you absolutely must, you would do well to follow the advice, counsel, understanding, and wisdom of those who have made such deals before you; who have contended with Other Forces and bent them to an acceptable compromise; who have wrought chaos into the world in controllable form; who have brought forth the Salamander, the Naiad, the Stone Talker . . .*

Aelis realized that the age of the book put it squarely in the age of extremely long sentences set off by semicolon after comma after dash until she found herself rereading each long period two or three times to make sure she had the sense of it.

"This is going to take longer than I thought," Aelis sighed, but she resigned herself to it.

+ + +

The knocking on her door startled Aelis awake. She shook her head to clear it and winced as she felt the Death Curse oozing inside her mind, awaiting release. Her room was dark but for a dying fire. She had not made it to bed, but rather fallen asleep in the chair she had been reading in. Her feet were cold, her lamp was dead, and the candles she'd lit were mere puddles of wax on the table.

A hand thudded on her door again.

"*Aelis,*" a voice hissed. It was Miralla. "Wake up. I've got news. And it isn't great."

Aelis found her alchemy lamp, fiddled with a dial, and it flared to life.

She unbarred the door and saw Miralla in her nightdress, maps under her arm and her box of silver tacks in one hand.

"What hour is it?"

"Coming on fifth," Miralla said. "But I was pulled out of sleep by my tracking spell just . . ." She snapped her fingers. "Sheared like a thread. It woke me up enough to buff up my Countersign, because let me tell you . . . that box passed through some *powerful* magic. Get me a flat surface."

Aelis was still sore and the room was still cold, but moving helped, and soon she had her empty dinner tray moved out to the hall, where it should have been placed before the turn of the day to make life easier on the servants.

Miralla threw her maps down on the table. "When I lost my spell, I could still hold a kind of . . . echo, a trace, of where it went." She slid a silver tack into the map she placed on Aelis's table.

Aelis lifted her lantern and looked down at the map. It was of the Lyceum, the well-spread out constituent Colleges connected by broad walks and avenues. It was too much space to have walled, and a kind of support town had grown up around each college; wineshops, eating houses, and outlets of the major wizards' suppliers who headquartered here in Lascenise. But where Miralla had placed her tack was dead in the center, in the oldest cluster of buildings that were the ancient center of wizardry in the Three Kingdoms.

Aelis felt her heart sink as she and Miralla locked eyes.

"The Vaults," they said in unison.

♦   ♦   ♦

Tired as they were, there was no use attempting to go back to sleep at that point. The jolt of finality, of knowing where the shipment had gone, had stunned them both into a kind of wakefulness. Aelis felt the situation called for coffee, maybe with brandy in it, and a dash of feeling sorry for herself.

Miralla was more of a talker, and she was doing so, at length, in a low murmur.

"Archmagisters, Aelis. Archmagisters have access to the Vaults, and only *that* through the Porters, and do you have any idea how powerful those are? Do you know how restricted access is?"

"I'm going to call for coffee," Aelis said in response to Miralla having pointed out the rarefied circles they were now *certainly* swimming in. "Would we like anything with it?"

"How about brandy?"

"I always did like how you think," Aelis said as she pulled the bell rope.

Miralla opened her mouth to speak again, but Aelis held up a hand and said, "Please, Miralla. Until coffee can kick my mind into compliance, please let me stew in silence."

They didn't have to wait long until there was a light knock. Aelis opened the door to a slender young man. "Coffee," she said, "a large pot. Two cups. And a half carafe of Tirravalan brandy, please."

"I do not know if we have Tirravalan brandy, Warden."

"Let me know what it costs to find some," she said, and the servant bowed.

She shut the door and slumped into a seat.

"I knew that I was likely up against powerful wizards," she murmured. "I knew that. Influential wizards. But the Archmagisters who have access to the Vaults . . ." She lowered her head and cradled it in her hands. "This could not get worse."

"Sure it could," Miralla said. "You could have a headache."

"One is well on the way," Aelis said.

"You could have a headache and no help."

Aelis chuckled humorlessly, then heaved herself up to open the door when she heard the rattle of crockery on a tray. She opened it on the startled servant, who recovered quickly, glided in, and set the tray down on the table seconds after Miralla snatched the map off it. It took Aelis a few moments to locate her purse, until she realized that it was still tied to the swordbelt hanging from a peg on the wall. She slipped two coins from it without looking at them and held them out. The servant bowed low and, in that trick all of Cabal Keep's servants seemed to have, made the coins disappear before vanishing himself.

Aelis poured each of them a cup with a splash of brandy.

She brought Miralla her cup and sipped her own, feeling the warmth spread inside her.

"Aelis," Miralla ventured, after her own first grateful sip. "You have to ask Bardun Jacques to plead mercy."

"He would die first."

"This is going to destroy him," Miralla said. "It doesn't have to destroy you."

"I do not turn from a challenge."

"It's one thing to face an attacker straight on even ground," Miralla said, "and it's another to evade an uneven fight while you search for ways to flatten the odds, and it's another still to stand in place while an army rolls over you."

"Hired knives and hard-case street thugs are not an army."

"No, but the right Archmagister might as well be. What if it's Tagliaferro? Lavanalla? Duvhalin? What if it's all three of them? You *cannot* take them on."

"Do you believe Archmagister Lavanalla Elysse Ymiris Cael Na Tenyll, the First Sword of the Lyceum, the Living Ward, the Bronze Scale of Stregon, is part of a conspiracy to steal magical artifacts?"

"It's unlikely, but we must assume any Archmagister could be part of the conspiracy. How much more time do you have?"

"Seven days," Aelis said.

"Not much. Can you buy more?"

"The lawyer told me she'd already exhausted every trick she had. They want a frame-up, and they want it swiftly." Aelis took a deep breath. "I need to find out directly who is in the Shadow Congress, and how to get leverage over them."

"Leverage over an Archmagister? How would you even . . ."

Aelis had a sudden thought. It struck her like a bolt of cold that even the coffee couldn't stand up to, and she set her cup down to stop her hand from shaking.

"Miralla," she said carefully, "I seem to recall from my curtailed study of divination that it is *easier* to track something that is, itself, magical."

"Well, of course it is. Ordinary objects, then precious materials, then magical. If it's powerful enough, you can use the artifact itself as a kind of battery; a spell as small as a tracker isn't going to drain it. Can even hold it against wards and counter-spells. Unless you're using the damn thing to plot circumnavigation . . . which Aenri the Farseeing supposedly tried as a method of establishing surefire nautical charts by corresponding his own tracking spells with fixed, enchanted objects on land—" She caught sight of Aelis's eye and stopped herself. "Right. You never had any patience for the long answer."

"Does that mean the short answer is yes?" Miralla nodded, and Aelis went to her trunk in the far room, the one she had dragged from Lone Pine, the one she'd left a trunk full of clothes on the side of the High Road for.

She opened it and took out the cloth-wrapped bundle tied tightly with cordage, wider than it was tall.

"Mira, I need absolute secrecy if I am to tell you what this is."

"Of course, I . . ."

"I need it sworn on your power."

Miralla set her coffee cup down, her eyes wide. "Aelis, it cannot matter . . ."

"Miralla. For having this in my possession and not reporting it yet, I could be *immediately* remanded to the censors. For life. *Swear.*"

Aelis's words, as well as something in her face and bearing, had a chilling effect on her friend, who stood up. "I don't have my sword."

"Use mine."

Miralla drew Aelis's sword and sniffed as her hands took its weight. "Could club someone to death with this. Heavier than Peyron's three-eyed gaze." She came back before Aelis and held the sword out, the blade balanced on her palms.

"I swear upon the power I wield, by Peyron and Stregon's moons, by my sight and by my wards, to speak to no one of what you are about to show me. If I do, may my trances turn against me; may my wards never hold; may the God of Seers and the God of Warriors both turn their gifts from me."

Aelis felt the power of the words settle over them both. With great solemnity and care, she unpicked the knots that bound the cloth and let the fabric fall away.

"It's a candlestick holder." Miralla still held Aelis's sword, though now by the hilt, the blade pointing down.

"This," Aelis whispered, reverence and fear in her words, "is Aldayim's Matrix."

Even among wizards of different schools, some names were so powerful, and carried so much weight, that anyone who'd been inside a Lyceum lecture hall or put on a scholar's robe could not help but know who they were. The closest to that who was still living was Lavanalla; Bardun Jacques was a legend among *wardens*, but not every wizard esteemed him. Among diviners there were Leria the Loresong and Aenri the Farseeing; invokers had Urtan the Flame Undying and Charosh the Many-Forked Bolt. But none of them had quite the mononym magnitude of *Aldayim*.

"Aldayim's . . . it can't be, Aelis. That would make it the most powerful magical artifact either of us has ever seen."

"Miralla," Aelis said, "I've used it. I've spoken with the mind-construct of the Master himself. He's . . . not as helpful as he could be, frankly."

Miralla took a deep breath and picked up her coffee cup. She refilled it so that it was at least a third brandy, took a long sip, then said, "So . . . you want me to track that? The same trick?"

"Something like that," Aelis said. "What I need to do is contrive some way to report it found or let them think *they* found it. Unlikely I can plant it on the smugglers again."

"You've got one in the cells here," Miralla said. "He could probably be induced to go back to work in exchange for a lighter sentence."

"Now we're thinking like wardens," Aelis said. "Admittedly, the next part is complicated."

"And that is—?"

"Once it arrives in the place we expect it to . . ." Aelis took a deep breath. "We'll have to figure out how to break into the Vaults."

"Oh. Oh. Is that all?" Miralla threw back the rest of her coffee and set the cup down again. She picked up the decanter and sniffed it. "Is this actually poppy brandy? Because I just heard you speak like a drug-addled fool."

"Any vault can be opened," Aelis said. "It's just a matter of leverage."

"Oh, is that all? And here I am thinking it might be hard. What'll we need, just a little alchemy to melt the lock? Start with some phoenix feathers . . . a dragon's eye, willingly given, of course, otherwise that spoils the humors. Say, two pints of blood of the specter, a ton of purest gold untarnished by living hands . . ."

Aelis sighed and Miralla stopped mid-sarcasm. Aelis held up the iron candlestick holder. "I found this in the vault of Mahlhewn Keep. A Calabris and Dolovkin Vault."

"Should those names mean something?"

"Well, I have two associates who are keenly interested in that sort of thing and I am assured they are the very best."

"Oh? Locksmiths, these friends? Security experts?"

"In an amateur enthusiast kind of sense, I suppose. Regardless, if I tell them there's a hidden Vault beneath the oldest buildings of the Lyceum, that it can be accessed only by the college Porters . . . themselves magical constructs of

very ancient provenance whose workings I barely understand . . . they'll beg
to be taken to see it. They'd pay a fortune for a glimpse. And if I told them I
wanted their help breaking into it, once they finished swooning, they'd probably offer to adopt me."

Admittedly, Aelis didn't see Timmuk and Andresh as *swooners*, but now
that she was rolling into her pitch, she could imagine it: a perfectly timed,
flawless penetration of perhaps the most secure hiding place of magical artifacts and wealth in the world. A perfect, intricate operation of magical clockwork that she and the Dobruszes would carry out with unstoppable dash and
efficiency.

Miralla stared at her for a few moments. "You fucking mean it, don't you?
But why? Why in the world?"

"Because I have a strong suspicion of one name in this *Shadow Congress*.
And if he is made to know that *this* is within his grasp, he will absolutely not
hesitate to use it."

"So you want to make an Archmagister who is already trying to have you
killed *even more* powerful?"

"The Matrix doesn't work quite the way you think. And I happen to know
that when a new user takes it up . . . they get a glimpse of how the *last* user
acquired it. If I pass it on to one of these assholes and then get it back . . ."

Miralla stared at Aelis for a moment and then nodded slowly. "But . . .
then he'd know that you had it?"

"Onoma help me, he probably already does. You have to get up pretty
early in the morning to outmaneuver the man I'm thinking of." In her mind's
eye, Aelis saw the Death's Head seal on a sheaf of letters, the large ring and
chain of office that Duvhalin always wore. She didn't want to speak aloud
her suspicion that he was involved, but it positively reeked of his methods,
she thought.

"Aelis, this is insane."

"Probably."

"And there's no point in wasting my breath trying to talk you out of it, is
there?"

Aelis shook her head.

"One question."

"Fair. Go ahead."

"Why all this for Bardun Jacques?"

Aelis took a deep breath and bent to retrieve the wrappings she kept the
Matrix in. How to explain this at all, this bone-deep affection for a cantan-
kerous old man who'd told her not a week ago what a pain in the ass she was?

She sat and began bundling up the twisted iron. "Because he never, not
once, treated me differently from any other student."

"I know I said one question, but I'm going to need some clarification . . ."

"Every teacher, Mira, *every single one*, at some point, somehow made it
about my family. Money. Influence. Privilege. What did Lavanalla always

call me? *Rich Girl.* When I met Bardun Jacques, I was ready for that, for those prodding insults; could the rich girl *really* be serious about being a warden? Hadn't my pampered life made me want to quit this run, or beg out of sword forms, or given me a false sense of how smart or strong or fast I really was? Did I need a tutor to come explain something to me, like those I'd had in one of my father's palaces? *The insults never came.*" Aelis hid a sudden upsurge of emotion behind raising her empty coffee cup and then clattered it onto the tray. "When Bardun Jacques criticized a room, sure, that was full of obscenities and questions of parentage and the failures of our entire generation, but that's all . . . a *character.* The angry old battle-mage raging against the ruinous *youth.* It's expected. But when he corrected a student *personally,* when he criticized in training or in a classroom, it was about something I had just *done.* It was never, not once, about who I was. He made no assumptions. He saw the student I was and the wizard and the warden I *could be* and did everything possible to make me that without ever making me feel like I hadn't earned it. It was never easy. But I knew he meant it."

"You could've stopped, like, three or four revealing sentences ago," Miralla said, grinning.

"So you just let me go on embarrassing myself?"

"You would think that revealing that you have actual feelings is embarrassing, Aelis. All it means is you're just like everyone else . . ."

Aelis stopped her with a wave of her hand, and they poured the last of the coffee and brandy.

"Are they serving breakfast yet, do you think?"

"Not for another hour," Miralla said.

"It's too late to go back to sleep. Why don't we go down to one of the training rooms and have a little sparring?"

"Only if you promise to leave no bruises on my arms," Miralla said. "Not with this dinner coming up."

"We'll be there to thwart an assassination attempt, Mira, not to find dalliances."

"I can do both at the same time."

"Fine, any bruises, I'll heal them before the dinner. Chances are I won't lay a touch on you; I've not even done forms in a month. Go get dressed; I'll meet you down there."

Miralla gathered up her chart and box of pins, Aelis set the tray on the table outside her door, and dressed for exercise: blouse, trousers, new jacket, which she'd probably swap for a gambeson once she was down there. She paused to gather writing materials and make a new list for herself. She was too suspicious of others to write things down plainly, even if she vowed not to let the list leave her person. So she abbreviated.

1. Inform B
2. Visit patient

3. Polish the iron
4. Soiree plans

"I'm not going to remember what any of this means in an hour," Aelis said, but pressed on anyway. When she finished, before she left her room, she rewrapped Aldayim's Matrix in its cloths, retied the thongs that kept it wrapped, replaced it in her trunk, and warded it. The package would open with a concentrated magical attempt, but it would also let her know that it had been breached.

◆　◆　◆

Two hours later, sore with exercise, full of breakfast, and clean from the quickest bath she could make herself take, Aelis hurried up the steps to Bardun Jacques's cell. When she came within reach of the censors and her ability to manipulate magic slipped away—all of it except the Death Curse rattling around in her already rattly brain—she felt the grungy buzz that always accompanied not having slept enough. It was not helped by having already had a pot of coffee and a quarter carafe of brandy, but she was reasonably sure the day would even itself out.

Her visit with Bardun Jacques was uneventful, except for the slip of paper she dropped into his hand while she mixed and administered medicines. He unrolled it in his palm with one thumb, said *tsk* and then seized his breakfast fork, pressed it into his thumb until the skin broke and blood welled up, then pressed it on to the paper.

"Too complicated," he murmured. "Be there between midnight and three." He scratched out an odd phrase, something about "the eye of Anaerion," and slid it back to her.

Aelis lifted her eyes off the slip of paper. Could getting into the vault be that simple? *Will a Porter accept his blood-seal?*

Bardun Jacques read the question in her eyes and shrugged. Then he muttered, "I'm still an Archmagister, and I have a hand in the Porter who watches the vaults at those hours. Trust me." Here she was, spinning thoughts of cracking open an impossible vault with the Dobruszes—she was halfway to smuggling Andresh, or maybe Mihil, inside the vault on a fume-hooded alchemy cart—when all she might have to do is hand the thing over, with a slip of paper, to Brass Bob or the Sandyman?

But I still need to track it. And retrieve it.

And to do that, she needed Miralla. Again.

"Go to the Lyceum," the Archmagister whispered while she listened to his heart and his dragging lungs. "Today. Take someone you can trust. *Not* another wizard."

Aelis felt her day rearranging around her and the pulse of the Death Curse behind it, threatening a headache.

"Right. I'll get two extra days' supply of medicines made up and . . . hire an assistant," she said brightly, rubbing her eyes as she went to the door.

"Don't you have a prisoner to interrogate?"

"Yes, Archmagister. Thank you, Archmagister," Aelis said mechanically as she left. When she passed out of the censor's field and felt her power and magical senses return, light danced behind her eyes. She leaned against the cool stone wall, hoping no one saw her, till she could right herself and find the guest rooms.

+ + +

"Do you want a job? Longer-term, I mean."

Mihil looked a bit stunned as he sat behind a teapot in the guest room he'd been allotted. It had taken Aelis a few trips up and down the stairs of various towers to find the official charged with housing guests before she tracked him down, and then several long minutes to rouse him from sleep. But now he sat at the small table in his room, with Aelis opposite him, looking blearily at the tea he'd asked for, which a servant had just delivered.

"What'd you say?" he muttered, after finally finding the strength and co-ordination to lift the teapot and pour himself some.

"Do you want a job? For as long as I'm in Lascenise."

"But do I get paid on results, or . . ."

"No. Daily wages from the warden service. Supplemented by my own funds occasionally, if warranted."

Mihil stood up long enough to pour tea into Aelis's cup. She stared at the stuff, a limpid brown in the cup, inoffensive, but not the least bit enticing. *Why would* anyone *choose this when coffee exists?*

"Don't suppose you've got any whiskey to pour into this?" he inquired hopefully, holding up his cup in two hands.

"No."

"Gin?"

"Absolutely not."

"I don't suppose it's worth asking about brandy, rum, arrack . . ."

Aelis set her cup down. "We're getting off-track here, Mihil. I'm offering you a comfortable bed every night, and as many meals as you can eat here in the keep refectory, in addition to a salary. A warden has discretionary funds to hire specialists."

"Sounds like you're after a dogbotherer, not a specialist . . ."

"I'll put you down as a bodyguard, if that assuages your conscience."

"It don't much. Why would you need bodyguarding from me, anyway?"

"Why indeed, Rigging Sharpshooter? I saw you working that hand-crossbow. Maybe the deadliest thing I've ever seen, and I was taught by an elven sword-mistress twice as old as you and I put together, who could slit your throat so fine you wouldn't realize it till a quarter hour had passed."

"Those days are behind me . . ."

"Mihil," Aelis said, leaning across the table. "Good wages, better than average in this city for a skilled tradesman. Food. That bed you just slept in for the last twelve hours, or a better one. And yes, you can drink when you're not working, so long as you can handle your tasks."

"Been a long time since I slept on a featherbed," Mihil said. He stroked his chin. "It beats a hammock hollow, I'll admit. You know, some hands come home from the sea, pretend they have to sling a hammock rather than sleep in a proper bed. Fools, the lot."

"I'm not running a charity, mind. You can letter and cipher, yes?"

"Find an illiterate gnome and you've found a newborn," Mihil shot back. "What's my first job?"

"Shadow me as I go speak to the prisoner we took. Run a note for me over to my outfitter's, then we leave for the Lyceum this afternoon."

"Elisima," he muttered. "What would the boys at the Sow say, they saw me working out of Cabal Keep?"

From what I saw, they'd probably just lean on you to buy their next round, once they knew you had steady employment.

"Remember," Aelis said instead, "this won't last forever. I will wrap up this case and head back north."

"I've never been that far north."

"You aren't missing much," Aelis said flatly. "Now do we have a deal? There'll be papers to draw up, and I'll be run off my feet by noon."

"Sure," Mihil said, throwing a hand in the air. "Why not? I can always drink myself to death tomorrow."

Aelis decided to let that go. "Great. Paperwork, go see the prisoner, then I come up with a list of people I need you to see."

"Right." Mihil struggled to his feet and went to fetch his sky-blue Naval Infantryman's coat, freshly laundered and brushed, hanging on a peg on the wall at exactly his height. "There won't be a uniform, will there?" He flicked his eyes to Aelis. "Black was never my color. Shows the unhealthy pallor to my disadvantage."

"Not unless you want one," Aelis said. "But I can stand you some new clothes, new boots, at my outfitter's, if . . ."

"Just got these broken in proper," Mihil said, shifting his coat onto his rumpled bed and then slipping underneath the frame to pull up a pair of hole-strewn brown boots. "But I could stand a new dress pair."

Aelis waited outside in the hall while Mihil finished dressing. He finally made it out, scratching at his graying jaw, managing to slouch inside his coat without even moving, looking as tattered as if his clothes hadn't all been laundered, dried, and pressed while he bathed the night before.

"We have an agenda today?"

"Like I said, paperwork, talk to our prisoner, then I'll send you over to

Manxam's to get a bag, boots, anything else you need to keep up, and see if they have anything to pick up for me, which they might. Then to the Lyceum."

"Why there?"

"Probably one of those things you just need to trust me on," Aelis said, then flagged down one of the ubiquitous keep servants and asked him to guide Mihil to the paymaster's office, there to be enrolled as her retainer. She herself went to the apothecary, to order fresh medical supplies for Bardun Jacques.

While waiting in the infirmary for her fresh medicines and ingredients, she made the apprentice come up with some pen, ink, and paper. She scratched a quick note.

T: father throwing a party end of next week. Expect noise; lots of it. I need a coachman and a footman and I would prefer you and your brother. Bring a groom if you have need of one. Would like you to keep servants safe in event as bad as feared.

She folded this up and decided it would have to do without wax for now. She looked in on the apprentice's slow, careful gathering of boxes, canisters, and flasks, and said, "I'll be back."

Aelis stole out of the infirmary before anyone could answer and made her way as quickly as she could to the opposite tower, which mostly held bureaucratic offices. She quickly found the paper with the stamp she needed to officially hire an assistant. One didn't graduate from three of the Colleges of the Lyceum at once without a solid grasp of *exactly* where to find official paper. Aelis prided herself on an ability to look at any academic or warden office and know who to speak to and what to say. Failing that, she'd gotten good and fast at rifling drawers. It didn't come to that; the sword on her hip told any keep functionary, wizard or otherwise, that she was a warden, and they were her support staff. A quick conversation with a spectacled gnome and she was hunting out Mihil, whom she found almost immediately on the stairway.

"This place is a fucking maze," Mihil said as Aelis tapped him on the shoulder and pulled him to a turning-alcove off the stairs.

"Not so bad once you get used to it."

"I prefer small spaces. And before you make any crack about gnomes and burrows, it's the years I spent at sea. Two hundred souls on a ship no more than fifteen yards at the beam, and maybe three times as long. Everything in its place because if it's not, you might all die, and everyone to their place because if you don't, you might all die. All this space," he said, gesturing at the massive enclosure of gray stone of the inner keep, which Aelis found rather oppressive herself, "just gives rise to indolence and greed."

"Come along now," Aelis said. "Time to interview a prisoner."

Aelis was happy enough to slow down to allow Mihil to keep pace with her, as she was feeling slow and woozy. They made it to the infirmary without her needing to pause and rest against a wall, but she fumbled slightly with the pen when she signed in. The Death Curse beat in her skull like the worst hangover headache she'd ever known.

She found her prisoner dozing, one hand curled protectively around his stomach. Clean, out of his rough laborer's clothing, under solid conjurer's lamps, he looked young. No more than her own age, to be sure. Probably younger.

Without waking him, she drew her anatomist's dagger and delved him, simply laying the blade against the bare skin of his arm.

She was satisfied with the surgery that had been performed on him; she'd rather she had her own hand in it, and thought some of the suturing less elegant than she would've produced, but all in all she couldn't complain; the analgesics were doing their work, and any infections would be regularly purged by an anatomist until the prisoner's tissues had knit together.

He slept through the Delving, but Aelis decided a physical examination was in order; a surgeon who relied *only* on their magic and never on what they could see, feel, and smell was a surgeon who was going to kill a patient eventually. So she shook him awake, gently at first, then more insistently.

He sat up at last, then clutched at his stomach, where bandages were tied in place. Blinking away sleep, his eyes focused on Aelis, and he let himself sag back into his bed.

"Come to finish what you started?"

"If you mean saving your life, then yes."

"Wouldn't have t'do that if you hadn't gutted me."

"Do we need to talk about who assaulted who? Attack a warden, don't act surprised when you get cut."

He said nothing, only tried to draw up the blanket over his wound, but Aelis snapped it out of his hands and tossed it to the floor. "We'll get you a clean blanket when I'm done," she said. The dressings could stand to be changed, so she cut the wrappings and began to carefully peel them back.

The wound was livid, smeared with ointments to encourage healing and alchemical conductives that smelled strongly of camphor and alcohol, to ease the passage of both magic and medicine into his skin. But it was still ugly, and it would scar.

"What's your name?"

"Why d'you care?"

"If I don't know your name, I can't argue for lenient sentencing when you're brought before an Assize."

She let him sit with that for a while as she first spread strong triple-distilled spirits over her hands, then went to the long black stone counter in the center of the room. Upon it sat a silver bowl; Aelis could feel the necromantic magic that lurked within it. She directed a simple pulse at the stone and waited for it to recognize her, which came with a faint, eerie black light limning the bowl that only she could see. Then she plunged her hands into it.

The water tingled, and Aelis forced herself to count three before she pulled her hands from the water, now free of any possible contaminant.

"Ryne," he said, finally, as she came back to his bedside and commenced inspecting the wound with her hands. It wasn't appreciably warmer than the skin around it; he winced, though did not show signs of serious pain.

"Ryne," she echoed. "How did you know we were down in the tunnels yesterday?"

He clamped his mouth shut and turned his head away from her.

Aelis sighed. "You don't have to die here, Ryne. Especially not if I ask for lenient sentencing. But you were part of a mob that attempted to murder a warden . . ."

"A warden trespassing on our patch . . ."

Aelis felt one of her hands curl up with the itch to slap him. "Listen very carefully and do not talk, or I swear I will think about ripping this wound back open and casting Leonhid's Fast Fester upon it, and we will both sit here and watch and smell your belly *rot*."

Ryne's eyes got very wide, but he still kept silent.

"Understand that everywhere in this city is *my* patch. I'm not a wall-walker who can only operate in the outer ring of the city, between the outer and inner gates, and I'm not an armsman of any of the three kingdoms who can only act to defend his nation's keep or his principal ambassador, and I am absolutely not some guild-hall thief taker whose commission is only good in Ruby Chapel or the Tremont or between East Canal Street and the Liberties. I can go where I want, kick open whatever public door I want, seize and bind anyone I jolly well feel like, and I can *definitely* kill a mob of dirty-handed canal rats if I want." Aelis paused for breath and hoped her color hadn't gone too red. "But I *don't* want to do most of that. I might stab you in the belly in the heat of a fight, but I will try to heal that wound when the fight is over and you are no longer a threat. So answer my questions, tell me what I need to know about the Saltmen, and you'll live to see your home and family again. Refuse, force me to compel you, and you might spend your last moments dancing on air."

Aelis's stomach roiled at her own words; she didn't want to condemn this man to the gallows, but since she was short of both time and useful information, she needed to apply whatever pressure she could.

Ryne turned his head emphatically away from her once more. Aelis slipped her wand into her hand and prepared a targeted compulsion, setting her dagger aside and laying her hand over his wound.

"How did you know Mihil and I were in the tunnels yesterday?" The compulsion slid into him; the alchemical conductives meant to aid his healing were just as good for enchantment as for necromancy.

Ryne slowly turned to face her, then answered through gritted teeth. "Someone saw the lock gone; we look for these things. Then he saw footprints—gnome size and human. We guessed the rest."

"How do you move things to the Lyceum?"

"I wouldn't know. I'm a canal-side boy to my bones." His voice was distant. "Never been more than a mile outside Lascenise."

"You must've heard something, from someone. A name."

"Nicholas, or something like it."

"Nicholaz? Arstan Nicholaz?"

"That sounds right."

Here, though, Aelis's willpower snapped, and with it, her connection to her magic. The tip of her wand went dark; Ryne's eyes went wide and angry with betrayal and he tried to rear up from the bed only to find himself still cuffed to it.

"You wizard scum," he spat. "You made me betray my family, my . . ."

"I don't care, Ryne," Aelis said, knowing she was lying at least a little. "You had the chance to cooperate. We'll do this again another day."

"You don't know my family," he went on. "You'll never sleep well again, you . . ."

She turned quickly on her heels and left, Ryne still sputtering and cursing at her. Mihil lifted his hand and pointed his finger and thumb at Ryne like a crossbow, winked, and followed her out of the infirmary.

Once they were back in the dark of the hallway, she sagged against the wall and raised one hand to her head.

"You well, boss?"

"I will be," she said, pushing herself upright with effort. "Now I need you to head to Manxam's . . . He'll bill me for whatever you need, though it may take a day or two to make or mend. Then I want you to take a note to the Dobrusz brothers. The proprietor of Manxam's will know where to find them."

"How will he know I represent you? You said you'd give me a note of hand."

"Right." Aelis thought for a moment, then tugged the ring she'd bought just a few days ago off her smallest finger and held it out. "Show him this. I bought it through him, from his preferred jeweler."

"He might think I nicked it."

"If he says that, tell him this; that if you could've pickpocketed me, I'd deserve to have lost it anyway, and ask him how you'd know to come to him asking to shop on my credit."

"Fair." Mihil slid the ring onto his index finger and stuffed his hand into his pocket. "Remember, no uniforms."

"Not on my account," Aelis said. "Just whatever you think you need to keep up with me."

"A bag, new boots. Maybe a knife and a sheath."

"Manxam's isn't a smithy, but I'll be surprised if Drewic doesn't have a preferred bladesmith and a few samples on hand."

"And these brothers you want this note sent to? They hatmakers or belt-weavers?"

"No," Aelis said.

"If they don't do that, what business will they have with Manxam's? What do they craft?"

Violence, Aelis thought. "They're bankers, of a kind. Regardless, Drewic will pass the note I've given you to them. They also may have another spot to meet, so don't get too used to Manxam's coffee."

"Right," Mihil said. "Carry the message. Buy myself a new wardrobe on your account."

"I said, whatever you needed to keep up with me."

"Oh, don't worry," Mihil said as he started away down the stairs. "I'll keep the silver thread to a tasteful, elegant minimum." With that, he disappeared, and Aelis lingered in the dark coolness of the hallway until the throbbing in her head receded. Then she walked as quickly as she could to her own rooms, mindful that she needed to see Miralla but intent on talking to someone else first.

Aelis hurried to the chest in the corner and pulled out the cloth-wrapped spiral of iron. After she unwrapped it, she grabbed two lit candles and stuck them in the wrought-iron holders that were the skull's eye sockets. She went into her larger medical kit, took out a small glass jar full of dirt, and sprinkled the tiniest pinch over the flames.

Instantly Aelis found her mind in that formless gray nothingness that she experienced when she used the Matrix. The voice, calm, assured, that she finally allowed herself to think of as Aldayim, or an echo of his mind, at any rate, came immediately.

"Ah, the self-operating abjurer-enchanter-necrobane," he said. "It has been some time. Do you come for more secrets?"

"What do you *do* with all these secrets, Master?"

"I do nothing, for I am merely an echo of the mind of the wizard who made this device."

"What does the Matrix do with all these secrets?"

"That would be a secret, and you know what the price is."

"My surmise is that they are retrievable, and that it is a mechanism put into place to prevent the Matrix from being used for atrocities or too much in the way of self-aggrandizement, because to have done so, you must have opened your own soul to it. It only makes sense that those revelations are accessible."

There was silence for a moment; Aelis had the sense that the mind within the artifact was half-pleased with her.

"That is an interesting surmise. I will not confirm whether or not it is true."

"I will trade a secret for the method of unlocking the stored secrets."

She was met with silence and decided that was as good as a yes.

"I have with me, in a spirit trap, something that was acting parasitically on the Sundered soul of Dalius Enthal de Morgantis un Mahlgren, warden commander of Ystain. Something that had driven the remnants of him insane, to evil. I should probably have it identified at the College of the First Art."

"Why haven't you done so?"

"Why, Professor!" Aelis imagined herself smiling. "That would be a secret, traded for free."

There was a dry chuckle. "You would be surprised how many times that has worked."

"I don't think I would. I think it worked on me, when last we spoke. So. How to unlock the stored secrets?"

"There is a ritual. It must be done in the night air, under Onoma's moon. Grave dust, cedar oil candles . . . and the sacrifice of something important to you. Something you valued. It must be burned, and the ashes sprinkled over the candles with the grave dust."

"Please help me understand the definition of value we are working with."

"Not gold. I suppose, perhaps, if you had a lucky gold coin or a particularly treasured piece of jewelry, that might do."

Aelis was already doing the math on reducing gold to ash. A calcination oven could do it, but only a truly powerful and well-reinforced calcination oven; they would have them in the alchemical laboratories at the Colleges. But she did not treasure gold and was getting carried away thinking about the technical aspects of a problem she didn't even have. Yet.

"I suppose buying something expensive and then burning it will not suffice."

"No. A childhood toy or a treasured letter . . ."

"I did not have a toy-filled childhood." Aelis thought a moment. "Tell me then, once the ritual is complete, how may the secrets be accessed? In exchange, I answer your question from before—I do not want anyone to know that I have it."

"Why not?"

"Really, Master?"

"You are at least thinking carefully now. That is good. Once the ritual itself is complete, you must expend Orders of magical energy to search the index."

"You did not make this easy."

"Power should *never* be easily accessed. This Matrix is a repository of learning, true, but it is full of knowledge that made the man who created it powerful beyond the ability of most to measure. That he turned that power to healing, instead of bending life and death to his will, does not mean that others would not subvert it."

Aelis wanted to say that she wouldn't, to reassure this echo of Aldayim's mind that she would never seek power for its own sake, or that if she did it would be for the right reasons. But she remembered when she used the Matrix to strengthen and broaden her own necromantic abilities, how swiftly she had been seduced by it, how close she had come to turning it against Rhunival for being an inconvenience.

And in truth, there was probably no magical power she would not bend to free Maurenia from her cursed imprisonment, no taboo she would not break, no line she would not cross.

"When I first used the Matrix, I had a vision of it coming to the hand of the previous owner. When it passes to someone else, they will have the same vision of me. So, my last question today, Master: Is there a way to erase that vision from the Matrix? In payment, I do not want anyone to know I have that spirit because I fear I may need to turn it on a very powerful wizard or wizards before too long, and if it comes to that, I want him—or them—to be surprised."

"That is a dangerous secret to share."

"Shared it was. And now I will be paid."

"There is not. You may see the index, but you may not alter it. The Master who created it did not even allow that power to himself. If you use it for ill, the next hand to have it will know it."

"Thank you, Master," Aelis said, and already the gray plane was receding.

As the walls of her room began to take shape again before her eyes, she heard a quiet voice say, "Welcome back, boss."

Training kicked in; Aelis leapt to her feet and ripped her sword free from her belt, turning on a smiling Mihil, who was sitting in her extra chair several feet out of lunging distance.

"What are you doing here?" she exclaimed.

"Bringing lunch," he said, pointing to a tray and a bottle that sat on her desk. "After carrying out my assigned tasks. Was sort of hoping we might share that bottle, but you seemed to be engaged in some significant magical whatnot, I thought it best to stay quiet and out of the way, and to have the wine close to hand for when you finished up."

Aelis sheathed her sword carefully, taking inventory of her limbs and her racing heart as she did so. "How'd you get in here?"

"All the security in this place is focused outward," Mihil said with a shrug. "Once you're inside the walls, it's a piece of piss."

"What do you mean?"

"The locks in here are shit. I'm no great shakes as a locksmith. I mean, I can jimmy a door open as well as any other odd gnome, but these don't even give me pause. Once someone is inside this place, they can go just about wherever they like and do whatever they want."

"There's paperwork to get hold of anything dangerous from the apothecary or the armory."

"Do you have to declare what you're carrying when you walk through the gate? Do they take your weapons away?"

"You have a point," Aelis said. "I'll bring that up with the commander."

"Right," Mihil said. He stood up and preened. He still wore his sky-blue coat but it had been expertly patched and brushed, and even Mihil couldn't make it look shabby anymore. The gnome was wearing all new clothes beneath it, none of them black, down to his boots. He also had a bag slung over his shoulder and a new horn-hilted curved knife with a shiny knuckle-guard on his belt. "We off?"

"You're off to secure a coach," Aelis told him. She found her purse on a table and tossed it to him. "Fastest, straightest trip available; pay them to wait if you need to. I have two stops to make, and I'll met you outside the Infirmary."

"Wouldn't it be faster to hire a couple of horses?" Mihil asked. "Well . . . a horse and a pony, anyway. Maybe just one big horse . . ."

"We aren't sharing a saddle, Mihil, and while riding to the Lyceum might save a little time, we'd arrive too tired and sore to get any real work done. Now, off you go."

"Right," Mihil said, and slouched off out her door.

She gathered up her pack and went to find Miralla.

19

MORE FAVORS

"It's not locked."

Aelis knew her friend's voice well enough to know she was distracted, so she slipped in quietly after the answer to her knock. Miralla was seated at her desk set against the open window, one pen in hand, another tucked behind her ear, making careful entries in a book.

When she was finally done, she set down her pen and closed the book, then turned to find Aelis with a rucksack over her shoulder. She smiled.

"Finally taking the hint and running off?"

"Mira, I think you know me better than that."

Miralla sighed and stood up. "Why would you ever do the thing that's right for your career, Aelis?"

"I'm trying to do the thing that's right for a mentor," Aelis answered. "And I'm afraid I need to ask for help again."

Before Miralla could respond, Aelis unslung her pack, removed the wrapped bundle that contained the Matrix, and unwrapped it.

Miralla came forward to look at the wrought iron again, extended an elegant finger to gingerly touch a glob of melted wax where one of the candles had sat.

"Just had a chat with the greatest wizard of your school, hrm? How does that go, exactly? Knock on the candlestick-holder and leave a calling card? His valet or his secretary make an appointment and you get in his favorite wine and dainties?"

"No," Aelis said. "Just light the right candles, add some grave dirt, and it just sort of . . . happens." She thought for a moment about mentioning the secrets but then it occurred to her that one she had traded concerned this very friend and decided to let it lie.

"Is there an artifact that'll let me chat with Rosfar the Seeing Knife? I could use some pointers, polishing up my close guard form."

"I have no idea what you diviners get up to, or what your magical regalia might be like." Aelis thought for a moment. "Have you seen an orrery lately? I haven't been paying much attention. I know the blue moon must be up, as I feel wards easier to call, but . . ."

"Stregon is descendant, Midarra ascendant, full in two days. Onoma will replace Stregon in the sky."

"How soon?"

"Three days till she's visible, to those with the lenses to see it."

"Or the eyes," Aelis muttered. "So . . . a week till fullness." She took a deep breath, looked to the small fire in Miralla's grate. "Just enough time to get to the vaults, for us to get it out, and me to do some work upon it."

"*Us* to get it out of the vaults?"

"Need you to pinpoint it," Aelis replied.

"I'll draw you a map. But I am also drawing a line." Aelis looked at Miralla's face, which was set, her lips flat, eyes hard. "I am not going to be part of a scheme to crack open one of the Lyceum's vaults."

"What if I need the . . ."

"Aelis, do you realize how far out of my warrants and purview I already am? Knowing that you possess this thing, believing it is what you say it is, and not having reported it *already* opens me to dismissal from the warden service. Not to mention all the other schemes you've revealed to me. I have a career, too. I have goals. And while this may be a shock to you, neither of those is to be a footnote in your chapter of *Lives of the Wardens*."

Aelis was taken aback by the force and emphasis of Miralla's words. They stung like a slap on a cheek.

"I—" she began slowly, "I am not good at . . . appreciating friends, Miralla. I know I have a tendency to use whatever people will give me of themselves, and ofttimes that is too much."

"If you know that, why can't you change your behavior?"

Because there's too much to do seemed the obvious answer, but Aelis thought better of saying so. "If I pause for self-reflection and chastisement right now, everything will fall apart. But I will stop asking things of you."

"After this," Miralla said, pointing to the wrought-iron skull with cedar-oil candlewax drying on it. "And after the party. And after . . ."

"You don't have to come to the dinner," Aelis said. "Amadin and I and the Dobruszes could manage it."

"I am *not* missing a dinner party given by the Count de Lenti un Tirraval, even if it *is* at a distant townhouse and not at your proper palace, where I'm sure the wine cellar alone is larger than the house I grew up in."

"It's no more than a couple underground acres if you don't count the aging caves." Aelis wished she could cram that defensive reply back into her mouth when Miralla's face broke into sudden laughter.

"Gods, you have no idea, do you? Let's get on with it before you reveal how your dolls had diamond rings and their swords had rubies set in the pommel and it never occurred to you that anyone else's didn't." She dug into her desk for her box of pins and needles and other diviner's gear, grabbing up a few needles that sat loose inside a drawer and stuffing the book she'd been recording in away.

"Lewyd's Distance Beacon and Dahja's Hound are not going to do this time, I think," Miralla said. "Set that down," she added, pointing to the Matrix. She studied it intently once Aelis set it on the desk, poking it here and there, running a finger along the curve of the sinuous metal. "Far too smooth for iron worked by hammer," Miralla muttered. "I doubt I can flake any off like I did with that ring."

"I'd hope you wouldn't try."

"Which is why we're going to rely on Sympathy," Miralla said. From another belt pouch she produced two glass jars, each part-full of a clear liquid.

"Double-refined spirits?"

"Finest and clearest," Miralla said. "One for direction, one for elevation." She pursed her lips. "Now we need some wax." She began rummaging about, but Aelis dipped a hand into a belt pouch and found the black stick a hawker had pressed on her in Halfton. "Will this do?"

Miralla turned around and took it in hand, eyeing it critically.

"Well, the color is a bit on the nose . . . but it seems fine enough quality."

"There's a gnome wax merchant in Halfton who'll be delighted to hear that. Now how are we going to put sympathetic wax divination targets on this and not have them be scraped off the instant anyone sees them?"

"We use the natural camouflage of the item itself. After all, it's a candleholder, isn't it?"

Aelis grasped her friend's idea quickly. "We put thin spots of wax, then melt other wax on top of them?"

"Exactly. Nothing more natural on a candleholder than wax, after all. Give me the stick. I might as well enspell the whole block of it. Peyron knows, by the time you're back you'll have three or four more things you'll want tracked with it, and before you ask: make two thin wafers, stick one to the thing you want tracked, carve an arrow in the other. It's not elegant or perfect, but it'll do. Understood?"

"Many thanks, Mira. I owe you more than I . . ."

"You do. And if this all works out and you suddenly find yourself in a position of authority and power, don't forget it, hrm? Now . . . do you have tweezers?"

"In more sizes than you can imagine. What do they need to hold?"

"Quicksilver."

"How much?" Aelis dug her traveling medical kit out of her pack and snapped it open, pulled back an interior kidskin flap to reveal a row of gleaming instruments held in tight loops.

"No more than a few grains."

Aelis produced a long, thin pair of silver tweezers with a tiny tension gear. "Do you want me to apply it?"

Miralla's intense brown eyes flitted to her with the same scrutiny she'd been applying to the Matrix. "Can I trust your hands?"

"I'm a surgeon, you know."

Miralla held out a jar and Aelis saw the dull, semiliquid sheen of the nearly pure alchemical quicksilver within. With calm assurance, she dipped the tweezers in and seized up a globule of the stuff; with quick motions of her fingers she formed it into a ball. It wasn't a stable ball, but by slowly turning the tweezers first one way, then the other, Aelis could keep it from dripping away.

"Now rub it all over the Matrix," Miralla said, and uncapped one of her jars of spirits. "While I begin casting." She settled her diadem over her head, the white gem sliding into place on her forehead like a third eye, its faint white glow suffusing her natural eyes, then took up the stick of wax in her hand. Aelis heard Miralla issuing a stream of words that she could not quite grasp, so rather than try, she concentrated on her task.

Aelis picked a spot on the wrought iron of the candelabra and began running the quicksilver at the tips of her tweezers along it. She was careful not to press it in, just to touch it, as if she were performing the most delicate of surgeries, such as, say, removing a shard of poisoned arrowhead from where it touched, but did not pierce, one of the major veins of her father's heart. She tried to cover the entire surface, every whorl and twist, but found that the coils of iron that made up the Matrix evaded her if she tried to follow them precisely.

She began to feel dizzy.

That's also when she felt a buzz coming off the artifact, then saw the quicksilver she was working with dissolve.

"The wax," Miralla said, her voice distant as if she were speaking softly from the end of a hallway. She set it down; Aelis swore it glowed as well, and she took a scalpel from her kit to slice off four thin wafers. Miralla immediately took one and applied it with the tip of her index finger under one of the holders, then repeated with a second.

Then, her eyes still glowing, Miralla used a silver pin to carve on the other two wax wafers that sat on her desk, her motions quick and confident. She dropped the wafers into the jars of spirit, which frothed. The wax writhed and curled in on itself. Aelis feared something was going wrong, and was about to speak up, when suddenly all was still.

Two black wax arrows floated in the jars, pointing directly at the Matrix.

Aelis wanted to ask questions. *What is the range? Will it somehow convey distance? What next?* But Miralla had not stopped her ritual; her diadem and her eyes still shone, and so Aelis kept those questions in her own head. Miralla spoke a few more words, and in each jar, the wax arrows split into two parts.

Miralla stopped her casting and immediately fell, hard, into the nearest chair. Aelis, not wanting to show weakness on her part, placed a hand lightly against the tabletop and tried not to lean on it.

Miralla held the cork of the first jar out and said, "Seal them."

Aelis did as she was told, wedging the waxed cork into place, then repeated with the other jar.

"Why two jars? Redundancy?"

"Right," Miralla said. "Give the second jar to someone you trust. *Not me,*" she quickly added. "The two arrows in each jar . . ."

"Direction and elevation?"

"Aren't you clever," Miralla said, her breath still coming a little shallow. "I thought if it's going down into a vault . . . or perhaps up into a tower . . . you'll need to know it." Then she tapped a finger against each of the sealed jars, carefully; the black wax arrows bobbed but held steady, still pointing at the Matrix. "Right. Time you're off then, I expect to do things I do not want to hear any more about. And you owe me."

"Three more bottles of wine?"

Miralla stared at her as she slowly stood.

"Six?"

"It's a start."

"Mira," Aelis said. "I'm sorry. I know I've asked a lot of you. Whatever you need in repayment . . ."

"You'll be the first person I call on when I'm going up against a secret congress of the most powerful wizards alive," Miralla said with a wink. "With my luck, though, you'll be one of them by then."

Miralla leaned over the table and put one hand on the cool metal of the Matrix, spoke a few more words. Her diadem flared, briefly, and she took a long breath, then helped Aelis rewrap the artifact. They shared no further goodbyes as Aelis went back out into the corridor.

Once in the infirmary, she was almost glad to find Ryne asleep, still bound to his cot. She spoke with the duty necromancer and looked over the logbook of what medicines and procedures he'd had, found that he'd had some minor knife-work overnight to remove tissue showing signs of rot; it was advisable that he be left to sleep.

She borrowed a pen and added some notes. *Patient is a criminal. Dangerous. Do not allow to go unbound, do not allow him anything that counts as a weapon. Assaulted a Warden. If healed enough for discharge before I return, remand to the dungeons.* She signed it, stamped it with a stick of black wax that was to hand, which made her think of the enchanted wax in her pocket and what uses she might have for it. Mihil was waiting for her just outside, bearing a paper-wrapped package.

"What's this?" she asked. He held the parcel out to her.

"Gift I forgot to bring to your rooms. Got it at Manxam's, but it was ordered for you by your associates."

She tore it open, puzzled, and unfolded a construction of supple leather, black, and wider than she could see an immediate use for. Mihil read her confusion quickly.

"It's a shoulder belt," Mihil said. "Can hang your weapons from it, pouches across the chest for oddments, clever little loops over buttons. And—" Mihil gestured and Aelis handed it down to him. "Your friend noticed you were a bit handicapped in the use of your knife, something like that. So . . ." He tapped what looked like a simple decorative piece of metalwork along the strap that would've sat on her right shoulder. "Go on," he said. Aelis slipped her hand on it and found that the metalwork was, in fact, the bottom of a hilt. She drew a few inches of the blade out, marveling at how it sat completely flush inside the strap.

"A second one," Mihil said, tapping another ring about a foot's length down the belt. Aelis tapped out and felt the same suggestion of give. She drew one out completely, felt its weight in her hand. Only a few inches of blade, not as long or as heavy as her anatomist's blade, and not enchanted in any way; just plain steel, though light and cunningly worked.

"My guess is you could learn to throw those," Mihil said. "Though it's a fool who throws a knife instead of drawing it out and swinging it, unless it's a fool in desperate need."

"Why would I need more knives?" Aelis had only murmured this in confusion, but Mihil responded as if she'd directed the question at him.

"Don't want to die for lack of being able to fight back. If you'd had a spare blade when those thieves wrapped that chain around your arm, you could've filled your hand with one of these."

"Fair point." Aelis slipped the belt over her shoulder and felt its weight settle comfortably on her despite the fact that she was already wearing a swordbelt. She felt a tad ridiculous, but at the end of it all there was a point to the gift; she could not use her anatomist's blade to attack anything but an undead animation, and she'd recently seen how easily her sword arm could be disabled. She tugged at the shoulder belt and resolved to give it a fair try.

"It won't fit right without the weight of a sword on the end. Let me." Mihil went to her left side and slipped her scabbarded sword off its frog, then into position on the far end of the shoulder belt. He gave it a few adjustments and tucked the belt down, and Aelis felt it settle more comfortably, the weight pulled taut against her. She checked the draw of her sword and found it a little higher than she was used to, and she said as much aloud.

"Pretty sure your man Manxam can fix that. Now," he said, shifting his own new belt under his patched coat and adjusting the lay of the fresh satchel that sat on his right hip. "I believe there was a coach to catch?"

"Right. How are we . . ."

"Meet me in the kitchen. Not the refectory; the baking kitchen, down in the sublevels."

"I don't know where that is."

Mihil sighed dramatically, rolled his eyes. "Helpless," he muttered. "Better stick with you then."

20

THE LYCEUM

"The security here really is terrible," Aelis said with some dismay as Mihil led her out to the streets from the baking kitchen. *But at least, for once, I'm using that fact against them.*

"Every kitchen the world over has a way to the street," Mihil said. "Whether one was built in, or whether tired staff figured out how to make it themselves. Now get your hood up and follow me."

"We do have one more stop to make."

Mihil stopped and eyed her. "Really? All this 'we must get out of the city immediately, and . . .'"

"I need to stop by the Urdimonte. It'll take a quarter of an hour."

Mihil closed his eyes, and she could almost see him doing the mental recalculation necessary to get her there, then suddenly he opened his eyes, nodded, and said, "Follow."

They used *mostly* major thoroughfares with one or two detours into alleys or through someone's garden, until Aelis saw with a start that they had arrived at the outer wall and iron fence of the main Urdimonte branch. True, they had to backtrack along it to get to the entrance, but once there she hardly had time to say "Aelis de Lenti, to see the Fiduciatrix" before Carlassa herself was greeting her. Aelis handed her one of the jars Miralla had given her and wrote out a quick list of instructions, and was back on the street with an impatient Mihil in good time.

"What was that all about?" Mihil asked as they plodded off the main thoroughfare into his comfortable backstreets.

"Something important left with people who can't be bought, bullied, or threatened," Aelis said. "And an opportunity for the ambition of minor clerks, who are going to have to stare at a little jar and record any movements it makes for the next several days."

"I wake every day thankful that the gods spared me the curse of ambition," Mihil said, then lapsed into silence.

Aelis thought she knew the city of Lascenise well, but as she hurried to stay behind the gnome's quick pattering steps, she realized she was in the presence of someone who was natural to it in a way she wasn't. She had no idea where they were as he darted through alleys, across sad little gardens, over ashpits and open grates and through markets selling things she didn't want to look at too closely. Occasionally she'd recognize a major street as they passed it, or crossed it, but eventually they emerged at the tradesman's entrance of a major post-coach inn. The coach was in the front yard, the horses stamping and shaking their harness with a merry music.

"Made it just in time," Mihil said as they hurried toward it, and the beaming coachman tipped his hat at them. "Lucky for us, I paid the man well."

"Paid well with what?"

"With my expense money," Mihil clarified, as Aelis slung her bag and followed, shaking her head. She didn't allow herself to relax until the coach had passed out of the city walls. Only then did she exhale and start thinking through the night ahead of her.

However, she couldn't discuss any of it with Mihil, because there was one other passenger on the coach, a gray-robed student. She could not stop staring at Aelis's black robes, her sword, and the slashes on her sleeve.

Aelis tried to busy herself with ordering her thoughts by writing but didn't get very far with the student's eyes on her the entire time. She could see the girl's large brown eyes dancing with questions she wanted to ask, so after a while, without looking up from her notes, she muttered, "Which Colleges are you in?"

"Abjuration and illusion," the girl blurted out. "I'm only finishing my first year. I hope to join warden training next year."

Aelis made a noncommittal sound. "Want a tip?"

"Absolutely." The student was far too eager and Aelis could see Mihil wasn't even trying to hide his smirk.

Aelis closed her notebook and settled her writing-stick hand overtop it. "Start a vigorous program of running now."

She immediately saw that her advice didn't penetrate the girl's enthusiasm. "Running?" Her voice had the same disappointed note of someone asking if a shopkeep was *certain* of the price.

"Vosghez will run you into the ground before he even teaches you a single Combat Ward. Show up prepared, it won't be as bad. You work with a sword now?"

"I . . . don't come from wealth," the girl said. "I'm at the Lyceum under scholarship given by the Estates House, specifically from the Baron de Mentzis."

"That come with a stipend?"

"Yes."

"What've you been doing with it?"

"Eating better. Sending some home."

"Start using it for fencing lessons. And I don't mean with a fashionable small-sword. With something that can hurt someone."

"How will I afford a sword?"

"Any decent master will have practice blades. And before investing in one, you'd want to know what sort suits your arm. If you make it through warden training, the Lyceum will make you one anyway."

The girl's disappointment turned back to excitement at the thought. Aelis

didn't really blame her. She remembered the day Lavanalla had handed her
sword over. It had seemed the finest thing she'd ever owned. It was far from
her first sword; it wasn't even the first that had been made to her measurements. But it was a sword she had *earned*, not a sword she'd been given as a
gift or bought on a whim. The scabbard had been plain, though Aelis had
quickly replaced it with something a bit finer, and the hilt had no gems, no
fancy work, no designs upon the willow-leaf blade. But Aelis treasured the
sword as well as the memory of the Archmagister of Abjuration handing it to
her to fix to her waist.

"Is it unusual for a warden to have necromancy as the primary school?"

Aelis was jerked from her pleasant reverie. "I suppose. Comes in handier
than you would think."

"Does it? I suppose you can summon the various forms of . . . deathly
claws and ritual daggers and the like . . ."

"I can also perform any surgery you care to name and many you can't, and
mix medicaments for the ailments that surgery can't fix. *That* is more what
I meant."

"Apologies, Warden." Aelis must've put more sting in her voice than she'd
intended, because the girl's cheeks had colored and her eyes had turned to
the floor of the rattling coach. "I am sorry for questioning you . . ."

"What's your name, student?"

"Caryn," the girl said, still looking down.

"Look at me." Aelis tried to smile, knowing the expression sat uneasily
on her face. "A few further lessons. First, a warden is never sorry for asking
questions. That's half the job. Second, *weapons* are not a warden's primary
tool. *Ward* is right there in the name."

"Thank you, Warden," Caryn said, turning her eyes away again.

"Third and last, never be afraid to look *anyone* in the eye." A pause. "Unless you come across a catoblens, which isn't really an *anyone* so much as an
anything, or an enchanter who has Elisima's Maddening Eye up their sleeve.
But . . . those exceptions aside—" Aelis leaned forward—"look everyone in
the eye." She held the girl's gaze to prove the point. Caryn looked away again,
but it took her a while, at least.

Aelis nodded and sat back. "Onoma's frigid milk, that's more talk than I
meant to do. Mihil, have we got anything to . . ."

Before she finished the sentence, Mihil had reached into his bag and
pulled a dark case-bottle free.

Aelis accepted the bottle from him and carefully pulled the cork, then
took a sniff. "Pear brandy?" Mihil nodded and Aelis took a draw. It burned,
but had a sweet undercurrent. She held the bottle out to Caryn, who looked
uncertain.

"If you're not used to brandy, I'm sorry that this is your first impression."

Caryn took the bottle and had a tentative sip, coughed but choked it down.
"I don't taste pear at all."

"There was probably a basket of browning pears near the barrel it aged in," Aelis said as she took the bottle back and held it out to Mihil.

The gnome took it and had a pull that equaled what the other two had drunk combined. "Not my fault I can't afford the stuff with your name on it."

Aelis sighed as the girl sent a puzzled look back and forth between them. "I never introduced myself," Aelis said, and held out a hand. "Warden Aelis de Lenti." She paused. "Un Tirraval."

The girl took Aelis's hand and shook even as comprehension dawned.

"Still just a warden," Aelis muttered. "Names are nothing but that, in the service. So help me, if you start calling me Lady, I'll visit Vosghez and tell him to watch out for you in particular."

Aelis must have found the right tone, because the student laughed, the bottle went round again before Mihil put it away, and they settled into basic small talk. Where Caryn lived in the Lyceum; a tower that wasn't near anything, reserved for scholarship students. What had her early classes been like, Aelis misremembering her own as either easier or harder, depending. By the time the coach pulled off the road at a post inn, Mihil and Caryn both had to be woken up so Aelis could buy them a plain yet hot and filling dinner of a stew thick with potatoes and a hint of beef, bread, roasted carrots, and perfectly average wine before loading back on for the remainder of the trip. With the heavy meal and a couple bottles of wine aboard, it wasn't long till the swaying rattle of the coach had them all fast asleep.

◆   ◆   ◆

By the time the coach rolled up to the outskirts of the Lyceum, the sun was setting. And because the sun was setting, Aelis pulled down the partition and asked the driver to stop for a moment as the rise of the road gave a good view of the center of magical learning in the Three Nations.

Towers. More towers than in all Lascenise, for certain, in a much smaller area, for fewer souls. There was something in a wizard that loved a tower, that needed to build them, make them centers of power and legend and learning, fill them with treasure and artifacts and instruments of measurement, precision, alchemy, knowledge, danger, and destruction.

And where there were more wizards per square mile than any other profession, there were bound to be lots of the bloody things. Tall and short, round, square, some walled off inside their own enclaves like keeps, though Aelis couldn't imagine the army mad enough to try to besiege any of them. The towers were not so carefully color coded as the wizards who inhabited them, but she picked out some of the landmarks. Aldayim's Needle, slim, graceful, spearing the sky just above the Dome of the First Art, a temple to Onoma and the building where, by tradition, *all* necromancy exams took place. Gunthar's Bulwark, the most keep-like of them all, battlements and supporting towers and walls, home to the Archmagisters of Abjuration, with a practice yard Aelis knew all too well, having shed a good deal of sweat and not a little blood there. In the fading light they were simply spires and shapes against the sky, no colors or insignia visible.

Caryn stuck her head out the window, waiting expectantly like Aelis. After a beat, frowning, Mihil did the same.

"What are we waiting for, bo . . ." The rest of the word died on his lips as the sun sank just a bit lower and the Lyceum was suddenly bathed in light. On the domes and spires of temples, insignia glowed: Onoma's scales in pale ghostly silver; Stregon's flail in a steady blue; Anaerion's flaming lance in a red so vivid it outshone the sunset behind it.

"That," Aelis said. Even as she spoke the lanterns that floated along the many streets and avenues began lighting as well, giving the entire open, unplanned mess of streets a carnivalesque quality. They twinkled like merry yellow stars.

"When you live in it for years, it's easy to overlook the grandeur," Aelis said. "I'd like to say I meant to pass by at just this time, but . . ."

"But you couldn't plan a piss-up in a brewery," Mihil muttered. "Still, it's lovely."

The coachman cleared his throat, and the horses made muffled noises and shook their harness impatiently. They resettled themselves and the driver resumed their voyage.

After the driver pulled up at the inn that Aelis remembered as being just *outside* the Lyceum, but which was slowly being overtaken by new housing, administrative buildings, and the foundations of one or two new towers, she paid and tipped him for the ride for all three of them. When Caryn alighted from the box, Aelis slipped her a golden tree.

"Treat yourself, and some of your friends tonight," Aelis muttered, suddenly sheepish at her own gesture.

"I'm heading to the abjuration library to study one of the kept copies of Dwergoch," Caryn said, though she took the coin right enough. "But I thank you for the gift, Warden."

Aelis watched the student, bag slung over her shoulder, begin her swift way up the street, toward the first cluster of lanterns.

"What's wrong with the youth today? Going to the *library* instead of a tavern, on her first night back at the Colleges?"

"You hate to see that kind of work ethic in a child," Mihil agreed.

Aelis could do little but sigh. "Let's go for a walk, then."

"What's wrong with the post inn?"

"Mihil, I lived here for five years. I know all the best spots, and I know where we can get the best food in the Lyceum. Come on. It isn't far."

Aelis had to slow her pace for Mihil to keep up, burdened as he was with his seabag. Frankly she was glad of the respite, because she was a little thrown off by the new construction, and it took her a moment to set her bearings between the Needle, the Bulwark, and the Diadem of the Sky, as the diviners called their most prized tower.

The main footpath they took quickly divided into five separate paths; Aelis knew precisely which one she wanted. As they passed a floating lantern, she trailed her hands across the fabric that enclosed the light within, and it followed them a pace or so behind.

"Is this place so full of magical toys?"

"It is the center of several traditions of magical knowledge," Aelis said. "It's more full of magic than anywhere in the world."

"Would not these kinds of lanterns do poor folk a world of good?"

"They might, if poor folk lived around a never-ending tide of ambient magic that conjuring apprentices could turn into wychlight." Aelis glanced down at Mihil. "We *do* try to help, you know. That's what the wardens are, after all."

"Doesn't stop you from living well."

"In Lascenise or the Lyceum? No. But you haven't seen the tower in my permanent post, my friend."

"Oh, I'm sure it's a veritable oubliette. Dark bread and sour ale? Maybe the occasional rind of cheese?"

Aelis sighed. If she were honest with herself, Mihil's words rankled her largely because they had the ring of truth. Coming back south after the year she'd spent in Lone Pine *was* driving home how differently wizards and wardens lived from the folk they guarded. Especially when that warden happened to be the daughter of a count.

"Would you let it go if I promised to make a large donation to the next . . . I don't know, orphanage we pass?"

"No," Mihil answered. "Anyway, I'm just a sour old salt. I can point out your sins all day, but I'll cut the bastard who calls out my own."

Aelis couldn't bring herself to laugh. She was too unsettled, and not just by Mihil. Something felt off on the streets of the Lyceum, even though she'd been there just a day ago. She felt unwelcome; Bardun Jacques's warning echoed in her thoughts, bouncing off the Death Curse.

Her mood lightened when they came to her destination, though; a three-winged, three-story public house, with a silhouette wearing a pointed hat and a long robe on its sign.

"The Academical," Aelis said. "Best drinks in the Colleges, best food, best rooms."

"What'd I just say about fine living? Got over your guilt fast."

"You would too if you knew what wonders the Academical's cellar holds," Aelis said. "Come on."

When they swept in through the wide double doors, Aelis thought for a moment that she'd erred, that even here in one of the most cherished institutions of the Colleges, something had changed forever. She searched the lantern-lit interior for a familiar face, in vain.

Then she heard a booming contralto voice call, "*Lady de Lenti!*" and she let out a sigh of relief.

"Oliria." Aelis turned to face the owner striding toward her, hands out. She extended her own hands. "I am so delighted to see you. Tell me you have . . ."

"Rooms available? Is this the Academical or isn't it?" Oliria smiled, her plump cheeks creasing.

The going theory was that Oliria was half-elven, but Aelis could never have said for sure. Nor could she have said how tall she was, not exactly. Not short, but not towering. Nor could she have described her general shape as anything other than plump, but not really, not so that anyone would really notice. Her hair was dark, except sometimes when the light hit it the threads of silver made it seem less so, and it always, without fail, covered her ears. At this moment, the woman's eyes appeared hazel in the shadows of the many fires and lanterns that were lit inside her inn, but Aelis had seen them at other times and would've sworn them to be green.

"Two rooms, adjoining if possible. Whatever food is ready. And . . ."

"And a bottle of Tirravalan crowberry from the year of your father's ascension?" As they spoke, Oliria had guided Aelis and Mihil into a snug, and they were seated even before they realized it.

"I . . . could hardly say no to a glass of that."

"It'll be along directly."

Oliria glided away, the long skirts and apron she wore concealing her feet.

Mihil watched her go, then turned a rather stunned face to Aelis. "Is she a wizard?"

"Not at all."

"But . . . she's magical, right? This whole place?" His eyes ran around the inside of the room, comparing it with what he'd seen from outside. "The dimensions don't match, and there's so much fire it ought to have burned down twice since we came in."

"Mihil. There's a *lot* of ambient magic sort of . . . floating around the Colleges. I wouldn't get too obsessed with cataloging all of it, or even looking for explanations. If all the wizards of our three nations, and many besides, can be trained here and accept the odd mystery without tearing it down, so can you."

"But it . . ."

"Relax. Enjoy your dinner."

Soon, dinner indeed began coming out. There was no bill of fare at Oliria's establishment, and rarely had Aelis had the same dish there twice. Even now a servant in a long dark robe and white collar glided up with a covered tray. He set it in front of Aelis, as well as a long oval plate that held both a covered cup and something wrapped in a cloth before Mihil, then glided away.

Aelis whipped her cover away and gasped in delight. There were two stacks of perfectly round, perfectly browned oatcakes, and three cheeses. There was a rich Tyridician veined with green, from some seaside cave; she could smell the salt off it already; a hearty block of stolid, clean slicing Ystainian loaf-cheese, the marching food of armies as long as there had been a Ystain; and an oozing

Imravalan cream that released faint smells of pasture and vine and cattle. Aelis bent deeply over that one and inhaled.

For a moment, she was home. In the countryside just outside Antraval. Golden light and rippling terraces of vineyards and red-hatted cowherds urging their pampered milk cows to their secret chosen pastures, jealously guarded by each family. Blood feuds, nay, near wars had been fought over the paths to those pastures. And this cheese was the product of all that trouble.

Aelis felt her eyes fill with tears. She bit her lip and blinked them back.

"I have never been homesick in my life," she muttered, then looked up to see what Mihil was eating.

He'd uncovered his bowl and stared at it, only going as far as slipping his spoon into it. "This is . . . this is Krisindeen hot pot," he said, amazed. "This is a specialty of the gnomes along the rivers and bays of Tyridice. This was a treasured dish in the navy."

Aelis could smell the spice coming off it, searing her nose, and saw chunks of fish and shellfish floating in the thin red broth.

"Of course, it's not complete without . . ." Mihil swiped the napkin away to reveal a basket of crackers about the size and shape of a large pebble. He selected one, holding it delicately between two fingers, and slipped it into his mouth. Aelis saw him shift it to the back of his mouth and bring his molars down on it and heard the *crunch* as he chewed. To her, it sounded painful, inedible.

Mihil looked like he might cry. Swiftly, he picked up three more in his fist and ground them against one another, over his bowl. Thick chunks of cracker fell from between his fingers, then smaller bits, then finally a rain of crumbs and crystals of salt.

"I haven't had this in years. And Midarra knows it never tastes like this aboard ship."

They both ate then, quietly, Aelis marveling at the taste of sun and hay and home in every bite, Mihil taking each spoonful of hot broth and cracker slowly, cautiously, like he was praying over each bite.

When they looked up, baskets of bread had appeared, and bowls of butter and a small dish of herbed oil, as well as the wine. So dark it was nearly black, already opened, left for Aelis to pour, probably out of deference to her family name on the bottle.

"This . . . this place is magical, right? Just tell me that. Tell me I'm right," Mihil said, as he turned another cracker around in his fingers, admiring it.

"Of course it is. But we don't ask, and we don't bring it up, and we don't question it."

"But you're wizards, that's your job, it . . ."

"Because if we did, maybe Oliria would get tired of us, and disappear," Aelis said.

Mihil nodded as if accepting the wisdom of that, then popped the cracker in his mouth, savoring it like Aelis had her cheese.

She poured a glass for each of them and contemplated the nearly black surface of the wine. Before she'd even had her first sip, she regretted that she wouldn't spend *nearly* as much time in the Academical that night as she wanted to.

21

THE VAULT

Aelis went gratefully to her room, saw Mihil off at his, and went through every appearance of going to bed. She unpacked her rucksack, pulled down the bedclothes, smoored the fire, took off her boots and her dress.

Then she sat in a chair and waited, trying to call on some of the calming mindfulness techniques she'd learned as an abjurer. She tried reviewing her actions of the past several days and found them wanting on every account.

I should have sniffed out the purpose of that ambush on the road. I should march into Archmagister Duvhalin's rooms in the Dome of the First Art and arrest him right now. That thought gave her pause.

"On what charges?" she asked herself in a whisper. "Being an asshole? With what evidence? I have nothing. I have to wait for him to take the bait. I must be patient."

Patience is not among your virtues, she remembered Urizen telling her as she waited to see if the results of an alchemical process would be viable or not. *But no one is an alchemist who cannot school themselves to patience while assembling their reagents, while combining them with utmost care, while awaiting the results of oven or alembic. Impatience is the father of haste, which is in turn the father of error.*

She was sure she'd made errors as a warden. Sometimes she felt as if her career so far had consisted of making errors and then attempting to correct the problems she created. She hadn't seen the magic in the gold coins the Thorns had brought back until it was too late. She had been forced to kill Nathalie instead of pacifying or detaining her because she'd maneuvered poorly. She'd had to face and kill Dalius twice because she hadn't been strong enough the first time. She'd unleashed hundreds of animations from the barracks-crypts across Old Ystain. She'd caused Maurenia to be imprisoned in Rhunival's valley and, so far, had no clear idea how to fix that, only impenetrable old books that told her very little.

"So much for mindfulness." Aelis looked out her window into the darkness just before midnight, put on her darkest clothing, some of the new working clothes Manxam's had made for her since her arrival, with no slashes of her alternate schools, only the sleek, dark black of necromancy across all of it. She slung her shoulder belt over her arm, slid her wand up her sleeve, and fixed her dagger in a more prominent position on the front of her belt. She clipped her alchemy lamp onto one of the rings on her new shoulder belt, slung on her rucksack, now carrying only the cloth-wrapped Matrix, and levered her window open.

Her room was on the second story, between two eaves and above an awning over one of the Academical's porches, one she was sure she'd spent many a night drinking on. Tonight, though, it was empty of drunk students, which made Aelis consider the date.

Must be exams, she thought. The timing was right; spring heading into summer. The Colleges weren't nearly as abuzz with carousing students as they might have been. Once the week of exams had been the focus of her yearly schedule, the terror of her nights and the days around which her life had revolved. Now, barely two years since her last exam, she could hardly remember them.

Aelis considered the rather more practical exam before her, and decided on a simple magical course. She went feet first through the window, perched on the edge, and summoned a ward just beneath the awning as she let go and dropped onto it. The ward gave her just enough cushion not to stress the wood and cloth of the awning as she slid down it with ease. She saw the ground, dirt with a fresh layer of crushed nutshells and rushes, summoned another ward, and landed directly in its center, hovering above the ground for just a moment before she found her footing.

Then, adjusting her weapons, Aelis set off north, with the stars, and Aldayim's Needle, brilliant above the huge shadow of the Dome of the First Art, guiding her steps.

She avoided any lamps, ducking off the path onto the carefully manicured grass, or even leaning into a hedge to keep from accidentally brushing against them. As she neared the Needle and the Dome, Aelis felt the ground itself change subtly beneath her feet, the very stones and paths becoming familiar.

Aelis was pointed straight at the Dome, and she no longer doubted her destination or herself or needed to check on other towers to orient herself.

There were no guards, and if there had been, the dagger Aelis carried would've been enough to win her entry. There were no locks, no security, no metal plates requiring her hand or a drop of her blood. The door simply creaked open.

Of course it creaks, she thought. *It wouldn't be a Temple to Necromancy if it didn't.*

It was then that she realized precisely which part of the Dome she was in, where her steps had led.

The Temple to Onoma.

There were chapels in the various towers and lecture halls, of course. But an outer slice of the bottom floor was itself nothing but a Temple to the Goddess of Death, and Aelis had just entered it from behind the altar.

Aelis could only see the black basalt of the slab and the pillars running along the smooth marble floors. Onoma's Temples had no benches, no pews, and no seats.

Slowly, her steps as soft as she could make them, Aelis made her way around to face the altar, which was as tall as she was, and featured in its center a bas-relief of a woman's face, the shadow of a robe hiding her eyes. The face itself, Aelis knew, could look old, young, or an ageless in-between, depending on the angle of one's approach. But it was too much in shadow now for her to see much, only the suggestion of the features, the sharp nose, the strong chin.

Door of the Next World, She who Stands on the Threshold, Mistress of Secrets and Vaults, Mother of our Last End, Source of the First Art, Aelis thought, *I may be a poor servant to you, but I swear I am not come to rob you.* She thought on this a moment. *Only to rob someone who serves you . . . wrongly.*

Aelis winced at her own unspoken presumption. She reached into the belt across her chest for her alchemy lamp, then stopped as realization struck.

She could see.

She could see just as if Onoma's moon was in the sky, and she had been able to since she walked into the Temple. Aelis had spent any number of hours here during her university days.

Never once had this happened before.

Though time was precious, she forced herself to stop for a moment to think. *This Temple, and the facility beyond it, has absorbed more necromantic magic than any other place on earth, save perhaps the ancient army-building platforms of Ghadask, which are so ancient and so little attested that Aldayim, Kheverian, and Diaw put the city-state on two different continents and no proposed location is within a thousand miles of another.* She cut herself off with an audible huff. *The point is . . . this place has absorbed so much necromantic energy, and so much ambient power floats around it, that undoubtedly that is what's causing this effect.*

With two steps back to look at the altar again, still finding the bas-relief of Onoma's face in shadows, she knelt, briefly. She felt a small thrum in her chest, like the feeling she had long ago when poring over books made some theory or new spell at last snap into sharp focus.

Then she set about her business. She looked for exits and saw one, set to the side of the altar, that did not lead back outside but curved inward into the dome. Aelis thought it was the one used by clerics and attendants when a liturgy was read, or funeral rites for a prominent necromancer were held, or whatever else clergy did, none of which she'd ever had a burning desire to learn. She tried it and found it locked. Inspired, she slipped one of her new thin knives out of her shoulder belt, inserted it in the crack of the door near the lock, and pulled it upward. She felt the blade catch and move something aside, and the door slid open.

She slipped into the vestry, or sacristy, or chantry, or whatever it was called, not bothering to question her luck. She felt strongly, though she couldn't have said why, that any entrance to a vault from inside the Dome would be hidden.

Immediately Aelis tried a row of cabinets, finding the first full of dark vestments. She felt along the back and sides but came across no pressure plates or hollow spaces or secret compartments. The second, likewise. As she shifted the various stoles and chasubles and cassocks and robes about, she snorted.

"Couldn't we have a little *gray* or even the occasional thread of gold among all this black?" She shut the second cabinet, opened a third and saw it full of scrolls and prayer books. She shut it without poking around and sighed.

Aelis settled her roiling thoughts, narrowing her eyes till they were nearly closed, till the room blurred around her.

Stop overdetermining. Do not look with a goal. Look at the entire room to find what stands out.

Aelis opened her eyes and began looking slowly, methodically about the room, without anticipating, without expecting, just letting her eyes take in every feature in turn.

Her gaze landed, suddenly, on a row of statues above a door on the far wall. There were five of them, all robed female figures, posed as Onoma's aspects. The first stood before a closed door, one hand on it, the other beckoning the viewer closer; the second stood in an open doorway, arms crossed, hands hidden in the sleeves of her robes; the third stood before a chest as high as her waist, a naked dagger in her hand; the fourth was leaning behind a grave obelisk, one hand wrapped around it, the other held out; the fifth stood with both hands out, one holding her dagger again, the other a small bottle.

With no doubt in her mind, Aelis strode forward, reached for the third statue, and tugged. She met with resistance and had to put both hands on it. She pulled hard. There was a great mechanical groan, and the three cabinets all pivoted forward along the black stones of the floor, revealing a stairway.

"I knew it," she muttered as she turned for the stairs. She was five steps down when she realized she was leaving a trail behind her. As she turned back to the hidden door she'd left open, she considered.

"This is likely not the only way in," she told herself, "and if it is, it has to open from this side as well." She found an iron bar along the back of the block of cabinets, which she grabbed, pulling it close behind her, finding the motion easier than she expected. The secret door sealed shut with a click, and Aelis hurried down the stairs.

And down the stairs. And down the stairs. It was a long way, and she noticed her vision beginning to fade, darkness swimming in, the steps before her losing definition. She turned to her alchemy lamp and found that the stairs she descended, and the tunnel around her, were no longer hewn of the dark basalt of the Dome of the First Art but appeared to be a more common gray stone.

Eventually the stairs level off into a tunnel, and that was quickly joined by a second, giving Aelis the surge of joy that only *being right* about something could. The tunnel widened, until it finally stopped dead.

"A wall of bare rock?" Aelis unclipped her lantern and held it high, spreading its beam wide, brightening it as much as she dared. She swung it from side to side, then down, finally realizing the massive scope of the rockwall before her and then the half circle of metal inset at the center, meeting the stone of the tunnel floor.

She took a few steps forward, looking at the steel vault door. It was runebound, carved not only with reliefs of Onoma but of Peyron, too—with a gem inset on his forehead, clutching a scroll—and in the center, a sphere, inside which sat a featureless humanoid form.

"The Worldsoul," Aelis muttered as she came forward. "It's a . . . puzzle lock of some kind? Maybe?" There were large locks, wheels and dials whose purpose and design she didn't understand. She no longer thought she was going to have to try to break in, but she couldn't be sure. So she did the only sensible thing.

She set her lantern down, sat, pulled out her notebook, and began to sketch every part of it that she could see. She rendered the reliefs of Onoma, in her aspect as Guardian of Secrets and Vaults, of Peyron—she did not know his aspects—and of the Worldsoul, which showed no gender or other characteristics.

From what Aelis remembered of what little theological study she'd done, and the tiny amount of that which had been devoted to iconography, artists of any given era tended to depict the Worldsoul as man or woman depending on what aspect was ascendant in their own lifetime. This sort of depiction, a bare form with no aspect, was highly unusual. Regardless, Aelis sketched it as best she could. Occasionally she would stand to take in a detail she couldn't see well, holding up her lantern with a tight beam and leaning close between each stroke of her stick.

She was so lost in her task she did not hear the footsteps until they were nearly upon her. Her heart leaped and she wanted to flee, but she steadied herself, clipped her lantern to her shoulder belt, and waited.

The steps themselves were hard *chunks*, like iron boots. But behind each one was a soft whirring, like the sound of sand poured through a sieve.

Every part of her wanted to run, because the sound was so unnatural, so strange, so unnerving.

But every student of the Lyceum who'd been in a College-on-College brawl, or been out after a curfew imposed after a College-on-College brawl, or broken into a building to take revenge for losing a College-on-College brawl, or any of the other nonsense Lyceum students got up to against the institution's wishes, knew that you could not run from the Sandyman.

Aelis took a deep breath as the iron-framed glass construct came into view. His limbs were long and square as was his body, of clear and well-made glass. Aelis knew that in places, the lower ends were thickening, showing his age, and on the top of his head and his shoulders there was a purple tint from the sun. The construct's head was roughly the size and shape of a human skull, oddly small against the length of its body, and it had a beard painstakingly sculpted out of glass.

Inside the glass, the machinery that drove it was clear to see, though Aelis's mind would bend itself in half trying to understand it. Each limb contained hourglasses, full of fine sand, and each hourglass was itself encased in a stabilized matrix of curved metal pieces that would swing with its movements. The falling sand powered its leg as it stepped forward, and then the impact of the step flipped the metal cage about and the sand began pouring again.

The steps were solid, hard, loud, and the glasses rattled a little in the iron frames that held them steady. But behind each one was this rain of sand, this nonstop susurration as the machine powered forward.

It came to a stop, looming over her despite being a sword's-lunge length away. Not that Aelis would lunge at the Sandyman, or any of the Lyceum's wondrous Porters. Within the first week of arrival every class at the Lyceum watched as Magisters demonstrated precisely why the Porters were not a target for foolery. Stout guards threw spears and axes at Reticulate Rex, a beautifully ornate suit of black-enameled armor trimmed in gold, and those it didn't dodge it simply knocked away.

Aelis particularly remembered the Sandyman's part in the demonstration, with guards wheeling up an ancient ballista and firing it once. The machine had caught the bolt. The second time, they fired with a conjurer having imparted extra force to the bolt to drive it faster.

The blunt bolt had gotten home, landing square on the Sandyman's chest. The construct had staggered back a step. The bolt bounced off and landed at his feet, doing no damage.

The Sandyman came to a halt, and for just a moment the sound of whooshing sand stopped, leaving a silence all the more eerie in its place.

Then, with a sound like wind across a dune, the magical machine spoke.

"You cannot be here."

The voice was a whisper, but a forceful one. Sand whirred inside its head; Aelis thought the voice sounded like handfuls of sand thrown against a window while the listener was in a deep sleep. The kind of sound that forced you into a reality you might not have wanted or been prepared for.

"You cannot be here," it whooshed again.

"I am a warden," Aelis said, "entitled to go where I will in the lands ruled by the Tri-Crowns and the Estates House. My way cannot be impeded."

There was a pause as the construct processed her answer. Aelis studied the rough glass features of the head for any clue or sign, and found none.

"Wardens may not go into the secret places of the Colleges unless warranted by the College. You must leave these grounds. I will see you to the edge of the grounds."

"I am on an errand from Archmagister Bardun Jacques." She unfolded the slip of paper and the wadded-up cloth. She could not see the drop of blood in the light of her alchemy lamp, but she knew it was there, could feel it with her necromantic senses, felt the vestige of life that remained in it. *Onoma, please let this work.*

"Archmagister Bardun Jacques has lost his privileges while he is under suspicion . . ."

"The Eye of Anaerion opens," Aelis said. The Sandyman stopped in mid-sentence and lowered its long central body, as if peering closely at her.

"The heart of fire burns beneath His gaze," she finished.

The Sandyman ignored the piece of paper she held, but took the blood-spotted cloth and held it against the center of one delicately engineered iron hand.

"What does the Archmagister require?"

Aelis, too startled that the phrases had worked to wonder at it, unslung her rucksack and removed the bundle. It felt heavier in her hands than ever before. Through the cloth and the cordage she could feel the sinuous iron, the smooth curves that could not have been shaped by any hand-held tool. Forcing herself to speak was difficult; her voice came in a hard whisper.

"He wants this stored in the vault," she said. "With the latest shipment from Lascenise."

"Very well."

"He will want reports on whether it has been moved, by whom, and for how long when it is returned to him."

"I cannot promise this."

Well, that's why we build redundancies, she thought. The construct took the bundle from her hands. Aelis wanted to curl her fingers around it, to yank it back, to clasp it to her chest.

She didn't. She let it go, and it felt like some bright hope, some secretly guarded flame was being snuffed out.

"Are there any conditions on its storage?"

That question surprised her, and for a moment she was too stunned to answer. The sand inside the construct stirred and brushed against the glass; the delicate metal armatures clicked and swung.

"Yes," she finally said in a rush. "It cannot be removed for more than two hours at any time." That, at least, should preserve it, guard it somewhat.

"Very well. You must go."

"I can show myself out." Aelis tried to dart around it, but the construct extended one implacable arm to bar her way.

"I will escort you. Wait there." With the Matrix clutched carelessly in one hand, the Sandyman turned to the Vault. Aelis kept still, fearing that if she turned her light on the vault to see exactly what the Porter did, it might somehow ruin the moment. She heard a whirring sound of metal on metal, hinges in want of just a little grease creaking heavily, and the clanking steps of the Sandyman as it disappeared. It was gone for only moments, then the Vault clanged shut with a finality that tolled like a bell in her chest and a moment later the Sandyman was standing in front of her, whirring.

"Follow me," it whispered, and she had no choice but to do so back along the tunnel. The Sandyman went off to the right when the single tunnel split into two branches and Aelis resolved to pay attention to any twists and turns it took.

At least I'll know two ways to the Vault.

At one point as they walked, the Sandyman's head turned around to face her, sand still whirring within.

"I will need your name."

"I am a warden working on behalf of Archmagister Bardun Jacques." They were still winding up the tunnel, and as long as the Sandyman didn't halt and block her path, she did not care what questions it asked. Slowly its head turned away.

Finally, they came to a door. Each of the Porters, no matter how strange their form and manner, had a heavy leather belt girding its middle, from which tools, or in this case *keys*, were hung. One of its thick glass fingers tinked against the heavy iron keys for a moment before the Sandyman selected one and opened the gate.

It was a plain, unobtrusive side door in an alley halfway between the Dome of the First Art and the Diadem of the Sky, and once she had location of that door memorized, Aelis immediately bolted for the path that would take her back out of the Colleges proper and back toward the Academical.

She had to try. She knew what every student knew; you can't outrun the Sandyman. Old Stone was slow and methodical and too heavy to follow you up any stairs. Brass Bob and Tick-Tick were so loud you could always hear them coming, hide, and count on them not finding you. The Silk Lady was easy to evade; get across any amount of water deep enough to get your ankle wet, and she would go three blocks out of the way to try to circle around in order not to cross it.

But the Sandyman was inescapable. Possibly the oldest of the constructs, certainly one whose secrets were well hidden, or even lost. Aelis had read that the Lyceum relied on a particular family of glassblowers to provide the glass panels strictly to their specifications in order to replace any panels that had thickened too much to sit safely in their frames, or any that had become damaged or unsightly.

She made it half a dozen steps before the rapidly sped-up *chunk-whir-chunk-whir* of the Sandyman's steps caught up with her and the machine slid before her, barring her path yet again.

"Do not run," it said as the head slid around on the body to face her. "I will not be evaded. I must have your name."

"Nathalie de Morgantis."

Aelis did not, in general, like a lie. They felt ill in her mouth, like eating cheese a day too late or drinking corked wine. But that one had come to her lips before she truly realized it. *I hope this fucking thing hasn't got a roster.*

"I will have to report this name," it said, in its strange blowing-whisper-voice. "If you run again, I will have to take you with me to report to a warden of the watch."

"Then am I free to go?"

Sand blew around the machinery inside its head. The glass of its face and beard was thicker, and somewhat frosted, obscuring whatever lurked inside, unlike the clear gyroscopic sandglasses that powered the rest of its body. But Aelis could see a faint glow, tints of yellow and blue sparks among the blowing sand.

"I must observe you walk a sufficient distance away from the restricted point."

"Wardens are not restricted within the Three Nations. I have the Warrant of the Tri-Crowns and the Estates House."

"You were in a restricted area and must move a sufficient distance from it."

"Who restricted it?"

Again the sand whirred, again the faint hint of sparks, the sense of moving machinery she could neither see nor understand.

"It is restricted."

Aelis racked her brain for what she remembered of the games students would try to play with the Porters, or whether the Sandyman had any notable weaknesses or exploitable logic loops in his directives. But he had always been the one they'd known the least about, and the one that seemed the most frightening, even dangerous.

She could also see, from the position of the moons and the stars, that she was out later than she meant to be, and that she needed to return to the Academical if she wanted any sleep at all before a long day tomorrow.

Aelis could not resist noting how far away she could walk before the Sandyman would stop focusing on her. So she walked five paces, turned, walked five more, turned, and so on. Until, on the count of one hundred paces, she turned to find it had disappeared.

She made a note and hurried on her way back to the Academical.

She reached the inn with a clearer mind; at least one step had worked. *Can another Archmagister countermand the orders I gave it?* There were too many things she didn't understand about the Porters and the Vault to make any useful guesses.

Aelis also realized that she had no good plan for getting back into her room. She looked up at the awning she'd nearly crumpled. There were no tables or chairs out on the patio, and she didn't feel up to the ward-climbing trick.

Then she heard a throat being discreetly cleared. Oliria's voice followed.

"Come in by the front door, Lady de Lenti," she said.

Aelis felt shame creeping onto her cheeks but she fought it off. She walked around the building and found the front door opened by Oliria, who stood watching her.

"I hope that the hospitality of the Academical is not so far fallen from what your memories made it that you need to escape from it by the window," she said, genuine hurt thickening her voice.

"I could not be seen exiting. Please do not take it as a reflection on you, most gracious of hosts."

"The Academical *does* have a back door, dear Lady de Lenti. A simple talk with a member of staff would've led to you to it."

Aelis fought the wince that threatened to seize her face but felt it inwardly nonetheless. "I am not accustomed to seeking help in such matters."

"And yet it finds you nonetheless. Think of the gnome sleeping well in the room adjoining yours. Does he follow you only for the promise of vines in his hand?"

I have had absolutely enough interaction with cryptic mysteries tonight, Aelis thought. "I don't suppose I know, Oliria. He is a bit closed to me."

Oliria sniffed. "You play a very, very dangerous game, Lady. Your opponents see more of the board and have had much longer to prepare their moves. Yet if you had that time . . . would it even avail you?"

"It isn't chess I'm playing . . ."

"I daresay not. Chess has rules, and prescribed movements, and clear lines. What you do has none of those. Which may be your undoing, or perhaps your only strength. Who can say?"

"I must have some sleep, Oliria."

"Of course." She swept past Aelis to lock the doors of the public house, and as she did, she whispered, "Beware the Colleges, Lady de Lenti. They are a perilous place for you, and they will remain so."

Aelis bowed her head, could not come up with any suitable answer, and plodded off to her room. She barely got her shoulder belt and boots off before she collapsed into bed.

22

VISITING

She did not want to dream, much less remember her dreams, but she could not seem to help it. Once more a labyrinth of forests. This time there were pursuers; the Sandyman, for one, and Demon Trees like the one she had fought with Tun, but wearing the ornate robes of Lyceum Archmagisters, waving Enchanter's Wands, smoke billowing from their mouths.

When she finally woke up, she threw open the shades on her window and found that it was not as late into the morning as she'd feared, but washing, dressing, and, sadly, breakfast were going to have to be greatly compressed to make her schedule. She threw off the clothes she'd skulked about in, went to the bath chamber adjoining her room and found the copper tub full of hot water. With a blessing of thanks to whatever the Academical really was, she resisted the urge to sink into it and relax, instead washing quickly and furiously and gathering her wet hair loosely at the back of her neck. She put on new robes, formal for visiting, equipped herself, and opened her door.

Mihil was lounging just outside, sipping from a mug of coffee that seemed enormous in his hands.

"There's more on the table outside," he said, pointing to a door at the end of the hall that she knew led to a small veranda. "And some almond-paste buns in fine gnomish style. Haven't had the like since I left home to join the navy."

Aelis marched outside, drank a cup of coffee as fast as she could, ate one of the buns Mihil pointed out, and wrapped the remaining three in the napkin they nestled in and stuffed them in a pouch.

"Are we stealing the linen now?"

"Oliria will add it to the bill. Come on, we've got visiting to do."

"Where to?"

"One of my old Colleges. Enchantment. I hope to catch up with a favorite teacher, and since he's a gnome I thought some fine gnomish-style pastry might provide a present."

Aelis didn't encounter Oliria on the way out, but she was met by a smiling member of staff who almost had the proprietor's effortless glide down pat, who presented her with an itemized bill. Aelis took no time to scan it, handed over a small stack of gold and a larger of silver, said, "Always a pleasure. Please tell Oliria," and sallied out into the daylight, Mihil dragging behind her.

The College of Enchantment, being one of the less favored and less well-endowed schools, had an unenviable position beyond the major quadrangles shared by the bigger, flashier Colleges of Necromancy, Abjuration, and Evocation. But the walk there had its charms; Aelis struggled not to become bogged down in memories. The urge to dart back into the library was almost overpowering, but she needed to talk to Urizen again first.

"On our way back, we may go in there. If I stay for more than an hour," she said, pointing to the bronze double doors with images of pens and quills stamped on them, "shoot me if you have to. Once I got the scent of the books in my nose, you'd never drag me out of there. I simply haven't got the time right now."

"Books?" Mihil yawned. "Never saw the appeal. I like a tale as much as the next gnome, but . . ."

Aelis snorted and quickened her pace. With every step she passed another memory trigger—a tree under which she'd sat to read; a bench where she and Miralla had sat all night speaking of their ambitions; a building where a favorite abjuration class had taken place; the tiny, cramped building where she'd first roomed; the small satellite library where she'd done most of her enchantment research and which had become a favorite spot for writing out her papers and theorems.

Even the sounds of young abjurers running on a distant gravel-strewn square, bootfalls hitting in time, and a senior student, probably a warden trainee, calling out their cadence brought back a certain nostalgic glow.

I hated that when I had to do it, Aelis thought, *but there's comfort in knowing someone else has to.*

Coming at last to the far edge of the abjuration campus, she saw the cluster of thin, graceful, somewhat neglected towers that made up the College of Enchantment and made straight for the one that bore the rather-too-grandiose-for-it name of the Wand of Elisima. It being a stump squat of a building with actual battlements on it, students had long since dubbed it Elisima's Molar, or just the Molar.

"Isn't anyone here going to ask to check our weapons, or ask us our business, or . . . ?" Mihil, she knew, wore his small crossbow under his coat and his new knife with its sharp brass knuckle-guard openly on his belt.

"Well," Aelis said, as she paused to orient herself in the familiar-but-still-strange confines of a building she hadn't set foot in for over a year, "in the first place, a warden going armed is hardly likely to excite comment from anyone." She suddenly remembered her way and immediately turned to her left, heading for one of the staircases built into the corners of the keep, "In the second place, can you think of a worse place to come with the intent to do violence than the Lyceum?"

"Probably," Mihil said, "but thinking of bad places to do violence was sort of my trade for a number of years."

They trotted up the stairs, Aelis restricting herself to taking them one at a time so as not to lose the gnome, though it had long been her custom to leap two or three at once. "If you try *magical* mayhem here, you'll be sorted before you can do too much damage. You'd simply better hope the Porters get you before an Archmagister shows up."

"Porters? Never known one to stop a stabbing."

"Well, you've never met Old Stone or Reticulate Rex or the Sandyman. Our Porters are not old men given a nice job for services rendered to a noble patron. More like unsleeping, independent magical machines. But there are, at a first guess, at least six people in this building right now who could convince a man with a knife and bent on mayhem to *stab himself* with a wave of their wand. And we're going to talk to one of them."

"Remind me to keep my hand away from my knife, then."

Aelis found the floor she wanted and strode down the hall, past old banners, tapestries depicting great enchanters such as the Living Riddle and Alphiran the Mist-Minded, stopping outside a slightly cracked door. She paused, took in the smell—coffee, *good* coffee—heard the scratch of pen on paper, could smell the books, ink, and old wood.

She knocked very lightly on the door and pushed it open. As she expected, Urizen was standing on, rather than sitting behind, his desk, with a gnome-height lectern holding papers in front of him, over which his pen floated, marking and notating while his hands were clasped behind his back.

"Good morning, Archmagister," Aelis said, noting that even alone in his office, Urizen wore his new robes with their three golden chains and the gold cord over his shoulders. *If I earned those, I'd wear them nonstop for weeks. Maybe months.*

"Miss de Lenti," Urizen greeted her as his pen floated to a resting place on the desk at his feet. "Two visits in a week. How delightful. Please tell me you bring me something more interesting than Introductory Magical Theory Exams."

"You could fling them down the stairs and grade them based on how far they travel?"

"Elisima spare us all the day you're appointed to a professorship," Urizen said. He peered past her at Mihil, who was lingering in the doorway, and spoke a greeting in the quick, musical tongue of the gnomes.

"Sorry," Mihil said, throwing his hands up. "Can barely understand your accent."

"Where did you grow up, then?"

"Mostly on saltwater in southern Tyridice."

"Ah." Something about Mihil's answer seemed to mark him as someone Urizen could ignore, and he focused his attention solely on Aelis. "To what do I owe the pleasure, then?"

"Can't a graduate of an esteemed College visit her adviser now and then?"

"Well, she can," Urizen said, plucking off the spectacles that were clipped to the front of his long nose and beginning to polish them with a handkerchief. "But based on what she told me a few days ago, her days are likely to be quite full."

"I will admit that my duties are many, and I can't stay long, but I did bring you something." She produced the linen napkin holding the gnomish pastries and it *immediately* tugged free of her hand and floated toward Urizen. "My associate informs me these are of a fine gnomish recipe."

Urizen's eyes flitted to Mihil and he frowned, his lips just barely puckering.

"Mihil Angleton. Enrolled and paid at Cabal Keep. You can say anything you wish in front of him."

"Then I say this: if you are seeking some help in proving Warden Emeritus Bardun Jacques innocent or attempting to obfuscate the case in order to free him, I will not provide aid willingly. I do not like the man; he is a stain on wizards generally and on your service in particular. If you have some questions for me on the case, I am afraid I will answer only through his lawyer. I believe he is likely guilty."

Aelis summoned all the stoicism she could muster as a Count's daughter. She was used to keeping a blank face to withstand withering criticism or stern disapproval or even extreme boredom. But Urizen had known her too long and too well not to read the sudden mask that came over her features.

"I do not say this to upset you, Aelis. I say it because I would like to see you flourish in your chosen career. Jacques has gone too far, finally, and will pay for it. I do not want to see you go down *with* him."

"I understand all that, Archmagister," Aelis said, forcing her voice to become smooth and politic. "In truth, I *did* hope to discuss the other matter with you."

"Ah, good," Urizen said. "Let me pour us all some coffee. And perhaps a bit of brandy . . ." He turned a questioning look at Aelis, who shook her head no, and then at Mihil, who nodded enthusiastically. Urizen carefully descended the steps from his desk and went to the sideboard in his office, which was compact but so neat as to seem large, and poured three cups from the steaming pot Aelis had smelled on her way in. She'd never once known Urizen not to have coffee to hand. But she frowned as he reached for a decanter full of a pale yellow brandy.

"I recall you having strict rules about drink before noon, Archmagister," she said.

"Strict rules are for *magisters*, Miss de Lenti. And one does need an occasional jolt to get through these early student exams. Now, what exactly was your question?"

Aelis looked down at her notes and gathered her resolve. "I brought something for you to look at. And I must admit that my search for the titles you recommended was largely in vain. I did manage to find a copy of another text, Hughinn . . ."

"Hughinn was something worse than an amateur. A wizard with opaque methods, nonexistent documentation. He ought to have known better and expects us to take everything on faith due to his *experience*." As he spoke he brought mugs of steaming coffee to Aelis and Mihil, who took them gratefully.

"He does direct anyone who reads his work back to a basic understanding of Urquhardt and Barston," Aelis pointed out.

"A second-year student of conjuring has basic understandings of *them*. You said you had something to show me, and I assume it's not a dusty copy of Hughinn that would'e been better left forgotten?"

Aelis savored her coffee. Wherever Urizen got it, it was typically the best to be had in any of the Colleges, she knew. Better even than what was served at the Academical. She reached into her bag and removed the carefully wrapped stack of pages. She stood and set it down on Urizen's desk, unwrapped it. He clambered up to look at it, bending low. She turned to the leaf that had the drawing of Rhunival's rod.

Urizen stared at the drawing with an intensity that Aelis could feel.

"Tell me again," he said, "everything about this creature. Everything about your dealings with him, everything he said."

She launched into the story again. She did not spare any of the details, no matter how badly she wanted to. Speaking again of Maurenia's imprisonment, and her dreams—she avoided discussing physical changes—wrenched her heart. Mihil fell noiselessly asleep in the chair as she went on. Early in the tale, Urizen's pen floated to his hand, and he began to take notes. Occasionally he made Aelis stop and repeat something, specifically the distance Maurenia could travel and the things she seemed to know. He showed very little interest in the dreams Maurenia described, and Aelis balked at describing any of those she herself had had.

They're just my mind repeating the things Maurenia had told me about her own dreams, she reasoned.

"This is all very bad, Aelis," Urizen said when she'd given him all the information she thought important to produce. "I am not sure I see an easy solution."

"It doesn't have to be easy."

"It may not be possible."

"Archmagister, there has to be something."

"You *should* have used the rod that summoned it to banish it yourself rather than giving it over. You may well have given a malevolent entity—I am not prepared to commit to calling it a woodshade—the ability to incorporate and discorporate itself at will. However, you suspect it was shed blood that sealed the woman there, yes?"

"From the injury I treated, yes. That was her understanding as well."

"It is possible that blood could be traded . . ."

"I do not think she would forgive me if I trapped another person there in her stead."

Urizen stared at her for a moment. "A year in warden service has not made you a better listener, Miss de Lenti."

"Warden de Lenti," Aelis said, faster and more sharply than she had intended. But she was tired of hearing Urizen strip her of a title she'd earned.

"The point remains, I did not suggest trading a person for her, only that blood might suffice."

"Sufficient quantity?"

"Well, I would not rush to exsanguinate all the local fauna in an attempt to find out."

"Specific type, then?"

"That would depend on the nature of the original binding, and precisely what creature was bound. If you knew that, you might know some enemy, or some creature that had power over it, and a ritual done with their blood might be able to supersede this Rhunival's wishes or power."

"Is that name in any way familiar to you?"

"Not at all. I could assign a senior student to research it exhaustively, if it would help. I am curious myself."

"I would be very indebted to you if you were willing to help in that way, Archmagister."

"You can call me Urizen, Aelis," the gnome said, his eyes flashing over the bright crystal and silver of his spectacles.

"I . . . do not think I can, Archmagister. I was raised in a formal house."

"Right. Well, if you could do one more favor for me; write down precisely where this Rhunival's hall was found. That may assist in narrowing down any potential references." Urizen pursed his lips. "And he appeared as human to you?"

"He did."

"And to your companions . . . ?"

"I . . . never asked."

"The first thing you ought to do when you suspect that you are dealing with anything that is summoned and bound, Aelis, is to compare notes with anyone else who has perceived it. The differences may be startling."

"I do wish I had taken your classes on this subject, Archmagister."

"Well, when your warden service is done, you could always return to the Lyceum and enroll in a new College . . ."

"I am no conjurer, Archmagister."

"Did I say the Conjurer's College? I seem to recall some divination professors suggesting in early discussions of your class that you may have had more potential than you showed. Professor Dondas in particular thought you had intentionally failed an exam."

Aelis smiled. "Come now, Archmagister . . . who among us would ever turn aside from the chance to command a fourth school? To walk so immediately into the annals of history?"

"One needs to do more than pass a test and wear a sword to earn a chapter in *Lives of the Wizards.*"

Not the book I aim to be in, Aelis thought, but once again didn't say.

"Thank you, Archmagister," she said instead. "I am afraid I must head back for Lascenise as soon as I can. I wish I had more time to spend here at the Lyceum . . ."

"You'll be back some day," Urizen said. "Your potential is limitless, Aelis, if you make the right choices. A professorship, even an endowed chair . . . these things are not beyond you."

"You are too kind, Archmagister," Aelis said, sweeping her eyes to the floor. Her heart soared at the praise from a beloved teacher, but her mind recoiled from the idea of a professorship, from teaching, from being chained to a desk and a schedule, with the responsibilities of students and papers and grading.

Urizen, seeing something of the clash in her careful features, leaned forward. "This is why I worry for you in this role as advocate. Greatness is less likely if you are tied so closely to a political anchor like Bardun Jacques."

Mihil suddenly uncurled from the tight ball he'd been sleeping in. "Anchor aweigh? What? Is it four bells already?" He looked blearily from Aelis to Urizen, his eyes red-rimmed and his face haggard.

"Calm, Mihil," Aelis said as she stood up. "But we must away."

"I assume, Warden de Lenti, that you have not forgotten how to write everything besides official statements, reports, and dutiful letters to family?"

Aelis felt a flush of shame. "It had . . . not occurred to me that you would want correspondence, Archmagister. But I would be delighted . . . I warn you that my day-to-day in Lone Pine is quite dreary."

"Well, I will include only one meal eaten at the Academical per letter then, out of kindheartedness and old affection, and so as not to drive you to distraction."

"Truly, there is nothing I would like to hear better than everything you eat and drink there. Or at Tausner's, if you make it over to Lascenise. Or the latest fashions at Manxam's . . ."

"Manxam's? As if I can afford that frippery on a professor's pay. No, no. Roepert's will always be good enough for an old gnome."

Aelis laughed and bent to help Mihil, who was struggling to get out of his chair. "Thank you for your time, Archmagister; I know it is valuable."

"Where can I forward any information relevant to you?"

"Cabal Keep would be best. If I am gone, they will know how to forward it."

"Very well. Take care, Warden de Lenti. I hope to call you a colleague one day."

When Urizen's door closed behind them, Mihil stopped to lean against the wall for a moment, yawning and blinking. Finally, he resorted to slapping himself in the face, a couple of quick strokes, which seemed to get him back to wakefulness.

"A bit of brandy in coffee has done you in? Doesn't seem like the gnome I met on the floor of the Fallow Sow."

"That was something more than brandy or I'm a water-hob," Mihil said. "I'll walk it off."

Aelis set a brisk pace back to the library. Mihil struggled to keep up but perked up at the sight of Old Stone lurking in front of the library, checking weapons.

In many ways he was the simplest and least person-like of the Porters. At least, he was so from a distance. He was a round boulder of mixed gray and brown stone, though one that could sprout limbs as necessary, two of which were at the moment holding several belts with swords, knives, and other weapons and implements absolutely still.

Once Aelis came within a few feet, a face appeared in the stone, and a bright, friendly voice said, "Good afternoon, Warden! May I hold your sword?" The accent belonged to an impeccable great-house servant used to a public-facing role.

She was a little bit satisfied to see Mihil jump a step backward when it spoke.

"Thank you, Stone," she said as she laid her belt carefully along one of his outthrust limbs.

"Enjoy your time in the library, Warden." Then the face rolled its eyes with an audible grinding noise to regard Mihil. "Your companion must disarm himself as well."

"I don't like leaving my tools out where anyone can take them."

The stone face smiled, which even Aelis found unsettling. "I assure you, good gnome, I will not allow anyone else to walk off with your knife or your handbow. Now, if you would."

Stunned, Mihil unbuckled his own belt with his new knife, and his handbow cradled in a holster along the back, and laid them over the arm.

As they passed the Porter and entered the library, Mihil stared backward.

"How did it know what weapons I carried?"

"Old Stone knows what every stone knows, and how he knows he does not tell," Aelis replied in a singsong voice, as if she was repeating some old childhood verse or doggerel.

"That doesn't clear it up," Mihil hissed as they passed into the dignified, quiet bustle of the library.

Aelis hoped the same student-assistants might be on duty, but that hope was dashed as she saw no gnomes, nor any Reference Diviner. She didn't need one, though, for she knew what she wanted this time.

"I need a study room key and the copy of *Primal Forces of Magic*. It's a locked book, so I will need the key."

"Do you know where that is, Warden?" The assistant who asked was a young dwarven woman, all helpful smile and braided blond hair.

Aelis dropped a gold coin on the desk. "No, but I'm sure you can find it." She smiled and added, "Study room key, please."

The student handed her a key and made the coin disappear with one impressively fluid movement, and Aelis led Mihil up the stairs.

"Do you have to spread coins *everywhere* around this place?" Mihil slumped into a chair as soon as Aelis had unlocked the door.

"It's expected," Aelis said. "Makes everything run more smoothly."

"It's a wonder some good fast-talking confidence gnome hasn't winkled you people out of all your money by now," he said as he curled his legs up under him and let his head fall onto his chest.

She decided to let Mihil sleep and waited with her typical ill-patience for the student to arrive with her book. Briefly Aelis pondered Mihil's words about the gold she'd dropped at the reference desk. *Totally normal part of warden service life*, she told herself, but she had no conviction in it.

The door opened, and that dwarven student came in, gray-robed and blond-braided, but grimacing rather than smiling.

Most importantly, she was empty-handed.

"I'm sorry, Warden . . ."

"For *what*, exactly?" Aelis said, coming to her feet and clearly not managing to keep her anger as in check as she might've wished given that the student took a prudent step back.

"That book is . . . no longer shelved. It appears the Dangerous Books Committee revised its guidance, and the book has been moved to a secure vault."

"And how do I get access?"

"You need to submit a request in writing to the Dangerous Books Committee, and have the professor overseeing your research approve it before you . . ."

"I am not a student. I am a warden; there is no professor overseeing my research."

"Then perhaps the warden commander? I am afraid I don't know protocol, but I know that Forbidden Books can only be accessed by writing to the Dangerous Books Committee and getting on their docket."

"How long does that usually take?" Aelis knew that was a doomed question, but she needed to be sure.

"The committee meets every three months. But getting on the docket usually takes two to three meeting cycles . . ."

"So perhaps in a year."

"Six months?" The student tried another smile, but it was as half-hearted as Aelis's question had been.

"Thank you for your help," Aelis said, and advanced out of the room at a pace that forced the student to back up. If she'd been expecting another tip, it wasn't forthcoming. "Mihil!"

Aelis roiled with anger as Mihil chased after her. She hadn't regained enough composure to trust herself to speak by the time they'd retrieved their weapons from Old Stone. She even met the Porter's legendary courtesy with a grimace and a curt nod. She hadn't recovered herself fully until they were seated at the post-house waiting for the coach back to Lascenise. Mihil had fallen asleep once again, and she decided to focus on a different problem.

"Let me check if you are suddenly ill," Aelis said. She drew her dagger, pushed back his sleeve, and laid it against the skin of his arm. While the colors that sprang forth in her mind were not the picture of health, many of them with a dull yellow sheen over whatever color they ought to have been, she saw nothing immediately worrying. Mihil woke up and looked at her quizzically.

"What've I got? The hockogrockle? Don't tell me it's the marthambles. Anything but the grippem; say it's not that."

"You're fine," Aelis said. "But there are sicknesses that come on suddenly, and fatigue is a symptom of some." She tried not to dwell on the fact that in this case, "fine" included a liver that was possibly in irrevocable decline. "Water'll do you good."

"It'd be the first time," Mihil said, taking the cup the server delivered and drinking half of it, his face twisting into a grimace as he swallowed. "Midarra, you can taste the fish."

"No, you can't. This water's been cleaned by Tzat's Vermintide. There are no parasites and no fish in it."

"Cleaned by what now?"

"A necromantic spell. Makes stores last longer. Did they not use it in the navy?"

"Tyridice has never been great with necromancy. Never saw one in the service."

"Then who does your surgeries?"

"Whoever is sober enough to hold the saw straight but drunk enough to pick it up in the first place."

Aelis held in the lecture on medicine that sprang to her mind, sipped her own water, and was grateful when the coachman began calling for his passengers.

Mihil was asleep before they were out of sight of the Lyceum, and despite her notebook calling to her, and her copy of Hughinn nestling inside her pouch, she gave in to the swaying of the coach and fell asleep on the cushioned bench.

23

A LONG NIGHT

When they reached Lascenise that night, Mihil was still so sleepy that Aelis told him to take to his bed and send for her if he felt any worse.

"I feel fine," he said through a yawn. "Just tired."

"I could pop down to the keep apothecary and get you something that would keep you awake. But . . . I'm concerned this is a reaction to returning to drinking after pausing."

"Warden. What makes you think I'd paused?"

"At the very least you lowered your intake. Your color is better, your eyes were more alert, response time and reactions improved, you had more appetite."

"Fine, fine, fine. One glass of brandy didn't hurt me. Just more exertion than I'm used to these days."

"For the both of us," Aelis said. "I'm feeling my own exertions."

"You mean from sneaking out last night?" Mihil paused at the door to his own small set of rooms. "I'm accustomed to taking orders and not questioning them. Much. But you are no sneak thief, Warden. You clatter like an armored knight falling down a flight of stone stairs."

"I do nothing of the kind. And . . . you don't want in on every part of my business, Mihil."

"Why the hell wouldn't I? Most fun I've had in years. And frankly . . . while the beds here don't compare to the finest gnome-made goose-down, they aren't the floor of the Sow either, you take me? You could at least do me this, Aelis; tell me your plans, and I'll let you know if I mean to be part of them or no."

"I will take that under advisement, Mihil. I will. What I have planned next is dangerous, foolish, and unlikely to work . . ."

"As opposed to all your other plans that fell apart like wet bread?" He yawned again. "I'm for my rack. You do as you will. That seems your specialty." He opened his door and disappeared into his rooms. Aelis intended to go back to her own, but duty sent her trudging to the tower where Bardun Jacques was imprisoned.

When she came within reach of the censors and her ability to manipulate magic slipped away—all of it except the Death Curse—she felt the grungy buzz that always accompanied not having slept enough. She smelled food as she came close, and indeed she felt she had possibly interrupted some kind of censors' meal break, as one was slipping his helmet back on, and their nearby table held plates of crumbs and large, empty cups.

"You are late," one of the censors said. She was fairly sure she'd seen this censor before, and that there was a woman, possibly an elf, behind the feature-obscuring helmet and mail. "The condemned is asleep."

"The what?" Aelis took half a step back from the door.

"You heard me. Come back at another time."

"As both his advocate and his physician, I will see Archmagister Bardun Jacques at any hour of the day, and your only job is to allow me in the fucking room. Are we clear?"

"It is not your place to tell censors what we are to do." The censor and her partner had both shifted their stance, Aelis noticed, to make their long blades easier to bring into play, she thought.

"If you continue to bar my way, I will rouse the Cabal commander out of his sleep," Aelis said. "And from him, I *will* have your names, because as an advocate I have wide investigative powers, and you are currently interfering with my access to my charge." She narrowed her eyes. "Do you want to find out how good I am at keeping secrets, censor? I have a feeling in this case I might be just *awful*."

That gave both censors pause. Censors weren't guaranteed anonymity, exactly. Their uniforms and helms more or less granted it to them, but that was custom, not law. Other wizards *did not* like them, did not wish to be near them, did not wish to serve or associate with anyone who had worked as a censor. There were rumors, never substantiated, that during the orc war, former censors among the wardens had been the recipients of any number of awful wounds of spell or blade. In their backs.

"You wouldn't." The censor's voice had that weird hollow quality, but Aelis thought it was a little less than confident.

"Then let me in, and we never have to find out."

That, apparently, was the breaking point. She was searched, had to set down her wand and sword, but continued in with her dagger and her medical kit.

Unsurprisingly, she found the Archmagister asleep. But he did not rouse when she shook his shoulders.

Immediately Aelis's mind split into two; one half that was calm and present in the moment and capable of dealing with whatever this was, even if it was a new crisis, which it probably wasn't.

And one that was terrified that something had slipped past her and filled her stomach with a cold, roiling fear.

She checked his breath and pulse and found the former wheezing and the latter weak and irregular. Aelis slipped her dagger out and pressed it to his wrist.

She knew immediately that he had been poisoned, but she could not tell with *what* or how it was affecting him. His breathing and his heart, yes, and with his lungs already damaged and the work his heart had done—invokers tended to ask a great deal of their bodies—she feared for those systems, and she feared he wasn't getting enough air as it was. She pushed against the clinging, syrupy block that suffocated her hold on magic. She could just barely eke out a First Order Aldayim's Bellows, which encouraged his lungs to fill, and empty, and fill again. That much, at least, steadied his breathing.

While holding that in place, Aelis ran for the door and threw it open.

"The Archmagister has been poisoned," she told the censors. "I need you to cease blocking me."

"How do we know this is not a ploy?" the woman censor said, turning to face her from behind her helmet. "We will do no such thing."

"It requires the permission of the Keep commander, under whose orders the prisoner is held," the other censor said, and she heard a touch of detached amusement, perhaps disdain, behind the words.

"By all means, go and wake him," the first one said as she contemptuously turned her back on Aelis.

"He may not be dead by then, but he will be irreparably harmed. I can keep him alive while you seek out the permission . . ."

"We are not to leave our post except at gravest need," the first one said, with her back still turned. "You were so full of threats earlier; make good on them if you can."

Anger like none Aelis had ever known blew up inside her. Her hands itched for her sword, and she sized up the censor's mail for gaps where the tip of the blade might go.

She knew a mad lunge for her sword had no chance; in a swordfight she relied on wards, which at the moment she could not cast.

Not really thinking about what she was doing, she cast her eye around the room and settled on a heavy piece of firewood. Before she could stop herself, she seized it, marched up behind the shorter censor, and brought the wood down like a mace on the back of that mirror-bright helm. She stepped into the blow, though in truth it was not as hard as she could've made it, nor as hard as she *wanted* to make it. Some tiny shred of self-preservation stayed her arm.

The resulting clang was incredibly satisfying. The firewood broke in her hand. The censor dropped to the floor with a visible dent in her helm.

Aelis tossed the broken wood aside and stepped back even as the second censor brought up his sword.

"Do you want to save her life in addition to the Archmagister's?" As she spoke, she raised her hands. "I'm the only anatomist in this keep who can deal with a fractured skull." She was lying and she knew she was lying; at worst the censor moaning on the floor had a cut scalp and a bad headache, but a dent in the helmet *looked* much worse to an untrained eye.

"Drop. Your. Field," Aelis ground out. "Fetch the Cabal commander if you must. But do it now, because I promise you, I will let her wound carry her away first."

Somewhere in Aelis's mind a voice was *screaming* in alarm, wondering what in seventy-seven hells she thought she was doing. But she was desperate and past caring.

"I will return," the censor said, ominously. "And I will clap you in irons when I do."

"Try it," Aelis spat back, even as she felt the censor's field slip away from her and magic flood back into her awareness. She picked up the sword of the wizard groaning on the stones and threw it down the stairs, then carefully pulled the helmet free.

It was much as she'd suspected; the blow was a stunner, and perhaps her initial assessment of "headache" needed to be upgraded to "minor concussion." But she refused to feel too badly about it.

Aelis went back to Bardun Jacques's bedside and Delved him. The poison was the kind that slowly paralyzed the heart and lungs; probably extracted from some kind of sea-creature that used it to subdue prey. Someone had fed it to him in extreme quantity.

Aelis refreshed the energy that kept the Bellows working on his lungs, finding it much easier now. She considered Aldayim's Blood Purge but dismissed it almost immediately, as the poison was collecting in muscles, not suffusing his blood. She might be able to concoct a cure from what she had in her kit, and she certainly could do so from the Keep apothecary, but that would take hours she did not have.

Casting about for a solution, she settled at last not on a Purgative but on an order known among anatomists as the Lodestone.

Holding her dagger parallel with Bardun Jacques's chest, Aelis concentrated her will through the blade and down the hilt, which slowly lowered until it came in contact with his skin.

She dug into her medical kit with her free hand and produced a clean rag. With the dagger's hilt against his bare skin, she began drawing all the poison from his infected tissues, gathering it together, coalescing it back into the form in which it had been given to him.

It was exhausting; it was pushing a stone her own size up a hill without placing her hands upon it, moving it only with her shoulder or her knee; it was sword drill for hour after hour, till the skin of her palms was torn and bleeding; it was days of running with no break.

But after some moments of this enormous effort, droplets of dark liquid appeared at the tip of her anatomist's blade. She swiped at them with her rag, careful not to let it touch her skin. She watched to see if there was more, but her blade told her that Bardun Jacques's breathing and pulse had returned to near normal, then one of his eyes opened halfway, boring into her.

"What in seven hells, de Lenti?" His voice was just barely above a croak.

"You were poisoned, Archmagister," she said. "And I might've had to . . . um . . . halfway brain a censor to save you."

"Might be time to make a run for it," he grated.

"Best that you don't," came a new voice, as strong as burled oak and as calm and deadly as a drawn sword.

"Commander," Aelis said, rising from Bardun Jacques's bedside. "I have drawn the poison from *your* prisoner. Whom *these* censors were meant to protect."

The second of the pair who had been guarding the door had returned with the commander, who had dressed hastily and looked about as grim as anyone she'd ever seen that wasn't a corpse, and no small few who were.

"You're making a lot of accusations for someone who assaulted a censor, Warden," the commander growled.

"I have proof right here that the Archmagister has been poisoned," Aelis said. "Under any oath you like I will swear to the magical processes by which I saved him. Any diviner or necromancer will confirm what I say of this: it is the poison extracted from the lesser sac-fish out of the southern waters along Tyridice, and it was given to him in a strong dose. Under their noses. And yours." *I really hope I'm right about the sac-fish,* Aelis thought, letting her tongue run ahead of her.

"And yours, Warden," Mazadar pointed out.

"And mine."

Meanwhile, the second censor had moved to help up the one she had clubbed with the firewood, to much groaning and clanking.

"I can treat her very easily," Aelis said.

"I think you've done enough," the taller censor shot back.

"Let the warden see her wounds," Commander Mazadar said. "She will heal them before I decide what to do with her." With a heavy sigh, the dwarf walked to Bardun Jacques's bedside, grabbing a chair from the table and dragging it behind him before sliding into it. "Archmagister," he muttered. "I'm sorry this happened in my keep . . ."

Aelis let this conversation slip away from her as she helped the censor she'd attacked stand up. She was an elven woman of fine features with dark hair cut close on the sides of her scalp. Blood crusted the back of her head and neck from the dented helm; her eyes had a glazed and faraway expression.

"Come and sit," Aelis said; the woman presented little in the way of resistance. Even with her small kit, it was hardly any work to stop the bleeding with a coagulant cake, clean the wound with astringent and yet more rag, and then sew it back up in tight, neat stitches.

The censor was quiet while she worked; Aelis assumed she was still stunned and used the Delving powers of her blade to find out. There was, in fact, a gray shadow over the bright silver color of her brain and down into her spine.

This, Aelis thought, *is going to hurt.* She braced herself, called a Fourth Order Tranzid's Transference—the Refresh she'd used on Mihil's hangover would not do—and dragged the pain, the wound itself, to her. She could not, as she had done for Mihil, spread it out; since Mihil's fatigue and dehydration were generalized, it was much easier. This had to go directly to creating an equivalent wound.

Her first instinct was to swathe herself in an armoring ward, but this wasn't force, it was just going to be pain. She held her breath, tightened the muscles of her stomach, and let it seep into her.

Suddenly she felt as if she'd been kicked in the stomach by a horse two days ago. A small horse, maybe, and perhaps she'd just dodged the worst of it, but it hurt, it was going to continue to hurt, and there was nothing she could do to mitigate it until she could get to the apothecary.

Aelis let her held breath out slowly, feeling it in each rib, determined not to let anyone else know what she'd just done.

The censor, her pain and fog gone, leapt off the chair and turned on Aelis with fury.

"You coward! By my right as censor, you are bound by law for assault . . ."

"No, she isn't," Mazadar said suddenly, standing up from Bardun Jacques's bedside.

The elf's cheeks flushed with anger, her eyes bright but watering. "Then I demand satisfaction."

"You can fucking have it right now if you want it," Aelis said, bolting out of her seat and biting the inside of her cheek to keep from wincing. "When I got here you referred to this *accused* Archmagister as the *condemned*. Then I find he is poisoned, and you interfered in my attempts to save him. After I humiliate you on the green, I will drag you before an Assize . . ."

"No, you won't," Mazadar said again, with a growl that demanded silence. "You," he said, pointing to the censor, "have been wildly remiss in your duties. Your job is to guard the prisoner, not merely censor him. You will be dismissed from this Keep."

Aelis's flush of victory rapidly dissipated as Mazadar turned on her. "And you, assaulting a fellow wizard . . ."

"Who was trying to kill the wizard for whom I am acting as advocate and physician . . ."

"That's a lie!" the censor shouted, and Aelis turned on her anew.

"The next one of you," Mazadar said slowly, "who speaks to me unbidden will be broken from her service, if I have to expend every favor I have collected in thirty years as a Warden and fifteen as a Magister. If that is understood, nod."

Aelis swallowed her bile and nodded; the elf did the same.

"The pair of you," Mazadar said to the censors, "report to your quarters until I give you further orders." He waited until they left, then gestured with his fist; the door closed and locked itself.

Aelis swallowed hard. While not a display of great power per se, Mazadar had just shown superior control over his conjuring with wood and metal.

"Warden de Lenti," he addressed her. "I am . . . disappointed."

Aelis wanted to ease her stance, to lower into a chair, to take some pressure off her now aching stomach, but she absolutely was not going to let herself do that.

"I am disappointed because two assassination attempts have been made in my Keep, under my very eyes, and a warden fresh out of the Lyceum, barely into her second year in the service, has had to foil both. Since you apparently are better at seeing to the security of my own keep than I am, what am I doing wrong?"

"Oh, Stregon's balls, Mazadar," Bardun Jacques croaked, "there'll be no living with her if you start out that way."

"Commander," Aelis said, "I am not a security expert. I do not even know how the poison was introduced to the Archmagister's system. That would be the first question to ask . . . and, Onoma help me, I do not have the time or the energy to answer it."

"It would seem to fall into your purview as advocate and physician."

"It would," Aelis said, frantically scrambling for a way to not say *I am fighting a shadowy coven of wizards more powerful than I am, a guild of assassins, and some thieves, and I need to figure out how to break a curse someone is under, and all of it's on a clock.* "But I have no relevant experience or training here . . ."

"No time like the present to get some," Mazadar said. "Just speaking with your gut; what would you do about the poisoning situation?"

"Have a necromancer and a diviner examine every item that enters the Archmagister's rooms," Aelis said. Then, with a deep breath and a glance at Bardun Jacques, who may or may not have given her a tiny nod, "and . . . I think the censors, and many other people in this keep besides, may be compromised."

"Aelis." Mazadar spoke only after a measured silence. "You are accusing other wizards, other *wardens,* of being complicit in attacks against you and against Archmagister Jacques."

"I am, Commander." Aelis felt weariness catching up with her. "I am accusing them because it clearly happened. The censor whom I attacked— which I did only to force them to drop the field they held over me so that I could save the Archmagister's *life*—referred to him as *the condemned.*"

"That is troubling, but a slip of the tongue does not indicate . . ."

"Oh, come off it, Mazadar." Bardun Jacques's face was twisted as though he wanted to spit out something curdling on his tongue. "Are we so naive as to think politicking among Archmagisters doesn't come down to murder now and then? How many people that we both know would love to see me slip quietly away in my sleep? I can think of a dozen out of hand."

"There's a dozen for whom it might be convenient, but how many would . . ."

"All of them!" Bardun Jacques sat up straighter. "Corbin, for certain. Duvhalin has never scrupled to grab whatever power was there to be got. Kyriasis just to prove she could. The better question is . . ."

"You are giving too little credit to your colleagues, as you always have, you . . ."

"MAGISTERS!" Aelis shouted. "This is getting us no closer to any of the practical matters at hand. If you want to avoid poisoning, then winnow out every source of food and drink that was being served to prisoners."

"Most of it comes from the same stores as are serving the rest of the keep," Mazadar countered.

"Commander, I've been eating in the Wardens' Refectory and I doubt any of the same carvery stations are being set up to feed any prisoners."

"Every scrap of meat I've seen has been burned to a crisp," Bardun Jacques muttered.

"If I throw out every source of food, the keep goes hungry for a day or two. Maybe three or more, and we buy out the city replacing what's here. It's too big an operation to stop and restart."

"Then everything served to the Archmagister must be vetted by a diviner or a necromancer, better yet, both. I cannot commit to being present at every meal."

"I'll work up a duty roster for it," Mazadar said. "But how do we know the assigned wizards aren't, as you suggest some may be, corrupt?"

"I think whoever tried poison is unlikely to do it again, and letting some through would implicate the wizard in question, no?"

"It's hardly secure," Mazadar grumbled.

"I've trusted my life to less," Bardun Jacques said. "But I want you to shut off the censor's fields."

"Conditions absolutely forbid that."

"Then give him his Wychwood leg back," Aelis said. "You can do at least that much."

"I suppose I can allow that," Mazadar said. "I'll go to the storage rooms myself."

Aelis felt something in the air change, something settling over her; she heard footsteps, heavily booted, in the hallway, and then a censor's field was laid over her again. She saw a shadow pass Bardun Jacques's face, saw him crumple a bit against the pillows he'd wedged behind his back to sit up.

She went to the bedside and took his wrist to check his pulse. As she did, she slipped a piece of paper from her sleeve into his while Mazadar had his back to them. She said nothing, didn't even look to the Archmagister's face for a reaction, just turned and left with the commander, who was grimly silent until they parted ways.

24

AN UNEXPECTED VISIT

Aelis trudged back to her rooms, her mind buzzing with exertion, pain throbbing in her stomach, and a growing feeling that she should give up on sleep and just call for coffee. She decided on sleep and was halfway into bed when there was a knock at her door.

"Mihil, unless there's an emergency, for the final embrace of Onoma, let me sleep!" Aelis shuffled back to the door. She opened it and was shocked to find not Mihil but the elven censor she'd clubbed just an hour ago. Without her armor, helm, or flamberge it took Aelis a moment to recognize her.

"May I come in?"

"If you're here to take revenge, get it over with," Aelis said. "I'm too tired to stop you."

The woman did not laugh, but there was at least the ghost of a smile on her fine features. There was no hint of the concussion Aelis had feared she'd left, and probably little of the scalp wound.

"I want to talk."

Concealing an enormous sigh, Aelis stepped back and opened the door wider to allow the elf to enter. In response, she got the least perceptible nod she'd ever seen, a minute inclination of the chin. It was a fine chin under sharp cheekbones that led to the startlingly green eyes she'd only seen on elves or half-elves.

"May I sit?"

"Suit yourself." Aelis, despite feeling weak in her legs, stood.

"My name is Melodyn," the elf said, perching herself lightly on the corner of Aelis's bed.

"Aelis."

"I knew that." Melodyn briefly closed her eyes, then went on. "I owe you, and Archmagister Jacques, an apology. Allowing someone, even a dangerous prisoner, to be poisoned while under my care is an unforgivable breach of my duty. My partner and I deserve the punishment."

"Why'd you come here to tell me this?"

"Because, in short, Warden de Lenti, I think we were enchanted into allowing it."

Aelis lowered herself slowly to the opposite corner of her bed, biting the inside of her bottom lip to keep from wincing.

"You don't believe me," Melodyn said.

"I don't know what to believe," Aelis replied. "You admit to an *unforgivable breach*, your own words. Now you go looking for an excuse."

"Warden de Lenti, I *do not remember* much of today . . ."

Well, that could be because of the injury I inflicted on your brain, Aelis didn't say.

". . . and neither does Holborn," the elf added.

Aelis was jolted. "Your partner?"

"Yes."

"The one who *didn't* take a blunt-object strike to the skull?"

Melodyn grimaced. "Yes. That helm will have to be repaired, and . . ."

"A man was dying. A good man, whose life is mine to save," Aelis said. "You were hindering that work. I had few options. Now, if you were Enchanted, how did someone get close enough to you to do so?"

"You may be overestimating the powers of a censor. I don't feel every spell cast around me any more than you do; only those aimed at me, or whose power I am caught in. And the field requires constant attention, constant power, and a constant struggle to contain anyone who fights against it."

"Yes, your plight is very terrible," Aelis said. "Get to the point."

"It could've happened anytime I was not on duty. Or it could have been alchemical. If the poison came in through the Archmagister's food or drink, why couldn't other poisons or substances have been applied to us?"

"That's possible."

"You would know more about poisons and enchantments than me. Can't you check to see if I have been?"

"To be quite honest, Censor, I don't think I can tonight. By tomorrow the marks may be gone . . . but if you find me in the morning I will look." She paused. "Have you told the commander any of this?"

"I don't wish to incur his wrath more than I already have."

"I don't blame you, but it does seem rather a large security risk."

"When I know if I've been enchanted, I'll go to him. Until then I have nothing but suspicion. In the meantime, I have to pack for my reassignment."

"Why did you call Bardun Jacques *the condemned* when I came to check on him?"

"I told you, I don't remember much of the day. Think what you will of my service, Warden, but I take it seriously. I do not know if Bardun Jacques is guilty or innocent, and it is not for me to decide. In my right mind, I believe I would never have said that."

Aelis considered this for a while. "If you're looking for an apology for picking up that firewood, you aren't getting one."

"I know." Melodyn paused. "You're not going to do an Enchanter's Excavation? You have expended so much power today that . . ."

"If doing it will get you out of my rooms, I'll try it. But be ready to catch me." Aelis took her time gathering herself. Her head swam as she gained her feet. Melodyn stood up to meet her, and they came close, face to face. The elf was shorter than her, which was unusual in her experience with elves. She was lovely; that was not.

She drew her wand out of her sleeve and tapped its glowing point against Melodyn's temple as their eyes locked. A piece of her magical senses traveled from inside her own mind to the other woman's. Aelis felt like fire being pulled by a draft. She would have had a difficult time putting what she felt into words, but it felt like walking down a long hallway in a palace or great house, looking for a door that was open but should've been shut, or that was shut but should've been open.

But when she rocked back to her own mind, and to her own sense of herself, she realized she'd seen nothing. Aelis tried shaking her head and nearly tumbled over with dizziness.

"No enchantment I can find."

"Are you sure?"

"Yes," Aelis said. "Now get out."

"Why do you hate me?"

"I don't know you enough to hate you," Aelis said as she sank back to her bed.

"I didn't ask to be a censor, you know. I wanted to be a warden. But do you know what happens as soon as it's discovered that, as a student of abjuration, you have the capacity to create the censor's field?"

"I'm sure it's very sad," Aelis said, her voice flat.

"Any other training you're doing stops. Alchemy, another College, holy orders. Everything. You're rushed to and through an Abjurer's Test. You hone that field at the expense of all other arts, disciplines, and strengths. If you pass, you owe the censors the best years of your life for the mistake of having their gift. I may be strong in raw power, Warden Aelis, but I know nothing but the most basic disciplines of wards. I was a student of divination as well, and that was my true passion, my calling." Melodyn shook her head slowly. "And I learned almost none of it. I owe the censors four more years, at least, before I'm free of it. And if my punishment for today doesn't tack on two more, I'll be very lucky."

"You could always quit if you hate it so much."

"Under pain of death if I ever worked magic again. There are none of us in the censors who are volunteers, Warden. Think on that."

Melodyn turned to go.

Aelis had a sudden thought. "Wait. Wait." She pushed out of her chair, went to her swordbelt on the wall and drew her dagger. "Let me have your wrist," Aelis said.

The elf laid her hand in Aelis's palm. "You expect obedience so casually. How many shy away from your touch? Wearing the black, one of Onoma's Daughters . . . not so long ago, as my people measure things, no one would've given you their hand."

"Spare me," Aelis said. She laid the flat of her dagger on Melodyn's wrist and, gritting her teeth and blinking away spots in her eyes, she Delved.

Almost instantly, despite the headache blooming in her skull, Aelis's eyes flew wide open.

"You weren't enchanted, Melodyn. You were *drugged*."

"With what?"

"To know, I'd need a sample of your blood. I'm going to write out an order for the infirmary, to draw your blood and hold it in a flask sealed by an abjurer until tomorrow. Then I'll . . ." Her head swam, her vision darkened. "I'll design some alchemical tests." Her brain traversed the foggy landscape of the past few minutes slowly, like a limping traveler with no lantern. "Wait, you expect to be reassigned immediately?"

"I imagine I'll be gone by noon."

Aelis fumbled in her belt pouch as Miralla's words sounded in her head. *Peyron knows, by the time you're back you'll have three or four more things you'll want tracked with it.* She came up with the half a stick of black wax she still had.

Melodyn cocked a thin eyebrow but said nothing as Aelis cut two thin rounds from it, carving the runes Miralla had shown her.

"Do you taunt me with the art I was denied, Aelis?" Melodyn's voice was cold and distant, but Aelis thought she detected genuine pain behind it.

"I'm no diviner. Fortunately, I know a good one." She held out the first of the wafers to Melodyn. "You said you want to make up for your failure today; let this track you, and if I or my agent come looking for you, come back to the keep. I may ask you to testify at the Archmagister's trial."

"Why?" Melodyn reached out and took the delicate wax in the palm of her hand.

"Because if we can prove that you *were* poisoned, or enchanted, or some combination of the two I can't understand without alchemical testing of your blood, it may help my case. It may help save the Archmagister's life."

Melodyn nodded faintly and carefully wrapped the wax in a thin square of silk she'd produced from somewhere on her person. "If the person who comes to me is not you, how will I know they come from you?"

"Pick a password. Right now, something only the two of us know. Write it down if you fear to say it aloud."

Melodyn nodded as she tucked the silk back into her own belt pouch, thought for a moment while she looked at Aelis.

"Daughter of Onoma," she murmured.

"Fine," Aelis said, nodding, and then felt her head swimming unpleasantly. She clutched at a bedpost and took a ragged breath. "Melodyn, I need you to put me in bed."

"That's a quick swing from hate."

"That's not what I . . ." Aelis began, then fell forward, overwhelmed by the pain in her skull, the weariness of her muscles, and the sheer amount of energy she'd expended that day.

25

OBSTACLES

Aelis woke later the next morning than she would've preferred, and skipped breakfast in her hurry to check on Bardun Jacques.

There were censors on duty, but their field was less onerous, as if not extended as far or as heavily as it could be, though she certainly did not test it. Nor did they argue over her dagger.

"We will allow thin threads of necromancy, as ordered," said the taller of them, features obscured by that great mirror bright helm. He unlocked the door. She found the Archmagister at his small writing table, and he stood to greet her.

"Well, de Lenti, you made good on another promise at least," Bardun Jacques said, and she realized that he was walking toward her without a crutch. "Got my Wychwood leg back. Mazadar brought it up himself, gave it the charges it needed to run for a while."

"I'm glad of it, Archmagister." She leaned forward, cleared her throat, and whispered as softly as she could, "It's in the vault beneath the Dome. Confirmed. We can get it out whenever we want."

"And my case?"

"Once I can prove who took possession of it, it'll melt away."

"De Lenti, you already have proof that wizards were behind the smuggling of artifacts, with a smuggler in custody. That alone should prove my innocence . . . or at least muddy the water enough to have me released."

"That . . . is true," Aelis said, somewhat crestfallen. "I'll send for Khorais and have her take sworn statements from the thief in custody. But . . . there are many other plans in motion, things I could achieve."

"Oh, I see. And an old invoker-illusionist would be of no help with any of these plans?"

"I would . . . think you'd want to stay clear of them, Archmagister."

"Nonsense. You get the sworn statements, get me the absolute bleeding fuck *out* of prison and away from these Midarra-damned censor's fields, and then we'll see about the Shadow Congress."

"Archmagister Urizen will soon have a report for me on the curse we discussed.

"Archmagister?" Bardun Jacques looked surprised.

"Archmagister. Something to do with enchantment and alchemy."

"Alchemy's no *proper* magic. Anyone with the tools, tables, and time can make that work." He snorted again. "He said he was going to come visit me, you know. Never did."

Aelis found that statement hard to reconcile with the Urizen who'd warned her away from helping Bardun Jacques, but she didn't press him on it.

"Regardless, he's generously offered some assistance in the matter of my friend. I need as much information as I can get before I head north again."

"Had he any suggestions?"

"Other than make different decisions when I met the creature responsible? No. Something about blood possibly sufficing, but I found nothing of that in Hughinn."

"Nor will you. Hughinn stresses looking for loopholes, actionable points in the compact. He urges a lawyerly attention."

"I had a teeth-chimera the size of an elephant bearing down on me," Aelis said. "My attention was anything but *lawyerly*."

"The answer will present itself," Bardun Jacques said. "Now. Send a runner for my lawyer. Get on with the business that brought you here."

"Yes, Archmagister." She stood and started to sweep out of the room, then paused, seized a scrap of paper and a writing stick, and scrawled a message.

Chances of success?

Bardun Jacques looked at her message, lifting his chin and squinting, then refocused his eyes on her. Slowly, though eloquently, he shrugged.

Aelis nodded slowly and made her way out.

♦   ♦   ♦

She decided not to rouse Mihil and hired a runner from one of the courier services that kept small shacks near Cabal Keep. *Everyone believes wizards are too lazy to run their own errands*, Aelis thought. *Why stand out?*

"Nobody ever lost money catering to the ease of wizards," Aelis muttered as she lingered in the courtyard of the keep, waiting for a coach or a pony or whatever conveyance or animal Khorais might arrive on. *Perhaps, just perhaps, things are loosening up. If I can have Bardun Jacques free before the dinner at my father's townhouse, everything will be a great deal easier.* She had half a bottle of decent wine, the stones of the keep held the warmth of the late spring sun, and she leaned against them as she sat on a bench.

She sipped from her huge clay mug—people stared if you drank straight from the bottle, but if you poured the same liquid into a plain clay mug, they paid you no mind, she had long since learned—and thought about her leverage over the wounded Saltman in custody. She wanted to interview him with Khorais once the lawyer arrived.

"I could dangle lighter sentencing for cooperation again," she muttered.

If she was going to simply Compel him to say everything he knew, she needed another warden present to take the evidence and swear that she had only compelled him to speak the truth, and she'd already asked too much of Miralla.

She decided to consult her wine and found it offered no good alternatives, but it was generally agreeable on whatever points she might make up her mind on.

It wasn't too much longer before an extremely well-appointed coach drew up. Small, sleek, lacquered black and with the coat of arms of some Court Inn on the door, drawn by four matched blood bays. Aelis watched as the coach's footdwarf hopped down, set out a stair, and opened the door. Khorais Angleton, looking well composed in her lawyer's robes, stepped carefully down, holding Aelis's eyes the entire time.

"Pyriot and Gleese travel in style . . ."

"We do when we are *summoned* to Cabal Keep." While her features were composed, her words were clipped angrily.

"That . . . is a poor choice of words on behalf of a messenger, and I apologize. I think we may have a break in the case."

"Oh, do we? Do *we* have a break in the case?" Khorais leaned forward and Aelis fought the urge to take a step back. "*We* haven't been working on it. As best I can tell, *I've* been working on it while you have been off stirring nests of sand-spikes and drinking with my layabout cousin . . ."

"We best have this discussion privately, Khorais," Aelis said, leaning down and keeping her voice low, trying to hide her own rising anger. "Where I can fill you in on exactly why I asked you here."

"Fine. But know that I started billing the moment I left the Inn."

Without any further acrimony Aelis ushered Khorais into the central keep, where the warden of the watch had set aside a small meeting room for them. It had a fire going, several candles standing ready, and the steady blue-tinted light of a conjured lantern hung over the table. A water pitcher, two cups, and a bell sat in the center of the circle of light it cast.

"If you want anything . . . food, coffee, tea, wine," Aelis said, tapping the handle of the bell with one fingertip, "do not hesitate."

Khorais threw open the leather satchel she carried and slapped a heavy leather folder down on the table, rattling the pitcher and cups. "Explain."

Aelis shut the door. "We are going to be very quiet, because there are possibly unkind ears nearby. At times I will merely write down what I want to say and shuffle the paper to you. Do you understand?"

"If secrecy worries you, why aren't we simply meeting at the firm?"

"Because the prisoner whose sworn statement I want you to take is here, and I cannot have him moved."

Khorais paused, hand inside her satchel. Slowly, she drew out an inkwell, and then a handful of capped wooden pens. For a moment, Aelis admired the grain of the wood and their silver mountings. "The what?"

"Prisoner. From the Saltmen. He can provide sworn testimony as to the nature of the smuggling operation. Magical artifacts came to Lascenise, they smuggled them to the Lyceum, and I can prove they've been taken to secret vaults. It is precisely what Archmagister Bardun Jacques said he was investigating when he was seized."

"That doesn't exonerate him if he broke any laws in the pursuit of this investigation."

"But exposing the existence of said operation, or even threatening to expose it, should frighten those who are behind it into dismissing the charges."

"And they are?"

Here Aelis took a slip of paper, inked her pen, and wrote, *A secret coven of very powerful wizards. The less you know, the better.* She slid the paper into the light of the conjured lantern above them.

Khorais read Aelis's paper, frowning. Then she wrote, *Why would wizards need to smuggle artifacts? Don't they own them?*

Aelis shook her head and wrote *Tri-Crowns, Estates House.*

"Just to be clear," Khorais said in a whisper, "your plan to have my client freed is to make a number of very powerful people angry, and to do so using less powerful but still dangerous people you have compelled?"

"The properly prepared and ever vigilant abjurer is the antithesis of danger."

Khorais stared at her, unblinking.

"I'm an abjurer," Aelis added, hoping she didn't sound petulant.

"Right. Well, go have this prisoner brought in. I'll prepare the necessary documents to record the interview. We'll need a witness."

"Will I serve?"

"No. Has to be someone unconnected to the case."

"Need it be another warden?" Miralla would do it, if pressed, Aelis knew that. She didn't want to have to press.

But she knew in her heart she *would* press and Miralla probably *would* do it.

"Provided they have had no connection to the investigation on either side. They don't need to be present the entire time, only to watch the swearer sign their statement, and to countersign that they were not compelled."

"Damn," Aelis muttered. "Well. I can ask Mazadar to assign someone. Would you like me to rouse Mihil? He's been sleeping the day away, but he could at least keep you company."

"I would not mind dining with him after the work is done."

"Noted. I'll send a servant for him. Time he was about the day anyway."

Aelis started making a mental list of where she needed to go; to the Infirmary first, to grab Ryne, then to Mazadar to arrange a witness on the way back. She flagged the very first of the endless stream of Keep servants she saw and asked them to find her adjunct and have him meet her at the Infirmary.

She spent the entire walk making plans, imagining Bardun Jacques's release, the congratulatory dinner she would treat him to, the vindication of her loyalty, but most of all, the easing of her many worries. Putting down any one of the worries she was carrying—Bardun Jacques, Maurenia, the Saltmen, the Shadow Congress, the Hidden Skulls, Pips's future, Lone Pine under Rhovel's hand, her father's dinner—would be almost unimaginably sweet.

She was practically writing Bardun Jacques's speech of thanks, which she knew in reality would mostly amount to *that took too fucking long*, when she reached the Infirmary.

There was an older necromancer on duty there, in shabby black robes; she found him rubbing his hands dry at the front desk, an empty mug at his side. From the smell of it, he'd been drinking some kind of awful herbal tea. *What do people see in that stuff when fresh coffee is to be had at all hours?* She forced a smile as he looked up at her.

"Hello. I need to borrow the wounded prisoner who's been confined and convalescing here. Ryne. Surname unknown."

"Prisoner? Confined? I have a couple of mild injuries, someone fell down a stairway, someone cut badly in training, but no prisoners." His voice was a little slow; Aelis assumed his attention was wandering, nearing the end of a boring shift in another boring day in a boring career.

Aelis felt a cold ball of dread form in her stomach. "You have no prisoners? No one named Ryne?"

The necromancer flipped open a ledger on the desk. "He was released."

"*When* and *by whom?*"

He bent down, peering over the ledger. Aelis snatched it away from him, ignoring his sputtering. Ryne's name and the condition of "released" was so freshly written she could've smudged the ink. The signature was illegible.

"How long have you been on duty?"

"I . . ." The necromancer stared at her, glassy eyed. Aelis was turning to dash away when he fell bonelessly forward, hitting his chin so hard on the desk she heard his teeth click against one another.

Her anatomist's training took over. She vaulted over the desk and assessed the damage, pressing her blade against the skin of his neck. His brain was rattled, but that was the least of her worries.

All the other colors her dagger showed her were turning gray one by one, a tide of gray that Aelis knew could only be held back by one thing.

Everything in her wanted to pursue whoever had released Ryne and the Saltman himself, if that foolish boy wasn't already dead.

But running away would mean letting a fellow necromancer die, and, staying behind meant she might save his life.

She Bound his soul with Aldayim's Refinement, holding it in place despite the damage overtaking his body, and with that Second Order throbbing within the hilt of her dagger, silver runes flaring to life along the blade, she reached for something stronger, a Third Order, Aldayim's Stasis. It took her two tries to grasp the power; the first time it slipped away from her, the words not coming to her command, the Death Curse ricocheting in her mind and robbing her of the focus. She shoved it away, got the Stasis out, and felt it settle into the necromancer's body. Immediately, the spreading gray halted.

None of it *reversed*, though, and the man's life was very much hanging in the balance, but in the moment, with both his soul *and* his body held in her magical grasp, Aelis was doing as much as anyone possibly could.

And yet she still had to yell for help, and she did, great raw sounds escaping from her throat, filling the infirmary and the hallways beyond.

It was probably only a few moments till a servant came running, but it felt like an eternity, like she was poised with a weight she could barely lift in each hand, her arms extended, and that if she dropped one, the man would die. Her concentration, her entire world, dimmed to simply holding those two things with her hands and her mind, not letting them go, until she heard more running feet around her. Eventually she felt both of her burdens taken up by someone else, by multiple someones, and she burst back into awareness of the world.

Her knees hurt. She was slumped on the rug-covered stone floor of the Infirmary, now surrounded by others. A brown-robed apprentice was kneeling over the other necromancer's body, with a black-robed elven woman she did not know but could guess was the Keep Apothecary. After a moment, a group of servants carried the wounded, poisoned man into the infirmary on a litter.

Aelis pushed herself off the floor, staggered, found Mihil standing by her. He guided her hand so she could lean on his shoulder, then turned to face Mazadar, whom she had not noticed before.

"It seems the security of my keep is still too lax." His deep, ponderous voice had an almost accusatory tone, and Aelis was too tired to mind her tongue.

"You're damn right it is," she snapped. "Another wizard poisoned, possibly dying. Try to be less of a bureaucrat and more of a commander." She turned from him and let Mihil guide her into the infirmary.

"I love the smell of bridges burning," the gnome murmured. "It's followed me my entire life."

"Let me worry about it," Aelis muttered. Mihil guided her to a cot but she refused to lie on it; she simply sat on the edge and bent her head back to take deep breaths.

Slowly, color came back to her vision, the feel of the world, the air moving against her skin, the straw-stuffed mattress beneath her, the stones beneath her feet, the smell of blood and astringent that permeated the room, all these sensations settled into place again.

"Mihil, I left your cousin in a meeting room. Ask a servant for directions and get her, please. She is going to be very disappointed. And bring the lantern that's hung above the table." Then she pushed herself up, stared at Mihil until he walked off. The black-robed elven woman she had noticed earlier was standing over the poisoned wizard lying in his cot, an anatomist's blade poised over his stomach. "What can I do?"

"Leave me alone while I draw the poison from him," the elf snapped. Just then Aelis became aware of someone else standing behind her, and she moved aside as the apprentice approached, holding out a small box. The elf flipped it open and removed a green stone that glittered darkly in her hand. She had cut away the black robes over the man's stomach, and now laid the stone upon it, holding it in place with the flat of her dagger.

Aelis watched in wonder as the tall elf spoke harsh syllables. Aelis could feel the necromantic power moving through the stone and the woman who held it, and wondered if she could match the feat she was seeing. *Not right now*, she thought. *But if I was fresh?* "I never thought I'd see a Sovereign Stone," she murmured.

"It's kept locked in the cage." The apprentice overheard, and turned to her, eyes wide. "Only the Keep Apothecary may unseal it."

They both watched the man's stomach convulse, saw the veins and arteries of his wrists and neck and forehead bulge and move strangely. The stone that lay against his skin gleamed, something like smoke moving behind its facets. The elf bent over the stone, her fingertips barely stroking its surface; her dagger's blade blazed with the light of its runes.

Suddenly, she stopped. She scooped the stone up and held it out toward her apprentice, who stared at her dumbly.

"The box, idiot!" The apprentice quickly snapped it open. The Apothecary all but threw the stone in, and Aelis heard it hiss against the velvet lining. The elf shook her hand as if it had been burned.

"Warden de Lenti," she said as she continued to cool her fingers. "What you did earlier . . . That was . . . powerful work. If Hristo lives, he will owe you many thanks."

"Thank you," Aelis answered. "Commanding a Sovereign Stone is impressive."

"Well, it is not as crude as the binding and the stasis at once, by yourself; did it not occur to you to attempt to draw from the power in the Necromantic Circle?"

Aelis was surprised. "There's . . . a circle inside the infirmary?"

"Well, to be precise, the infirmary is inside a Necromantic Circle. It's all beneath the stones, you see. Had no one told you?"

"Not until this very moment." She was trying very hard not to grit her teeth. "You would think it might be mentioned to visiting necromancers."

"We are somewhat set in our ways here. We don't always think of the more obvious things when someone joins us."

"Perhaps there should be a folder of orientation documents," Aelis said.

"What an excellent idea. You should suggest it to the commander."

"I will do that." Aelis had the sense she was speaking to a superior on at least one axis, and it was all she could do to force the words out through clenched teeth.

The Apothecary hefted the box. "Best get this back to the cage and the dampeners in its lockbox." She swept out of the room, a half cloak that was just a step closer to charcoal gray than true black flaring from her shoulders.

Aelis admired the sense of style but wanted to scream. *What a lax, vain, ridiculous post this is! Living so far from danger that they don't even take it seriously when it tries to kill their own.*

"Excuse me, Warden de Lenti . . ." She turned to find the apprentice staring at her. "You really did hold the Binding *and* the Stasis at once. Why? And how?"

"The Binding because I needed his soul . . ."

"*Anima*," the apprentice muttered, with the reflexive debate-me energy of the student. Aelis knew it well, having indulged in it herself, but at the moment her eyes widened in anger and he recoiled.

The apprentice looked as if he wanted to say more, but she brushed past him, because Mihil was leading Khorais in. The lawyer's eyes were heavy-lidded with anger.

"Warden. I take it we won't be meeting this witness."

"No. But I think we have a case anyway. At least a circumstantial one."

"Oh yes, *circumstantial* evidence. Judges, especially those of a secret wizard court, simply love that. Can't get enough of it."

"Hear me out," Aelis said, "while we talk to the third person who was poisoned by unknown actors in pursuit of this case. I can produce all three of them."

"The words are only just out of your mouth and I already don't believe them." Khorais took a step closer to Aelis and suddenly reminded her of Urizen, demonstrating that trick of forcing the taller person to adjust their eyeline. Perhaps it was something gnomes learned to be taken seriously by taller folk.

"Listen to me," Khorais hissed. "This case is a loser. I don't like admitting that, because I don't like losing. But the Archmagister needs to admit guilt and plead for mercy."

"No."

"No? Do you think you have veto power over the legal strategy?"

"You say you hate losing, Khorais. Everyone hates losing. Not everyone feels sickened by it. I don't admit the possibility, do you understand? Now, we're going to talk to the necromancer who was just poisoned. Quickly, while his memory might still hold something."

She set off and Khorais was forced to hurry after her to keep up as she went to Hristo's bedside. He was asleep.

Aelis was about to seize Hristo's wrist when the student assistant came hurrying over, his brown robes billowing.

"Warden de Lenti, please, the man's condition is very fragile! He needs rest."

"You'll do then. What's your name?"

"Malcon de Maunsel, Third-Year Necromancy—" Aelis cut him off with a stare.

"Malcon de Maunsel, meet Khorais Angleton. She's representing Bardun Jacques, and I need you to confirm some facts for her."

Malcon gave Khorais a small bow. For her part, she hopped onto an empty cot and unslung her bag to draw out paper, pen, and ink.

"Malcon, this man was poisoned, yes?"

"Oh, definitely," the apprentice answered. "We are not sure with what. It may have been Hanged Man's Blood."

Khorais's pen stopped and she looked up abruptly. "That is not a real poison."

"It is," Aelis said. "And you do *not* want to know how it's made."

"It isn't . . . the blood of a hanged man, is it?"

"Not *only* his blood," Aelis said. "But note at least that it is a very expensive and very deadly poison. And I thought it was sac-fish bile. Doesn't matter." *If that little pest Malcon is right, I will be so angry*, Aelis thought.

Khorais went back to writing, but Aelis thought she caught a hint of the gnome suppressing a shiver.

"This man was poisoned. And just before the poison took effect, he had released a prisoner . . ."

"Patient," Malcon corrected her.

"A prisoner," Aelis went on, "whose testimony I was counting on."

"What a coincidence," Malcon muttered.

"*Is it?* He was not scheduled to be released. He had been arrested on my authority; I should have been told, and I would've stopped it. Malcon, would you be so kind as to get the log from the front desk?"

When the apprentice vanished, Aelis turned to Mihil. "Lantern?" From under his coat, he produced the still glowing conjured light that had hung above the table where she and Khorais had met. She seized a blanket off the nearest cot and shrouded it, then went to a casket bracketed to the wall and rummaged in it. She pulled out a small wooden box, set the blanket-wrapped lantern on the floor, and surrounded it with a circle of dust poured from the box.

"Silver salt," she said, "excellent for preventing putrefaction in a wound, and for clearing out suppurating pus and the like. It also just cut off the sight and hearing of whoever was spying through it. Mihil, I cannot leave here just yet, so if you would be so kind as to go to the warden of the watch and ask for Warden Miralla Despatia, please."

"Aye," Mihil said, knuckling his forehead as he went.

It was about then that Malcon returned with the log. Aelis took it from him and looked over the pages authorizing the release of two prisoners.

"Look," she said, turning it toward Khorais. "Is any of that legible?"

"Not especially."

"Because the prisoner was not legitimately released, and the man respon-sible for ensuring his health and safety had been poisoned. If I hadn't hap-pened upon him, he'd be dead."

"I see what you are getting at, Aelis, but . . ."

"Yesterday, Bardun Jacques himself was poisoned, and so were his guard-ing censors. Someone has penetrated the defenses of Cabal Keep to attempt to either kill him, or to interfere with my ability to act as his advocate. Surely this is a pattern."

"It might be," Khorais admitted. "But you would have to be able to prove all three incidents happened."

"I can do that."

"And are linked . . ."

". . . I can make people strongly suspect that."

Khorais eyed her. "You aren't allowed to use magic in court."

"I'm not enough of an enchanter for that anyway."

"Fine. We can pursue this angle; it may muddy the waters long enough for you to produce something better."

"At this point, that's all I can really ask for," Aelis admitted.

Mihil led Miralla in just as Khorais was packing up to leave. From the set of her friend's mouth, Aelis knew she wasn't happy.

"Sorry to drag you from . . . an early dinner?" Aelis's guess was haphazard at best. She really had no idea what time it was.

"With a *friend*," Miralla said.

"I'm sorry, Mira. I strongly suspect I was just spied upon in a meeting." She pointed to the blanket inside its tiny circle of silver salt.

"By a blanket?"

"Underneath the blanket is a conjured-light lamp from a meeting room."

Miralla immediately bent over the blanket, pulling up a corner until she could just make out the soft blue glow behind the glass. She stroked her fin-gers over its surface; Aelis saw her eyes shimmer with white when Miralla looked up at her, nodding somberly.

"There's a full scrying suite in that lamp. I suspect the edges of the glass and the inside of the iron, rune-etched to make it easier. The Long Eye, of course, but also the Wordfetch and Obscurant Mirror just in case anyone attempted to backtrack . . ."

"Excellent. I'll be taking that lantern into evidence. Would you be so kind, Warden Despatia, as to take me to where I can get a null-cage to store it in?"

"Absolutely, Warden de Lenti."

"I'm even more in your debt, Mira," Aelis murmured as Miralla straight-ened her back and walked past her on her way out of the room.

"You have no idea how deeply." Miralla's voice was positively acid now.

Aelis quickly wrapped the lantern back up in the blanket and tucked it under her arm, hustling out behind Miralla. Mihil sighed heavily and fol-lowed them.

Commander Mazadar was waiting just outside the door, his thick arms crossed over his chest.

"I have not given you permission to leave, Warden de Lenti," he said.

"I didn't ask for it, Commander," she shot back. "I am not asking you for anything pursuant to my investigation any longer."

"If you take that tone with me, I will . . ."

"Do *what?*" Aelis wheeled on him, letting her frustration and anger shatter whatever last bits of decorum she had been clinging to. "Allow *another* wizard under your command to be poisoned? Do *nothing* about it? Take no measures to improve security because doing so might mean taking *responsibility* for this keep and the souls within? I am not impressed by bureaucrats, Commander. No matter how much conjuring they show off . . ."

Aelis felt the air around her stiffen and her words stalled in her throat. A cuff of air, unbreakable, irresistible, wrapped around her ankle.

"Listen to me, Warden de Lenti, I will not be spoken to . . ."

Aelis's attention was focused on the furious dwarf who was but a step away from her. Mihil was suddenly standing in front of Mazadar.

With his handbow. Loaded, charged, and scant inches away from the commander's eye. She hadn't even seen him move.

"I've seen abjurers at work," the gnome said, very calmly. "I know it's impressive. But is it 'stop a gnomish handbow from this close' impressive?" Mihil clicked his tongue. "I have my doubts."

Aelis felt the cuff unwind from her ankle, and the fingers of air that stopped her throat dissipate.

"De Lenti," Mazadar said, "I know your tagalong is *not* pointing a weapon at me."

"For what it's worth, Commander," Miralla's voice came from down the hallway, "*you* were using magic against a fellow wizard, a warden engaging in her formal duties, with no warning, no formal challenge, and without any reasonable suspicion of criminal behavior. *That* is a crime. And I witnessed it."

"This is insubordination," Mazadar growled. "I will . . ."

"Be lucky not to impale your eye on this bolt if it bulges any further," Mihil said softly. Aelis's mind was spinning in many directions, but she could not ignore how danger transformed her companion. Mihil's voice was steady, detached, calm. His hands did not shake. Since he'd drawn his bow, either too fast or too subtly for her or anyone else to have noticed, she didn't think he had moved.

"This is madness," Aelis said softly. "It is not insubordination to let slip hasty words. Put your bow away, Mihil, please."

The weapon disappeared under his coat like it had never been seen at all.

Mazadar's glare didn't diminish an iota as Mihil stepped off into the shadows. "I will not forget this." His voice grated like stone against iron.

"Neither will we," Aelis answered him. Mazadar turned and strode away.

There was silence in the corridor for a long moment.

"Once you've got sparks caught on the tinder, why not throw some oil on it?" Mihil's voice had its mocking quality back.

Miralla turned and stalked down the corridor so fast that Aelis had to hurry to catch up. She knew just from the cadence of Miralla's footfalls that her friend was furious.

"Mira, I'm . . ."

"Just don't, Aelis," she said as she turned and headed up the stairs. "Let's get that thing in a cage, and I can worry about what I've just done to my career later."

"You haven't done anything to your . . ."

Miralla's pace increased and Aelis decided to drop the subject, though it ate at her. Mazadar had been negligent in his duty, he obviously had terribly lax security, and he didn't appear to be taking steps to fix it.

Generally, one's career is not advanced when an associate points a weapon at the commander of Cabal Keep North, who may have a direct say in your next assignment, or even your continued service.

Miralla led them up two floors, to a locked gate in front of a locked door, both of which answered to keys from her belt.

"Wait here," she said, and Aelis peeked over her shoulder into the storeroom.

It was a treasure trove of magical and alchemical equipment. She saw orreries, alembics, beakers, flasks, ring burners, and alchemy lamps aligned on racks. Numerous books, chests that must have contained alchemical ingredients, and racks of weapons; swords long and short, axes, even a Dwarven mattock-spade with a curved pick at one end and a flattened blade on the other.

"I didn't even think those were *real*," she muttered. "How would anyone even wield it?"

She could only see a tiny part of the storeroom, but the lure of iron-bound chests full of ingredients was strong, and she was just about to pop in and have a look at them when Miralla returned, blocking her view and firmly closing the door behind her.

She held a cedar box, slid the top open. Aelis tossed away the blanket and slipped the lantern into the box. The top of the box went back into place and Aelis had to work embarrassingly hard to seize on a single First Order ward and discharge it. She felt it engage and the box let out a faint chiming note.

They both kept hold of the box.

"If you're entering this into evidence . . ."

"Not here," Aelis said. "I don't trust the security in this keep."

"What place could possibly be safer?"

"A place where three people haven't been poisoned in the past day. A place where my conversations with the lawyer I am meant to work with aren't being spied upon."

Miralla clearly didn't relish the argument, so she let go. "I am certain that by now my companion has either fallen asleep or abandoned me," She turned the full force of her glare on Aelis and walked away.

"Still on for dinner tomorrow night?" Aelis tried not to sound too plaintive as she called after her.

"Maybe."

26

TIRED OF FOLLOWING ORDERS

Mihil tailed Aelis silently back to her rooms. They didn't see even a single servant on the way.

They didn't talk until she had closed and warded her door.

"Where are you taking that?" Mihil asked, pointing a finger at the box under her arm.

"Nowhere," Aelis said. "I'm going to lock it in the chest and sleep with my arm around it tonight. And in the morning, I am going to make anyone who is watching think I am taking it to Manxam's."

"Do I want to know?"

"There are ways for wizards to know I am carrying a null-cage with me . . . that's a catchall term for anything that dampens the magical potential of an artifact, possibly to nothing, using any of a variety of techniques. This box, for instance, is two layers of cedar built over a latticework of silver and thinnest glass filled with silver and copper dust, and . . ."

"Pretend I don't care about any of that," Mihil said.

Aelis frowned. "At any rate . . . I am going to have a null-cage with me. *Two* of them. Then I am going to keep one of them with me and bring it back here. If anyone *is* watching me with magical eyes, they shouldn't have any reason to suspect I'd leave it at a tailor's, and I'll do my best to make them think I'm carrying it everywhere I can."

"If you had one already, why didn't you use it for this lantern?"

"It is . . . occupied."

Mihil narrowed his eyes. "Do I want to know with what?"

"You'd probably sleep better if you didn't."

"What will happen if someone does come here looking for . . . whatever it is you've already got?"

Then I guess they'll learn whether they can fight the spirit that possessed Dalius. "I'm not sure, but . . ." Aelis winced. "It'd be bad."

"Right. I definitely don't want to know." He looked at the door, then back at her. "Listen, boss . . . I think it might be best, sleeping wise, if I stayed here. I can bunk in a chair easy enough. Just . . ."

"No one is coming to murder me in my sleep, Mihil."

"I'm not worried about *you*. I'm the one just threatened the commander, eh? He didn't seem like the type to hold a grudge so much as the type to immediately settle scores . . ."

"He's at the top of my chain of command, but as an advocate I have wide latitude. He can't order me to do things that interfere with that mission. And he certainly isn't going to have my adjunct murdered in the keep. However, if it will make you feel better, you may certainly move in here."

"Still strikes me odd that a warden accused of serious crimes gets another warden *solely* devoted to their defense. Does anyone else in all three realms get such personal service?"

"I imagine one of the crowns or a prominent member of the Estates House might have access to an advocate if they were credibly accused of a crime, though most would have a wizard adviser already."

Mihil shook his head. "Best of everything for you lot, eh? Magical servants, magical inns, endless amounts of good grub, good wine . . ."

"We provide a lot to the three realms, Mihil."

"I saw wardens in action in the war. No lives saved by your black-clad lot, but plenty claimed by fire-throwing red-robes, and ships kept afloat only because a wood or water conjurer was belowdecks. I know what they can do, when they've a mind. But when you put this many of them in one place, so much power, it just . . . it makes everyone in its orbit a *little* bit shittier. And since people are all pretty shitty to start with . . . I'd bet your commander there has the best intentions, largely. But he's got a career to think on, promotion and glory . . ."

"I'm trying to help a man here, Mihil. A man who means a great deal to me, to my service, and who was wrongfully stitched up by other wizards, *truly* grasping, avaricious, power hungry, mean-minded wizards."

Mihil shrugged. "What would I know about any of it? I just wonder if you aren't doing the world more good up at your tower in the wilderness than you would be here. I wonder if you don't like yourself better up there, too." He looked at the door. "Suppose I'll chance my own room. Been too long since I had one, and I owe you for that. Coming with you in the morning?"

"I would like you to accompany me as an extra set of eyes, yes. But I'd mostly like for you to follow at a distance, see if you can spot any tails, anything out of the ordinary. Then I want to put you in touch with my friends, so you can join them on the carriage we'll be taking to dinner."

"Through the servants' entrance, I take it?"

"My father won't allow you armed through the front door. But going in the back door, you and the Dobruszes can bring in as much ironmongery as you like."

"My handbow and knife are all I'll need."

"Well, I'm sure Timmuk and Andresh will each carry enough for you in the bargain. Good night, Mihil."

The gnome left but returned soon enough with his seabag slung over one shoulder and his old, hole-ridden boots dangling from one hand.

"Appears my quarters are no longer mine, by order of the commander. I'm supposed to vacate the premises but . . . I don't feel like following his orders."

"You know what? Neither do I," Aelis said, closing and warding the door behind him. Then she returned to brooding over the events of the day.

"I should've checked on the prisoner earlier in the day. First thing. Or last night," Aelis said suddenly.

"Won't help to second-guess yourself."

"Lives depend on me getting things right, Mihil."

"And lives are going to be lost even if you get *everything* right, boss."

"What's going to become of Ryne? What's going to become of the woman whose hand I cut off? What is . . ."

Mihil clicked his tongue to slow her recriminations. "Both of them were trying to kill you. Can't afford to lose sleep over defending yourself. Should you have gone to see that prisoner earlier? Maybe. But did you really have any reason to suspect someone would be listening to you and Khorais?"

Aelis sighed. "Let's just order dinner and then I'll stew in silence."

Mihil stared at her. "You have handed me a pun, boss. I won't take it up, because I'm a gnome of taste and refinement." He pulled the bell to summon a servant.

Aelis ate and drank without tasting or even noticing what was sent up, keeping her doubts and recriminations to herself. She was in bed preparing for a dark and hopefully dreamless sleep when she bolted upright and seized her alchemy lamp.

"What is it, boss?" Mihil came quickly to wakefulness, bouncing out of the chair he'd curled up in.

"I want to make sure I can track down the necromancer who was poisoned in case someone tries to get him away from me." She got up and went to her swordbelt, hanging on the wall, rifling through it till she found the nearly spent block of black wax. She hoped Miralla's magic was still potent.

"Need a watchful eye?"

Aelis frowned. When she'd first arrived at Lascenise, the idea that she'd need someone to watch her back inside the walls of Cabal Keep would've seemed absurd.

"Probably best," she said, took down her swordbelt, and buckled it on.

◆　◆　◆

The necromancer who had been poisoned was still under care, but sat propped up in his cot, reading by conjured lantern. As she came into his circle of light, he attempted to stand up, but Aelis, like any good physician, urged him back into bed.

"You had a rather close brush with death, man," she said. "No need to be on your feet just yet."

"That isn't true, Warden," he said. "First, of course, is that there's always too much work to do around here, and too few hands. I intend to take my shift tomorrow." Aelis glanced around at the otherwise empty beds, the perfectly clean floor, and the presumably well-stocked medicine cabinets and supply chests in the infirmary.

"Second is that I need to properly thank the warden who saved my life," he added, reaching for her hand and clutching it in his. Aelis resisted the urge to pull away from his soft, clammy hands. "I am in your debt, Warden . . ."

"De Lenti," Aelis said, "and I promise that you aren't. I only did what any necromancer would've done for another."

"Nonsense! He finally let go her hand and Aelis discreetly dried her palm on her robe. The Refinement *and* the Stasis? At once? And for as long as you did?" He gave his head a shake. "That is impressive stuff."

"It was the Apothecary who cleansed the poison using a Sovereign Stone," Aelis said. "I only kept you alive until that moment."

"Anyone can command a Sovereign Stone," he said, waving her protestation away. "Not everyone can demonstrate the power, control, and clarity of mind that you did."

"If you say so, ah . . ."

"Hristo Osiric," he said. "Please call me Hristo."

"Well, Hristo . . . can you go over the events that led to the release of the patient?"

His brow furrowed, as if thinking on this problem caused him a great deal of irritation, if not outright pain.

"It is . . . hard to grasp," he said. "I got a cup of tea sent up from the refectory and then a stranger appeared . . . when I try to recall him, I simply cannot." His face screwed up in concentration. "You know, I don't even know if it was a *he*."

"And this stranger signed for the release of the prisoner?"

"He . . . let's stay with he . . . had a paper," Hristo said. "It had the appropriate signatures and seals. Or . . . I thought it did? Did he have a paper at all?"

"If you do not mind, I'm going to . . . check something." She slid her wand into her hand and leaned over him, repeating the same minor ritual she'd conducted with Melodyn just the day before.

She blew the last syllable out as a puff of air into Hristo's eye. She felt instantly transported, as if she were rushing through a grand building, doors opening before her, something just out of sight traveling ahead.

Something was there, definitely, but it was faint. So faint that she could see only a vague shape, not even an outline. And as soon as she tried to focus, it was gone. She was ejected from her projection as quickly as she'd entered it.

Aelis's mind came back to itself in her own body with a start. Hristo looked slightly dazed.

"You were definitely enchanted," she muttered. "But I don't know how, exactly."

"To use malign magic on another wizard of the Lyceum is a high crime!" Hristo was offended and pale, as if he couldn't imagine that anyone might do such a thing.

"I know. Which is why I'm going to need to ask you to testify to the fact that it happened. And to speak with a lawyer . . . and to be very, very careful in the coming days. Listen to me, Hristo, can you take a few days of eating necromantically purified food and drink?"

"If I must. But it does so take the zest out of things."

"It does, but the alternative is to watch every single thing you consume being prepared, and to make someone else drink first from every cup you raise. I'll let you decide which is less onerous, but if you want to live through the next few days . . ."

"And what of attack from other ways? What of simple force, and assassination?"

"If things go as I hope, you'll be in protective custody very soon. But I'm going to give you something before you leave here," she said, producing the stick of wax.

27

FINAL FITTING

Aelis dreamed she was back in Lone Pine, in her cold and drafty tower, feeding charcoal into her calcination oven and warming herself while it worked. She did not know what formula she was creating, and every time she went to check her notes she could not find them. When she looked for the book she was working with, she couldn't find the right one, and spent endless time shuffling through endless pages.

When she woke, there was barely any light coming through her shutters, and her shoulder hurt from having her arm wrapped around the lantern in its cedar null-cage.

Mihil was already gone, having left a note.

I'll follow. But let's not be seen too close together this morning.

She got up, washed, and dressed in the most nondescript clothing she had, a plain gray cloak she'd been given in Lone Pine worn over the clothes she'd nearly ruined on the road. She hurried down to the refectory for coffee that she slurped hotter than she liked, and decided she'd walk to Ruby Chapel and Manxam's, carrying both null-cages slung over her shoulder in a bag. She saw Mihil exactly once, while she ate. The gnome had winked at her, and in the next moment when she'd bent her head to take a sip of her coffee, he'd disappeared. So she set out, confident that he was following and that any attempt to find him would just complicate his life.

"Onoma, I've forgotten how to dress for civilization," she muttered after she'd made a mile. The cloak and bag were totally unsuited to the warm morning, and all the city stonework that had been soaking up the spring sun for days was now warmer than the grass and pine forest she'd grown almost used to.

She also felt bad for referring to Lascenise as civilization, thus casting Lone Pine as its opposite.

"Going soft," she chided herself, and pulled the cloak tighter. With that on, and her rucksack, she was to all eyes a servant or a soldier about on an early errand, or on their way to an employer's house, her clothes too shabby to draw much attention despite the sword on her hip.

Every so often she paused and adjusted her pack and belt and took the chance to scan the few other early-morning foot travelers.

What I wouldn't give for Tun to be watching the crowd for me, she thought, then once again felt bad. Lascenise was no place for Tun; he would've been miserable, and she would've had no right to ask him to come with her, no matter how much she'd wanted to. She had very little choice but to trust Mihil at this point, and no reason not to. To the contrary, in fact.

But as much as she was coming to like the gnome, he *wasn't* Tun. *But who could be?*

She shook off her strange impulse to reminisce and picked up her pace, working up a sweat by the time she got to Manxam's.

It wasn't open yet. It hadn't occurred to her that Manxam's *closed*. That it had business hours the way any other tailor or outfitter or merchant would. She was standing there thinking about how to kill the time till it opened when she heard a voice behind her.

"Lady de Lenti?"

She turned, her hand falling to her sword, only to see Drewic standing a few paces away, a ring of keys in one hand and a grease-stained bag that smelled like frying oil and sugar in the other. She dropped her hand to her side.

"Sorry, Drewic, I'm just . . ."

"Quite eager to be fitted for the dress I have made for your father's dinner this evening?"

"Yes." Aelis saw no point in disagreeing.

"Good. Give me a few moments; if my favorite client saw the shop before it is put into visiting state, my grandam would haunt me to the grave."

He slid keys into the several complicated locks and eventually got the door open. Aelis could see lamps and lanterns being brought to life inside and heard rattling and scraping and, a few times, the tinkling of that tiny crystal bell. Eventually Drewic stuck his head back out and waved her in.

"I have been working on this dress for a few days now," he said as he led her to a back room. Once again he was in his gartered shirt and silver vest, crystal spectacles clamped over his thick nose. "You know, if *most* people had arms like yours, so used to sword work, they'd be perfectly happy to go sleeveless, but even I did not want to pick that fight with a wizard so determined to hide a wand up her sleeve."

He closed the door behind them. In the middle of the room was one of the wheeled racks, a single dress displayed on it.

It was a wrap dress like those she'd been seeing around the city as the weather warmed, but of a lustrous black silk that drank in and threw back what light there was in the room. The cuffs and collar had the faintest silver thread, and as Aelis drew close she let out a soft gasp.

"Magda mentioned how you felt about the skull and dagger motif on the jewels," Drewic said. "So I thought . . . why not repeat it on a statement dress?" Indeed, the cuffs and collar were highlighted with tiny silver skulls and daggers.

It was also when Aelis was that close that she realized that, as the fabric of the dress moved and shimmered, notes of dark green and blue surfaced in the silk.

"Let's get it on you, Lady, so I can take final measurements and make any last adjustments."

"Oh, Drewic, I'm too sweaty to . . ." she protested. She turned around, only to find one of the side panel doors opening and an assistant in a gray vest wheeling in a cart that held a bowl of faintly steaming, rose-scented water and a pile of thick towels.

"Lady de Lenti, please do not underestimate us here at Manxam's."

Once she was inside the dress, Aelis did not want to take it off. She even appreciated that it would leave her shoulders bare and make any sword work she might have to do that much easier. It fit as well as anything she'd ever worn.

"Drewic, I am very afraid that this dress will be ruined in an evening of . . . hard wear," she said to the dwarf as he swept back into the room with his black measuring roll in his hand.

"What Manxam's has made once, Lady de Lenti, we can make again and again."

"I am going to need yet another swordbelt, as much as I hate to say it."

"As if I had not already anticipated that, Lady." The crystal bell appeared, rang, and a servant came forward with a thin paper-wrapped bundle.

Drewic unfolded the paper, revealing a black leather belt with silver fittings. It looked only just strong enough, if at all, to hold her sword, but Drewic buckled it on her and she felt it grip her waist and knew that the interior was lined with steel and the belt would hold. She looked down and saw, in the silver that ran the length of the belt, the skull and dagger motif repeated.

"Where did you get this design, Drewic?"

"Our archives are a storehouse of lore in their own way, Lady de Lenti. Since you insist on black, I paged through the various designs we have provided to those of your college over the years. It seems this motif harkens back to the days when all wizards were scholars and priests both."

"So . . . these were on the robes of priests of Onoma?"

"Yes," Drewic said. "Or roughly so; I updated the design a bit, to reflect the contemporary pattern of the necromancer's dagger, such as you wear."

Aelis wasn't sure how she felt about making a priest's regalia part of her eveningwear, but then, *all* the robes, gowns, hoods, braids, cords, belts, and implements that wizards wore had been inherited from priests.

"If you wish, since your friends the Dobrusz brothers and your gnomish compatriot were very insistent that you needed to wear more ironmongery than *just* a sword and a dagger, the ring-hilted knives from the shoulder belt we made can be slid into this one as well."

"They have their reasons, Drewic. Speaking of which, I have two very important things to pass on to the Dobruszes today."

"I do expect them, but later in the morning." He paused in making the minutest adjustment to the fall of her dress and the fit of her belt. "Are you quite sure you want to have so much to do with them? They are . . . thoroughly disreputable, even in Halfton, much less here in Ruby Chapel."

"Disreputable they may be, but they have many useful skills, "Aelis retorted. "They were good friends to me in difficult places and, in truth . . . I owe them an extremely great debt."

"Violence is a useful skill? Extortion? Intimidation? Arson?"

"In my line of work, yes," Aelis said. "I'm given to understand they can pick locks, too."

"Fine, fine. Do you need a message passed, or a physical object?"

"Both, and before you ask, it is best that you know nothing of it."

"I don't like to think Manxam's is engaging in a criminal conspiracy, even for you, Lady."

"Quite the opposite."

"I shall take your word." Drewic finished whatever he was adjusting to his satisfaction. "Can you move as you'll need to, for dancing and so forth?"

Aelis stepped down off the small wooden platform Drewic had placed her on. Her swordbelt was hanging on a peg on the wall; she drew the blade out and went through a series of steps and guards for close-quarters combat. She gradually increased the width and length of her steps, finding the silk giving as she moved, not impeding her at all. She guided her sword from a close parry through a riposte and then a close strike, as if she'd slipped inside an enemy's guard.

Her shoulders moved easily, and the split sleeves laced around her arms and elbows had a comforting, compressing effect. After a few more short sequences, she returned her sword to its sheath.

"It's perfect, Drewic."

"What kind of dancing do you Imravalans get up to? That climate, so hot and dry . . ."

"The climate is why we make the best wine in the world, Drewic. And now, I must . . . with great regret . . . shed this dress and go back to my preparations. Ah . . . has Warden Despatia been fitted here?"

"Oh yes. Somewhat similar to your own dress, though with a bit of a collar piece and lower neck, and she has the good sense to show off *her* arms entirely," he added.

"Add her bill to the note you send to Urdimonte for me, would you?"

"Shall I tell her so before or after her bill is totaled?"

"After," Aelis said. "I don't need to go adding a diamond and adamant diadem to the tab."

"Warden Despatia *could* wear a diamond and adamant diadem, you know, Lady de Lenti . . ."

Aelis laughed. "Miralla could wear absolutely anything, Drewic. Now, if I could leave a note for the Dobruszes."

"Of course. I'll go and fetch pen, ink, and paper myself." He sketched a light bow and turned to leave, then turned back again, fingers darting into a pocket of his vest, the light of something suddenly remembered in his eyes.

"I believe this is yours, Lady Warden de Lenti." He held out his hand, which held the smallest-finger ring she'd given to Mihil days ago as her vouchsafe.

"Thank you," she said, slipping it back on to her finger.

He bowed and disappeared. Aelis changed back into the clothes she'd worn earlier. When Drewic returned, she thought over the note and then wrote it out swiftly.

> *The coach tonight, at the main entrance to Cabal Keep, an hour before dusk. Please come armed, but discreetly. As for this package, please ensure that it is held somewhere not even you could break it out of.*
>
> > *Regards*
> > *A.*

Once she'd signed the first cost estimate of her dress, belt, stockings, and boots, suppressing a gagging note of panic at the sum of gold it represented, she decided she hadn't the time to walk back and took a coach.

She went straight to her writing desk and found Mihil stretched out on his makeshift chair bed.

"How'd you get back in here?"

Without even opening his eyes, he said, "Told you, the security is shit."

Aelis left him to sleep and sat down to write a note to Khorais, asking her to draft "writs, or summons, or warrants, or whatever they are" for Hristo, Melodyn, Miralla, Malcon de Maunsel, Holborn, and anyone else she could think of that might help her wreck the case against Bardun Jacques. When she had that letter done, she tapped Mihil on the shoulder.

One eye, slightly less bloodshot than it once had been but still not healthy, opened immediately and fixed on her.

"Care to run an errand to your cousin?"

"Oh, I'm sure Khorais will be just *delighted* to have the shame of the family darken her office door," he said, though he unfolded himself and took the letter from her hand.

"Going to have any trouble slipping out?"

Mihil snorted as he tugged his coat on. "Please, boss . . . I don't ask you about your witching or sorcery or whatever it is you do."

"I do *neither* of those things, Mihil."

"See? I don't even know. And *you* don't know anything about skulking."

Aelis thought about creeping through the woods north of Lone Pine with Tun and wanted to protest, but Mihil had left, with light and careless steps.

28

WAITING, POORLY

Mazadar hadn't been happy to see or hear from her, and it had been difficult for Aelis to summon the necessary appearance of repentance and sorrow. But in the end, he'd agreed to put Hristo in protective custody and to allow Melodyn to join him if she wished.

"In retrospect, perhaps I shouldn't have hit her as hard as I did," Aelis murmured. For most of the rest of the afternoon she was going to be stuck doing something she hated more than absolutely anything else; more than drinking plain water with dinner, more than running, more than weighted-vest sword forms, more than sitting the divination exams she'd deliberately failed.

She was going to have to wait.

Aelis was one of the world's all-time worst waiters. She tried reading but got no more than a few sentences into any book she picked up. She tried pacing, but if there was anything she hated more than waiting, it was waiting while doing something pointless and repetitive. So she snatched up her sword and stomped off to the training rooms. After she'd warmed up with basic forms, guards, and steps, she took up a wooden sword and sought out sparring partners. More than one fellow abjurer left with bruises after sizing up the length of her practice sword and underestimating the speed of her first few steps. She took a few lumps of her own, she realized once she left the sparring rooms for the baths.

With the lightest of touches, she applied Drazim's Blood Ward to make sure no bruises would show, at least not until another day or two had passed.

Then, at last, it was time to dress. She had trouble lacing up her split sleeves and had to calm herself with her Abjurer's Litany more than once, but eventually she was dressed. She slid her new swordbelt on, amazed again at its light suppleness, slid one of the ring-hilted knives into the slot she found for it, just at the back, where it would be hidden by the sheath for her anatomist's blade. Her wand was tighter than she was used to against her left wrist, but she tested it and could still drop it clean into her hand, which was all that mattered.

Then there was the question of her hair, which she was saved from having to answer by Mihil's arrival.

He'd replaced his faded sky-blue coat with a longer one of severe black, had his hair washed, and tucked a pair of gloves under his belt.

Aelis felt no anger when Mihil sized her up; she was confident the gnome was only giving her a professional soldier's eye. Her instinct proved true when he gestured to her hair.

"Surely you're not about to leave it unbound like that when you're expecting a fight."

"If I let a two-vine assassin from the Tremont get close enough to me to get a handful of my hair, I'll deserve whatever happens."

"They're trickier than you think. Come here." Mihil waved her over to the small table in her front room and climbed up into a chair. "I'll plait it for you, sailor's style."

"Not entirely sure that is an appropriate style for a townhouse dinner."

"Then set a new fashion. Aren't you the count's daughter? Let everyone else take their cue from you. Get it?" Mihil laughed.

"Get what?"

"You know, cue, queue . . ." He hefted the strand of hair his fingers were already nimbly twisting. "Oh, never mind. I betray my principles to make a pun and you don't even laugh."

With Aelis's hair securely plaited and lying lightly against her neck, they set out for the courtyard. Amadin was waiting for them there, wearing a vibrant red mantle over a dark blue jacket and trousers. His sword was belted at one side, his white crystal-topped staff, in its short form, hanging from his belt.

"Warden de Lenti." His mutter, his sneer, the arms crossed over his chest; he would rather have been anywhere else.

"Good evening to you too, Warden Amadin."

"Can we get on with this farce yet?"

"My father was never much given to farces," Aelis said, smiling blankly. "If he put on entertainments, he always preferred reenactments of military engagements, or perhaps a morality play. Especially the kind that emphasized duty to family above all else."

"How delightful."

"My mother once paid to have a mummers' troupe enact such a series of tales for us; something about a daughter gone to ruin because she insisted on knowing the delights of the city," Miralla said, having snuck up on them. "Tamra's Misery Amid the Towers, or some nonsense like that. Didn't stop me from leaving for the Lyceum the next year, though." She sidled up to Aelis and grasped her hand for a moment; Aelis squeezed her hand and palmed the ring Miralla had placed there.

Aelis turned and instantly felt inadequate next to her friend, as though she were aping every bit of style Miralla exuded. Her dress had puffy, diaphanous sleeves that highlighted her strong arms, which gleamed darkly in the twilight. She wore a gauzy silver half cloak off her right shoulder, matching the diviner's diadem her curled hair was carefully piled around. Her belt was white where Aelis's was black, but they shared silver fittings, and the only hints of abjurer's blue were faint pale threads at the neckline and the hem.

Her sword, longer than Aelis's but shorter than Amadin's, was in a new scabbard, white to match the dress and belt and worked with a pattern of eyes and stars Aelis could only just make out. There was also a small silver buckler dangling from her belt that someone who didn't know might mistake for an ornament, but Aelis knew Miralla could use it as an aid to her wards with great precision.

"You are stunning, Mira," Aelis said, with genuine admiration.

"I know." Miralla's lips curled into a smug, teasing smile.

"Are we there to defend against assassins or have a fashion show?" Amadin said petulantly.

"There's no law saying a warden cannot look good while discharging her duties," Aelis said.

"Even if it does seem to be a tradition," Miralla muttered.

"Most of the senior wardens in the service cut their teeth in wartime, you know," Amadin went on. "Armor and helmets and long marches don't leave much room for decoration."

"I've seen any number of uniforms worn by my father, his siblings, and my oldest brother and sister that say otherwise," Aelis said.

"Oh, and what did your puissant relations do? March around a city square in bright parade uniforms?"

"The Count's Own Tirravalan Light Horse were at Three Rivers, engaged the first orcish elements at the Floodplain, and were responsible for answering the plundering raids by flying columns and riverboats," Aelis snapped. "My sister did not lose an eye playing at garrison or leading parades."

"I touched a nerve," Amadin said. "I apologize."

His tone didn't convey contrition, Aelis thought, but before she could take any further umbrage a coach rolled up, with two familiar shapes hulking together atop the box. The Dobrusz brothers were clearly much less comfortable in sober black jackets than in the studded and iron-banded leather Aelis knew them to favor. If the jackets looked a bit too bulky, or Andresh's coachman's gloves were rather too large and perhaps had blacking rubbed over the metal studs over the knuckles, well, she wasn't sure anyone besides her would notice it.

Timmuk clambered down via the wheel and threw open the doors; Andresh set the brake and followed suit.

"Good evening, wardens," Timmuk greeted them in his sonorous, rolling voice. "Here to convey you to the de Lenti townhouse, at the very north end of the Azare Courts, in style and comfort." Belatedly, Mihil clambered down off the back of the conveyance and unfolded the step that would help them mount.

Miralla was the first aboard, with both dwarves granting her unnecessary hands to help her along. Aelis allowed them to do the same, and Timmuk leaned close and winked.

"If our Renia could see you now, Warden, she'd be dumbstruck enough to walk straight into a wall."

Aelis gave Timmuk the best smile she could manage. In the moment between entering the cab of the coach and arranging her dress and swordbelt so she could sit comfortably on the cushioned seat, she allowed herself to be completely and utterly heartbroken, to feel waves of longing and guilt lash against her heart till she thought she might crack into a horrifying and undignified sob.

The control she was raised with, the dismissing of emotions her family would've thought unfit, asserted itself. She did dig the nails of her left hand into the sword-hilt callus of her palm, and if Miralla noticed, she was too kind to say anything.

"One of our coachmen is wearing studded gauntlets rather than driving gloves," Miralla said as Amadin sat lightly down on her side of the coach, angling his lean body as far away from both of them as he could manage.

"And I'm sure I caught the outline of knives under their coats," Amadin added with a sniff.

"And I'm sure they're both wearing more steel than any of us," Aelis said.

"Does that fact comfort you?" Amadin raised a fine brow. "Might they not try and murder us along the way, dump us in a canal?"

"Amadin!" Miralla's voice was sharp, chiding. "Do you think Aelis doesn't *know* them?"

"The Count limited my guests to two," Aelis said. "He said nothing about a limit on servants. And I happened to have friends available."

Amadin rolled his eyes and turned his face toward the corner of the cab.

"So." Miralla dismissed the elf's grumbling and focused on Aelis. "Any hints about tonight's menu?"

"If I know my father, everything will be presented with the postwar austerity he clings to; I'd expect no great fancies, no crystal punchbowls with floating ice sculptures, no extravagant towers of effervescent Tyridician white."

"Oh, is it to be hardtack and camp stew? Reminders of his hard days in the field?" Amadin's sneer told Aelis what he thought of the idea.

You do not need to prove anything about your family to this traitor, Aelis told herself, and turned to answer Miralla's curiosity.

"Of course, presentation is one thing, but the Count also knows he cannot allow the de Lenti to be accused of failing to feed guests properly, of not showing out when it comes to the *quality* of the food. I'd expect shellfish to start, a cheese between each course, and something that will show Antravalan cuisine well; rare beef with truffles is a fine bet." Aelis felt stirrings of hunger and anticipation.

"Should I head to the kitchen and attempt to search out any poison when we arrive?" Miralla's question took Aelis away from imagining the food and finding time to enjoy it.

"Probably for the best, though I don't know that these Hidden Skulls are that subtle."

"They want to kill you specifically," Amadin muttered. "Poison would be too unlikely to work *and* too likely to result in collateral damage. If they killed a roomful of nobles they weren't being *paid* to kill, no one would cross their palm with a bent copper leaf ever again."

"I'll speak with my father and make him see reason. We'll place wards at the major points of entry after the guests have all arrived. Timmuk, Andresh, and Mihil will be among the servants, and I expect they'll be able to discourage any attempts from that direction. At the first sign of attack, I'll give a sign to my father to herd the guests to the donjon."

"Your father's *townhouse* has a donjon?" Amadin said with disbelief.

"The de Lentis have not always been popular; no family is, and never with everyone. Assassinations, even open attacks, have not been unknown to us. Enemies have taken advantage of proximity in Lascenise before; I bet if you take a hard look at any of the places owned by Estates House families in town, they've all got a fortified core that the family and retainers can retreat to, for a few hours at least."

"Such ridiculous games you families play." Amadin settled back into his corner, sullenly pushing himself against the cushions and thrusting his feet out.

Aelis and Miralla shared a look; both settled back in their seats, Aelis calling to mind her Abjurer's Litany. *The ever-vigilant and properly prepared Abjurer is the antithesis of danger. Thus, she does not fear.*

She gathered her will around her, thinking on how much power she might be able to call up in the event it was needed. The Death Curse rattled around in her head, distracting her, tying up some of her available strength; she eyed Amadin, who sat with head back and eyes closed, for just a moment. The noise of the Curse had abated, and it seemed smaller, calmer; perhaps it had to do with his proximity? *If the Curse does not have to reach as far to its target, it draws less strength. I should've done some research on it.*

Then she thought for a moment about how that research would've gone. Walk into one of the libraries at the Lyceum and say, *Hello, I need to figure out exactly how Death Curses work. What forbidden works can you point me to?*

Not that Death Curses were forbidden, but it was a touchy subject. Aelis shook her head and tried to fall into meditation, and failed, so she settled for looking out her window as the city rolled by. As they had headed north from Ruby Chapel, the streets became wider, smoother, with fewer pedestrians mobbing them, with more coaches, horses, carts, and the odd carried chair moving along the walks.

They were in the Azare Courts now; what businesses they passed were discreetly signed, the kind of places one had an appointment to shop at, where money was never discussed even while enormous sums of it changed hands. Jewelers, smiths who specialized in ornate parade plate or presentation swords, private dining clubs, those kinds of things.

Then the streets spread out a great deal, into large drives of crushed rock behind wrought-iron gates and decorative stone walls, leading to country homes built in miniature, palaces reduced to their core elements. Great halls cut in half and stuck in front, a residential wing reduced to two stories, three at most, and servants' quarters in the back where they couldn't be seen from the street. The coach slowed and gradually turned into one of the drives. Aelis felt a surge of emotion she hadn't expected—pride? belonging?—when she saw the de Lenti arms, a leafy tendril wrapped around a forked polearm.

She didn't have much time to contemplate it as the wagon pulled to a stop. The door was opened by a uniformed man, but he was no regular servant; he wore the pinked-edged blue tunic of the Count's Own. He was unarmored, but he had a sword at his belt, and it was no court affair, no delicate small-sword but a true horseman's saber.

There was a bit of jostling between the soldier, Mihil, and Andresh as to who would set the step and begin to hand the guests down, but they got it sorted out with the soldier standing to one side, pressing his fist to his chest and bowing shallowly.

"Lady de Lenti," he rumbled. Aelis smiled, but could not let the breach of protocol go, even now.

"Warden de Lenti," she said, glancing for any knots of rank on his chest. "You owe me no obeisance tonight, rider," she added, "but I thank you for the courtesy."

"The allegiance of the Count's Own transcends any rules set by the Tri-Crowns, the Estates House, or the rules of your own service, and it will not be breached while I am in earshot." It was not the soldier who answered but a stronger, sterner voice, and one Aelis knew well. Her head snapped up, looking for the speaker, and found her quickly. She was the very picture of an officer: knee-high riding boots polished to a high sheen, sword hanging precisely, balanced by a heavy knife, cap pinned to her coiled dark hair, with silver epaulets at her shoulders, and the pink of her tunic picked out in silk. Aelis restrained the urge to dash to her side and embrace her—in general, an unusual urge for a de Lenti. And one did not hug Colonel Delphine de Lenti un Tirraval, commander of the Count's Own, fierce in her scowl and blue eye patch, even when she was one's eldest sister.

"Delphine," Aelis said, slipping into the reserve she was raised with like a familiar garment. "I did not realize you would be attending."

"Aelis." Delphine inclined her head so slightly Aelis genuinely wondered if either Miralla or Amadin could detect the movement. "I am not attending the dinner so much as I am attending our Lord Father. The Regiment was passing near the city, and he asked for a detachment to be assigned tonight in case of . . ." Here, Delphine lifted a hand in a vague, dismissive motion, "threat." The way she uttered that single syllable indicated that the very idea of a threat being present inside the gates of the Count's townhouse was a fancy akin to flying horses.

"Allow me to introduce my companions," Aelis said, as by then her fellow wardens had joined her. She saw Mihil and the Dobruszes scattering to their spots on the coach, then the horses clattered away and disappeared around a bend. *Stregon go with you*, she thought.

"Warden Miralla Despatia," she said, indicating with her right hand, "and Warden Amadin Mauntell Carrafhyn. I have the honor of introducing Lady Colonel Delphine de Lenti un Tirraval."

Amadin made a graceful bow; Miralla floated forward to take Delphine's hand. She paused for a moment, searching Aelis's sister's face, and smiled as she came back to Aelis's side.

"If you would allow us, Colonel," Aelis said, shoving aside her burning curiosity over whatever Miralla had seen in her sister's face, "we do have some minor augmentations to make to your undoubtedly flawless security plan for the evening."

Delphine stared hard at Aelis for a moment. "Am I going to do anything besides waste time if I press you for details or say that it's unnecessary?"

Aelis offered a de Lenti family smile in return, a twitch of the lips so faint most mortals would never have detected it.

"I thought as much. Do what you must."

Aelis, Miralla, and Amadin separated, began walking a full circuit of the building, each on separate timing, with Aelis going clockwise, Miralla widdershins, and Amadin crossing his feet one over the other as he went.

Aelis pulled a small silver disc from her pouch and rubbed a thumb over it, repeating a short set of words with each pass her thumb made over the disc. Mairead's Walk began to gather around her; she felt it, and felt the way the wards being laid by her fellow abjurers were also taking hold. Miralla's power, she knew; her friend was a diviner first and second and an abjurer third. Amadin, though, was a closed book to her. She'd seen his invocation on the road, in the ambush she hadn't been meant to survive, but had that been his real power? Had he dampened himself, hidden it away from her? The Ward she felt going up was at least the equal of her own.

When they met again at the starting point, all three were holding silver discs that thrummed with power. Miralla and Amadin placed theirs into Aelis's hands.

Aelis looked for Delphine in the crowd; more coaches had arrived, and immaculately dressed guests were moving off the rocks and proceeding up the stairs into the great hall, where her father, no doubt, was greeting them.

She caught sight of her sister's cap of rank and a flash of silver epaulet and made straight for her.

"Lady Colonel," she said, holding out the three silver discs. "If you would be so kind, keep one of these, and give the other two to soldiers you trust. When the last guest has arrived and is safely inside the grounds, snap the disc in half. Not before."

"What will happen then?" Delphine held one of the discs up to her eye, catching the light of the torches and lanterns that flared along the front wall.

"Nothing," Aelis said. "Until someone who was not already within the grounds crosses one of the paths we laid."

"And if they simply come in above it, on a rope or the like?"

"Lady Colonel, I do not ask you questions about the disposition of your guards, do I?"

Delphine lowered the disc and favored Aelis with a smile, just for a moment. A real smile, with the affection of an elder sibling in it, not the reserved mask of nobility. "Not for several years now, no. But if I were to pay you back question for question, Aelis, we would stand here all night," she said, dropping her voice.

"And if I had leave, Delphine, there is very little I'd rather do," Aelis admitted in a similar whisper. "Another night."

Then both were behind their courtly masks again, and Aelis, with Miralla and Amadin flanking her, set out along the path and up the steps into the hall.

29

A GRAND DINNER

Aelis's father stood like a statue in the entry to his great hall, albeit one that favored passing guests with a brief dip of his head or a few murmured words of greeting, but never anything as broad as a smile.

That did not change when Aelis and her companions approached. He fairly gleamed in a court cloak of royal blue, a heavy silver chain of office worked in the de Lenti "vines and tines" pattern of leaves and polearms, and a similarly worked silver circlet, with deep purple amethysts in the shape of the grapes on the leaves. He also wore a sword, but it was more thin court sword than military saber, unlike those of the troops answering to him outside.

He extended his hand to Aelis, who took it between both of hers and bowed faintly. Still clasping his hand like a dutiful daughter, she turned to the other wardens.

"My Lord de Lenti, may I introduce Warden Miralla Despatia and Warden Amadin Mauntell Carrafhyn. My fellow wardens, allow me to introduce Lord Guillame de Lenti, Count un Tirraval."

Miralla and Amadin both made restrained, soldierly bows, though Miralla's was more graceful. The Count covered Miralla's hand with his own.

"Warden Despatia, it is good to see one of Aelis's friends from the Lyceum flourishing in the service, and here, within the very heart of civilization."

Aelis felt the sting of that, felt it like an invoker had just lit up her nervous system with a disabling shock. She kept her face pleasantly neutral through long training, even though her mind was running with angry retorts.

To Amadin her father did not extend a hand, but he did offer a greeting in the fast-flowing, light, clipped Elvish tongue. Amadin's face assumed an expression halfway between a smile and a grimace and answered in the same tongue.

"My lord," Aelis said, "before we go inside, I must beg your attendance upon one point. If we may?" Aelis indicated a dark corner of the hall with a door where servants might circulate unnoticed.

"Yes, Warden?" Her father had a small smirk on his face as they drew near.

"If I or the other wardens give you a signal, we will need you to gather all the guests and head to the donjon."

"Do you mean the cellars, Warden?"

"I mean a defensible place with one door in," Aelis said. "And you should send a guard to make sure no one is already inside it."

"Why so much concern, Aelis?" His amusement faded into his default unreadable blankness.

"There are credible threats."

"Which is why there is a troop of the Count's Own stationed outside."

"These are threats that they may not be as well equipped to detect or deal with as three wardens. Please assure me that you will meet this request."

"Very well. It should provide a week or two of gossip."

"I do not want anyone to bleed for gossip, my lord," Aelis said, then, with a calculated breach of expected decorum, she spun and turned away from her father. She joined Miralla and Amadin, who were holding glasses of wine in their hands.

"Your father's Elvish accent is . . . curious," Amadin said after taking a delicate sip of the bright red liquid in his glass. "He came very close to wishing me a good boot cleaning."

Miralla snorted into her glass. Aelis looked around for a servant carrying more wine and saw none. "It's an impossible language to pronounce, Amadin."

"No, it simply requires concentration and long study. Which would explain why so many humans do find it impossible."

"I read it fluently," Aelis said, brushing past them, laughing in one compartmentalized part of her mind at the idea of her father mispronouncing anything. She desperately wanted to tell him, if only to see how he would explain or justify his pronunciation; it would be Amadin, the actual elf, who was wrong, of course. Aelis almost let herself laugh at the image, but then they were past the entryway and into the circulating area of the great hall, and she had to stop for a moment and remember what *civilization* was like.

The number of white wax candles burning in the hall was likely more than the entire village of Lone Pine, including all outlying farms, burned in a season.

Aelis took a quick glance over the brilliantly polished silver-and-crystal chandeliers that sent dazzling light all across the long blond-wood room and changed that first assessment to *in a year*. And this didn't even take into account the lanterns, mundane and magical, that stood on the walls and columns. There was not a tallow candle or a rushlight in evidence, and Aelis would be surprised if, on a night like tonight, such burned even in the servants' areas or the kitchen. The smell or sight of such a thing would provide infuriating gossip for as long as rival families could make it.

There was a stream of well-dressed humanity moving about the room in an apparent chaos that, to an accustomed eye, would reveal patterns easily. There were those who moved about the room, seeking conversation, attempting to show off, and those stood more or less in place, waiting for others to come to them. This second group was far more powerful. With one glance Aelis noted the Urdimonte Fiduciatrix Carlassa standing pat, chains glimmering across her chest and the cuffs and hem of her robes, men and women gliding to a stop near her to get in a word or two. She saw the Viscount de Antissa, splendid in the deep purple of his house, a gold chain of office settled over his shoulders, practically *leaning* against a column, only deigning to make eye contact when someone interesting enough came near.

"We'll all three do a short turn around the room," Aelis said, "within the columns. Do not stop and be drawn into conversation. Do not chase after a servant, even if they are carrying a tray with your very *favorite* dainty and you'll die if you don't eat it."

"I have been to dinners before, Aelis," Miralla teased.

Amadin muttered something in Elvish and took two quick steps, disappearing in the swirl of dresses and robes and mantles.

"Once you find a place to stand and stop, do it," Aelis said. "Power stays put. Desperation circles the room."

"And in this case, we are meant to have power?"

Aelis stared at her friend. "Mira," she murmured, "we're the only people here who have any that matters."

Aelis strode into the crowd, in the opposite direction from the one Amadin had taken. Training and experience had prepared her for this kind of combat *long* before she'd started learning abjurer's forms. She snatched a glass of wine from a passing servant's tray without a word or a glance and took the tiniest sip.

She concentrated on it, because she'd been taught to and also because it gave her mind something to focus on just as surely as her abjurer's mantra. It was a Tirravalan orange, though not from her family's private holdings. De Buissel, if she were to guess, and not very old. Their wines were always excellent young.

This also gave her something to chat about when she stopped at a pillar near, but not *part*, of a small knot of richly dressed guests. She did not have to wait long.

"Is it . . . the youngest Lady de Lenti?" The woman who spoke these words as she drifted over wore a dark green dress with a horribly out of fashion too-high neckline. Still, the diamond earrings she wore and the fortune of emeralds on her fingers and the slight exposed slice of her neck marked her as someone rich, if not important.

"It is *Warden* de Lenti," Aelis said, with a tight not-quite-smile. She couldn't place the woman, somewhere between her and Delphine in age, so she extended her hand.

"Illana, Marquesa de Tigair," the woman said, and Aelis registered her. A member of the Estates House, reputedly having bought her family's place with truly heroic levels of bribery. That gossip was years old at best, so Aelis decided that at least a touch of humility was in order.

"My father's house is honored to have you, Marquesa."

A few others had gathered around; men in coats of military cut but far too richly made for such service, or mantles with shoulder-capelets that suggested a rustic hunting trip despite being made of silk or brocade, the women in dresses that varied but tended toward the wrap style Aelis and Miralla wore, though hardly as splendid.

"As I am sure it is honored to have you. To think, a family with two daughters bearing swords at a dinner party; how very unusual in peaceful times and settled places."

"As a warden, I am obligated to bear the tools of my Colleges," Aelis said, which wasn't strictly true; she was obligated to bear at least the sword, but by putting the slightest emphasis on *Colleges* she had scored a minor point among the listeners. "And of course, my eldest sister is the commanding officer of our house regiment. Who among us would ask any of our own officers to go unarmed?"

"But if you wear a sword, oughtn't your dress be blue? Not that this black doesn't become you, of course . . ."

Aelis's not-quite-a-smile became even tighter. "I am a necromancer, first and always." A few people shuffled away, trying for inconspicuous and failing. *Hypocrites. I'd be the first person you ask if you suspected yourself ill.*

"How charming," the Marquesa said through a toothy smile. "I do hope we are seated close." Aelis held her eyes for a moment, until the Marquesa was forced to move on.

That's right, hag, Aelis thought. *My house. My territory. Keep walking.* She took another minuscule sip and fenced eye-to-eye with the next knot of over-dressed graspers to come nearby.

She corrected *Lady* to *Warden* three more times, greeted a Duke's son, a Count's daughter, and any number of minor gentry who simply *had* to talk to the Count's daughter, and a wizard, even a warden into the bargain, how splendid! She made it almost halfway through her glass when a servant stepped from a doorway and rapped a metal-shod staff against a metal plate on the floor three times, the signal to dinner.

Aelis drank the rest of her wine on the way to join the queue, where she caught up with Miralla.

"Have you seen Amadin?"

"Charming the stockings off a Contessa, I think. Possibly literally—he was walking her into the dinner seating arm in arm."

"A scandal in the offing. They won't seat us next to each other, but we ought to be close. I can have a servant change our seats if need be."

The throng advanced slowly. Aelis could smell mushrooms in pastry and a fiery soup that would have greens and spiced sausage sliced so thin you could *see* through it, and she had just allowed herself to begin to feel truly hungry. She and Miralla finally made it past the blue-clad servants and into the hall that had been turned into a massive dining room, two tables running lengthwise and two raised tables set perpendicular at either end, each space elaborately set with fine crystal and a spread of silver that could've sent a dozen smithing families' children to the Lyceum, when a warning blazon sounded in her head and a pulse of alarm raced through her mind. She turned to Miralla, whose face told her she had felt the same. Aelis looked for the tall figure of her father where he was taking a seat dead center at one of the raised tables.

She cut through the crowd who were being seated by servants, ignored the soft words of one woman whose lace collar indicated rank in the household, and barged straight up to him, pushing past one or two of the guests who'd been favored with a seat at his table.

"My lord," she said urgently, "you must take the guests . . ."

"Nonsense," he said. "This has gone on quite long enough, Aelis, and I won't have . . ."

His words were cut off by the high-pitched crash of shattered glass, followed by a ragged shriek and then several screams.

Aelis leapt over the table, drawing her sword and cursing the damage she did to the plate and crystal as she went.

The shriek had been from a black-clad assassin who'd come straight through the shattered window, a small crossbow in one hand, a knife in the other, only to have been *immediately* spitted on Amadin's sword. She was there in time to see the elf quite calmly draw his blade out and use the tip to slash open the attacker's throat, even as his free hand still held a glass of wine. The screaming had been from guests, some of whom might have been struck by tiny fragments of glass.

"EVERYONE!" Aelis yelled, "to the donjon!" She lifted her sword and pointed to a large wooden door at the far end of the room. "Through there; the Lord Count de Lenti will guide you to safety!"

Even as she spoke, there were more crashes, both in the dining room and outside it. Three more black-clad forms hurled themselves through the windows, and she and Amadin rushed to meet them.

All three lifted their small crossbows and loosed darts at her; all three met the resistance of her ward in midair and fell. Holding the ward in front of her like a shield, Aelis ran forward and bowled one of them straight to the floor. It was knife to sword work then, and her training took over. She had drawn two and Amadin one.

Her pair of attackers tried to go at it in a businesslike manner, drawing as far as they could to either side. *I'll want at least one of you alive*, Aelis thought, and slipped her wand into her left hand. She let loose the Catnap at the one on her left-hand side and he dropped, though she'd felt some resistance; she wasn't sure how much and she had no time to spare to investigate because the one on her right came at her, trying to get inside her guard.

If Aelis had been some ordinary swordswoman it would've worked, but the ward she projected from the pommel of her sword skirled the attacker's knife wide, and Aelis was able to take a curling step away from him into more effective range and slash him hard across the back.

When he fell, she didn't lunge forward with a killing blow. Instead, she bent low and dragged her sword's edge across the back of his thigh. He wore no armor and his dark, loose trousers offered no resistance to her edge, and he was hamstrung in one leg and out of the fight as effectively as if she'd torn his throat out. Out of *any* fight, without advanced anatomist attention.

She turned to find Amadin seemingly having the time of his life as he allowed his attacker to launch cut after slash after cut at him with his long knife. He turned each one with no apparent effort, grinning, even once bringing his wine to his lips and taking a sip.

Aelis ran up behind the knife-wielder and smacked her pommel against the base of his skull. She'd misjudged, not wanting to crack his skull and kill him, and didn't strike him hard enough to knock him cold.

But it did stagger him, and Amadin, deprived of his fun, buried a foot of steel in the assassin's gut and drew it out swiftly, contemptuously.

"Four assassins? Really? Is that what we were so concerned about? Four barely trained knives . . ."

Aelis, disgusted, turned toward the entry where she'd heard the sound of windows being broken. The crowd had mostly run for the exit she'd pointed out, though a few had stayed behind, and Miralla had marshaled them to barricade the door.

Aelis caught a glimpse of Miralla's whitened eyes when her friend turned to her.

"It won't hold!" she yelled. "Get down!" Mira grabbed the nearest helping hand, a Duke's son who'd made small talk with Aelis earlier, and shoved him toward one of the long tables, hard. He immediately tumbled over it, knocking crystal and plate awry with a crash, and Miralla followed him, hurling herself behind it.

"WARDS!" she shouted. Aelis put up the widest one she could, just in time to cover her and Amadin before the great wooden doors—carved with the de Lenti arms and bound in polished bronze—*exploded*.

The cloud of splinters bounced off her ward, and she felt Amadin huddling behind her. The blast was so powerful and the fragments so many that it took considerable effort to keep her shield-sized ward intact, and she felt a splinter graze her ankle.

She felt the rain of debris and the concussion dissipate and dropped the ward, expecting a swarm of knife-wielding assassins to pour through the breach.

No one came.

Miralla rose from behind the table, which bowed in the middle, broken by the blast. Crystal and silver were scattered everywhere.

"Aelis, my left. Amadin, my right," Miralla called, her voice oddly distant. As she came up to where Miralla had directed her, Aelis could see why: Miralla was so deeply into a diviner's trance that her eyes weren't just filmed over but *glowing* white. She held her sword in one hand and the buckler in the other, but both were loose at her sides, not held up in guard. She felt a bit intimidated as her friend turned to face her.

"Interior guard," Miralla said to Aelis, then, turning to Amadin, "Exterior. Length of her blade. Move in opposite circles."

Amadin looked ready to argue the point, though he'd at least lost his wineglass and put his left hand loosely to his hilt. Aelis gave him a shove in the direction Miralla had indicated. "You do not argue with a diviner in her battle trance."

"Naftali's Tower," Miralla droned. "Your left arm. Angle forty-five degrees!"

The ward Miralla called for was a powerful one; Second Order at least, though it could creep into Third if the abjurer wished. Aelis focused, drew power inward through the hilt of her sword, and imagined she could feel the weight of a shield settle on her arm. Wards had no truly tangible weight, but one of her peculiarities as an abjurer had been to often treat them as solid things. In this case, that meant that instead of simply erecting the Ward at the angle Miralla had called for, she fixed it to her arm and then tilted it forward.

Smoke erupted in front of her, then any number of darts spent themselves against her shield.

"MOVE!" Miralla called, and as Aelis went, she felt something more substantial clatter against the shield and bounce away. As she and Amadin passed each other, she caught the glimmer of his own ward, detached from his body, angled in the air.

Show off, she thought. She wondered, briefly, why Amadin wasn't throwing any fire or bolts of lightning, but indoors such things could well be incredibly dangerous.

"Swords!" Miralla shouted. "High guard left, step in to low right . . ."

Aelis simply followed Miralla's calls through the thick smoke. She felt her blade turn a knife, then a second. The diviner continued to call out directions, but Aelis stopped consciously hearing them, stopped demanding that her body follow them.

She simply *did*. It was as though her stance, her guards, her counters and ripostes and attacks were all under the controlling impulse of someone else, someone who knew better than her how to fight with her own blade. It became so natural that she countered and thrust by simply feeling the opening in her sense of her opponents. She disarmed one with a turn of her guard and slashed him across the chest, sending him reeling away, then crushed her pommel into the temple of another, whom Amadin had sent stumbling toward her with a swipe of his long sword. Smoke still swirled about her and she was flowing from knife to knife, delivering cuts and thrusts in response, not even realizing she had cast Isring's Life-Finder not once but several times, pulsing it out again and again, that somehow she and Amadin had fallen into Miralla's Battle Divination, and her companion wardens could *also* feel the results of the pulse, that the three of them were sharing their gifts with one another.

It was frightening to know she was open in that way to Amadin and Miralla, and exhilarating as well. She felt that they could take on an army; for all she knew, they had.

Miralla was stepping forward into spaces Aelis and Amadin vacated, raising her own sword, but never to guard or parry. She attacked, if it could even be called that; she thrust and slashed with quick, efficient motions that were somehow more terrifying for their complete lack of rancor or anger. She was taking foes from the fight, to be sure; killing some, certainly, wounding others too grievously to carry on. She simply knew where and when they would be unprotected, given the surrounding curtains of steel and ward that Amadin and Aelis were erecting around her, guided by her.

Then, just as soon as it had come, the attack ended. The smoke dissipated. Aelis took in the scene before them, the fine wood floor of the dining room slick with blood and viscera, bodies crumpled, some trying to crawl away.

"Miralla, check in on the servants' quarters," Aelis called. "I will go to the guests. Amadin, the gate, please."

As she passed him, she saw Amadin sneer at a man was was crawling away, leaving a smear of blood behind him, and lift his sword.

With the thrill of the fight still thrumming in her limbs, Aelis threw herself toward the elf and knocked his sword away, hard, with her own.

"Kill none who are wounded!" Aelis yelled. "We want prisoners, not corpses!"

Amadin struggled against her for a few moments; she saw fury, even naked hatred in his eyes, in the way his lips drew back over his teeth. She was taken aback by the bluntness of it. She didn't like her odds in a one-to-one swordfight against Amadin, not after what she'd seen of him. And not since, she knew, he'd saved his strength, shepherded it throughout the fight.

She hadn't, though, and doubted she had more than two or three orders of wards left if it came to it. But in the face of Amadin's anger, she smiled.

He could read that smile, and his anger turned to disgust.

"Go," she said quietly, "and do what I ask, before I make it a fucking order."

Aelis felt the Death Curse floating in her mind, soaking up whatever power she might have left. She didn't imagine he could feel it throb as she did, but he knew it was there, would perhaps have a distant awareness of it, a sword hanging over him, poised to fall.

Aelis stalked away, making the best speed she could toward the door through which all the dinner guests had fled. She had just begun to feel the weariness of battle in her limbs, of the expenditure of so very much energy, magical and physical, all at once. She leaned hard against the doorjamb to catch her breath, then rapped hard against it with the hilt of her sword.

"Who is it?" came a muffled voice after a few moments.

"Warden Aelis de Lenti."

She heard several quiet voices behind the door, arguing, she thought, but what about she could not discern.

"Prove it," came another voice.

"I am Aelis Cairistiona de Lenti un Tirraval," she growled. "Necromancer, abjurer, enchanter, *warden*. And, lest you forget, I am the daughter of the owner of this house. There is no lawful barring of my passage here. Now open this Stregon-cursed door before I find a way to rip it down."

There was no spell she could call on that would do so, of course, even if she had all her strength. Perhaps someone could summon a ward that would stand up to that kind of powerful force being exerted on it, but she couldn't. Taking down a door was the work of a conjurer first and an invoker second.

As she was pondering this, she heard bolts rattle and a bar move, and the door opened. Beyond it, candlelight guttered down a crowded stairway.

"Not everyone could fit in the locked cellar," someone said. Some of them were servants, though at least a few others were nobly dressed, with slim court swords to hand.

"Keep this locked until I give you the all clear. Is all well inside the donjon?"

"They appear to be exploring the wine cellar, m'lady," said one of the servants, who was holding a candelabra in one hand and a long carving knife in the other.

"Good. Will just be a moment. Lock this door again. Do not open it unless I give you the password—duskdrop. Do you remember that?"

The servant nodded, and Aelis made a note of the man; she would get his name, commend his service, and press for her father to make a sizable gift to him. Or do it herself.

"Duskdrop, m'lady," the man said, and she shut the door, heard it barred again.

Aelis found Miralla coming from the kitchen, her eyes wide.

"Who," she inquired, "are those dwarves driving our coach?"

"Let's just say that coach driver is not their first profession."

"What *was*? Butcher? Soldier? Professional *murderer*?"

Aelis badly wanted to go to the front gate but allowed Miralla to divert her to the kitchen. She stepped inside and saw a group of aproned cooks clustered together against a hearth, where a roast sat forgotten, burning on a spit.

In the center of the room, Andresh and Timmuk were piling bodies. There were at least half a dozen. The brothers' black cabdrivers' coats were slashed and torn and slick with blood. The left sleeve of Andresh's was torn almost completely away, the gleam of a steel bracer showing beneath.

"Aelis," Timmuk called, standing up from wiping a long, curved knife on the black garments of a dead man. "Eight of them came in through the tradesmen's entrance."

"Where's the other two?"

"In the garden. Mihil climbed up to the kitchen roof and peppered them as they came on. Good fellow, for a gnome."

254 • DANIEL M. FORD

Timmuk made the knife vanish inside his coat. "I'm afraid to tell you they killed an underbutler as they came in the door," he said solemnly. "Cut his throat. Poor lad had no chance, even if . . ." He trailed off, but Aelis knew what he had meant to say.

Even if you'd been here.

She heard one of the cooks give a sob. "Timmuk, if you would, please find out everything you can about him, and bring it all to me. I will see to his kin." Aelis spoke very slowly, forcing the words out so as not to cause panic. "And to everyone here who knew him, I promise you that this guild of murderers will not sleep two more peaceful nights in Lascenise."

Anger gave her a fresh burst of energy. She turned back and left the kitchen, gripping her sword hilt till her knuckles turned white and her hand began to cramp. She ignored it.

She did not quite make it to the main doors before meeting Amadin, Delphine, and two of the household troopers. Delphine's sword was out of its sheath but did not appear wet.

"They did not try the main gate," Delphine said, addressing Aelis immediately with no preamble. "But they did whip up a small riot . . . poor folk they drove up here from Slop's End and Old Canals, gave them rocks and torches and told them to start a ruckus, threaten some of the great houses. Had to waste time and troops keeping that from getting out of hand." Aelis had turned around and walked alongside her sister back toward the large dining room. "What happened here?"

"Must've come over the walls while guards were distracted. We lost someone in the kitchen, but I think all the rest are safe."

Delphine grunted softly. The way her sister's jaw clenched told Aelis everything she needed to know; Delphine was as angry as she was, as determined to do something about it, though not likely to say anything to that effect. Her sister's control was something she had long envied, second only to her height.

"We'll need to do a thorough search . . ." Delphine's words cut off in a rush and Aelis was thrown to the floor, her sister landing hard atop her, sword clattering away. Amadin darted off, his sword flashing. Aelis and Delphine disentangled themselves and Aelis got to her feet, then helped her sister up.

"There was one playing dead . . . had a crossbow." Delphine reached for her neck, where a thin line of blood had appeared. "Was aiming for you." Delphine's voice had grown curiously distant, and her raised hand began to shake.

Anatomist training took over. Aelis guided her sister's tall, sturdy form to the floor and leaned over the wound. It was shallow but bleeding profusely; the small bolt had grazed the carotid. She rummaged in her belt pouch for the tiny kit she had packed, little more than astringent, needles, thread, and a tincture or two.

"I will handle this, Delphine," she said calmly, but her sister's eyes had rolled back and Aelis leaned over the wound, sniffing at it. There was a harsh, medicinal smell in the wound, something like a sharply distilled spirit. Her knife was in her hand and she was reaching for two spells immediately: a Delving to identify the poison and a Ligature to stop the bleeding.

Both spells slipped through her fingers like thin ice dissolving into water. She tried again. Nothing.

Delphine was convulsing, her limbs thrashing. "Hold her down," Aelis said sharply, hoping that fear, even panic, was not creeping into her voice. There was no time for litanies or prayers.

She snuck a glance at Amadin, who had returned and was standing there with his sword bared, and shut her eyes.

She did the only thing she could.

Onoma and Stregon, hear me. I Abjure the curse I have wrought. I free Amadin Mauntell Carrafhyn of my death's venom. He is free; lift this curse and return the power I formed it with.

The curse vanished instantly, freeing her mind and enough power to do what she needed. The Pulse and the Ligature came to her immediately. The bleeding stopped while Aelis examined what the poison was doing.

It was quickly, violently attacking Delphine's heart, lungs, and the nerve impulses that controlled her limbs. Her heart was beating out of all control and rhythm; her arms and legs twitched; her lungs were contracting without allowing her to draw in breath. Aelis could not put a name to the poison, but she could fight it.

First, the Stasis; it stopped every system of Delphine's body precisely where it was. The poison could not advance an inch as Aelis's will seized control of her, arresting it as it traveled in Delphine's bloodstream, stopping her heart in its mad beat, forcing her lungs open.

Then, the Blood Purge. Delphine let out a ragged whistling sound that Aelis knew would've been a scream if her sister had any control of her body at all.

The poison, the intruder, was gone. There was still what it had done to Delphine's organs, but she rolled the Stasis into Aldayim's Restorative, a gentle yet powerful wave of magic that rolled each tissue and system it touched back to a calm equilibrium. Delphine would be sick and weak for hours, perhaps a day; but the poison would not have her.

Aelis opened her eyes with a gasp. Her hand had cramped around her dagger; unlocking her fingers hurt. Sliding it back into place on the back of her belt took three tries. Delphine was slowly sitting up; a crowd of soldiers, cooks, and other servants was watching from a few feet away.

"What was that?" Delphine's voice was cracked and low, barely audible.

"That was poison," Aelis said, her own voice little better. "One I can't name, but as bad as many I could."

"Whatever you did hurt worse than when an orc's fist crushed my eye," Delphine said, slowly sitting up.

Aelis stood on shaking legs, felt cold sweat collecting on her neck and the small of her back. The world swam and turned in her vision. "That means it worked," she was saying, when several odd things in her field of vision clicked into place. Time seemed to slow.

Miralla was running toward her, sword out, eyes glowing white again, pointing. Aelis whirled around, saw Amadin standing behind her. His sword was sheathed but his hand was curled around something. She stepped to the side, instinctively, as he stepped forward as if to help her.

Miralla reached them, her sword sinking deep into Amadin's stomach. The elf crumpled around it, his breath punched from his lungs in something akin to a sigh. Aelis was too stunned to speak, too tired to react as Miralla drew her sword clear, wet with their fellow warden's blood, and kicked his legs out from under him.

She turned to Miralla, her eyes wide, but her friend had anticipated the question. She pointed down to Amadin's crumpled form, blood pooling under him. His hand fell open.

One of the small crossbow bolts favored by the assassins, like the one that had grazed Delphine's neck, fell out of his slackened hand, its tip glistening wetly in the bright glare of the lights against the polished wood floor. Aelis ignored it and knelt at Amadin's side.

It took her two tries to get her dagger out, and he feebly slapped at her hands as she worked to assess his wounds. She needed no Delve but the Ligature she reached for to squeeze his severed blood vessels shut and stop the flow of blood proved too evasive. She cut away his clothing and reached for her kit while pressing one hand against the wound. She got the small bottle of astringent open and splashed some onto the wound, but the blood would not stop. Still Aelis kept reaching for a Ligature, even as Miralla brushed past her and kicked Amadin's sword away.

"Delphine," Aelis croaked weakly, "get everyone out of hiding, please. Tell them the password is *Duskdrop*. And by Onoma's last embrace, ask if any of them are a physician or a surgeon. Send someone running for the next-nearest anatomist." The world swam in her vision. She glanced up at Amadin's face, which was pale and drawn. He was mumbling something she could not hear so she leaned close.

"Go," she caught, and "done," and a smattering of Elvish she didn't understand.

"No," she muttered, "I . . ."

". . . compelled," he grated out. "The chance was too near. I could not . . ."

His eyes rolled back and Aelis pressed what little remained of her resources of will and formulaic thought through the hilt of her dagger, reaching for his soul, preparing to Bind it till better medical help could arrive.

Something, she did not know what, slapped her grasp away. She almost recoiled physically from the way her grasp had been denied, as if she were an annoying child reaching for something an adult did not want her to have. She grasped at it again and felt her soul recoil within her.

Amadin gave a gurgling sigh. Aelis felt the blood beneath her hand cease to spurt, no longer driven by the pulse of a beating heart. She staggered to her feet and turned on Miralla.

"Why?" She had tried to yell but the word came out a defeated whisper.

"He had taken up that poison bolt to stab you, Aelis. To graze it against your neck and let it kill you as if it had just been an assassin who'd shot you and the poison acted slowly."

"And there was no option? No . . ." Aelis broke off. Her vision swam again and arms caught her as she swayed. She stumbled as she was guided to a chair, and a glass filled with an amber liquid was pressed into her hand. She lifted it, intent on draining it, stopped to taste the first few drops of a genuine Tirravalan brandy, then gulped down the rest.

She sat with the glass in her hand, eyes closed, images swimming against the back of her eyelids. She heard the tramp of feet and the calls of soldiers, her sister's voice guiding the guests away, her father's voice apologizing.

Aelis was not sure how long she sat before she opened her eyes to find her father and Delphine sitting nearby, having pulled chairs back upright from the table that had been ruined by whatever force the assassins had applied.

"There's a dead underbu . . ." she began, but her father raised a hand.

"I know, Aelis. His name was Torasso. He had just come into our service. His family will be taken care of. I swear it."

Aelis nodded. "Where's Miralla?"

"Warden Despatia is securing the other warden's body," Delphine said, "as well as the assassins'. With the help of your . . . coach drivers." Aelis could hear her sister's professional doubt.

Aelis nodded again. She could feel the brandy's warmth flow through her.

"We're having most of the prepared food served to the staff and guards. But there's no reason we three, and Warden Despatia and your servants, cannot eat as well. And you look like you need to."

Aelis almost rebelled against the suggestion merely because of who had made it, but her medical self knew that she *did* need to eat, having expended so very much energy both magical and physical.

"Timmuk, Andresh, and Mihil are not my servants, my lord," she said instead, "they are my friends. And if they had not been here . . ."

"There would have been absolute carnage in the kitchen," Delphine said. "I know professional handiwork when I see it. Warden Despatia has sent to Cabal Keep for officials to come and take such reports as you must give. The civil government of the city will also want to be informed, so . . ."

"They can go on wanting," Aelis said. "Wardens do not answer to any civil authority this side of the Estates House or the Tri-Crowns."

"As a member of said house," the Count began, "I *will* demand that reports be made to the city's council and guards. Citizens were attacked on a large scale, Aelis. This cannot be swept away. I will handle all the inquiries and make any report."

"This is going to be an even longer night than it already has been, isn't it?"

"Thankfully there are two more bottles of that family-label brandy," her father said. "Laid down before either of you were born."

30

BORING CONVERSATIONS

Aelis prided herself on being able to spot a boring conversation from quite a long way away. So, when Lascenise guards attempted to pin her down on any point, she simply invoked warden authority. Finally, she told one guard that all he could possibly do was get in the way of her investigations and that if he wanted to attempt to arrest two wardens and their servants, he was welcome to try.

She was sitting outside, sharing an awkward silence with Miralla, when a coach rattled up the drive, careening so fast that sparks flew from the horses' hooves.

Miralla and Aelis came to their feet.

"I will testify," Miralla said suddenly. "I'll swear in court to my diviner's vision. In a mages' court that should be . . ."

"I'll ask Khorais if it's admissible," Aelis responded. "And thank you." This last may have sounded more grudging than she wished.

The warden coach came to an abrupt halt, discharging Mazadar and two wardens Aelis did not know.

"Despatia. De Lenti. What the fuck happened?" Mazadar was wearing a breastplate over a short-quilted gambeson in conjurer's brown, an axe clutched in one hand the way one might hold a walking stick. The other wardens wore swords; it was too dark for Aelis to make out much of their features or even the colors they wore.

"An attack by assassins. Professional, more or less. They used a diversion to distract the house guards, and then . . ."

"I mean what happened to Warden Mauntell."

Aelis and Miralla shared a quick glance.

"That is probably best discussed elsewhere, Commander," Miralla said.

"I will decide when and where we discuss anything, Warden, and I have decided *here* and *now*."

Mazadar curled his free hand into a fist and raised it, and Aelis felt a wind whipping up around them. She heard the wind as a kind of distant hum, but guessed that anyone on the other side of it would hear *only* the wind.

"Speak," Mazadar commanded.

Miralla and Aelis opened their mouths, but the confused jumble of their words made them both stop. Mazadar rubbed a knuckle against his forehead, then said, "de Lenti, you first."

"I was attending to a wounded person after the fighting had stopped. I was dimly aware that Amadin was nearby. When I had completed my work, Warden Despatia ran over and . . ." She tried to spur her overtired brain to find a kinder way of saying *carved Amadin like a side of pork* and came up with "ran Warden Mauntell through."

There was a muted grumble from the two wardens who had arrived with Mazadar. Leather creaked; swords shifted on hips. Aelis knew she was looking at swordsmen who were preparing to get aggressive.

"And why did you do that, Warden Despatia?"

"Throughout the fight, Aelis, Amadin, and I had benefited from my battle trance," Miralla said. "Against significant odds, we three came through it with minor wounds, if any. Such a trance can linger in bits and pieces even after it's been dismissed. In that moment I saw, felt . . . I *knew* that Warden Mauntell was going to attempt to kill Warden de Lenti. He had palmed a poisoned crossbow bolt . . . the exact same kind of missile Aelis was going to great pains to save Colonel de Lenti from. He was going to scrape it against her neck and claim she'd been wounded in the fray."

"What kind of poison was this, de Lenti?"

"I could not identify it, Commander. But it took me Five Orders worth of necromantic power to cleanse it from the victim."

"Who was?"

"Colonel de Lenti, commanding officer of the de Lenti Count's Own Horse." She paused and added, "My eldest sister."

"And is there any corroborating evidence regarding Warden Mauntell's action?"

"He had a poisoned bolt in his hand when he hit the floor," Aelis said. *And he, or something, prevented me from healing him. He wanted to die.*

"Why would Warden Mauntell attempt to kill Warden de Lenti?"

Now or never, Aelis thought, then she said, "Pardon me, Commander. But it was not the first time."

At this, Mazadar's eyes snapped up from the loose stones of the coach path. "What?"

"The night that an assassin breached the keep . . . that man had been after Amadin."

"Because?"

"Because Amadin failed to kill me on our trip to Lascenise. Or failed to see me dead in an ambush."

"And the relation to the assassin?"

"Sent by the people who had wanted Amadin to kill me in the first place." Aelis paused. "I think that when Amadin died he said something about being . . . compelled."

"And who are they? Who could compel a warden with forty years in the service? Where do you find anyone that strong?"

"He did not necessarily mean magical compulsion. There are other means of compelling behavior . . ."

"Answer my question, de Lenti."

Aelis had very little store of reserve left in her, but what was there, she called upon, blanking her face and resisting all the little nervous tics—licking her lips, or swallowing, or flicking her eyes.

"I cannot say, Commander." Aelis was aware that was a careful evasion and even more aware of the way Mazadar's eyes narrowed in their focus on her.

"Cannot, or will not?"

"I do not know who they are." *Technically true*, she thought. Given how things were going, she was not about to say the words *Shadow Congress* to Mazadar, as she had no way of knowing if he was among their number.

"So the longest-serving warden in my command is dead," Mazadar said, "at the hands of two wardens who haven't got three full fucking years between them."

"At my hand, Commander. And I will swear in any inquest or tribunal that I did what I did while experiencing the remains of a Diviner's Trance. My vision is corroborated by the bolt in his hand and his approach to Warden de Lenti."

"That may be, Warden Despatia, but I am confining you to your quarters and striking your name from the duty rosters, pending an inquest." He turned to Aelis. "I have half a mind to order you confined to your quarters as well."

"I am working as an advocate for an Archmagister. I do not think you can."

"What you mean," Mazadar said, very carefully, "is that I might not have the authority to do so, if one gives the traditions of the advocate a very generous reading. Do not doubt what I *can* do, de Lenti. I *can* have you both seized right now, dragged back to the keep, and clapped in cold iron and silver manacles."

"You are standing on land owned and under the protection of Count Guillame de Lenti un Tirraval," Aelis snapped. "And we are his guests. We will return to the keep under our own power, in a time and manner of *our* choosing, after we have secured my prisoners, unless you want to be hauled before the Estates House to explain your actions."

Mazadar's dome of air dropped and the sounds around them rushed back into Aelis's ears. Horses and their harness; footsteps on the rocks; the voices of Lascenise guards in kettle hats and byrnies chatting with de Lenti troopers.

"For you that may be the case," Mazadar said, "but Warden Despatia is very much under my command, and her confinement begins immediately. Come along, and give me your swordbelt."

Aelis looked at Miralla's face, expecting fury, even hatred. She found resignation, an enviable control of her expression. She watched as her friend unbuckled the supple white leather of her belt, carefully wrapped it around the slim scabbard and silver buckler and held it out. Aelis wanted to snatch it away, to keep it out of the hands of Mazadar and his warden guards, but the dwarf took it himself, handing it over his shoulder without even looking at the man who took it and tucked it under his arm.

"Your diadem," Mazadar rasped.

"Commander, please." Aelis could hear the quaver in her friend's voice. She shared the sudden wave of despair that she knew was threatening Miralla's composure.

"Your diadem, Despatia. You are, after all, capable of the Battle Trance. I'll not have you using that on any more of your fellow wardens."

Aelis wanted to intervene, wanted to tell Miralla she could damn well stay put here, that she was on de Lenti territory and while Mazadar's authority might technically extend there, she'd dearly love to see him argue it with the Count and Delphine and an entire troop of veteran Count's Own. But she didn't, because even if Miralla listened to her, she would be destroying her career.

Carefully, Miralla slid the band of silver from her hair and held it out. Mazadar took it in a hand that looked as if it could, even might, crush it simply to see how it felt. But he tucked it into a pouch on his belt.

"And you," he said, turning to Aelis. "Your arrogance will undo you, and I'll be there to see it. You will be called to an inquest. Do not fail to appear." Mazadar turned away, snapped his fingers. Miralla watched the warden carrying her sword glide past them and disappear into the coach.

Aelis ignored him and reached out to grasp Miralla's shoulder. "If it turns out that you do need an advocate . . . by Stregon's balls, ask someone better at it than me."

Miralla laughed, a wild trill of desperation behind the mirth.

"I will be at the inquest, if it even comes to that. I will corroborate anything you say. And you will spend no more than a few days in this ridiculous confinement. I promise you."

"Despatia!" Mazadar's voice called from the coach, and he banged a fist on the warden sigil on the door.

"Stop making promises, Aelis. We both know you're shit at keeping them." Miralla squared her shoulders and walked off.

Aelis forced herself to watch her friend step into the coach, to continue watching as the warden driving it seized the levers to power it and then as it completed a graceful arc on the crushed stones of the entrance path and went back out into the wide boulevard.

Only then did she go back inside to begin to face the various consequences of that evening.

She was met by Timmuk, Andresh, and Mihil, who were passing an expensive-looking smoked-glass bottle back and forth in the shattered doorway to the dining room. Beyond it, Delphine and the Count were speaking to guardsmen who had fancier helmets and colored pins on their half-capes, clearly officers of some kind.

"Tell me that we have a couple left alive," Aelis said as she took the bottle from Andresh's offering hand. She sniffed it and found the overpowering nose of wheated whiskey, not her favorite. She took a swig from the bottle anyway, then handed it to Timmuk, feeling the whiskey burrow, burning, into her stomach.

"Hate to lie to you, boss," Mihil said, "but there's just the one. And the local talent have scooped him up."

"Onoma's tits. How many dead?"

"Two dozen," Timmuk said.

"There was at least one still alive in here; how else did he shoot at me?"

"That elf warden did for him . . . looks like he might have done for a lot of them. Any number of torn-out throats," Mihil said.

"There's no need to weep for them," Timmuk said. "They were assassins. You paid them in their own coin."

"I wanted a prisoner to interrogate," Aelis said.

"We'll just have to negotiate that with the guards," Mihil said. "You know . . . the ones you called amateurs, and said they'd only get in the way of your investigations, whose questions you refused to even listen to? Piece of piss."

Aelis looked at the guard officer in his enameled armor and helmet and thought a moment. "If one of you could find out which station he's being taken to, we'll just pay a visit in the morning."

"Smart," Timmuk said. "Day shift won't know you." Andresh nodded, added some words of emphasis in Dwarfish. "Andresh says you might still need to slide some silver across a desk to get access to the prisoner."

Aelis nodded as if she'd been thinking that all along. She was as tired as she'd ever been and needed sleep before she could deal with even one more problem. It did give her better odds of seeing the prisoner, though. She wasn't going to risk taking him to Cabal Keep, not with what kept happening to prisoners there.

Her head swam as she considered all the possibilities and variables and the few days till Bardun Jacques was due in court.

"I need to bid good night to my father and my sister," she said. The guard officer they were speaking with had concluded whatever he had to say to them and was turning away. Guards were collecting bodies of the assassins from where they'd fallen. Aelis paused, watching them place the assailants' dropped knives, crossbows, and bolts into heavy canvas sacks that they wired shut.

The crossbows and daggers looked very familiar; she was confident that if she took one of the blades apart, she'd find a tiny skull hidden beneath the furniture.

"My Lord Count, Colonel," she said stiffly, "I must beg your leave to return to Cabal Keep."

"Of course, Aelis," her father said, also with stiff formality. "I, ah . . ."

"What our lord father means to say is that he regrets not having taken your advice from the very beginning and canceling this event," Delphine put in, just loud enough for the two of them to hear and no one else. "That he is going to make an extremely generous endowment for the family of the young man who was killed. And what I need to say," she added, clasping Aelis's forearm with one hand, "is that you saved my life, little sister. I will not forget that."

"I won't let you," Aelis teased, clasping her sister in return, grinning. She was still tired, bone-weary, furious at what had taken place there tonight. But she could not help but feel a glow of pride from Delphine's praise.

"If there is anything we can do to help in your . . . endeavor," her father said. His manner was stilted and he was looking at a spot on the floor rather than on her face.

"My lord," Aelis said, "you have long since done everything you could. The both of you. Now I must return to the keep to rest before I continue my work."

"You could sleep here, Aelis. You are always welcome . . ."

"I wish I could." She meant that; she knew any chamber she was given here would be more comfortable than the keep. The food would be made specifically to her taste.

But the room around her smelled like blood. A man had died here because of her inability to plan or convince her father to take her seriously.

"I take back what I said before." There was more force in her voice than she'd expected.

"Excellent," her father said, "we'll have rooms prepared . . ."

"Not about that. About what you could do for me." The Count looked at her expectantly.

"Take me more seriously in the future. A man, a young man, in our service, under our protection, died here tonight. He did not have to. That is on all of us, me as much as you. But I told you this would happen."

The Count drew a sharp breath, the kind that had long since led Aelis to expect a sharp tongue. Instead, he nodded, his face as grim as if he'd just bitten down on glass and decided to chew and swallow it regardless of how it cut.

"We will see to his family, Aelis," Delphine insisted.

"I know you will," Aelis said. "But we should have seen to *him*. What was his full name?"

"Torasso Malkin," Delphine said.

Aelis repeated the name in her head, once, twice, a third time, committing it to memory.

"I hope, if my business allows, to see one or both of you again before I leave Lascenise," Aelis said.

"Of course," Delphine said. The Count only nodded again.

Finally, Aelis turned to go, trying not to look at the bloodstains and the detritus of broken plates and cups and tables on the floor.

She was asleep before the coach had even gotten off the street. Mihil woke her when they arrived at the keep, and walked with her to her chambers.

Aelis heard him dragging furniture around to make up his sleeping pallet, but she was barely able to undress and get into her bed before sleep claimed her.

31

A MORE INTERESTING CONVERSATION

If I'm going to feel hungover, I could have at least gotten drunk first.

That might not have been Aelis's very first thought as she awoke the next morning, but it was the first thought she consciously formed. She had a throbbing headache that was only just the very tip of the various pains that radiated throughout her body.

Suppressing a groan, she threw off her sweat-soaked blanket and swung her legs onto the stone floor. Hunched, she staggered to the washbasin, picked up the jug meant to pour water into the bowl, and drank directly from it, feeling her throat loosen as water gushed into it. She felt her skin drinking up the rivulets that poured down her cheeks to her neck.

"Want me to get anything?" Aelis turned slowly, and saw Mihil, who, having dragged the only two chairs in the room together, was lying across them, directly in front of the door. He was motionless, practically cocooned in his blanket, but obviously awake.

"Coffee." Her voice cracked and broke in the middle of the word.

"You'll want a little eye opener before that. Trust me."

"I don't want a hangover cure."

"It's not that. Or . . . not only that," he said. He threw off the blanket and hopped nimbly down. "You'll, ah . . . want to clean your arms, Aelis."

"What?" She looked down and realized that blood spattered her bare upper arms, and stained the silk half-sleeves she hadn't even unlaced before she fell asleep. "Drewic is going to have my hide for this."

"Important bit is, it's all their blood," Mihil said, then threw on his faded blue coat and slipped out the door.

Aelis carefully unlaced her sleeves and set them down, then spent a frantic moment looking for her wand, which was not in either sleeve pocket, before finding it sitting on her worktable, along with a jumble of papers, pens, ink bottles, and other implements.

"What would Maurenia say?" she muttered. "Something devastating, I'm sure."

Aelis resolved to clean her rooms, stow her gear, and take better care of it all in the future. She started by finding the dress she'd worn the night before, a pool of black silk at the side of her bed. Carefully, she gathered it up and hung it in her wardrobe, apart from the other clothes, not having the heart to check it for bloodstains.

She used what water remained in her basin to wash her arms and hands and was not surprised that the water turned pink as the stains slowly scrubbed away. By the time she was done, she decided to, for once, make her bed.

Aelis was still struggling with that when Mihil returned, a liveried keep servant in tow. The servant looked around for a spot to set down her tray, causing Aelis to abandon making the bed and to gather up the papers and other detritus and, after glancing about for a moment, dump it all on her rumpled blanket.

The servant gratefully set down the tray, Mihil slipped something into her hand, and she scurried off. The tray held a flagon, a bowl of eggs, a large carafe containing a red liquid and a very small one containing an almost clear juice, as well as loaves of bread and large cups.

"Last night was the first time you've been in a fight that big, wasn't it?" Mihil glanced up at her and Aelis nodded.

"Thought so. Sometimes, for a little while, there's an odd kind of . . . euphoria, I guess. I've felt it, after big engagements." He calmly began mixing things from the tray, still talking. "And drunk myself to sleep after them, too. I know you didn't quite do the last, and I know you've fought before, but . . . that was something closer to real combat than a street fight. The intensity of it's like nothing else." He poured generously from the large carafe into each mug.

"Is that wine? Did you just mix the noble product of the vintner's ancient art with beer and *raw egg?*"

"No. This is juice of the fenberry. Alone, it curdles on the tongue, but mixed with beer . . ." He sighed. "Mixed with beer it's still pretty shit, but it won't turn the mouth inside out. This is whatever citron juice they could spare." He splashed some into each mug, took up a long spoon, and stirred vigorously.

"Drink this all, keep it down, follow with bread."

Aelis took the mug and sniffed it. The smell of new, sour beer was strongest, but there was something incredibly acrid about it as well.

"Checking the bouquet, are we? The nose?" Mihil stared up at her, lifted his mug, and started drinking. Aelis couldn't help but follow.

The beer was sour, but the combination of the citron juice and this unfamiliar berry positively roiled in her mouth, making her cheeks pucker and her stomach clench. She gulped every drop of it down, though, as instructed, and set her mug back on the tray with a thump just as Mihil lowered his.

She had exercised too much de Lenti composure the night before to hold on to it now. She grimaced and gave her head a painful shake.

"Onoma's tits, gnome. I have done the slop bucket challenge at the Sink in the Tremont, and I have drunk wine that was a quarter of an hour from turning to vinegar, but that . . ." She twisted her mouth. "That is the worst thing I've ever tasted."

"And yet it's full of things your body wants right now."

Aelis stared at him through narrowed eyes. "I'm the Lyceum-trained anatomist, physician, and surgeon, and . . ."

"And give it a few minutes while we eat bread and wait for the coffee to be brought up," Mihil said. "If it doesn't work, take it out of my pay."

"How much do I owe you now?"

"Figuring hazard pay, my brilliant ideas, my proprietary postbattle pick-me-up recipe, plus all the time I'm spending far away from my loved ones . . ." He paused and returned Aelis's stare evenly. "Arris counts as a loved one," he said. "I figure fifty gold trees by now, at least."

"That's more than a naval captain makes in a year."

"And I'm doing more work than a naval captain does in a year, so it works out." Aelis couldn't help but laugh, and Mihil joined her.

They got quiet. Aelis looked at the floor and felt Mihil's eyes on her.

"Tell me about the locket."

"The what?" She snapped her eyes up to meet his.

"The locket. That cheap little painting you took into that shop when we were book-hunting. You said to ask about it another time, when you weren't busy. Well . . ."

Aelis sighed and leaned back in her chair. "I found it on someone. On their body."

Mihil waited.

"On the body of the first person I killed."

Mihil showed an amazing facility with silence. He didn't ask another question, didn't sniff, move, cause his chair to creak, or even begin to form a question.

"I took it and thought . . . I'd find out who she was. Where she came from."

"Why?"

"Because I felt I owed it to her."

"Did you have to do it?"

"In a sense, in the moment . . . yes."

"But?"

"But if I had been smarter about it, it wouldn't have come to that."

"Permission to speak freely, boss?"

"Have you *ever* needed it before?"

"Why'd you want to find out about the locket, then? Find out where the woman came from? Find her people? And tell them . . . what?"

"I hadn't thought that far ahead."

"Got no particular wisdom about what you would've said to them, but . . . here's the part I was asking permission for. Did you want to find them for her, or for you?"

"What do you mean?"

"I mean, is it because you want to look her parents or her siblings in the eye and say, hello, I put a couple feet of steel in your girl's guts . . ."

"Cut her throat, actually."

"Midarra's eyes, boss."

"It's important to be precise."

"Okay then, let's be precise. Did you hope to find those people to make them feel better or to make *yourself* feel better? Because it doesn't seem like you're going to find them, and you're going to have to make some peace with that. You can drown it or bury it or, undoubtedly, some other, healthier third thing that I know fuck all about. But you're going to have to put it down. Somehow."

There was a discreet knock at Aelis's door, and she noticed two things. The first was that she smelled coffee; the second was that it did not turn her stomach or make her head ache. She lifted her head and drew in a deep breath, then caught Mihil's grin of triumph.

"There's going to be no living with you now, is there?"

"Was there anyway? Come on."

✦   ✦   ✦

Aelis soon found she had a proper appetite again, so coffeed, breakfasted, washed, and freshly dressed and armed, she and Mihil took a coach for the watch house where last night's prisoner was being held. It wasn't quite in the Azare Courts—such neighborhoods didn't have watch stations, largely because the various Estates House families who lived there wanted their own guards to have as free a hand as they might like—but it was just the other side of a street, at the very edge of Ruby Chapel.

The watch house itself was easy enough to identify—three stories, barred windows, a front door just large enough and heavy enough to suggest the word "gate," even a miniature battlement that overhung the front door and allow good fields of bowshot down every street that led to it. There were no taller buildings within a several-block radius.

As their coach slowed to a stop, Mihil said, "Let me have a little look around."

"Do you think they'll have circulated a description with orders that no guardsman is to speak to me?"

"Like any body of armed folk, city guards can be an insular sort. They draw together in the face of any kind of threat or insult. Just natural."

"What do you mean?"

"What if I told you the wardens were a sack of worthless, sponging shits, too busy looking to their own comforts and privileges to do any of the fucking good in the world they like to talk about so much?"

Anger flared in Aelis instantly. "I'd say you haven't seen *half* of the magical horrors I have, and you've had fewer good meals than Archmagister Bardun Jacques has life-or-death struggles that would freeze your marrow and . . . oh . . ." Aelis stopped, probably faster than she ever had when getting started on a good sharp rant. " I see."

"Right. Just . . . hang back a little." Mihil darted off for the main door, pausing to speak with the two staff-bearing, scale-armored guards standing outside. He glanced back at Aelis, who fought her natural inclination to hurry and followed at a leisurely pace, giving him just enough time to have slipped inside and start talking to someone.

Inside was the kind of orderly, near-military precision Aelis understood instantly. Barred, locked doors preventing further entry into the building, guards standing near the entrances, a ranking guard manning a central position behind a large desk.

"Sir," that guard now said, nodding at Mihil, then, rather more coldly at Aelis, "Warden."

"We'd like to speak to one of your guests," Mihil began. There were a couple of small steps in front of the desk, for shorter folk to stand on. Mihil hopped up and casually leaned one elbow on the desk. "Hauled in last night from the big fracas in the Courts."

"What kind of authorization have you got?" The guard, a woman of middle years, had flat eyes, a flat voice, and a flat aspect.

You can't decide you don't like someone this fast, Aelis told herself.

"Lieutenant," Mihil began.

"Guard First Class," the woman corrected.

"This organization just doesn't know talent when they see it, eh? Anyway, Guard First Class, you ever pass through the Dock Street nick down in Slop's End?"

She sniffed, stared hard at Mihil a moment more before uttering a predictable "No," in the same flat tone.

"Well, Sergeant Fitzwillow there, prime fellow, rock of the service, he'll vouch for me."

"And you are?"

"Mihil Angleton. Fitz and I go back years. Years. Named his first child after me. Awkward when she turned out to be a girl, but a bet's a bet." He winked.

Aelis was certain this was a losing strategy, but she decided to let Mihil flail a bit.

"Fine. We'll send a messenger down to . . . Dock Street, was it? And get written authorization from Sergeant Fitzwillow. Should take three or four days."

"We haven't got that kind of time, so perhaps just take the good sergeant's word for it."

"Please stop leaning on my desk."

Aelis glided up behind Mihil. "I was one of the wardens present yesterday at the aforementioned *fracas*. I would like to speak to the prisoner."

"Got authorization of any . . ."

Aelis leaned forward and tapped her sword hilt. "It's right here, as an abjurer, and a duly appointed warden answering to the Estates House and the Tri-Crowns. My way may not be barred."

"You may have to wait . . ."

"My full name is Warden Aelis *de Lenti*. The *fracas* happened at my father's house. Now, Guard First Class, do you want both the warden service and the Estates House asking questions of your watch station?"

She could see the guard weighing and testing the words, wondering, was Aelis serious, was she willing to cause that much of a headache, was it worth the very tiny threat that folk as lofty as Estates House Seats were going to enter her life for no good cause? Slowly the guard pushed back from her desk.

"Come around to the third door," she muttered, a little defeated.

They had to wait for several rounds of barred doors to be unlocked so they could pass through and then locked again. At last they found themselves in an office cluttered with piles of overstuffed folders and tall stacks of paper. The man seated behind the desk—Aelis knew an officer's tokens of rank, golden epaulets and insignia on a collar, when she saw them—was much older than her, trim and composed. He did not rise as the Guard First Class led them in.

"Captain Lannick, warden wants to talk to the prisoner from last night's de Lenti affray."

"Thank you, guard. Dismissed." The captain studied Aelis with hard gray eyes; the guard gave a poor imitation of clicking her heels and walked stiffly away.

"Why should I allow an interfering, arrogant warden to see my prisoner?"

Aelis was ready to lunge across the table at him but Mihil smoothly stepped in front of her.

"Now, Captain Lannick," Mihil began. "The safety of Lascenise is at stake; shouldn't the warden service and the esteemed guards work hand in hand for the good of all?"

"We should," Lannick said, "but all too often we are ordered about, abused, referred to as . . ." Here he scrambled for a piece of paper and held it up to the light of his desk lamp, narrowing his eyes to read. "Blundering amateurs who might have just enough imagination and skill to interfere with an actual investigator." His eyes slid back up to regard Aelis. "Does that sound familiar, Warden?"

"It does." Aelis wanted to spit the words at him, insist that they were true, but for the moment she stayed reserved.

"Technically, I have to allow a warden on an authorized investigation, with the proper paperwork from Cabal Keep, to speak to any prisoner or request any assistance I can render. But I don't have to do it immediately . . . after all, sometimes prisoners are hard to find. So, show me your orders, and come back in . . . let's say, two days."

"I am not on an assignment from Cabal Keep," Aelis said, "I . . ."

"Then get out of my watch station," Captain Lannick said.

"I am working as an advocate in a criminal case against another warden . . ."

"I hope you're better at that than dealing with people you think are *beneath* you."

". . . on behalf of Archmagister and Warden Emeritus Bardun Jacques, and I must speak to that prisoner."

Lannick sat furtherupright in his chair. "On behalf of who?"

"Archmagister and Warden Emeritus Bardun Jacques."

Lannick stood. He was neither tall nor broad across the shoulders, but there was a presence to him, though Aelis thought the golden bits of rank about his armor were ridiculous frippery.

"And how does this prisoner bear on your investigation?"

Aelis swallowed hard. "I think it is very likely that the people Bardun Jacques was investigating when he was arrested hired this coterie of assassins."

"There are no Assassins' Guilds in Lascenise," Lannick said automatically.

"Last night, at the . . . affray . . . your guards gathered many a knife off the bodies of the attackers. Take the furniture off one of them, search on the tang . . . drip a bit of etching acid if you must. If they don't have skulls on them, then you can assume I don't know what I'm talking about. If they do, then you do have assassins, and they're known as the Hidden Skulls."

"Follow me."

Lannick led Mihil and Aelis through a corridor and down a stairway to a basement room with a heavy iron cage, built floor to ceiling. He unlocked it, rummaged among shelves built inside it, and came out with a cloth-wrapped package; Aelis could see the shapes of blades inside it.

"Follow me," he ordered again, and they did, eventually coming to an armory. Rows of cudgels, staves, short stabbing swords, crossbows, and long poleaxes sat on racks. Scale byrnies were piled on heavy tables, haphazard stacks of iron and leather caps in various states of disrepair in every empty spot.

"Sergeant Brashgo," the captain called out. "A moment, please."

In response, a dwarf emerged from the dimly lit back of the armory. He wore a cut-down version of the watch's scale armor, his enormously muscled arms emerging bare from the adjusted sleeves.

"Yes, Captain?"

Lannick held out the roll of knives. "Remove the furniture from these three weapons. Tell me if you see anything inscribed on the tang of any of the blades."

"We already looked for a maker's mark on some of the stock that came in, Captain, there wasn't . . ."

"Did it sound like a request, Sergeant?"

"Right, Captain." From the wide belt stuck around his thick middle, the dwarf selected a couple of tools. He cleared some workspace by removing a stack of helms, the leather rotten and the iron rusting, and setting them on the floor.

Unlike when Aelis had taken one of the knives apart, Sergeant Brashgo needed no lubricant to pry the blade loose, only his small chisel, which pried out pegs and snapped off the smooth bone handles with ease. Aelis admired the facility and speed with which the dwarf laid three bare blades on the table, their hilts, pommels, and assorted other pieces laid aside.

Stregon, if ever you look over foolish abjurers, please do so now.

He peered down at them. "I don't see anything, captain."

"It's dark in here," Mihil pointed out.

"Not too dark for me to see the gray in your stubble and the yellow in the whites of your eyes, gnome." Sergeant Brashgo looked up sharply. "Dwarven eyes are used to the dark." He was running a thumb over one of the blades as he spoke, and suddenly paused. "Wait."

"A weak acid, if you have it," Aelis said, hope surging inside her chest, which she carefully kept out of her voice.

"Not a lot of call for fine engraving work down here in the basement armory of a watch station," Brashgo said, "but I've a rasp to hand." He dug in his tool-belt again and produced a square block of wood that had rough metal plates affixed to two sides. He carefully pulled it across the tang of the blade a few times, the scrape of metal on metal running right up and down Aelis's spine with an awful, wrenching echo. With one eye closed, he examined the blade for a long moment.

"I'll be dipped in shit . . . I mean, Captain, it, ah . . . looks like a skull engraved on the tang here. Worn, but definitely a skull."

The sergeant held the blade out and the captain came forward to take it. He carried it to one of the few lights in the dim basement and bent close over it. "And the other two?"

"Looks like similar markings, Captain."

Captain Lannick straightened and set the bare blade down. "Come with me, Warden."

Once again, Aelis and Mihil followed Captain Lannick through what would otherwise have been an impenetrable warren of stairs, hallways, and doors that opened to one of the small handful of keys that were chained to his belt. From the sounds and the smells that became apparent—low murmuring voices, snoring, unwashed bodies, the clang of iron-bound doors—they had come to the cells. Guards stood at the inside of the door and the far door, and all of them clicked heels and raised fists to breasts in salute as Lannick walked in.

Eventually they came to a long corridor of hardwood doors with a great deal of ironwork on them, heavy locks, and bars on the outside.

"Do you want a guard with you?"

"I don't see why I'll need one."

"He's dangerous," Lannick said.

"I'm an abjurer." Aelis's tone suggested that this should've been the end of any conversation on the point, but the captain apparently had other ideas.

"I'll need your sword and your dagger before you go in," Lannick said.

"I have no intention of hurting him," Aelis said.

"I do not want what is apparently a devoted assassin to wind up with a blade in his hands."

Anger flared in her. She thought that none of it showed on her face any more than the twitch of an eye, but Mihil quickly stepped between her and Lannick. "I'll hold on to them, boss. I'd just get in the way in there."

"Fine." Aelis unbuckled her shoulder belt, wrapped the whole length of it around the two scabbarded weapons, and left the package in Mihil's arms.

"You have a quarter of an hour," Lannick said. He sized Aelis up carefully. "Do you want a truncheon? Just in case?"

"I don't need a heavy length of wood to get anyone to talk to me, Captain." *This man is helping you for unclear reasons and could decide not to at any moment*, she reminded herself. *Do not ruin it.*

"Fine." Lannick snapped his fingers, and the nearest guard sprang toward him. He took a set of manacles from the guard's belt, knelt in front of the cell door, and opened a slot. "Prisoner. Come forward and place your hands through the slot . . ."

A dry chuckle was the only answer he got.

"This is truly unnecessary, Captain," Aelis said. "Just let me speak to him."

"He's very dangerous . . ."

"I killed at least half a dozen of his comrades last night. I can handle him."

Lannick looked doubtful, but he closed the slot, and finally selected one of the keys on his belt. He swung open the door just enough for Aelis to enter, then closed it behind her. She heard him lock it, but no bar fell across it.

Not far from her, a man in all black clothes lounged on hard wooden slats that hung from the wall on leather straps. He was ordinary looking, so ordinary that she would not have remarked him in a small crowd; a few days' growth of beard, gray mixed in with the brown, plain dark eyes, balding. There was a hollowness in his eyes, a sharp edge to his cheekbones, that bespoke something out of the ordinary, but it disappeared as soon as she tried to grasp it.

"Ahh, Aelis de Lenti un Tirraval." She'd expected his voice to hold some hard edge, some threat of violence, the whisper of a razor. Instead, it was the plainly cheerful voice of a man trying to sell her something.

"*Warden* Aelis de Lenti un Tirraval," she corrected. Her first thought had been, *How did he know my name?* but she quickly recalled that he, or his fellow assassins, had been hired to kill her.

"My apologies." He made a faint bow from the waist, still seated.

"And you are?"

"Oh, bound for the hangman's noose, I expect. Or the wheel. You can't go trying to kill people in the Azare Courts and not expect the worst."

"You did manage to kill one," Aelis said. "Just none that you targeted."

"That was deeply unprofessional. If I knew who was responsible for that, and any of my guildmates were still alive, I'd have them punished."

"So you're a ranking member then. Maybe a guildmaster?"

Surprise flashed across his face; eyes widened, nostrils flared, then his face went back to that composed facade of blandness.

"No, no. We haven't ranks or any of that nonsense."

"Let's not start lying to one another. Since you have the advantage of me, I'm forced to ask more directly: What's your name?"

The man flicked his eyes from side to side of his narrow stone-walled cell, then back to Aelis. One foot tapped on the floor.

"I don't think that matters." he said, pausing before going on. "You know, we . . . serve the same deity." He pointed a finger at his own black tunic, then pointed to her. "In different ways, and different aspects. But we do both serve She Who Stands on the Threshold."

"Do we, now?"

"Of course. You don't think we could be mere assassins, do you? Nothing but tradesmen, taking gold for our skill and our labor? No. It is a holy thing."

"Is it? Passed down father to son, then? Marked at birth in some way?"

The man broke into a laugh. "I'm not going to reveal any secrets." He smiled widely, eyes suddenly sparkling. "Or perhaps I'm simply full of shit. Maybe all anyone has to do is cross my palm with the right weight of gold or silver and I'll kill anyone they name, in any way they choose. Man, woman, child, I'll kill a fucking horse or a dog or a cat if that's what the person desperate enough to find us and hire us asks."

His foot tapped on the floor again, then stopped. Aelis heard his boot grate across the stone.

"There is one thing, though," he said. "We *are* professionals. When we do take that money, we finish the task."

He hadn't been tapping his feet, not really, just slowly spreading his legs to find purchase to spring. His hands had curled around the leather straps of his cot to help propel his body forward. For all that he wasn't in an ideal position and that he had neither eaten nor slept well, it was a good lunge, his hands aimed straight for Aelis's throat. For many targets, it would've worked. He could've done irreparable damage to *someone's* throat by the time a guard came in and killed him or dragged him away.

If *someone* was not an anatomist of the Lyceum, trained to know exactly what the body could and could not do, who had read the shifting muscles and the way he gathered himself and had known without any doubt what he was preparing to do. If *someone* was not *also* an abjurer and a warden, trained in close combat by the likes of Magister Vosghez and Archmagister Lavanalla. And especially if that *someone* was not Aelis, whose reaction time, first step, and first strike had been extraordinary among her class.

Her first impulse had been to simply drive her fist into his nose to shatter it. The pain and the humiliation might do him a world of good, but there was the slim chance that she might drive the bone in too deep and do some real damage, so she discarded that idea. She also discarded her second option, to step to one side and use his own momentum to guide him face first to smash into the door of the cell, but that might rob him of consciousness or rattle his brain in a way she didn't want to deal with.

She settled on slipping down and to the side and driving her knee into the cluster of nerves just below his sternum and above his navel, causing him to fold over in the kind of immediate and overwhelming pain that instantly changed anyone's priorities.

As he struggled for breath on the floor of the cell, she heard a key rattling in the door.

"I'm not done, Captain," she called out. "And as you can see, I'm not in any danger."

She looked down at the man, who was even now trying to rise, and sighed.

Her wand slipped into her left hand, its light bright green, and she traced dizzying patterns in the air before his eyes, which glassed over.

The Beguilement, also known as Iacop's Pattern, was not her favorite quickly disabling enchantment, as she'd always been partial to the Catnap, but she needed him awake. It was a draining spell, though, climbing in orders the longer the enchanter kept it up. She only did it long enough to make him drag himself to his bench and sit on it.

She finished weaving the tip of her wand in the air and bent to tap him on the crown of his head with it, laying a simple but heavy Charm on him. Then she stepped back.

"What's your name?"

"Topas." His voice was distant, dreamlike, but completely open and friendly. He stared at nothing, sat immobile on the bench, though still slightly hunched over, one hand pressed to his stomach.

"Who hired you, Topas?"

"His name was Arstan Nicholaz." The name landed oddly.

"Arstan Nicholaz is dead."

"That may be. I have not seen him since our one meeting, and that was two weeks ago."

"He has been dead for much longer than that."

"That is the name he used. It could have been a lie."

"Was this man a wizard?"

"Yes, or so we who dealt with him thought."

"Why?"

"He had the arrogance. Assumed he was the most important person in any room. Confirmed when asked."

"Did he carry any implements? Any items that he would not relinquish?"

"Not that I saw. No sword or dagger or staff."

"What did he look like? Was he human, elf?"

"I . . ." Topas turned his eyes up to Aelis, blinking. For a moment she thought her Charm was wearing low, but he just shook his head. "I cannot remember."

"You met this man but you cannot recall what he looked like, not even whether he was a human or a gnome?"

Slowly Topas shook his head.

"Fine." She'd had a new mystery dropped in her lap and she didn't like it, not one bit. "Was he acting for himself, or representing someone?"

"Oh. Something about . . . immortal wizards. Would-be immortals? He was arrogant, and talkative, and generally we don't want to know too much of that kind of thing."

Aelis saw him blink, as though his vision was returning to normal, so she decided to hurry to the end.

"Topas, I don't suppose you'd mind telling me where you live. And where all your workmates lived, and where you met with them to discuss your contracts . . ."

"Of course," he said. "I live on Orlop Court in the Tremont. We meet in an undercellar at the Riverman's Doxy, which one of us owns, and . . . and . . ."

Damn. Those were useful pieces of information to be sure, but not as much as she'd wanted.

Topas came back to himself and she backed away a few steps, though she kept her wand dangling from her left hand, its tip faintly glowing.

The assassin immediately grimaced and clutched at his stomach. He tried to rise to his feet again and Aelis stared hard at him.

"Try it again, assassin. I got what I needed to know from you. This time I won't hold back."

"You . . . plunged magic into my mind. You ripped things from me. Things I would not have said." He sounded aggrieved, horrified.

"And?"

"That's not . . . that isn't right."

"Topas, you killed people for money. You bragged of it just a few moments ago. You and your guild have tried to kill me, twice now. Your opinion on what is *right* can be safely ignored."

"But . . ."

"I'm sure even now the watch captain standing outside is sending guards to raid your house, and your tavern and meeting spot. Your kind are done in Lascenise. And you, as you so mockingly said when I came in, are bound for the noose."

"But I gave you information! I helped . . . I should be shown clemency, I should be . . ."

"I won't have any say in what the civil authorities decide to do with you, Topas. If you had volunteered information, I might have helped you appeal. But you didn't. And if I am still in Lascenise when the day comes, I will go to the platform at the outer wall, and I will watch you hang. And then I will never think about you again. Murder is not a *holy thing.*"

Aelis very pointedly turned her back and went to the door, rapped on it twice. She moved slowly and calmly but held her legs ready to take a stance and drive her heel groin-high in case Topas decided to charge her.

But Topas simply sat where he was, deflated, defeated, silent.

Outside, in place of the captain she found a younger watch officer and Mihil. The gnome handed her back her swordbelt and she buckled it on and pulled it in place over her shoulder. Then she looked expectantly at the young officer who was positioning the bar over the door.

"Captain Lannick ran to gather guards to carry out an action based on the new intelligence that you, Warden, ah . . . gathered. He did ask me to bring you to his office before you left."

The young officer led them to Lannick's office, clicked heels theatrically, and disappeared.

"Warden," Lannick greeted her. He was standing behind his desk, busily signing papers shiny with new ink and bundling them together. "I will not keep you. I wanted to thank you for the intelligence. We have guards on their way to that tavern already."

"I don't suppose you would consider sharing any pertinent information you find, Captain."

"If you do the same, Warden." He finished binding up the documents in seals of blue ribbon. "And I wish you success in freeing the Archmagister from his current difficulties."

"You know him," Aelis said, thinking back. "Your entire attitude changed when I mentioned his name. Why?"

"Because Bardun Jacques is the kind of warden who gave us help whenever we asked. Many Lascenise guards are alive because your Archmagister was standing next to them when they rousted some villains. When he needs something from our service, he gets it."

"Thank you, Captain." Aelis swallowed hard. "I will try to remember that."

Captain Lannick nodded, and Aelis quickly made her way out, Mihil in tow, chewing on her embarrassment at Lannick's gentle but unmistakable reproach.

Once they were back on the street, Aelis pulled Mihil aside. She was filled with nervous energy, a desire to be somewhere, doing *something,* immediately. It was a struggle to calm herself and set priorities.

"Mihil," she said, "I need you to take a note to Khorais. Then, with Khorais, check on the Archmagister, and convey to him everything that's happened yesterday and today. Do not say any of it out loud; write it down, show it to him, cover it with normal talking. They may have tried to kick you out of the keep, but they cannot deny him a meeting with his lawyer."

"Where are you going?"

"The Lyceum. I need answers, and they're only to be found in the Records office."

"Are you sure you should travel alone?"

"At this point, I'd welcome them having another go at me," Aelis said. "Another attack means someone else I can grab and wring information from."

"Isn't the trial in just, what . . . two days?"

"Something like that. Please, beg Khorais to do absolutely anything she can to delay it further." She handed Mihil a purse that contained roughly half the coin she had left.

"What's this for?" He hefted the bag in his hand.

"Bribery. Any that you don't need to spend, you get to keep."

"I should've tapped into the wizard economy years ago," Mihil said as he made the bag disappear in his tattered coat.

32

REGISTRARS, RECORDS, AND REX

Aelis hired the fastest coach she could find. About halfway to the Lyceum, realizing she was probably in for an overnight trip at least, she lamented her haste and the lack of any extra clothes or equipment, but with the six-horse coach rattling its springs along the road, there was no turning back for an extra set of robes or something to sleep in.

She did count the money in her purse, and finding it a bit light, frowned.

"Well, many places ought to still accept my notes of hand," she said. *Better save the coin I do have for bribes. Shouldn't have given so much of it to Mihil.*

She had no time for reminiscences of her university days, nor to marvel at architecture or displays of power. She didn't even stop to eat when the coach pulled into the inn; she simply paid to take the next fast conveyance diretly to the Lyceum.

She went directly to the cluster of administrative towers that had, centuries before, been the entirety of the Lyceum. There were six towers and one dome; Aelis knew well there were tunnels between each structure, connecting them beneath the street and offering the administrators easy access to the vast quantity of paperwork upon which an institution like the Lyceum ran.

"If there's one thing a wizard loves more than wine, it's writing things down," Aelis muttered as she made a beeline for the Registrar's tower, a graceless block of stone, its only beauty found in stained-glass windows, done mostly in red, featuring Anaerion, wizards throwing improbably vast quantities of flame, and the phases of the red moon.

Aelis could see just a hint of that moon, a sliver, rising off the southern horizon, while the blue, larger but duller in the still-just-light sky, came on from the opposite direction. Her robes and sword carried her past several of the external offices without a word of challenge or even a look. A warden *belonged* here in a way no one would think to question.

Almost no one. Once she reached the main registrar's office, she had to deal with typical bureaucratic nonsense. A central desk where she was handed a wooden tag with the number 3 graven and gilded on it. Aelis took it from the unsmiling secretary, a middle-aged man who looked disappointed in her appearance, and in the world in general, and glanced around the waiting room.

"Three? Where are one and two?"

"Sit and await the number you were given."

There was a scattering of hard wooden chairs, poorly worked and uncushioned, against two walls. Besides her and the disappointed man there was but one other person in the room, at a desk in the far corner, scratching away at sheets of paper. Aelis watched him work for a while, amazed at the speed at which words seemed to flow from his pen. Soon she realized he was a scrivener, and was merely copying one sheet, speeding up as he went. When he finished the necessary numbers of one page, he slid it into a folder and removed a second, then began the process again.

The man who'd given her the number sat his desk, staring at nothing. Occasionally he trimmed the wick of his lamp.

She waited for long, agonizing minutes. Finally, as she was repeating her Abjurer's Litany and running through various calming mind-stilling exercises, the disappointed one called out imperiously, "Th-ree." The way he said it somehow made the simple word into two syllables. Aelis stood and approached the desk, holding the tag out.

He took it from her hand and pointed to a door on the wall opposite the scrivener. Aelis briefly wondered what horrors awaited her on the other side, but it was just a row of desks with wood panels partitioning each one from those next to it.

"Three?" Her voice was more plaintive than she wanted it to be. A hand emerged from one, the fingers long and gnarled, the back of the palm dry and wrinkled.

She went to the desk and found, indeed, an old man, though wearing the gray robes of a student.

"And how can I help you, Warden?" Old he may have been, but his voice was clear and sharp and his eyes were bright blue under heavy gray brows.

"I need to see the records for a student. Well, a former student, I expect, and likely a confirmed wizard. Possibly works in the Lyceum somewhere."

"Do you have proper authorization to see these records?"

Aelis stood opposite the man, staring. He stared back, placidly.

"I'm a warden," she said, finally. "It is pertinent to an investigation."

"But our records contain significant information that could be dangerous to the student or to the wizard."

"Like what?" Aelis inquired.

"True names," the registrar said, still placid and unconcerned.

"I am a graduate of three of the constituent colleges of the Lyceum, and the only thing I can do with a true name is craft a Death Curse."

"Well, that seems quite dangerous indeed."

"I would have to die for it to matter."

"Nevertheless." The improbably old student tugged at his sleeves. "We have certain standards to uphold."

Aelis had slipped her hand into her purse and now she set a heavy gold coin on the desk. The light of his flickering desk lamp caught it and threw the three crowns on it into sharp relief.

"Standards *must* be . . ."

Aelis had only just set a second coin down when they both disappeared up a gray sleeve, and the man smiled broadly.

"And what is the name you wish to look up?"

"Arstan Nicholaz."

"Very well." The man stood, slowly, seized a worn walking stick that stood propped against his desk, and said, "I'm off to the catalog. I'll be back in a few moments with your records."

Aelis was no more patient with this waiting period than she had been with the previous one. A quarter of an hour passed, then another. Down the line of desks, lamps went out, and soon enough Aelis was sitting in a small pool of light in an otherwise dark hall.

She was just about to get up, clamber over the desk, and go in search of her man when she heard his stick thumping on the stones on his way back. She composed herself, clasping her belt with one hand, carefully posed as the picture of patience and poise.

"I am afraid this is rather odd," the man said. He set down a leaf of paper, with a few lines written on it. "That name repeats in the archives." He cleared his throat. "Twice in the last seventy years; I went back a hundred and found it a third."

"What is recorded in them?"

"Well . . . it is hard to say. Arstan Nicholaz is recorded as entering the Lyceum, or graduating, but there does not seem to be a great deal of consistency in the dates."

"I want to see the records."

"I am not usually permitted to allow visitors into the catalog, it is . . ."

Aelis placed another gold piece on the desk. The older man stared at it, then at her.

"Pick it up and take me in, or don't, and start thinking about how you're going to stop me."

He snatched up the gold piece quickly and said, "There's a swinging flap that will let you behind the desks three stations up." He then took up his desk lamp, adjusting the wick as he walked in front of her.

He led Aelis to a cavernous hallway, full of dim magical lamps. "Been a while since a conjurer came in and touched these up," he muttered, looking distastefully at the non-magical lamp he carried. Aelis, one fist clenched, had to fight not to shove past him and rush to the end of the corridor, where massive doors awaited her.

These swung open easily to his touch, and she felt a breeze. Beyond the door was a railed stairway, and a massive column of wood and stone, starting twenty or thirty feet above them and descending in a spiral hundreds of feet below.

"Is that . . ."

"The catalog, yes," the clerk replied. "Follow me. There's an interface point two stairwells down."

As he picked his way down the stairs, soft shoes scraping against the stone and metal, Aelis tried not to goggle at the size of the artifact before her, and the amount of information it must contain. The long column had a snaking line of wooden drawers with the glowing patina of long handling. The drawers curled in a long serpentine coil around the huge column. She almost missed a step as she marveled, drawing a sharp look from the clerk, and resigned herself to following him to the interface.

The landing at the end of the second stairwell was much longer and broader than the one they'd entered the records chamber on. At its far end was a long sloping table, built of what looked to Aelis to be the same wood used in the column and the steps.

The clerk stepped right up to the desk and lifted the desk top to remove paper, pen, and ink from underneath it. When he closed it, he set his lamp down in a convenient depression on the sloped surface that must have been designed for precisely that purpose. Aelis crept right up behind him to see the details; there was a hollow metal bowl in the middle of the table.

"Now, I ask the catalog for records of Arstan Nicholaz," the clerk said. He dipped his pen in the ink bottle and scratched out some words on one of the slips of paper. He put it, facedown, on the concave metal.

For a moment, nothing happened. Then the serpentine line of drawers began to move, slowly picking up speed. Just as it reached a pitch that Aelis feared was certainly too fast, it stopped, and a drawer smoothly opened, extending all the way to the clerk.

"Now, I put it on the last thirty years. As far as I can tell, there have been two Arstan Nicholazes entered into the Lyceum records in that time." He reached into the drawer and took out the first two folders, both of which stuck slightly above the rest. "They are very curious records."

"Curious *how?* Be as specific as possible."

"Well, ah, he is entered but with only the barest detail. Tuition payment is recorded as *other* but there's no indication of scholarship, remedy, or sponsorship. The bursar would have those records, of course. There is a date of entering . . . for this first one, as I said, thirty years ago. But his date of graduation is . . . well, look."

He held out the folder so Aelis could see an entry he indicated with a gnarled finger.

"It's illegible," Aelis said.

"Indeed. And that might not be so odd . . . even here at the Registrar's office we make mistakes, of course. But there is no record of his entry into any Colleges, his exams, implements issued, service entered . . . simply an entry date, and a graduation date."

Aelis felt a tiny hope flare up inside but tamped it down. *They cannot possibly be this stupid, can they?* She bit the inside of her lip to keep from smiling. "And what about the next one?"

"That one has even *less* detail, if that's possible. Entry date. No mention of tuition, exit date . . . and yet he has the graduation stamp." Once again he held out a sheet to Aelis and pointed to a complicated stamp at the bottom-right corner of the page. Aelis's eyes widened at something in the center of the stamp.

"Did you try entering 'Arstan Nicholaz' with *no* date range? All the results that could turn up under that name?"

"I . . . if this name keeps cropping up that could be dozens of records. It could take hours and . . . I do have a lecture in the morning."

There were a dozen questions Aelis wanted to ask of a man old enough to be her grandfather but wearing student's gray.

But more importantly, she was increasingly certain she'd just found exactly how to free Bardun Jacques. Or at least how to dismiss his most serious charges.

"Then let me do it."

"I have to lock the doors behind me and . . ."

Aelis took her purse off her belt and dumped its contents into her hand, held them out. "I'm a warden. Those kinds of rules don't apply to me. If anyone comes along, I let myself in. I don't even know your name. I've forgotten your face and all identifying details."

He looked at the small pile of gold and silver—mostly the latter—and swept them into his hand.

"Good luck, Warden. I want to ask what you're about but . . . I do not think I would want to be responsible for knowing." With that he took up his cane, left her the lamp, and tottered away.

✦   ✦   ✦

Aelis wasn't sure how much time had passed, but she had amassed quite the pile of documents. According to the records in this registrar's archive, there had been no fewer than eight wizards by the name of Arstan Nicholaz to enter the Lyceum in the past two hundred and fifty years. Only the first one had any of the significant details listed, like Colleges, but no graduation.

Most importantly, Aelis had noted, and confirmed, what she suspected was imprinted in the center of every graduation seal.

A drop of blood.

That was standard practice, of course. There was undoubtedly a drop of her blood on her records. But she had done some quick Delving—to do more she'd need her alchemical kit—and the blood samples on the most recent three such documents were all taken from a still-living person. The most recent document featured blood from at least two different races.

Arstan Nicholaz *did not exist.*

And if Arstan Nicholaz did not exist, and she could now prove at least three ways that he most certainly did not, Bardun Jacques had not killed him, and that most serious charge melted away.

And she would have a chance to expose the Shadow Congress in court.

I really cannot believe they are this fucking stupid, she thought. Then she pondered whether it was stupidity, laziness, or arrogance, and settled on a heady mix of all three. The name was obviously shorthand for them; she lamented whatever poor students or hirelings or just-powerful-enough-to-graduate wizards got saddled with the name "Arstan Nicholaz" and sent to do the bidding of people much more powerful than them.

But any member of the Shadow Congress would know that a message coming from, or delivered by, a person with that name was coming from another Shadow Congress wizard. That spoke to a kind of deniability among their membership. Perhaps some way of staying anonymous but still communicating; send him from one group of wizards to another group, and any Congress wizards would hear something just slightly different in the message. Or perhaps it was a way of keeping their membership from knowing too much about one another.

"I am going to drag every single one of them into the light," Aelis muttered.

She had to take the original records, of course. There was no recourse for that. But she was not going to simply steal them. She was carefully writing receipts for each one, noting the date and stating that *I, Warden Aelis de Lenti, have temporarily taken possession of this record in my role as advocate on behalf of Archmagister Bardun Jacques. I will keep it safe and return it as soon as practicable.*

She had a pile of papers worked up and stuffed into a folder she'd purloined from one of the drawers, and was busy writing her last receipt when she heard heavy footfalls, metal on stone and wood, on the stairs behind her.

"Shit." She clenched her teeth and wrote faster, tucked the receipt into the drawer. She turned around to see a nearly seven-foot-tall suit of perfectly made tournament armor walking down the stairs toward her. The gilding on the black-enameled plate caught what light there was. The cuirass was embossed with the seals of the Colleges of Conjuration, Evocation, and Abjuration.

"Hello, Rex," Aelis said.

"Good evening, Warden." The disembodied voice echoed hollowly inside the Porter's beaked great helm, a padlock holding the visor shut. "I must ask you to leave. The archive is closed and has been for some hours now. You may return when it reopens in four hours." For a moment, she marveled at the voice's refined accent, the way it precisely marked each letter of each word.

"I am just leaving," she said, gathering the folder.

"Those documents may not leave the archive without the Registrar-General's permission. Please give them to me."

It extended one hand, a lobstered gauntlet that clicked mechanically as it opened.

"What are your duties when in this building, Rex?"

"To ensure the safety and integrity of the archive. To escort unauthorized persons out. To protect all residents and visitors at the Lyceum from threat."

"I see." Aelis took up her lantern and had one deep breath to steady herself. *I hope he said that bit about the archive first for a reason.*

Then with as much strength as she could muster, she hurled the lamp over her shoulder and offered a quick prayer for forgiveness to any of the seven gods who might be listening for threatening a room full of paper with a lit lamp full of oil.

Reticulate Rex reacted instantly, with a speed and precision beyond any mortal being. He sprang forward, Aelis forgotten, and threw himself into the air. Aelis felt the entire platform she stood on shake beneath the force of his leap. She had the good sense to start running but couldn't help looking over her shoulder as she reached the stairs.

Rex twisted in the air, the armor contorting in ways that would've torn anyone inside into pieces even she couldn't have put back together, and *caught the lantern in midair.*

Expecting a deafening crash, Aelis ran, banging her feet more than once on the stairs in the near pitch darkness of the huge room. None came, but she did hear a loud but smaller-than-expected squeal of tortured metal, then a heavy thump of metal on stone.

"Please stop, Warden."

The voice was below her, but not so far below that she did not find an extra level of fear that gave her feet a speed they did not naturally possess.

She was already considering the route she'd take. Straight out of this building and across the manicured park that lay between here and the College of Necromancy. If she made it to the Dome of the First Art, there were ancient traditions that would protect her, if she decided to invoke them.

Aelis hoped they wouldn't be needed, so she ran as fast as she could, tearing down the corridors. She heard a door explode open far down the hall but did not look back.

When she got to the long line of desks, she cut an angle toward a dim light, and found herself praying again.

Thank the Worldsoul for clerks who forget to turn off their lamp.

Instead of heading for a partition entryway, she slid across the desk, grabbing the lamp and throwing it behind her at a nearby wall. Then she was out the door, running, her heart pumping, clutching the folder of records before her likea child she was saving from a raging fire.

Which she deeply, truly hoped she wasn't leaving behind her.

33

TRIALS AND TRIBUNALS

Aelis made it as far as the park before she realized she could no longer hear the pounding of heavy footsteps behind her, or the clank of armor. She came to a stop by a small stand of trees, trying to find her wind and hoping no students out for a secret rendezvous would bump into her.

She knew what students used this park for, after all. She'd done it often enough. She slumped against a tree, one hand against its rough bark, catching her breath and waiting to hear the crush of Rex's boots against the grass.

In the stillness of the late night that had slipped to very early morning—the red moon that had been just rising when she entered the Registrar's tower was now on the other side of the sky entirely—she did hear some muted laughter, a few soft moans, but nothing more ominous.

I have stolen files from the Registrar. Reticulate Rex knows it. Rumor has long been that when one Porter knows something, they all do. Quickly, if not immediately. I need to get back to Lascenise, but a post coach is out of the question. I could probably buy a horse with a note of hand, but that means waiting till morning to do anything.

She was suddenly very aware that she had not eaten since early that morning, and one thought immediately occurred to her.

The Academical.

It was a bit of a walk from where she was, but it was open at all hours, and she'd never seen a Porter near the place. She suspected, too, that Oliria wouldn't give her up.

There was a direct route there, if she simply found a main road out of this park heading back toward the Lyceum's gates and the administration buildings she'd fled. She decided that haste and openness were her best disguises, at least until morning. No one would look twice at a wizard hurrying along a path in the Colleges, papers clutched to her chest. They would notice a woman skulking in the bushes and darting furtively from statue to statue.

So, tucking the folder under one arm, she set out on the road. She tried to look like a tutor or a young professor on her way back from a late night in an alchemy lab, perhaps, or laboring over a paper.

"As if anyone could believe me a professor," she muttered. The only time she'd ever been out on the streets this late was after closing the pubs.

Despite her weariness, she did not let her guard down as she walked. She saw hardly another soul, and no sign of any of the Porters. By the time she was on the outskirts of the Lyceum, where the taverns, wineshops, chophouses, inns, and saloons clustered, it was light out and some hardier folks were out running. She even saw one small formation that must have been abjuration students aiming for warden training, running together in a group.

By the time she reached the steps leading up to her destination, the sky was the gray blue of dawn *just* about to break, and Oliria was outside her establishment, sweeping the top step.

"Good morning, Warden." Her voice was casual, barely audible above the whisk-whisk of her broom on the stone.

"Good morning, Oliria. Do you have . . ."

"Vacancies? Why do you keep asking, Lady? Honestly, it may one day offend."

"Thank you." Aelis suddenly felt so tired she wanted to collapse and sit on the steps, but she forced herself up them, patting the folder to make certain she still had it.

"If I may say, Warden, I think you need a good sleep more than you need breakfast, or even coffee."

"That is very tempting, Oliria, but I'm afraid . . ." Aelis stifled a yawn. "I'm afraid I will need a cup or two to get me through writing a letter and hiring a swift messenger to carry it."

"Of course." Oliria set the broom down and glided into her domain, closing the doors behind Aelis. "Coffee and the first morning's bread and a writing case," she called out, then guided Aelis to a table.

Aelis collapsed into the chair and set the folder down on the table, unwilling to let go of it. She didn't have long to wait before an aproned server brought a tray and set out a mug, a small pot that steamed decadently, and a slim leather writing case. Aelis set the case on top of the folder and poured herself a cup before she could order her thoughts for the letter she wanted to write.

Once she had half the cup down, she opened the case and took out thin sheets of paper, a fine pen with a gold nib and fittings, and a tightly corked bottle of ink.

By the time this letter was received and acted upon, she'd be cutting it very close for showing up at Bardun Jacques's trial. On her walk, she'd settled on a plan, and her best route back into Lascenise without getting caught.

She set pen to paper, and began, as one did, by naming the person she addressed.

Dearest Elder Sister.

✦   ✦   ✦

The wait was simply interminable.

True, there were worse places to wait out the better part of a day than the Academical. Aelis ate two excellent meals, as well as a bit of elevenses before lunch and a late tea after dinner, not that she drank any of the stuff it was named for. She did cut a swath through the small sandwiches and pastries that came with her coffee and brandy and was just reaching for the decanter when six dust-covered Count's Own Horses trooped into the Academical's second parlor, led by their Colonel.

"Aelis," Delphine's strong and precise voice boomed in the intimate space.

"Ah. The cavalry I ord—asked for," Aelis responded, catching sight of a thunderhead gathering on her sister's face at the suggestion of the word *ordered*. She poured two generous measures of brandy and kicked out a chair.

"This is the favor, you know," Delphine said as she came forward and folded herself into the chair, stripping off her dust-covered leather gauntlets.

"For saving your life?"

"Given the urgency of your letter, might I not be doing the same?"

"It might not be my life," Aelis admitted, "but it's the life of a man I admire."

Delphine picked up her glass in one broad hand. Anyone seeing them together would not miss the resemblance: the same hair color, the same nose, a similar build. Delphine was simply built on a larger frame than her sister, though Aelis was not small. They sipped with the same motion, the same casual assurance.

"Should we not be rushing to horse?"

"If there's one thing our lord father taught both of us, it's to never rush through a good glass of brandy."

Delphine shifted her eye down at the glass, down at the glass, then back to Aelis. "Are you going to provide one?"

"Do not dispute the quality of the Academical's cellars where Oliria might hear you," Aelis cautioned.

"I hear everything," the landlady said, appearing in the door of their otherwise private anteroom. "And, Lady de Lenti the younger, we have a changing room prepared for you."

Aelis threw back her brandy and stood. Delphine didn't, lingering with her glass.

"Thank you for the spare uniform, and the . . ." Aelis was brought up short when her sister, finishing her own drink, held up two fingers.

"One, little sister, the uniform is not a spare." She looked up. "It is *yours*. I know you are in another service now, but there is always a commission in the de Lenti Horse the moment you want it. Keep it. Bury it in the back of a closet if you must. But keep it."

"And two?"

"Two is that I need no thanks." Delphine stood, unfolding herself with an unhurried grace Aelis had always admired. On horseback or on foot, her eldest sister had the calm of someone who was always doing *exactly* what she meant. "You are my blood. If you had needed the regiment to ride here with sword and lance to cut a path through all the wizards of the world, we would have done it."

"Let's . . . hope it never comes to that," Aelis said. Before emotions could spill out of her in front of Delphine, her sister produced a letter.

"Lawyer sent this to the townhouse and said it needed delivery to you immediately."

Aelis looked down at the green wax seal with a stylized P&G stamped into it. She slit it open and read quickly.

Your commander refused to reveal the location of your witnesses. Said protective custody meant protective custody, and it did not matter who asked, he did not have to produce them for a trial or release them at all until he decided it was safe. You have to find them on your own or do without them; it was made clear to me that the services of any diviner were going to remain out of reach.

Aelis crumpled the letter in her hand and felt certain that Mazadar had either been against her all along, or had been turned. Either way, what she needed to do was clear, and also probably impossible.

"Pardon me, Colonel. I will be a few minutes."

With the paper-wrapped uniform in hand, Aelis called out a couple of orders to the nearest member of the Academical's staff and headed into her changing room.

+ + +

She changed into the uniform, emptying her mind, starting by not thinking about how it fit or admiring the silk of the pink highlights or how the vines and tines were threaded with silver. She noticed them, cataloged them as she would the symptoms of a disease or the things she meant to fix in a surgery.

The tunic was loose, as it would've been meant to go over light horse soldier's armor. The boots were taller and stiffer than any she owned, but richly crafted, and hardly suited for walking any distance. But in the saddle, set in stirrups, they'd do well.

The strangeness and newness of the clothes allowed her to split her mind somehow, to separate her focus from her consciousness.

A servant came in, leaving behind a tray and a map. Aelis hardly noticed. She poured herself a cup, just to do something with her hands; she tasted nothing . Then she set it down, admiring the leather-lined teakwood tray that the pot, cups, and sugar and cream dishes sat on. She focused on some of the decorative carving on the side of the tray. Vines. She smiled, allowing herself to imagine Oliria picking that motif specifically for her de Lenti custom.

She continued to focus her vision on that tray as she unrolled the map and dug the discs of wax out of her pouch, all without taking her eyes off the vines.

She let her eyes unfocus. Some dots filled and swam and pulsed in her field of vision, a kind of overlay, like swirling snow. She'd seen such a thing often as a child and had learned to ignore it, but its springing back into her vision was a sign that she was approaching the kind of focus she was looking for.

Aelis didn't see the tray or the vines now. Her physical vision had slipped into something dreamlike, with its own internal logic but no clear explanation. The snow she saw formed a pattern, an impression, like a hand pressing up through thin fabric. She saw a woman, in armor, with a long sword. Her hands did something with one of the small discs of black wax.

She tried to let her vision wander farther but it snapped immediately back and there was the impression of a figure in robes seated by a fire, reading a book. Her hands once again pushed a wafer of wax across the map.

When she snapped out of the trance, she could feel strands of hair stuck to her forehead with sweat. She was so tired that opening her eyes was a chore. A headache began to pound in her temples.

And the two discs of black wax had settled, one atop the other, on a small farming hamlet, one of many that thrived in the environs of Lascenise and the Lyceum.

Aelis smiled through the pain of her headache and the leaden weight that bore down on her limbs.

"Four," she murmured to no one but herself, triumph in her voice.

Then she swigged the rest of the coffee in her cup, and her hand almost stopped trembling.

✦ ✦ ✦

She was not precisely intimidated by the squad of soldiers Delphine had brought with her, but they shared an intimacy, an understanding, a physical and mental shorthand with one another that she lacked. She felt as though almost anything she might choose to do or say would be wrong. hing.

"Subaltern Vintner." Aelis heard those words but didn't process them until she heard them a second time, directly behind her ear, followed by a cough. She turned and found a man at least a decade her senior, and looking twice that with his blunt, weather-beaten features. "Your mount and remount." He gestured toward the two horses he was holding by the reins: one strawberry roan, one gray. He held out the lines to Aelis; the roan was saddled with a fore-and-aft-peaked saddle with high stirrups, over a saddle blanket in the same colors as the unlikely uniform she wore. "Mind the mare. She is fast, hardy, but will want her own way. It would be better to start on the gelding," he said, nodding to the gray, "but she is saddled, and time waits for no trooper."

"Thank you . . ."

"Sergeant Hauser," he supplied. He held the mare's bridle as Aelis sized the horse up. Tall, lean, not huge in the quarters. She glanced at the high stirrup and thought for a moment.

"Don't hesitate, don't pause, don't think," Hauser murmured, barely moving his lips. "Just act. If you're uncertain what to do, look to me. I'll be on your right, M'l . . . ma'am." He stammered for just a moment and continued to hold the bridle as Aelis swung into the saddle.

She was briefly amazed at how quickly ten soldiers and almost two dozen horses formed up. The remounts were quickly led to the back by one who had to be the youngest member of the troop, a girl Aelis would've thought young to *enter* the Lyceum, but she wore a studded jack, a helmet, and a sword like the rest of them, and rode with the same easy confidence.

Aelis found the saddle harder than she was used to, but she would be damned if she complained. Her sword—it was still her sword, despite the length of the scabbard, the last half a foot or so of which flopped empty at her side—dug into her hip, and she realized she hadn't adjusted the belt for riding. She waited for a command to be given to move then heard Hauser's soft grunt behind her.

"Officers to the front."

Gratefully, but forcing herself not to turn and thank the man who was, in this moment at least, her inferior, she kneed her mare into motion and rode up to the front of the small column. Delphine sat her own horse, an enormous tall black with a white splash on his head and white socks, the way Aelis could sit a barstool or a bench; completely at ease, facing a world she understood and had mastered.

Aelis held out the map with the hamlet marked. "We need to stop here on our way to Lascenise."

Delphine took the map and held it closely to her eye. "Of course we can. But it's going to take time. How much of a hurry are we in?"

"Quite a bit, I'm afraid."

"Can you keep up, Subaltern?" Delphine handed the map back and narrowed her eye. Aelis felt the sting of sweat dripping into her eyes. "What did you *do?*"

"Brute forced some magic. It's not important."

"Very well. The Count's Own has never been late to the field, and I do not intend for them to be late now." Then, once Aelis had tucked the map away, she cleared her throat and spoke loudly. "Is the column ready to move, Subaltern?"

"Yes, Colonel."

"Then give the command to move." Aelis looked up at her sister and found the trace of a smile ghosting about Delphine's features.

"Giddyup?"

"Try again."

"Onward?"

"Are we in a storybook?"

"To death or glory?"

"Too often the same thing, I'm afraid."

"Forward?"

"Louder."

Aelis cleared her throat. "FORWARD!" she cried, and her unfamiliar horse lurched under her, getting almost a length ahead of Delphine's horse before she could be reined in.

"We're not out to take a gate in a charge," Delphine warned her. "Running down the foot traffic might be a bit suspicious."

"I suppose," Aelis said. They lapsed into silence as they passed by the late afternoon traffic. Happy students, done with lectures or tutoring for the day; tired magisters trudging to their offices to mark papers or hold conferences; clerks and workers in clusters, their jobs done, heading for their homes beyond the Lyceum proper or to the outer ring of taverns and public houses. Only once did Aelis see any of the Porters—Brass Bob, his gleaming armor unmistakable in the gloaming. Thankfully he was far in the distance, and she was sure her horse could outrun him, at least.

"What is this animal's name?" Aelis asked suddenly, feeling the barely contained spirit and power of the horse beneath her.

"A horse soldier does not often give a mount a name," Delphine said. "As much as I hate to say it, we have to think of them more as tools than as animals." When Aelis didn't respond, Delphine went on. "Of course, you can give her one. She is yours. As is the gray."

Aelis's head whipped toward her sister, who did not return her look. "These are too fine for my posting."

"Lesser would be unworthy of a de Lenti," Delphine said. "Unworthy of my sister. They are from my own books."

"I see." Aelis sized up her sister then, saw one of Delphine's hands leave the reins to stroke the strong neck of her mount. "And what's his name?"

"Stockings," Delphine answered absently, then turned to glare at Aelis. "If you repeat that, I'll . . ."

"Your secrets are safe with me, o dread colonel ma'am."

34

A QUICK TRIAL

The courtroom was in fact a reception hall inside Cabal Keep that had been hastily furnished for the day. A tall, boxy bench had been erected at one end atop a dais, with three heavy wooden chairs inscribed with the warden arms behind it, two long tables a few yards before them, then rows of chairs.

The room was more full of wizards than most. Three sat on the dais in those heavy chairs, all in formal robes, Mazadar in the center, in his richly brocaded conjurer's brown, his heavy golden chain around his neck. His orb—a perfectly round, smooth, heavy ball veined with yellow and green crystal—sat on the bench before him, a symbol of his power as well as a convenient hammer for bringing the court to order. On either side of him sat an elf in robes as green as a forest in the full flush of spring, and an aging human woman in invoker's reds.

At one of the tables sat Khorais Angleton and Bardun Jacques, the former in court robes that were outshone on all sides by what the wizards wore, and the latter at least allowed the dignity of his own invoker's red, under which he wore a vest of illusionist's yellow. He had his Wychwood leg and a stick to lean on, but his face looked like he had a mouthful of vinegar and was uninterested in pretending it was wine. Khorais was almost idly taking notes.

Between them and the judges, another wizard, in abjurer's blue, held forth on the many crimes of Archmagister Bardun Jacques.

There was not much of a crowd. A few wizards, most of them visibly growing bored. Miralla, anxiously looking at the door. Next to her, his feet tapping the chair in front of him nervously, sat Mihil, wrapped in his shabby sky-blue coat.

"And of course, the charge of murdering a fellow wizard by magic," the abjurer thundered. "For which we know the defense will have no answer! I put it to you, tribunal, that this Archmagister . . ." He pointed theatrically at Bardun Jacques, who looked for a moment like he was considering leaning forward and biting the extended digit clear off, "has acted recklessly, dangerously, even criminally, for his entire career, and that it is high time he paid for . . ."

The court was suddenly silenced by shouting outside the doors, cries of protest, a crash. Mazadar took his orb in one hand; there was a general shuffling as wizards all about the chamber took up implements.

The doors were thrown open. Behind them was a scene of some chaos. The two keep guardsmen who'd been charged with holding that door shut against latecomers or intruders were slumped to the ground, their polearms clattering away.

Two figures who seemed to have no business there, soldiers in blue-and-pink tabards, tall cavalry boots, and helms with chainmail havelocks, strode in.

"What is this? This is a closed court . . ." Mazadar trailed off as the shorter of the two horse-soldiers removed her helmet, struggling somewhat with the straps and ruining the intended effect by letting out a soft "fuck" as she disentangled it from her hair.

"Actually, Commander," Aelis said, at last handing the helmet to her older sister, "I have a great deal of business here."

From under her tunic, Aelis produced the folder she'd carried with her out of the Registrar's Tower. She hoped that word of what she'd done there hadn't spread to Cabal Keep yet, for she was keenly aware that she was risking a great deal on this one throw.

She stalked forward, struggling to keep from grasping her sword's hilt.

"What is Archmagister Bardun Jacques on trial for?" she called out, to everyone and no one in particular.

"This is not regular procedure!" The lawyer she'd interrupted with her entrance was slowly turning a shade of red not unlike Bardun Jacques's robe. "You must wait until I have . . ."

"Would someone on this tribunal answer my question?"

"You know the answer to that question, Warden de Lenti," Mazadar growled.

"Maybe say it for their benefit," Aelis said, sparing a look for the courtroom. Khorais had her head in her hands; Mihil was staring at the ceiling in despair. Delphine stood at the far doors, menacing everyone with her mere presence.

But Aelis did, in her quick sweep, note that Bardun Jacques was *almost* smiling.

"Malfeasance and . . ."

"Why don't we focus on the crimes punishable by death?"

Mazadar's glare could've melted silver. "Assault by Magic. Murder by Magic. Both against a fellow wizard, one Arstan Nicholaz."

"Interesting. Then based on the evidence I have brought with me, we can wrap this up quickly enough. Archmagister Bardun Jacques did not assault, much less murder, one Arstan Nicholaz. Because Arstan Nicholaz *does not exist.*"

"What a ridiculous claim!" the lawyer to her right thundered. "What is your understanding of procedure? What even is your standing to . . ."

"I am the Archmagister's warden advocate," Aelis said, turning slowly to face the abjurer. "And to answer your questions: none at all, and I don't give a fuck. This entire trial is a sham; it's been a frame-up since the beginning, and I can prove it now."

She walked over to Khorais's table as the courtroom tittered, and set the folder down on it. She could feel the eyes of Mazadar and the other wizards of the tribunal boring into her the entire time.

"Counselor Angleton, would you please tell the court what these documents say?"

Khorais unwrapped the ribbons that bound the folder and began to sift through them.

"They appear to be Lyceum records," Khorais began. "Of the entry and graduation dates of one Arstan Nicholaz. But . . ." She looked up at Aelis. "Should they have more information than this?"

"A great deal more. It seems our man . . . or gnome, or dwarf, or elf, because the documents are unclear . . . has matriculated and graduated from the Lyceum *eight times* in the last three centuries."

"It-it could be a family name," the other lawyer stammered. "A tradition of fathers and sons . . ."

"Twice in the last thirty years," Aelis said. She seized the most recent document and took it over to the judges. She set it down on the bench but kept her hand on it, forcing Mazadar to lean forward. "It has an entry date, and a graduation stamp of *six months ago*, and *nothing else*. No tuition payment. No Colleges attended. No exams or tests passed, no implements issued. This is a fraudulent document for a man who does not, in truth, exist."

"It does have the blood dot. Someone's blood was put on that paper, entering him into the various blood catalogs that would give him access to Lyceum buildings and . . ." Mazadar was scrambling for purchase; even his deep and assured voice was *too* fast.

Aelis carefully slid the paper off the bench and walked back to Khorais's table, taking up a second one. "Funny thing about that. The blood on these two documents, representing wizards who ostensibly attended the Lyceum thirty years apart, with the same name, is from different races. One sample is human. One is elven *and* human." She took up two more documents. "These two date to seventy and ninety-five years ago, and these samples were from the same person. I am prepared to swear to that under any oath or enchantment this court would like."

"These are wild allegations," the other lawyer began, only to be silenced when Mazadar rapped on the dais with his orb.

"I'm not finished," Aelis said in the silence that followed. When no one stopped her, she went on. "An assassin, a member of a *guild* of such blackguards here in Lascenise, was hired to kill me . . . by a man purporting to be a wizard, going by the name of Arstan Nicholaz. This happened days ago. I say once again: Arstan Nicholaz, wizard, does not exist."

"Surely, esteemed tribunal, this warden must produce this *assassin* to prove . . ."

"Captain Lannick," Aelis called over her shoulder. "If you would be so kind."

The court was once more thrown into an uproar as Lannick, in armor and boots polished so bright they could've been used as a mirror, marched in with two guards who were dragging a fettered Topas between them. Whatever fight had once been in the assassin was gone.

"Your Excellencies." Lannick marched to about spear-length from the dais and bowed stiffly under his armor. "I bring forward a prisoner to testify in this matter."

"This witness was not disclosed to us, nor were we given leave to examine him ourselves." The opposing lawyer had grown frantic at that point, sweating through the collar of his court robes. "This is highly—"

"Irregular? So is trying to send an Archmagister to the gallows on behalf of his political enemies in the Lyceum," Aelis said, drawing a sharp orb-on-wood rap from Mazadar.

"That will be quite enough of your casting aspersions on this tribunal, Warden de Lenti!"

"I will try not to do so again, Commander."

Mazadar turned his glare on Lannick. "What is the prisoner's name?"

"He has given it as Topas, your excellency. Topas of Orlop Court, in the Tremont. His putative profession is brewer."

"The warden advocate claims he is an assassin."

"That would accord with my own assessment, your excellency. He has confessed to as much in my hearing; I am prepared to swear so under any oath, or even enchantment, if it be the will of the tribunal."

Aelis had to admire the way Lannick handled Mazadar's gaze, having withered under it herself. The watch captain simply stared at a point just behind Mazadar's head, anticipated every question, and let his finely turned-out armor perform half his role for him.

"And what of the putative assassin himself? Will he have to be enchanted?"

"If it will save me from the gallows, no," Topas spoke up hoarsely. "I will answer every question honestly."

Mazadar sighed heavily. "Have you any other surprises to rain upon us, Warden de Lenti?"

Aelis cleared her throat. Delphine ducked into the hall and returned with Hristo and Melodyn, the former in his finest formal robes, the latter in her censor armor, helm under her arm.

Mazadar's face went purple. "I did not give leave for Wizard Osiric or the censor to leave their *protective* custody!" he shouted.

"Turns out, it's difficult to keep a censor under magical guard," Aelis said calmly.

"You were not to even know their location!" Mazadar fumed and smacked his orb against wood for no reason that Aelis could see other than to give vent to his own anger. She waited for him to stop, then continued.

"Warden Despatia will testify to Warden Mauntell's attempt to murder me," Aelis said, pointing to Miralla in the crowd. "Wizard Osiric and Censor Melodyn will testify to their experience of poisoning while involved with this case, and the shockingly similar ways in which their memories were altered by persons unknown."

Beside her, the opposing lawyer picked up a folder and hurled it at the dais, drawing a thundering rebuke from a purple-faced Mazadar.

"SEIZE THAT MAN AND CLAP HIM IN IRONS!"

No one in the court moved; no one appeared to be certain to whom that command had been given, and Mazadar looked in danger of choking at the scene of inaction before him, when the elven enchanter at his side said, carefully, "We haven't got the authority to do that, Magister." Aelis strained to catch what was said next, working hard not to lean forward and openly eavesdrop as the enchanter leaned closer to murmur into Mazadar's ear.

"... recess and a discussion with the advocate in private," she caught, while the rest was lost into Mazadar's bristling beard.

"Recess." Mazadar smacked his orb on the bench sharply once. "De Lenti! Come with me."

"Huh," Aelis said aloud, more for the room than for Mazadar. "I suppose I don't even *need* the enchanted lamp that proves someone was spying on my meeting with Counselor Angleton." This garnered a chuckle from the crowd.

On his way out the back door, Mazadar drove his fist into it so hard the wood splintered.

I fucking have them, Aelis thought. Khorais had flown from her chair, coming to Aelis's side, clearly intending to accompany her.

Then she glanced at Bardun Jacques, who sat stoic and unreadable until, just before Aelis turned away, he winked.

She almost stumbled as she followed the three wizards of the tribunal out of the courtroom.

Mazadar preceded Aelis into a small room, probably an unused storage closet, just a few steps outside the gallery, then whirled on her, still clutching his orb so hard his knuckles were red and white.

"What is the end goal here, de Lenti? We lose the charges of Malfeasance and Murder and . . ."

"All the charges," Aelis said.

"*Someone* died in all this mess, someone apparently a wizard."

"And since I was called to investigate it, almost two dozen more have died, one of them a wizard and a warden, and you know what, Mazadar? I don't see that he counts one whit more than an underbutler at my father's townhouse."

Mazadar growled and curled his arms as if he meant to raise his fists. His green- and red-robed fellow judges had not followed them into this room. Khorais had tried, but Aelis had stopped her, leaning close and murmuring a few words that made the lawyer's face go pale.

"I will admit," Mazadar said, "that there's simply no way for murder to stand up at this point. You've demolished that. So Bardun Jacques lives, for however long we're all so cursed by Onoma. But he cannot just walk away . . ."

"He can, Mazadar. And he will."

"Power is aligned against him, de Lenti."

"And being a wizard is not merely about power. It's about control. Subtlety. Application."

Mazadar snorted. "A fine thing to say for a barely grown girl less than two years out of the Lyceum. You do not understand what power is. Or subtlety."

"Perhaps not. But I understand a great deal about necromancy. A *great* deal. Whatever you think is taught under the Dome of the First Art, Mazadar, I'm certain you do not know the half of it. So, masks off. Cards on the table. Pick your cliché."

Aelis walked forward to the desk Mazadar sat behind and placed her balled-up fists on it, leaned forward.

"You go talk to the Magisters and Archmagisters who arranged this trial. The Shadow Congress." She let the words drip contemptuously from her lips. "Tell them something. The blood on two of those documents I have in my possession? From people who still live." She paused to let that sink in. "Ask them what they think . . . or know . . . that I can do with that. If you're not clear, I can tell you."

Aelis felt the air tremble around her under the force of Mazadar's glare. Undoubtedly it was the Magister before her conjuring air, though she did not think he would do anything with it. After all, if she didn't walk out of this room, there could be only one suspect.

"And what," he whispered, "might that be?"

"In a day, I can find them. If they die by the time I get to them, do not doubt for one moment that I can haul their ghosts back from Onoma's embrace and make them answer any question I want. And if it so happens that the person whose blood is on one of those pages appears to be sitting in a fine office in a desirable tower in the Lyceum? I'll make their fucking veins unravel beneath their flesh."

For just a moment, Aelis could not breathe; air ceased flowing around her. She didn't let panic show, but she was one more heartbeat from drawing her sword when she felt the air fill her lungs again.

"Back to the courtroom." Mazadar had paled. "Go."

Aelis forced herself to turn her back to him and walk with an insouciance she absolutely did not feel to the door.

Khorais was waiting for her, anxious and fanning her sweating face with a folder. "And?"

"It's good," Aelis said, forcing a smile. "It went well." *In that I think Mazadar would kill me if he could get away with it, but he knows he can't.*

Khorais glared at her, and they walked back to the courtroom together, nearly running into the other two judges on their way.

+ + +

It took Mazadar and the other judges nearly a quarter of an hour to return to the courtroom. She spent that time sitting in awkward silence between Khorais and Bardun Jacques.

Finally, the door behind the dais opened with a bang. Mazadar marched in alone, went straight up to the bench, and rapped his orb upon its surface, and announced, "The charges are dismissed. Archmagister Bardun Jacques is free to go, with all the rights, privileges, appurtenances, and perquisites of his position intact." He studiously did not look in their direction as he spoke. Then he smacked his orb back on the bench and retreated swiftly.

The courtroom sat in stunned silence for a long moment.

"Told you it went well," Aelis said to Khorais.

"What did you *say* in there?"

"You would be better off not knowing," Aelis muttered. "But . . . I honestly cannot believe it worked."

"What did I tell you?" Bardun Jacques didn't look at her; Aelis didn't look at him. "Be a pain in the ass."

"What do you want to do to celebrate, Archmagister?"

"I have a few ideas."

35

CELEBRATIONS AND PLANS

The first idea Bardun Jacques had involved Aelis running an errand for him. She found herself deep in the recesses of the keep, holding a damp piece of paper that a clerk had surrendered to her, with what she thought was Mazadar's signature on it. Eventually the servant she followed unlocked a thick door that was covered in sheets of lead, and used the candle she carried to light a few others placed around the walls.

And Aelis found herself staring at a literal treasure trove. Staves, wands, swords, daggers . . . all the implements of the wizard's trade laid out before her, carefully arranged on racks and tables. She saw bracers that would've erected shield-sized wards with a simple movement of her arm, gems that an illusionist could use to pierce any *other* illusion, and other tools and artifacts she couldn't identify. Her gaze stopped cold on a sword, a long blade with a plain crosspiece, paired with a targe. The blade was a dull gray; cold iron, she was sure. The sword practically sang to her, but in a discordant, atonal way; it was a menacing, dangerous thing, something that could drink her power away.

"That is a Wardbreaker," she said, pointing at the sword. "Why is it here? Why hasn't it been destroyed?"

"I . . . wouldn't know, Warden." The servant looked hard at the paper and then turned to Aelis, holding the paper out to her. "I don't suppose you could help me identify what, precisely, an Eye of Anaerion is?"

Aelis reached for the paper, still transfixed not only by the deadly sword but the shield next to it. Her eyes kept trying to read the spiral of the cold-iron studs that danced around the central boss, and finally she realized something.

"With that shield my wards would turn fire. Lightning. Cold. Like they were . . . nothing." She could do that already, but at the cost of a great deal of energy; that shield, a Targe of the Elements, would make it *easy*.

"Is that . . . an Eye of Anaerion, Warden?"

I could rob this place and make myself a legend. Aelis dismissed the thought almost as soon as she'd had it.

"No. An Eye of Anaerion is a faceted red crystal about the size of an egg. The one we're looking for is set in the handle of a walking stick. Lacquered dark wood, an iron handle . . ."

The servant went right to a rack of staves and picked up the exact stick. Aelis had heard its metal-capped end rap against many a lecture-hall floor.

The servant handed it over, and Aelis looked for a moment into the bloodred crystal held within the iron latticework of the handle. She had never studied invocation and the thing was just an inert, pretty rock to her. But she had read the legends, what this crystal could do in the hands of a powerful invoker. *The Lives of the Wardens* was full of tales of the advance of armies being blunted by a single powerful wizard with such thing to hand.

"I don't suppose you have any idea who is . . ."

"Commander Mazadar was very clear that I was not to let you take anything from here except the Eye of Anaerion," the servant said. "And that I was not to let you talk to me or ask any questions about any of it. He threatened to dismiss me from service, Warden, if I did not comply."

Aelis sighed, took the staff, and handed over a piece of silver. She had a long walk in which to contemplate the treasures locked away in a nondescript storeroom in Cabal Keep.

Why is a Wardbreaker *sitting there instead of in the hands of a warden, or, Stregon forgive me for thinking it, a censor? A Targe of the Elements? Why can't that be issued to me? Why keep such a trove hidden?*

She puzzled on this all the way to Bardun Jacques's new quarters, a generous suite of rooms on the first floor of a tower, windows facing the courtyard and allowing in a great deal of sunlight. When she arrived, the Archmagister was sitting in the parlor alone, a jug of wine and a meal ignored and cold on a silver tray before him.

He did hold a cut crystal glass filled with dark amber liquid in his hand as he stared at the window, legs stretched out before him.

"Do you know what a simple, gorgeous pleasure it is to not have your power barred from you, de Lenti? To know that you can rely upon the forces you've commanded for fifty years?"

Bardun Jacques seemed as tired, as run-down, as Aelis had ever seen him. Deflated inside his formal robes, looking every day of his age, he stirred the spirits in his glass and sipped at it lightly, making a sour face.

"I do not. But this might help." Aelis held out his staff. Bardun Jacques took it and set it against his chair. "Archmagister . . ."

He looked at her, raising one brow expectantly.

"Commander Mazadar is well aware of the Shadow Congress. Perhaps even a part of it. The keep has a huge trove of magical artifacts in a storeroom. Precisely the kind of thing they've been smuggling to the Lyceum."

"Mazadar may well be the most powerful conjurer alive. The most powerful since Isiros the Walking Flame perhaps. Is it any wonder that a secret coven of the most powerful wizards would target him?"

"I suppose not, but a trove of untouched artifacts does not accord with what we know of them."

"Then what are the possibilities? Speculate." Immediately the Archmagister's voice assumed the tone of the classroom: inviting, leading, authoritative but not overbearing.

"One: he is a member of the Shadow Congress, aligned with their methods, and keeping this trove for his own purposes, which may be some kind of accumulation of internal power, some dramatic purpose he wishes to effect, or because they measure power internally by the gathering of such things. Two: he is a member of the Shadow Congress and does not wish the rest of the members to have access to this trove because he is *not* aligned with their methods or purposes. Three: he is not a member of the Shadow Congress but is aware of them, and they are afraid to move against him."

"Could he be unaware of them and yet they be afraid to move against him?"

"I mentioned the name to him, Archmagister. He knew it. It was not the first time he had heard it."

"What exactly did you say to him in that private meeting?"

"I pointed out some of the things I could accomplish with the blood on those documents."

"Oh?"

"Archmagister, the blood catalogs that the Lyceum maintains for access to buildings, privileges, and so forth? Given those, a sufficiently skilled necromancer could kill every wizard alive."

Bardun Jacques's eyes shot open. "Is that so?"

"Theoretically, yes. I'd have to go one by one, two by two at best, so I imagine I'd be hunted down before I got too far. But if I had only one target . . . everything I can do to heal a body, I can do to harm a body."

"Aren't there oaths about that kind of thing?"

"Probably." Aelis shrugged. "Are you going to pour me some of that whiskey or am I just going to stand here, dry, after saving you from the gallows?"

Bardun Jacques laughed and produced a leather-wrapped glass flask from his sleeve, then poured two careful glugs from it into a matching crystal glass. "They'd never have sent me to an actual gallows. I'd have been allowed a graceful, painless death."

"Would've wound up in the same spot."

"We all will, de Lenti. Some of us faster than others."

Aelis sipped her whiskey. She did not generally love spirits other than brandy, but this whiskey had complex notes that weren't overwhelmed by its potency: vanilla, oak, fruit, earthiness.

"So, what's next?" Bardun Jacques croaked.

Race back to Lone Pine and free Maurenia is what Aelis thought. Instead, she said, "I was thinking I might eradicate a conspiracy of powerful wizards."

"How would you do that?"

"First, check on where the item I deposited in the vaults has gone. Second, retrieve it. Third, use it—and a particularly nasty little thing I have inside a spirit-trap and a null-cage—to threaten, or possibly kill, the people behind it all."

"And which people do you think those are?"

"Ressus Duvhalin, for one."

"This nasty little thing . . . what is it, exactly?"

"Whatever was animating the corpse of Dalius de Morgantis."

"And you caught it in a trap."

"Yes," Aelis said, trying not to show annoyance at the questions.

"And yet you think it will make an effective weapon against an Archmagister of Necromancy? The head of your College, and probably the most powerful necromancer alive?"

Aelis felt the cold wind of reality rush in and blow out the tiny flame of angry hope that had been building inside her.

"Then how do we destroy them, Archmagister?"

"This other item you have is . . . ?"

Aelis cleared her throat. "It is Aldayim's Matrix."

Bardun Jacques nodded lightly. "Well, then the course is clear." He was silent as he refilled his tumbler with the last of the whiskey from his flask, held it up in the light to admire it. "You're not going to destroy them, de Lenti. You're going to join them."

"WHAT?"

Bardun Jacques ignored her tone by having another measured sip of whiskey. "Think it through . . ."

"I am thinking it through, or trying. How does this achieve anything? It means they win. It means they *get away with all of it.*"

"They were always going to."

"Why? Why do we have to let them? Everything I've done, all the deaths since I got here, then, it's . . ."

Bardun Jacques held up a hand, asking for silence. Aelis gave it to him, unable to form a good argument, her anger still swirling in her mind.

"We aren't *letting* anything happen, de Lenti. Put anger aside for one moment, just one, and look at this square on. Can the two of us together hold off everything the Shadow Congress could send at us, if we went to war?"

"They've already taken their best shot at me. Twice. Maybe three times," Aelis pointed out. "It didn't work."

"Was it their best shot? Do we know what they're fully capable of?"

"We don't even know who's a part of it and who isn't."

"Exactly." Bardun Jacques shuffled to her and sat down at her side. "And if one of us gets a seat at their table, then we can learn."

Aelis curled her hands into fists and searched for a rebuttal.

"It has to be you," the Archmagister went on. "They'd never let it be me. And Aelis, we both know I'm not going to live long enough to bring them down."

She was unused to hearing her first name from Bardun Jacques, and she looked up.

"Archmagister . . ."

He raised his hand again and she quieted. "I'm not. We know it. You said so. What have I got left, a few years? Taking down a conspiracy of this magnitude will be the work of a lifetime. It has to be you. This can't be what wizards are. That we've let it get this far is a sin that *all of us* bear. We have to serve more than our own power."

"I'm not immune to it, Archmagister. They might corrupt me. What if I can't say no to it?"

"What did I tell you when I brought you here, de Lenti? No one I've ever taught needed the world to know who they were as much as you did. For the world to know what she'd *earned*. I can't be sure, but if I have to pick one person to go inside a conspiracy of the most powerful and privileged assholes in the three nations and learn enough to burn it down from the inside . . . I want you."

"I don't like handing this artifact over to . . ."

"You have to, Aelis," Bardun Jacques said. "This is how we must proceed."

Aelis hated every word that had passed between them. She hated knowing that Bardun Jacques was right. She hated everything she was going to do for the next several days.

36

A DIFFICULT CONVERSATION

Retrieving the Matrix was easy. The Sandyman brought it to her for the asking, and the first sign that it had found its intended target was that the plain sacking she'd wrapped it in had been replaced with a black velvet bag closed with silken cords.

She tried to keep herself calm and centered as she walked back to the Academical. A servant ushered her in to a side parlor that had obviously been made ready for her, including a stack of cedar-oil candles and a silver cellar containing what she assumed must be grave dust. The room was lit only by a small, shuttered lantern, and otherwise dark, the windows curtained, no fire in the grate.

Aelis lit candles from the lantern, stuck them in the eye sockets of the iron skull, sprinkled dirt over the flames, and immediately sank into a gray void.

The void was quickly replaced by a view from a desk. She hadn't seen it before; black stone veined with white and silver. She knew it was a desk by the implements on it: blotter, paper, ink bottles, sand cellar, pens, and other detritus, all finely made and silver mounted. She was put in mind of her vision when she first used the Matrix, from behind Dalius's desk, down to the entry of someone carrying a sack and rushing breathlessly to the desk.

"Archmagister," this figure, a black-robed necromancer she didn't recognize, said. "I was going through the latest shipments from our friends on the river," he went on, peeling the bag back excitedly as he set it down on the black stone desk, "and I thought this should come to you immediately."

A hand reached into her view, an older, age-spotted hand with a heavy seal ring on the middle finger, and caressed the iron.

"What is this?"

Even as a formless watcher of a vision she could not affect in any way, she felt equal measures of anger and triumph. She knew that voice.

"I don't know exactly, but it is necromantic, very powerful. I cannot figure out how to activate it."

"You did well to bring this to me," Archmagister Ressus Duvhalin said. "It will not be put with the rest of the shipment. I shall have to keep it for study."

"I am afraid there is a problem, Archmagister. The Porter who retrieved the shipment for me said this can only leave the Vault for two hours at a stretch. I shall have to fetch it back soon."

"Which Porter?"

"The Sandyman."

Duvhalin made a disgusted snort. "We'll search for a workaround. In the meantime, find something more befitting its status, and fetch me cedar candles and grave dust."

The necromancer looked perplexed. "Archmagister?"

"Do not ask questions, *Nicholaz*," he spat. "Remember your place, and how easily you may lose it."

Pale and trembling, the black-robed wizard who'd brought in the artifact rushed away, and the last thing Aelis saw in the vision was that same beringed hand stroking the iron.

When she came to, the candles had burned halfway down and the room smelled of cedar. She angrily pinched out the wicks and threw the stubs into the unlit hearth, stuffed the Matrix back into the repulsive velvet bag, and went straight out of the Academical.

♦   ♦   ♦

Aelis stood before the door she didn't want to enter, biting sourly at the inside of her mouth.

"I could just take this and flee back to Lone Pine," she muttered, but even as she said it, the word *flee* tasted like shit in her mouth. She thought back to her talk on this subject with Bardun Jacques.

Be a pain in the ass. She heard his voice echo in her head, and she shouldered the door open and strode in with purpose.

She knew the stairs and corridors without thinking on them, which was good, because if she had needed to stop, she might have flinched.

Not to the highest floor; those offices were tiny, and for new professors, minor functionaries, or recluses. One simple flight of stairs, and a short one, to a block of rooms that could look out at the dome, but also had windows facing the avenues and other buildings of the Colleges.

The door she wanted had no name or title on it, only a grinning skull knocker made of solid silver. Aelis steeled herself and rapped it twice, sharply, against the plate beneath it.

"Do come in." The voice was cheerful, even avuncular, and went on even before she had opened the door all the way, "Good afternoon, Warden de Lenti. I was beginning to feel hurt that you had not visited since you had been making regular visits to the Lyceum." Ressus Duvhalin sat behind an expansive desk made of black stone veined with white. If Aelis looked too closely at it she began to think it resembled more of an *altar* rather than a desk, and thought it might be long enough for someone to lie—or be stretched—across. But her focus was on the man behind it, pale-skinned, large-framed, hands folded together on his stomach over his richly brocaded black robes. A single overlarge silver ring, the Seal of the College, was prominent on his right hand.

"Good afternoon, Archmagister."

"To what do I owe the pleasure, Warden?"

Aelis resisted the urge to take a visible deep breath and walked up to his desk, setting her heavy bundle down on it.

Duvhalin didn't move except to raise one gray eyebrow at her.

"Unwrap the package, if you would, Archmagister," Aelis said.

"How do I know it's not a trap, Warden? You have been to many exotic places since you left us, if your letters are to be believed."

Aelis called upon all her calm to stay stone-faced, as if she were speaking to her father. "If I was going to make an attempt on your life, Archmagister, I wouldn't have come in the front door."

Still, Duvhalin did not move to touch what she'd set down, though he did sit forward somewhat. "You know, Aelis, we do need to discuss some of what you've achieved. Some quite stunning successes in the face of great difficulties. Did you ever sort out your . . . predecessor?"

Aelis stared at him but did not answer. He smiled, the expression broad and natural on his grandfatherly face. She hated looking at it.

"My suite is empty. We are the only two here. My secretary, my assistants, my graduate lecturers are all gone. Speak freely."

"He's dead. Permanently, this time."

"How do you know?"

"His bones . . . whether they were his, or simply those he'd appropriated, are now so much calcinated ash scattered to the compass points. The spirit that was continuing to animate him rests in a spirit trap inside a null-cage."

"Then I am right to fear a trap." Duvhalin chuckled. "How do I know that's not what's set in front of me?"

Aelis had enough. "Open the package and let's talk about the Shadow Congress, Archmagister. I don't have all day."

"You have as much time as an Archmagister decides to take, *wizard*," Duvhalin snapped, his eyes suddenly cold as a winter's night. Aelis saw the crack in his grandfatherly facade that she'd never believed and wanted to jump across the desk and throttle him.

Instead, she merely met his dark-eyed stare. Without moving his gaze, he unwrapped the velvet bag and looked at its contents with feigned shock.

"Ah." He took a deep breath. "How, exactly, did you find this?"

"Originally?" Aelis said. "The vault of Malhewn Keep. *Today?* The Sandyman handed it back to me."

Duvhalin's eyes flitted to her and he took another sharp inhale, the kind taken by someone who was trying not to let anger get the better of him.

"That was not in your reports."

"Would *you* have reported finding Aldayim's Matrix in my place, Archmagister? In fact, *did you?*"

Duvhalin smiled, and it was, to Aelis, like watching a snake or a dragon smile. Unnerving, unnatural, frightening. "No. I do not suppose I would have. What do you think this . . . *buys* you, as you said?"

"The Shadow Congress. I know it exists, I know you're in it, and I can prove it."

"I have never heard of such a thing. What could you mean by it?"

"I have blood samples of at least two members. One is a human male of between sixty-five and eighty years of age. Still living. What do you suppose I could do with that blood? Certainly I could go for Onoghor's Unraveling, but that is so ugly. I suppose I could give the unlucky bastard a blood-borne parasite, or really *any number* of interesting afflictions. I could also work with a diviner to simply *find him* and leave it up to a wizard tribunal to decide what would happen for manipulating Lyceum records, falsifying blood catalogs, creating profiles of false wizards, malfeasance, and half a dozen other crimes."

"Enough! What do you want, de Lenti? What is your price?" He slapped the stone desk, his cheeks pinched, his face a deadly white.

Here came the hard part. The test, the words Aelis did not want to say. But she leaned forward, assumed a pose of hungry ambition, placed the palms of her hands on the desk.

"I want *in*."

"Do you think this is how the organization you posit . . . I am not admitting it exists, you understand . . . do you think this is how membership is determined? Brash, unseasoned, barely graduated children demanding it?"

"Since this organization does not exist, then it will not mind me continuing to investigate using the proof I already have. Including letters from a suspected member directing me to destroy illegal caches of animated soldiers in barrack-crypts scattered around Old Ystain. Barrack-crypts that would've been illegal before that land was lost and ceded to orcs. Barrack-crypts that various members of the Shadow Congress almost certainly knew about. Or the documents I have under Urdimonte seal proving that this," she said, tapping the Matrix with one fingertip, "was moved into the Lyceum vaults several days ago and has moved in and out of them since. With a little applied math and a map of the Lyceum, I think they could even prove *where* it's gone. And that's just for a civilian court. I could also hand this to another necromancer, slap a couple of candles into it, and show them how to call up proof that you've accessed it."

"If that were even possible, would it not allow them to reveal your use of this artifact?"

"Indeed it would. I suppose it's a question of which of us has more to lose." She scooped the Matrix off his desk and made a show of heading for the door. "I can afford a large fine without missing it. And I'd long outlive the worst sentence of punishment they could give me. Can you say the same, Archmagister?"

From over her shoulder, Aelis saw rage flash in Duvhalin's dark eyes, but it passed, and he was all avuncular charm once more, his cheeks returned to a normal color, a gentle smile on his features. "Perhaps we should discuss a fitting reward for that achievement. Unearthing a conspiracy undertaken by a former warden commander, destroying it, destroying dangerous, uncontrolled magic, setting things to rights, without alerting the orcs."

His stone block of a desk had no drawers built into it, but there were wood and leather boxes stacked at its far end. He heaved to his feet and tottered to one, drawing it open and removing a folded piece of paper.

"All this requires is my signature," Duvhalin said, unfolding and setting the piece of paper down.

Aelis could not resist scanning it quickly, though she did not trust the Archmagister unless she kept an eye on him.

The formal, ornate hand at the top of the page read, *Commission and Warrant of the Title of Magister.*

This can't be real. It has to be a feint, she thought.

"I had this prepared as soon as I knew you were coming to Lascenise," Duvhalin said. "I know that you neither like nor trust me, de Lenti. I have known it since your first workshop with me. But you do not need to do either of those things to accept that I am an Archmagister of your primary College, and I can make your career."

"Or break it, by trying to send me to the most obscure post imaginable . . ."

"Did I?" Ressus looked at her with disarming intensity. "Or did I send you where you would best serve the needs of our shared calling? Do you think it an *accident* that so many mysteries fell into your lap? I had not counted on Dalius, no, not quite in that way. But I knew *some* power was working there and I suspected it had to do with that man's wilder experiments."

Aelis sneaked another glimpse at the commissioning paper on the desk, enough to catch her name written unmistakably across it.

Onoma's cold milk, I could be the youngest Magister since . . . since . . . Her mind could not supply an apt comparison and she let it drop, focusing on the Archmagister leaning on the desk across from her. All traces of charm, concern, calm mentorship had melted into a calculating hunger.

"If you want this," Aelis said, pulling Aldayim's Matrix closer to her, "I will have that commission. I will have an inroad to the Shadow Congress, and with it, guarantees of mine and Bardun Jacques's safety. And my other associates, Warden Despatia and Mihil and Khorais Angleton . . ."

"All of that, and as a personal thank-you, one more thing." Duvhalin settled easily back into his chair. "A Magister's Warrant brings the possibility of a new assignment." He drew out a sheet of paper from another one of his drawers and set it on the blotter before him, produced a heavy silver seal from one wide sleeve, and smiled widely at her. Aelis felt she was looking at a predator's display of teeth.

"Name the place," he said, picking up a pen with a shaft of polished bone and a golden nib. "Antraval. Your own beloved Tirraval. Perhaps one of the great Tyridician cities along the sea; canal-crossed Estazia, or Mizanta, over-looking endless leagues of emerald waters. You can be free of that wretched village. Leave Rhovel there to rot; it's no more than he deserves."

The longing Aelis felt for Antraval was suddenly painfully acute. Her time in Lascenise had made her feel soft, it was true, but Antraval was an older and a grander city, harder in its way. She would not live there in a walled Warden Keep, with servants at her whim, but in her own tower in one of the many sprawling districts. Perhaps she would have a view of Lightsmith's Way from her roof; a roof with a garden, chairs and a table to catch the cool breezes down off the mountains. She would be maintained by people who knew without being told what a warden was and how they were to be respected. She would eat at a different table every night if she wished and never grow weary of the fare. Even a poorer district of Antraval would be peopled by craftsmen proud of their trades and their white stone houses and washed floors.

"Lone Pine," she blurted out. "I will finish my term in Lone Pine, includ-ing extra months to make up for my travel and service here. And then accept the ruling of the warden service for my next assignment."

Duvhalin cocked an eyebrow. "Aelis, I am offering you what I *know*, what anyone who paid any attention to you while you studied here knows, is your heart's desire."

"Hearts change," Aelis said, stunned at the ferocity of her conviction. "I gave you my terms. My introduction or induction or whatever you prefer to call it. My commission. Safety for me and my associates. And only when those are assured do I hand this over." She snatched the Matrix off Duvhalin's desk before he could say another word, stuffed it into its bag, stood, and started for the door.

"Wait, wait, wait." He sighed deeply. "Do not leave the Lyceum. There will be a meeting of sorts, three nights hence. You will be summoned."

"Then I will see you in three nights, Archmagister." She set her hand on the door handle and began to open the door when his voice called out once more.

"Wait." She heard the tink of metal against glass and turned to see him dipping his pen into an ink bottle, then signing the commission before him with a flourish. "Let me be the first to congratulate you, Magister."

Aelis crossed quickly back to his desk, took the paper with its still-wet signature, and left before she could let one hint of pleasure show on her fea-tures.

✦ ✦ ✦

Aelis decided to walk back to the Academical. She passed any number of cabs and coaches, but somehow a walk in the piss-warm rain of an ugly early summer evening suited her mood.

She passed through the Academical's common room, brushing off all offers of food or drink, not even stopping to shake the water from her cloak or dry it a bit before one of the many hearths. She was too warm anyway. When she reached the parlor that adjoined the rooms she, Miralla, and Mihil had taken, she was shocked to see only Mihil and Bardun Jacques. They were both seated at a table facing a wide window that ran with water, a teapot and cups forgotten before them.

"Well," the Archmagister said, "don't leave us in suspense."

Both he and Mihil were smoking pipes, filling the parlor with the rich, faintly sweet smoke. Annoyed, she stalked over to Bardun Jacques's chair and snatched the pipe out of his mouth, turned the burning flakes out of the bowl into a silver ashtray, and rubbed them out with the wooden bowl of the pipe.

"I ordered you, as your anatomist, to stop smoking."

Bardun Jacques glared at her but there was something approving in it. Mihil leaned back in his chair, putting his pipe out of her reach.

"Are you going to answer my question?"

Aelis sighed, patted the carefully folded commission that was tucked inside her jacket. "He says there is a meeting in three nights, and I will be . . . inducted or introduced or whatever."

"Good. Going swimmingly. I told you, with that artifact in hand they'd never turn you away."

Aelis reached for the teapot and poured herself a cup, knowing she'd hate it but wanting something else to hate besides herself. She turned on Bardun Jacques, careful to keep her voice respectful.

"What's to become of the Matrix once I hand it over? Onoma knows what Duvhalin can do with *that* in his hands."

"Is it worth your safety? Is it worth breaking your lover's curse?"

Aelis felt that like a knife parting her ribs to seek her heart. "Why would that even matter?"

"Because if you do not make them believe it, then we will never make it that far north alive. Offering up Aldayim's Matrix? He can't resist that. It's leverage, and you'll find none better."

"And then they might just kill me anyway."

"I don't think so," Mihil said. "Oh, I don't doubt there's politics in this group, the kind that sometimes ends with knives in the back . . . but if they simply cut the throat of every applicant, there'd be a lot more dead wizards on your hands, no?"

"If you're concerned about that kind of thing, we leave a dead letter," Bardun Jacques said.

"A what?"

"A dead letter. We write out everything we know, with as much evidence as we can, give it to a source we trust and whom the Shadow Congress cannot touch. We set a date for it to be released. Say, a year. If we're not alive to push that date back further, it gets released."

"I see. But whom could we trust?" Aelis instantly thought of her father or eldest sister, but they wouldn't remain in Lascenise much longer and she was reluctant to involve her family any more than she already had. Then there was Khorais; she seemed trustworthy, for a lawyer. But a puff of smoke from Mihil's chair reminded her that Khorais was someone else's family, and the risk would be unfair.

"The Urdimonte," she finally said, and Bardun Jacques grinned at her knowingly. "That's what you meant about having a use for them."

"Capital!" Bardun Jacques proclaimed. "Let's get dinner in these rooms. I'll send to the local branch and start the letter."

"I," Aelis said, "am going to bed."

"Oh, come on, it's too early for that . . ."

"Archmagister, with all due respect, if you try to prevent me from sleeping right now, I will relight your pipe and make you eat it."

Bardun Jacques laughed, a deep gargling sound that wasn't particularly pleasant to hear. But he said nothing else as Aelis tramped into her room, set down her cup of cold, hateful tea, and began stripping off her clothes.

She dropped her cloak to the floor, tossed her swordbelt onto the bed, then sighed, thought of Maurenia, and placed them both on the provided pegs. She carefully removed her other garments and gear and set them where they belonged, then stretched out on the bed.

Sleep proved elusive, unusual for her. She thought of Maurenia still; she skimmed along the surface of thoughts about the Matrix and the voice inside that had instructed her a few times.

When next she woke, it was dark and silent and she listened at her door to be sure the parlor was quiet. It was, though a small fire gave her enough light to navigate to a window and peel back the curtains. She guessed that the gray tinge of the sky meant that dawn was approaching and she'd simply slept through the entire night. She looked around the room, saw empty bottles, plates with crumbs and smudges of food, but felt only a faint hunger despite how long she'd gone without eating.

There was a silver dome atop a tray, and she realized that the blocky object next to it was her alchemy lamp. She turned a dial to bring it to a soft ambient light and lifted the dome. There were a couple of folded pieces of paper, as well as a pen and ink. She took up the smaller page and unfolded it. A bold, hard hand had written, *Got to finish this dead letter. Urdimonte coming to get it early.*

There was no signature, but it was obviously from Bardun Jacques. She picked up the pen and unfolded the larger sheet, quickly scanned over what he'd written, and signed it. Most of it was the instrumentation of the letter; that it would be held in an Urdimonte lockbox under their names and no other and released—with the names of prominent authorities to whom copies should be sent—within one year, if neither of them did anything to prevent the release. Beneath that, he'd written a compact paragraph outlining the way he'd been set up and entrapped by a secret coterie of wizards known as the Shadow Congress, and so on.

Aelis picked up the pen, thought for a moment, and began detailing everything. The hiring of thieves to smuggle artifacts, of assassins to safeguard their operations. The multiple attempts on her life; the murder that was committed at her father's townhouse. The filing of false documents in the Lyceum archives, the hoarding of artifacts, the suborning of wizard tribunals. It didn't take long, but the outpouring of it angered her all over again. She felt fury at how much they had gotten away with, at how many conventions they'd broken, and crimes they'd committed, and how they were not only going to get away with it but one of them was going to be handed a powerful artifact in the bargain.

She finished writing the letter and sat there, fist white-knuckled around her pen, too angry to sign it.

"I hate this," she murmured.

"I'd worry if you didn't."

Aelis was startled to hear Bardun Jacques's voice behind her, and then the tapping of his staff as he came out of his room to take a seat next to her.

"Hold on to that hate, de Lenti," he muttered as he watched her sign it. "Don't let it consume you, but never let go of it. Think of all the things that wardens sacrifice . . . love, family, home, safety, our bodies . . . to keep other folk safe, while these soft and scheming bastards sleep sound in featherbeds and only ever look to their own power and comfort. And every time you meet with one of them, you smile at all the bullshit that comes out of their mouth, and you write all of it down, and you look for the moment to destroy them. It is not yet," he said, reaching for the letter and a stick of wax. "But it will come, if you are patient." He folded the letter, sealed it, and stood up.

"I'll take it. You order breakfast."

Aelis watched as her mentor, leaning heavily on his staff, took a letter that determined the course of the rest of her life as much as anything could, and shuffled out of the room.

37

ABOMINATION

Two nights later, in the finest formal robes Manxam's could produce—silver-threaded skulls on the collar and cuffs, silver buttons, all her implements in place, Aelis was sitting in a cab with Ressus Duvhalin.

She did not know where they were going. Duvhalin sat in one corner, she in the opposite corner, Aldayim's Matrix in its bag on the seat next to her. The Archmagister was beaming at her.

"Don't scowl, de Lenti," he said brightly. "This is a glorious day for you. The youngest Magister in fifty years, I'd guess. I'm sure you could number it to the month."

If anything, Aelis's scowl deepened, but Duvhalin went on regardless.

"You came to the Lyceum to pursue power. Do not pretend otherwise. And now you are about to see its true exercise."

Aelis didn't answer; she didn't trust herself. Duvhalin gave up and lapsed into silence. Eventually the cab rattled to a stop. The windows were heavily curtained and Aelis had no sense of where in the city they were. When they stepped out, the architecture was no help, as they were behind a row of houses.

Not the Azare Courts, she noted. *But not a much poorer district.*

Duvhalin waited as their driver pulled away, then led the way to the back door. It had no visible locks, handles, bars, knobs, or knockers. Duvhalin removed a small silver knife from his belt and pricked the tip of one finger, squeezing it just till a tiny drop of blood welled up. Then he pressed it against the door.

There was a metallic sound as the door unlocked and opened inward.

Aelis followed him into a small hallway that led to another door, this one more conventionally built.

"You must wait here," he said, "with the Matrix. Someone will come for you." Without waiting for her reply, he darted through the door before them, moving more quickly than Aelis had seen him do before.

She loosened her sword in its sheath, checked the draw of her wand, and wondered how many wizards she would be able to kill before they brought her down.

"Probably none," she muttered. "If they're all as powerful as Duvhalin."

She let that thought go and resisted the urge to try to commune with the Matrix one last time. The door before her opened suddenly. The person before her was indistinct; gray robed, with a hood pulled low over their eyes.

Their outline blurred, their height changing even as she looked. It became too difficult to focus on the glamour, and so she dropped her eyes to the floor.

"Warden Magister de Lenti. Follow me."

Aelis followed the figure down a corridor, through an absurdly normal-looking kitchen with banked fires in two separate hearths, into a dining room.

She couldn't help but let out a small laugh. There were five other figures standing around a heavy dining room table, blurred and opaque in identical robes.

"What is funny, Magister?" The voice was just as indistinct as the speaker. Aelis had no way of knowing who had spoken.

"Sorry, sorry," Aelis said, "just . . . this is your secret congress meeting house? You can't even find a proper dungeon somewhere? A stone circle? An empty alchemy lab, the old kind with runes of Stregon and Anaerion in bronze and silver engraved on the floor? Not even a lonesome promontory out in the wilds? Just . . . some townhouse that could be owned by a semi-prosperous merchant?"

"Silence, Magister!" snapped one of the glamoured figures. Aelis was was almost certain it was Duvhalin. "You come here as a petitioner. What do you bring us to earn your place?"

Aelis plunked the Matrix heavily down on the table. "Aldayim's Matrix. A repository of the knowledge of the greatest necromancer who ever lived. A device that empowers the wielder to achieve enormous feats of control over undead animations and . . . Onoma knows what else. I haven't used it that much."

"You ought not to have used it at all. You should be stripped of your titles and thrown into the deepest cell in the Larisha," one of the glamoured figures fumed.

"You're welcome to try it," Aelis spat. Her patience for the preposterous spectacle was at its end. Her hand settled around her sword hilt. She didn't see any of them carrying staves or swords, though the glamour could account for those if it was powerful enough.

"No more of this." At the head of the perfectly ordinary dining room table, one of the figures threw its hood back, and the glamour dissipated. It was, somewhat disappointingly, Ressus Duvhalin, the only person among the Shadow Congress Aelis could already positively identify.

"This bickering and infighting does not become this august confederacy," Duvhalin said. "Magister de Lenti has, perhaps unknowingly, come among us with precisely the requirement necessary to gain admission. She is of both sufficient rank and power . . ."

"The rank is recently conferred," one glamoured wizard said. "The ink is hardly dry."

"Is there something about that in the bylaws?" Aelis ignored the withering glance Duvhalin aimed at her for interrupting again. Now that she was face-to-face with the feared Shadow Congress, she found it hard to take them as seriously as she ought to.

"She does not believe in our work."

"I do not know what your work is. Perhaps you could enlighten me."

"It is time to do just that," Duvhalin said. "You will not find it disagreeable. Remove the Matrix from the table. It is too precious for what we will do. Someone, place another artifact upon the table."

Aelis watched as the Matrix passed, permanently, she suspected, out of her reach, one of the glamoured figures making it disappear into his cloak.

Her eyes widened as another glamoured figure set the Wardbreaker she had seen in Cabal Keep upon the table. It was a plain blade, with a dull gray sheen under the dim lights, straight and double-edged. It would have been a bit long for her, and heavy, but she could, she was sure, learn to wield it.

"What do you do, apportion these artifacts to who you believe should have them, or . . ."

"Be silent and learn, Magister." Aelis stopped trying to guess which glamoured wizard spoke to her, as the disguised voices all had the same whispery, indeterminate quality.

"The world needs the strong guidance of wizards," Duvhalin said. "And it needs that guidance to extend beyond the lifespan of men, or even of elves." He resumed his place at the head of the table.

Aelis started to say *That's why we have institutions, to carry on the work*, but was suddenly gagged with a block of Conjured Air.

"Wizards do not live as long as they once did. Perhaps the conjunction that turned the Worldsoul womanly and soft is to blame," Duvhalin went on, making certain to smile at her. "But we cannot wait to see if things are set right when the change comes again. Join me, brethren."

He extended his hand over the sword, and the rest did the same. Duvhalin began chanting and the rest joined in. Aelis could say nothing, but she could feel the necromantic magic that was gathering over the sword, and other magics with it that she could not have put names to.

Runes appeared on the surface of the sword, a deep cobalt blue rising over the gray of the steel. Aelis ached to have that sword in hand, thinking of what could be done with it, fearing what could be done to *her* with it in the clutches of an enemy.

The blue runes became almost white, too intense to look at, and Aelis was forced to turn away, shutting her eyes. When the glow no longer pressed at her eyelids, she turned back.

On the table, the sword was a pile of ash. Nothing of the blade or even its furniture remained.

Aelis's gag vanished.

"What have you *done*? That sword could have done good in the world. How many such swords even *are* there? There's never been enough starmetal to make . . ."

Duvhalin didn't answer her. His features were caught in a brief flash of joy, even ecstasy, like a man who'd just tasted a wine he'd remember for the rest of his life, or less savory images Aelis didn't want to entertain.

"What we did, de Lenti," he said in the whispery voice of a man shaking off remarkable pleasure, "was use the magic in that inert, outdated weapon to . . . renew our own bodies. With these trinkets, our lives should extend to the span *due* to an Archmagister. We can direct the course of the study of magic, of the Tri-Crowns, the Estates House, the world itself."

"It is the only way," said someone else. A second had taken off his hood, and Aelis wasn't surprised to see the figure shrink to the form of Mazadar, though the dwarf would not meet her eyes, or speak.

Aelis felt anger spread within her very core, not the kind of immediate, white-hot fury that would have driven her to do something foolish, like draw her sword and start laying about her, but a cold, calculating rage.

One word resounded in her head as she forced a mask of calm equipoise onto her face.

Abomination.

What these wizards were doing was a perversion of the natural order. Onoma's Embrace was the only thing every living person, be they human, dwarf, elf, gnome, or orc, wizard or not, truly shared. It could be kept at bay, be deferred or stemmed by her skill with spell, scalpel, or alembic. But to break down the magic bound in artifacts, magic meant to help wizards and wardens do their work in the world, *solely* to extend their own life span? That, she could not abide. Ths felt close kin to what Dalius had done in Sundering himself, trying to do more, to *be* more than was allotted to a mortal.

She kept all that in. She didn't even tighten her hand around her sword hilt.

Bardun Jacques was right. Smile, nod, learn everything you can, and destroy them when the time is right.

38

DEPARTURES AND HOMECOMINGS

Aelis came away from that meeting too angry to sleep that night. She met with Bardun Jacques and went over the meeting, repeating points and answering questions until he had wrung every detail he could from her memory.

"And will there be further meetings?"

"None for me as long as I'm posted in Lone Pine. But someday they'll drag me back here."

Bardun Jacques fixed her with a long stare. "You could've named your post."

"I did," Aelis said.

"That can't be what you want."

"Maybe I need to have less of what I want," Aelis said. "Maybe I need to work on living up to my obligations. Maybe we all do."

Bardun Jacques sighed. "Less than a month in Lascenise and look at all the good work you did. Imagine that over a span of years in Antraval, or . . ."

"Look at what I already did in Lone Pine. Dalius. The Matrix. Barracks-crypts full of animations that could've started a war or massacred a village, and I destroyed them all. And look at my failures there, like Maurenia, who I am no closer to freeing."

"Oh, we'll see what can be done about that when we get north. How many days to put your affairs here in order? Two?"

"Probably three," Aelis said, before what Bardun Jacques said had registered. "We?"

"I told you I'd owe you, and I told you I was coming north with you after this mess was over. I've broken more curses than you've had hot dinners. *We're* going north, and *we're* going to free your imprisoned lover, then I'm going to settle into a quiet retirement and you're going to rot out in a tiny tower in the wilderness. It's no happily ever after, but it'll do."

"Are you certain, Archmagister?"

"I'd be dead three times already if not for you." Bardun Jacques levered himself up with his walking stick. "Knowing Mazadar was among them hurts. He was a good warden, once. A friend. I'll have some words with him before we go. Three days, the Plain Gate."

"Three days."

✦ ✦ ✦

Those three days were a whirlwind of packing and goodbyes. She paid Mihil off with a considerable sum in gold, enough to fill two fat purses that the gnome tucked away in his faded blue coat.

"Mihil, do make me one promise," she said as she handed the coin over.

"You're not my boss anymore, so . . ." He grinned.

"Don't go drink every silver vine of that. You've got a life to live, if only you want it. I can't take you with me, but Khorais would keep you in work, or the Dobruszes would."

"Aelis," Mihil said softly. "You can't save everyone." Then he gave her a mock salute, slid off the stool of the coffeeshop they'd met in, and disappeared into the crowd.

♦   ♦   ♦

She rode the red roan mare Delphine had gifted her all the way out to the Azare Courts, only to find the house closed up but for a few servants and guards. Nothing more like her father than to have left without sending word, and she would've cursed the waste of time if not for the opportunity to spend some time on the horse.

Miralla was a more difficult goodbye, and the one she saved till last.

Her efforts to find her friend in her off hours had been fruitless, so finally she tracked her down while she was on duty as warden of the watch.

Miralla's face went flat when she saw Aelis standing before her desk. "I'm busy."

"I know," Aelis said. "But I'm leaving in the morning. I need to say goodbye. And thank you."

"You've said it. I'm busy."

The warden of the watch's office was empty but for the two of them. Aelis looked around at the empty chairs and bare walls, then back at Miralla.

"I have reports to write. Trying to stay ahead of them."

"Mira, you've never written a report in advance of the moment you absolutely needed to."

"Fine." Miralla dropped the pen she hadn't been writing with and stared hard at Aelis. "What is it you want to say? Thanks for all the help, for endangering your career to bolster mine, for endangering your life for my capers, for . . ."

"To say thank you, and that it won't be forgotten, and . . ."

"Oh yes, I forgot, you're a Magister now. Youngest in half a century, eh? Don't forget me as you climb up that ladder, Aelis. Remember that you stepped on my face."

"All I did was ask for your help, Mira," Aelis said quietly, trying not to show how stung she was.

"And kept asking, and asking, and . . . dammit, Aelis. I know exactly how this works with you. You just bull ahead, and you bend everyone around you into doing exactly what you want . . ."

Aelis wanted to interrupt her, to say that what she'd been doing was important, that her work mattered, that it had all worked out. Instead, she simply hefted something onto the table.

"I know all that. But I also know I owe you," she said as she pulled the paper back to reveal a leather-covered targe, its face studded with cold iron in a twisting runic pattern.

"What," Miralla said, "is that?"

"It is a Targe of the Elements," Aelis said. "And it's yours."

Miralla slowly stood up and took the shield from its loose wrapping. She stood, looking at the cold iron studs with a certain kind of awe.

"How did you . . ." It was an effort for Miralla to tear her eyes away from the shield, which Aelis understood all too well.

"You probably do not want to know that."

Miralla took that in stride and immediately slid the straps of the targe onto her left forearm, lifting it to feel the balance.

"And this is mine, clean? It has . . ."

Aelis removed a sealed scroll from her pouch and handed it over. "The Provenance. Correctly filled out, signed and sealed by me, witnessed by an Archmagister. The accession details are all fiction, but the document and the ownership are both completely legal."

"You could've kept this for yourself," Miralla said. "Why didn't you?"

"Never liked fighting with a shield," Aelis said. "Slows me down."

"Won't slow me down." Miralla raised the shield, assumed a guarded stance behind it.

"Because you're already slow."

"Come down to the sparring room and I'll make you eat those words, de Lenti."

"You know I would, Mira. But I am off in the morning, and I have so much left to do."

"Running from a fight, like always." A little of Miralla's friendly smile had returned.

"Mira . . . I'm sorry for endangering you. I'm sorry for not considering your career as I do my own. But with you around, these past weeks . . . I've had one wizard I could trust. You can't know how valuable that is. That shield is only a down payment on the debt."

"When they name you Archmagister, I expect an immediate commission to Magister. And an appointment wherever I ask. And an assistant."

"You'll make Magister long before I can deliver any of that."

Miralla's smile turned rueful. "I know you're trying to be kind, Aelis. But do you realize that in that answer, you don't doubt, not for *one moment*, that you're going to be an Archmagister one day."

"I'm not convinced I'm going to live out the month." Aelis spoke the words quickly, maybe too quickly. Deep down, she knew, she *didn't* doubt any of it. She never had. *Doubt leads to failure.*

"But you will. Even if those bastards come at you over this, you'll make them eat shit again."

"You watch out for yourself, eh?" Aelis leaned over the desk and whispered as low as she could, "And don't trust Mazadar."

Miralla's eyes widened, but she nodded. They hugged, a little awkwardly, and Aelis went to her last stop.

◆ ◆ ◆

Urizen's door was just barely propped open. Aelis gave it a couple of light taps with her knuckle and it swung open. She wasn't surprised to see a gnomish figure standing on the desk, at the lectern, but was surprised to realize it was a gray-robed student rather than the green-robed Archmagister.

"Is the Archmagister in today?" Aelis asked as she slipped around the door.

"Don't you know it's rude to barge in to an office uninvited?" The student was clearly flustered and fumbled to close a book, but kept her hand in the middle of it, marking a page.

"The door was open," Aelis said, "and I was under the impression I had a standing invitation to see him." She narrowed her eyes, as there was something familiar about her. "You're . . . Janine, yes? The student-assistant from the library. You helped me a few days ago."

"I help many people," Janine said. She looked at the door and then down at the book uncertainly, and said nothing more.

"Do you know when the Archmagister will be back?"

Janine pursed her lips for a moment, then said, "You should leave."

By now something had clicked out of place in the not-always-efficient clockwork of Aelis's mind. *She's hostile to me, upset about me being here, frightened, and it has something to do with the book.* Aelis decided to try a different tack.

"Is it standard now that Lyceum students do not respond to graduates with the titles they've earned?"

"Sorry, Warden," Janine said, with the air of ingrained reaction. Then, her face white, she said again, "You need to leave."

Aelis made the conscious choice not to be angry or to immediately threaten her.

But she did *not* take well to being given orders, even by people who were entitled to give them.

"A student does not give orders to a Warden Magister unless I am on your private property and cannot show cause for why I followed you there."

"This is private . . ."

"Don't try it, Janine. This is Lyceum property, and I'm a Warden Magister. Now, are you going to tell me where the Archmagister is?"

"He's packing for a trip. He asked me to bring him this book."

"Set the book down on the lectern, open to that page your hand is marking, then turn and leave this office."

"You don't have . . ."

"Yes, I do," Aelis said. "I can decide that you're trespassing and you're attempting to steal something from the Archmagister's office."

"But he . . . ?"

"Got a note, signed and sealed?"

The gnome shook her head, her cheeks white with fear, or anger Aelis felt a stab of shame, then something much more powerful.

That something was very wrong.

Janine set the book down and deliberately shuffled a few pages. Aelis stared her down until the gnome left the room, then she closed the door from the inside and threw a ward on the lock.

She hurried over to the book threw it open to see if she could find the page the gnome student had been focused on. She flipped a few pages and then was certain she'd found it.

There was no text, only a green-bordered icon of Elisima the Enchantress, wreathed in vines in a forest scene. In her hand she held a too-long wand, suffused with a green-white glow that showed real skill on behalf of the long-dead artist who'd painted this image.

The rod the Goddess held was was plaited of four separate pieces; one an impossibly gnarled piece of bone that resembled no actual bone Aelis recognized; one that was a twist of captured starlight; one that appeared to be smooth stone flecked with gold ore.

And the fourth was Rhunival's rod, or close enough to it. A living bough, flowering at the edges.

Aelis felt a cold stab of something far more akin to shock than to anger in her gut as she turned the book to its title page.

Primal Forces of Magic

And then, in smaller letters.

And the Taming Thereof

"Forbidden book my ass." She let it sit on the lectern for a moment, then snatched it up and tucked it under her arm. "Let him come and take it back if he wants it," she said, and slammed the door hard enough to rattle the walls.

◆   ◆   ◆

"It's not a surprise that you're coming back from the city with more than you entered it with," Timmuk said as he supervised the loading of her four trunks' worth of clothes, notes, effects, alchemical ingredients, replacement flasks, and other equipment. "I'm just surprised it's this much. Didn't take you for a clothes horse."

"The fourth trunk is nothing but coffee beans," Aelis said.

"You know we already *shipped* coffee beans up there for you on the last post wagon," Timmuk said.

"I do, but I have no idea what will have become of them, if Rhovel will have demanded them, or how fresh they'll be. This trunk," she said, tapping it with her toe before Andresh picked it up and handed it to a man clambering atop the long wagon that Andresh was personally loading, "is warded, which I can renew at will, and I can make certain it isn't opened until it's safe in my tower." As she was speaking, another, smaller wagon pulled up.

"Wine delivery for a Magister de Lenti," the driver called out. Aelis raised her hand. Timmuk glared up at her.

"Don't begrudge me the wine, Timmuk. It's only four hampers."

"You're going to help us load it," the dwarf grumbled. Aelis laughed and did indeed help lever the wooden cases, filled with straw so thick she couldn't even hear the bottles within clink, up into their designated spots on the wagon.

"We're sending our best teamsters with you," Timmuk said, once the wagon was packed and Bardun Jacques had climbed carefully inside, settled on a cushioned bench under the canvas canopy. "And our best hands for the horses."

Aelis reached out to take the dwarf's hand, and he just looked at it. "What's that for?"

"Goodbye and thank you?"

"Didn't I say we were sending our *best* teamsters, Warden?" He whistled, and Andresh appeared, handing Timmuk a wide belt with a broad-bladed dagger fixed on it. "Who do you think that means?" He buckled the belt on as Andresh brushed past him to climb onto the driver's board.

Aelis laughed. "Then who are the hands?"

Just as she spoke, there was a clatter of hooves. She turned to see two familiar forms ride up, each leading a string of mounts.

"You remember the Lashes, Aelis? Darent and Dashia, you remember Aelis."

The brother and sister, unmistakable in their resemblance, wore the sleek dark blue leather Aelis had first seen Timmuk's entire company in upon arrival in Lone Pine, back near the start of her service there.

"Timmuk told us you had a fine couple of mounts that would need seeing to on the way up," Dashia called as she slid from the saddle with an easy grace that Aelis envied more than she wanted to admit. "Can I see them?"

"Of course," Aelis said. "Just over here." She led Dashia to where the roan mare and gray gelding were hitched, both in light halters. The other woman's eyes widened.

"These are . . . incredible stock. From whom did you buy them?"

"I didn't," Aelis said. "They were a gift from the commanding officer of the Count de Lenti's Own Horse." Dashia's brow furrowed. "My eldest sister," Aelis added.

"Then their stablemates and siblings won't be for sale."

"I very much doubt it." Aelis sighed and reached out to stroke the roan's neck. "I'll want to spend as much time as I can with them on the long ride, carefully, of course. Been a long time since I had a horse to care for. I may need reminders."

"Well, let's get them on a line with the other horses, if you think they'll take it. We clear the walls, saddle one at the first pause, and you ride. No point in waiting."

Aelis busied herself with helping Dashia and Darent care for her new mounts. Having been well trained by a career officer of horse and her own hand-picked grooms and hands, both horses took every command as easily as Aelis could've wished. Before long, everything was ready and awaiting only Timmuk's command for the large flatbed, the smaller cart, and the strings of horses to move.

Aelis turned to take one look at the city, its streets bathed in the early morning sun. She took a deep breath, smelled the sun-warmed stones, the distant river and the canals it fed, the filth, the money, the beauty, the despair, then turned and climbed into the wagon.

Bardun Jacques appeared to be dozing, wrapped in a thick red wool cloak, though the day promised warmth. "A warden should travel light," he muttered, not opening his eyes, as Aelis slid onto the bench opposite him.

"Not when she's going home for another year or more."

His eyes popped open and fixed on her. "Won't pay to think of it that way, not when you'll have to leave it soon enough. I taught you not to get attached."

"Sorry, Archmagister. I have to say I disagree with your wisdom there, hard won though it may be. If we aren't attached to people, how do we serve them?"

Bardun Jacques grunted, closed his eyes, and settled back into his cushions. Aelis wasn't prepared for the wagon to suddenly lurch into motion, and was almost knocked over as it set off.

+ + +

The trip back to the very borders of Ystain was slow, hot, and blessedly boring. Aelis settled into a routine. Early mornings were for sword practice and general exercise before camp was packed up. Then she'd take one of her mounts along with Darent or Dashia to scout their route ahead. A few days out from Lascenise, she'd turned to Andresh on impulse and said, "Teach me Dwarfish," and since then her afternoons had been spent on the board with him, learning the basics of that musical language.

She wasn't likely to develop much more than a young child's facility and comprehension, but it gave her mind something to focus on besides worrying about Bardun Jacques's health. The warm weather and sunshine ought to be good for him, but there was still a great deal of moisture in the air from several late spring rains. She had to resume the regimen of medicaments she'd put him on in her early days in Lascenise, and he loathed the fuss made over him as she tried to keep him out of the rain.

Then there was his refusal to discuss whatever his plan was for freeing Maurenia. Anytime Aelis tried to bring it up, based on what she'd read in Hughinn, he'd dismiss the question with "I'll figure it out when I get there" or "Conditions on the ground will determine the method" or "de Lenti, if you don't shut the fuck up, I will *murder* you before we even cross the Ystainian border."

This did not generally deter Aelis from continuing to ask.

So her routine lasted for weeks. Scouting and working the horses in the morning, and never having an answer when Darent or Dashia asked her if she'd thought of a name for either the roan or the gray. Riding the wagon with Andresh and asking him, in halting Dwarfish, to give her the names of things they passed.

She pointed to a stand of pine trees, the first they'd seen after a week of steady northward travel along the High Road.

"Those?"

"Drszuk," he told her.

Aelis frowned and searched her limited vocabulary and came out with something that made Andresh shrug.

Timmuk thrust his head out from beneath the canvas. "We don't bother naming trees for what they are," he explained to Aelis. "It's the same word for wood. Drszuk. But bad drszuk, you say it differently, with a down note."

"What makes it . . . bad?"

"If it can't be used for tools. Axe and hammer hafts. Pegs. Squares, levels, saw handles . . ."

"You name trees based on what you can make from them, and nothing else?"

"Look, it's been thousands of years since we came up from the caverns, but it should be obvious that down there our language had no *need* for different words for trees."

Aelis had to agree with that observation. "So, pine trees would be . . . *drs*zuk? Because they're poor wood for tools?"

"Aye. Now, if you can emphasize the middle part of the word, that means it's good for burning . . . not for the forge, mind, never that, but for the hearth, for firing the distiller or roasting . . ."

Slowly, Aelis gathered words, and understanding, with her horses, with the new language, until by the time they came to landmarks she recognized and Lone Pine hove in sight, she could follow perhaps a quarter of what Andresh said at any given time, could read the body language of both mounts— she liked riding the roan better, but the gray would be less likely to panic in a crisis—and was longing for a soft bed and a cool glass of wine.

The first, at least, she would get when they arrived in Lone Pine late that night. The other, well, she might be able to create an alchemical effect that would flash-chill a bottle of Tirravalan orange, but she was so tired that there was a great chance she'd shatter the bottle into the bargain, and that wasn't an exchange she could afford to make.

The sun was setting, but they decided to press on because another hour would see them in the village proper. They'd already passed a few of the out-lying farms, and surely the word had spread that the post coach was on its way; a crowd would be gathered for letters, seeds, tools, luxuries, things that had been ordered and paid for months ago.

Aelis knew she was back in Lone Pine when she could smell sheep shit in the late spring air, over the rain and the wet earth, over the hearthsmoke, over everything. Sheep shit and wet wool.

Sure enough, a crowd was milling about just outside Rus and Martin's inn, knots of folk gathered on the green, most carrying mugs of sour ale or cups of brandy. The wagon pulled up to a bit of a fair-day atmosphere; people lit brands and lanterns as it slowed to a halt.

"People of Lone Pine," Timmuk bellowed, standing on the buckboard with one arm dramatically thrown back. "Dobrusz and Lash once again bring you the news and the fruits of the settled south!" With that he swung off, just before the wagon rolled to a stop.

"But most important of all," he added, and snatched up a long brand that had been stuck into the ground, holding it up so the light fell on Aelis as she dismounted, "we bring you back your warden!"

Aelis didn't know what kind of welcome she'd receive. Applause? Maybe. A cheer or two? Surely. People rushing forward to shake her hand or at least to pat her arm or have a word with her.

What she did not expect was pale faces, shocked mouths, wide eyes, a wave of murmured words she couldn't quite heart.

"I'm not a ghost," Aelis said, failing to garner so much as a chuckle. She saw the crowd moved aside by short but stout arms, then Rus, ever-present towel in hand, came to the front.

"Warden . . . Aelis? Rhovel told us you had died on the road on your way to the city. Said that he was the warden of Lone Pine now and . . . well, it's been an unsteady time."

"Has it now?" Aelis's voice and the look on her face sent the people of the village save Rus, back a step. Over her shoulder she calmly called, "Dashia, would you saddle whichever one of my horses is freshest? Please."

Aelis's tone sent the woman running to untie the mare from the line of horses she was leading, and her brother to clamber up to the back of the wagon for a saddle.

"Now, Warden," Rus said, "he's . . . not been a bad warden to us, treated illnesses and injuries. He's not as handy around as you, and . . . maybe he's been a little harsh. But there's no need to go . . ."

"Pardon me, Rus. I'd love to catch up, to eat whatever Martin has on the boil or the hearth, but . . . there is *every need.*"

Timmuk and Andresh had come up to flank her by then. Just by the way they stood, the way Timmuk's hand was nearing his dagger, the slight suggestion of Andresh's hands curling into fists, she knew they were absolutely prepared to do violence, immediately, to whoever she asked.

"This something you need us for, Aelis?" Timmuk's voice was low and menacing, like a knife leaving its sheath.

"No. Stay here. Unload the freight, give the people what they were expecting. This won't take long," she said, then went to help Dashia saddle the mare. Once she had it ready, having checked the stirrups and the girth strap and the bridle herself, she said, "Rus? Could I talk to you a moment?"

"Of course, Aelis." When he came to her side, he muttered, "There's not going to be a killing over this, is there?"

"Depends on the answers to some questions. Couple of things . . . one, the elderly man asleep in the back of the wagon will take a first-floor room, with the softest bed you can give him. And . . . do be warned, he's one of the most powerful and dangerous wizards alive, but generally speaking, his threats are worse than anything he'll actually *do*. But my tower is not suitable for him. I'll be by to see him in the morning. And last . . ." She dropped her own voice, leaned forward. "Is Tun around?"

Rus bit his lip. "He did not like Rhovel. Not at all. And Rhovel threatened him, called him a vagrant and a blackguard and a bad influence."

Aelis felt all the calm she'd accrued on the uneventful, even enjoyable trip back melt away in an alembic of fury in her belly. "Well . . . if I know Tun, he'll know that we've arrived. If you see him, tell him I've gone to my tower."

Rus's face split in a lopsided grin. "Will do, Aelis. Glad to have you back."

She was already mounting her horse when Bardun Jacques called to her as he was descending from the wagon.

"Where in seven fucking hells are you off to already, de Lenti? This isn't proper manners."

"I've got to go clean out my fucking tower," she said, letting some of her own heat creep into his voice. "Lone Pine . . . that's Archmagister, Warden Emeritus, and Aldayim Chair of Magical Practice Bardun Jacques. Probably the greatest warden alive today, and an enormous pain in the ass."

Then she reined her horse around and gave it a nudge with her knees; the mare broke into an easy canter, and Aelis was off into the night.

She didn't work the horse too hard on the ride; it was too dark to chance a real gallop unless it was truly a life-or-death emergency. She dismounted and led it the last fifty yards or so, tied the horse to a hitching post, and walked slowly up the stone ramp to the door.

Aelis didn't have to even seize her sword hilt to feel the wards on it; ineffectual things from a second-rate abjurer, but they'd keep her from entering unless she wanted to set off alarms.

So she rapped on the door instead, though not nearly as hard as she wanted to.

"What could it *possibly* be?" she heard a shout from inside. "My dinner was already brought up." There was the pounding of feet on stone from within the tower, the wards dropped, and Aelis gathered herself. As soon as she heard the bar withdrawn, she kicked the door as hard as she could, square in the center.

It rebounded off Rhovel's face and arm *hard* and sent him clattering back into the entryway. She was instantly upon him, balling up her fist and smashing him twice in the face, the second drawing blood. Rhovel looked up at her with unfocused eyes, uncomprehending.

Aelis looked down at him with disgust. "I'm dead, am I? Killed on the road?"

She felt the indrawing of power then; perhaps he was gathering a ward of some kind. She kicked him in the groin, and jumped back as he was noisily sick on the floor.

"You're the new warden of Lone Pine, eh? Is that the plum they promised you?"

She toed his ribs and he rolled over, face first into the pool of his own vomit. Aelis then put one knee in the small of his back. She grabbed the back of his head in her hand and raised his face so he looked her in the eye.

"You, replace me? In what *fucking* world, Rhovel? I ambushed you with your own door. Neither your sword nor your dagger was nearby to help you, not that they would've. Now you lie there while I get something to bind you with and try not to drown." She let his face drop and stood up, only just resisting the urge to kick him again.

A few moments later she dragged him outside, his hands bound, and walked him down the ramp to the grass, let him fall.

"Tell. Me. Everything."

"Or what, de Lenti? They'll kill me."

"You will address me as *Warden Magister*, Rhovel. Not by name."

"You have to be kidding me," he said, raising his head, managing a sneer on his vomit-smeared face.

"I could show you my commission, or I could shove your face back into your own sick."

"I don't believe . . ."

"You can answer me, or I can Enchant you, and if you make me do that, I will end by telling you to walk into the woods until your feet fall off."

"You aren't that powerful an enchanter . . ."

She slipped her wand into her hand and put everything she had into a Third Order Loquaciousness, more commonly known as the Gab. "Tell me everything."

It was about what she'd expected. Shadowy figures in the night, promises of promotion and advancement, starting with this small warden post, and he was never to ask any questions about what happened to her.

"Was one of your contacts named Arstan Nicholaz?"

"Yes!" Under her compulsion he brightly agreed with anything he could, so long as it was truthful. "I spoke with him a number of times."

"What did he look like?"

"I . . . I can't remember," he said, screwing up his features in concentration. "I want to say a man, but short . . . maybe average height? I want to say short."

"Right." Aelis knew she wasn't going to get anything else useful out of him, so she tapped him on the forehead with the green-glowing tip of her wand, and discharged the spell.

"You are no longer the warden of Lone Pine, Rhovel. No one here is obligated to give you food or shelter unless you can pay for it. You have a quarter of an hour to gather whatever belongings you need and get the fuck out of my tower."

"Aelis, I . . ."

She raised her fist and he cowered. She felt bad at that, so she lowered her hand and said carefully, "Warden. Magister."

"Warden Magister de Lenti, I . . . where will I go? They'll not take me in down in the village."

"If you can afford it, and I ask Rus to give you space tonight as a favor to me, he'll do it."

"But . . ."

"Your quarter of an hour is wasting."

Rhovel scurried back into the tower and she followed him, taking a look around as he gathered his belongings. He hadn't changed much; the layout of the tower didn't allow for a great deal of personal decoration. She did see that her books were in disarray, some left open atop others, and felt a fresh stab, if not of fury, then of serious indignation.

When Rhovel had gathered up some clothes, personal effects, and one or two books of his own, he went for his belt, which was sitting on a table, with sword and dagger on it.

"No," Aelis said evenly.

"What do you mean?"

"I mean, weapons and implements are forbidden to you within the bounds of my authority. When you leave the village, in the morning, you can have them back, but they will be peacebonded with as much knotted wire as I can string on them before I fall asleep tonight. Now go. I'll ride after you in a while."

"I have to walk?"

Aelis rose and one glance at her sent Rhovel scurrying out the door.

The absolute unprofessionalism of my enemies is the most insulting part of it all, she thought as she slowly walked out of the tower after the other wizard and watched him walk slowly, dragging his bag behind him, as Midarra and Peyron's moons rose, shedding a brilliant light on the pine forests in the distance and the cleared meadow between them.

"I'd hurry," she called out. "There are bears in those woods!"

She suppressed a snicker as he broke into an uneven trot. She waited a moment, then, without looking around her, said, "Hello, Tun."

There was too long of a silence before she got an answer.

"You could not have heard me approach."

"Not at all," Aelis said, turning around at last to find an enormous shadow lurking to one side of her tower, and smiling at the sight. "I only guessed." She hopped off the stone walkway and Tun emerged from the shadows, and they gave each other a friendly embrace.

"It is good to have you back," Tun said after a while.

"It's good to be back. I brought you more tea," she said.

"I am afraid I have no appropriate gift in exchange."

"If it was in exchange, it wouldn't be a gift, Tun."

"Sophistry. Are you back for good?"

"For a while," she said. "Going north soon to free Maurenia." *I hope.*

"And Bardun Jacques?"

"Come down to the village and meet him. Timmuk and Andresh drove us up; they'd stand you as many drinks as you want, I think . . ."

"In the morning. I have been too long out of the village. Rhovel . . ."

"I heard. What else did he do?"

"Well . . ." Tun sniffed. "He never learned. Not like you. Folk who asked for help had to explain why they *really* needed it. If he ever helped anyone put up a fence, I never heard about it. Then there was Pips . . ."

"He was supposed to continue her lessons."

"Yes, well . . . he tried, in a manner of speaking. Her uncles forbade her from returning after they found he had switched her palms for not having memorized a passage."

"He did what?"

"Aelis, I had far worse from tutors growing up. I daresay you did, too. It's not worth murdering over."

"Now she's months behind . . ."

"Well . . . I may have taken it upon myself. I haven't got the library you have, but . . ."

Aelis pushed thoughts of violence from her mind for the moment. "Tun . . . if Rhovel told everyone I was dead on the road, did you not think of coming to look for me?"

"No," Tun said. "I did not. In the first place, because 'the road' is indescribably large and even I can't track someone under that directive. And second . . . because I knew he was lying." Tun tapped the aquiline nose that would've given him a classically noble profile if not for his overly large jaw and protruding tusks. "Could smell it on him."

"Did you tell anyone that?"

"Pips. But I swore her to secrecy."

"How in seven hells did you get her to agree to that?"

"Told her I'd stop teaching her."

Aelis clapped Tun affectionately on the arm. "I've got to get back to the village before they murder Rhovel. In the morning?"

"Of course."

Aelis went back to the tower and shut the door, warded it properly, then unhitched her mare. She looked for Tun before she rode off, but he'd already disappeared.

She would've been disappointed if he hadn't.

39

HOMEMAKING

It wasn't the morning light or a sense of duty that woke her, but a pounding on the tower door, though the light in the tower told her it was midmorning. She buckled her swordbelt around the clothes she'd slept in as she went to answer it, only to be nearly bowled over by Pips rushing in and throwing her arms around Aelis's middle with as much strength as she could muster.

"I never believed 'em when he said you was dead," Pips said, her head buried in Aelis's robes. "Were dead. Tun's correcting my grammar. I never believed 'em. Tun told me it wer . . . wasn't true but I knew it before he said so."

"It's okay, Phillipa. I wasn't, as you can see." She tried to gently disentangle herself from the girl, who clung to Aelis's hand all the same, and peered into the sunlight. The Dobruszes' wagon was pulled up outside, and both dwarves were there, along with Elmo and Otto, Pips's uncles, carrying her trunks and hampers up the ramp to the tower.

When she finally managed to separate herself from Pips and start unpacking, she found that there was simply no getting the girl to stop talking. She was an endless stream of questions: What had she done in Lascenise? Had she fought any monsters? Was she going to be in *Lives of the Wardens* yet? Did she bring any new books home? Was Rhovel really gone for good? Aelis heard all about the books Tun had given Pips to read, including an Old Tyridician grammar and rhetoric with great speeches in it, a book of collected philosophies that sounded to Aelis like a standard tutor's text, and at least one military manual.

"I've brought some new stories, Pips. I won't make you read any more about the Cynemarean Philosophers and how they eschewed all personal possessions in favor of the pure pursuit of knowledge."

"Good, because they sounded fuc . . . they sounded stupid to me." Pips bit her lip. "Tun says that cussin' is . . . the words a small mind gropes for because it cannot find better?"

"That sounds like Tun, but you had better believe I've heard him curse before, too," Aelis said.

"You're sure you aren't leaving again?"

Aelis almost dropped the heavy case full of replacement flasks and measuring jiggers to replace those that her fight with Dalius had broken, which she was lifting onto her alchemical worktable.

"Well . . . I am leaving tomorrow. But it should only be for a few days. Three or four."

Pips only heard the first part, apparently. "But you just got back! You can't leave!"

Aelis set her box down and went to the girl's side. Pips was sitting propped up on her knees on one of Aelis's chairs.

"Phillipa. It's warden business. We have to go free someone from a curse."

"We?" Her eyes went wide. "I get to . . ."

"No," Aelis said quickly. "It's too dangerous. *We* means me and the other warden who came with me."

The girl's disappointment swerved immediately into curiosity. "There's another warden here? And not Rhovel?"

"Rhovel is not a warden any longer. Not while he's here. He may never be again. But there *is* another warden, down in the village inn. The greatest warden alive," Aelis explained. *Forgive me for what I'm about to do, Archmagister, but I need to unpack and put my tower right.* "If you go down there, and ask him nicely, I'm sure he will tell you some stories."

"The greatest warden alive?"

"That's right, and an Archmagister into the bargain. His name is Bardun Jacques."

Pips launched out of the chair to give Aelis a hug, then said, "I'll bring you the dream journal you asked me to keep later tonight. I have had some strange dreams . . . over and over again."

"About what?"

"Trees. And water, big open water."

Aelis held back a sigh. *One thing at a damn time.* "Pips . . . I have a feeling we're going to be sending you to the College of Divination in a few years. But it's going to take *lots* of study to make it possible."

"I know. Studyin's easier than farmin', believe me." With that the girl gave her one last squeeze and ran off at a speed that would have her catching up with the wagon before it reached the village.

Aelis let out a sigh and set to work. As she unpacked trunks, placed clothes in the wardrobe and chests provided for them, reorganized her books *properly*, laid in her alchemical supplies, her sense of being home grew. And that made her uneasy; she did not like to admit that she thought of Lone Pine *as* home. Home was a Tirravalan villa surrounded by terraced vineyards. Home was the Lyceum.

"Well," she muttered at last. "They were. And maybe they will be again."

Then she opened her large medical bag and let out a gasp of pure disgust when she saw the haphazard way Rhovel had organized it. She was going to take out every instrument, every vial, every roll of bandage and rearrange them, and sterilize what could be sterilized. It was going to be a gloriously fussy few hours.

◆   ◆   ◆

By the time Aelis was trotting on her gray horse down to the village, she'd set nearly everything to rights in the tower *and* composed a quick letter that she sent via her orrery, expending no small amount of her magical energy in the process. It detailed Rhovel's failures *and* that he'd tried to usurp her, and that she had sent him packing. She offered no further detail; that could wait for a letter she would send directly to Archmagister Duvhalin via conventional means.

She'd skipped lunch, and though it was early for dinner, she was hungry as she made her way into Rus and Martin's inn, then stopped in her tracks as she came upon an absolutely shocking sight.

Bardun Jacques was seated in front of a too-hot-for-the-season fire in one of the hearths, Pips on a stool next to him. The Archmagister was *smiling*.

Aelis took a few cautious, silent steps toward them.

"What're Maundean sep'ratists?"

"It means they denied the rightful government of Tyridice . . . the king and the Estates House. Bunch of rabble-rousing fools with more swords than sense."

"And you put their rebellion down? By yourself?"

"Well . . . they gathered all their leadership together after they'd won a battle, all of them prancing around a great hall in their pretty gilded armor. Do you know what happens when the Storm of Wrath . . . that's a Sixth Order Invocation . . . hits a big group of men in armor?"

Pips's eyes went wide, and before Aelis could interject, Bardun Jacques let out a gravelly chuckle.

"Cooks 'em right in it! Keeps bouncing back and forth between 'em like a well-made leather ball." He shook his head at the memory. "They say the hall of that castle *still* smells like roasting meat. To this day!"

"I see that the two of you are getting on," Aelis said as she came up to stand behind their chairs.

"Phillipa is a delightful child. Got a great appetite for stories, and she doesn't think she knows better than the teller of the tale. Asks a few too many questions, mind, but . . ."

"I'm sorry," Pips blurted out. "Please don't show me the Widow Grieving O'er the Waves again! I know it was just an illusion, but it was terrible!"

"But she can learn," Bardun Jacques said. He looked up at Aelis. "Is it dinnertime?"

"It will be as soon as I catch Rus or Martin," Aelis said.

"Excellent." Bardun Jacques stood, then was seized with a coughing fit and sank back into his chair. Aelis placed her hand on his chest; after long familiarity with him as a patient, she didn't need her dagger to Delve him, nor to ease his lungs just a bit, allowing him to catch his breath.

"Pips, would you go tell Rus he's got some hungry wardens with ready coin out here?"

The girl popped up and ran toward the back of the inn.

"Archmagister," Aelis said, "are you going to be well to travel?"

"I'm not going to get any better by waiting," he growled in response. "Just get me there, de Lenti. That's all I ask."

"I will," she said. "But it won't be pleasant. A cart can't navigate the country; you'll have to ride."

"Oh no, I might be mildly uncomfortable for a day or two? I'm not on my fucking deathbed. Now go. Get us some bread and cheese and . . . goat's brain or sheep's asshole or whatever they eat for dinner here."

"It's better than that," Aelis said, somewhat defensively.

Rus was already setting out beer and bread on their table when Aelis and Bardun Jacques entered the inn's dining room, and followed with cheese and wine and a soup that had small meatballs made of ground mutton along with root vegetables, and by the time they were tucking into seedcakes and brandy, the inn was filled with people. Some of them wanted Aelis's help writing a return letter, or reading whatever letters they'd gotten the night before again, to savor the news.

She was effectively separated from Pips and Bardun Jacques, but she didn't mind. Before she'd even noticed, the Archmagister had disappeared, probably to bed. Seeing that she had a free moment, Timmuk approached her, handing her a cup of ale, which she took with a grateful nod.

"Your Archmagister has warned us away from coming with you," he muttered. "Says he doesn't need any audience."

"Well," Aelis said, "it's a good thing I'm the warden here, isn't it? Be ready in the morning. We must get Bardun Jacques there safely. His health is failing, and he doesn't want to admit it."

"Oh, a wizard with a stiff neck? Never expected to meet one of those." The dwarf tapped his cup with hers in toast. "We'll be there, Warden. Me and Andresh for you and Renia; the Dashes for her, and because I pay them."

Aelis joined him in the toast, tossing her ale back in one gulp and suppressing the wince at the flavor—piney and sour—from her face.

"I should be off," she said.

"See you in the morning." Timmuk took both cups, seeking out refills.

Aelis felt a little bad, sneaking out as she did; there were other folk to catch up with. Elmo and Otto, Martin and Rus, Emilie, but she craved a glass of wine and her tower and, quite frankly, her bed, so she unhitched her roan horse and started walking it up the road out of the village.

She hadn't made it more than a few yards from the inn when a huge shadow appeared on the path and then stepped into a shaft of green moonlight. The mare reared in alarm and tried to pull away.

Tun frowned. "I forget that I can have that effect on an animal that does not know me. If I may?"

"Please," Aelis said, still struggling with the lead a bit.

Tun took the reins in one huge hand and stepped up to the horse's side, placing his other hand on its neck. He began to sing, very quietly, with no words Aelis could discern; perhaps it was more humming than singing, or it may well have been Orcish. The horse calmed quickly, and Tun stroked its neck gently.

"A beautiful animal. Must have cost."

"Not a stiff silver," Aelis said. "She was a gift, as was the big gelding I had up at the tower this afternoon."

"I smelled that one, but did not see it. A rare gift, then, two horses so fine."

"My eldest sister's stable is renowned, and she happened to be in Lascenise. And I happened to save her life . . ."

Aelis never got in the saddle; instead, as she and Tun walked slowly, she told him everything. The Shadow Congress, the attempts on her life, her father, the assault on the dinner party, the whole disastrous story.

By the time they'd reached her tower and he helped her unsaddle and brush the horse, then give it a light ground hitch that would allow it to wander on the grass a bit if it liked, she was almost through it. Tun joined her inside, and she finished the tale as they shared a bottle of wine.

"You tell this story as though it is a failure, Aelis. Yet your mentor is free and Maurenia soon will be. You have a promotion and entry into channels of tremendous power, and some new friends into the bargain. Mihil in particular sounds like a gnome I should like to meet."

"I don't like submitting to the Shadow Congress the way I did. I hated delivering them the power of Aldayim's Matrix."

"Compromise is not failure."

"It feels like it." Aelis stared into her glass.

"If the choice was compromise or be hounded to the very ends of the world . . . and the compromise buys you the time and the means to fight your enemies more effectively, well . . ." Tun turned a hand palm up. "I see this as victory, even if partial."

"I suppose I'd feel that way too if Maurenia was free. I still don't know how we're doing that. I sought out books . . . including one Bardun Jacques recommended. I don't know how I'm going to do it."

"I rather thought the Archmagister was."

"I am afraid the exertion might kill him, Tun."

"Aelis . . . how many wardens reach his years in active service, which I gather are near fifty?"

"Most never go beyond ten. Those we think of as dedicating their lives to the service . . . perhaps twenty."

"I do not underestimate my elders, as a rule. And I certainly do not underestimate those who become my elders while pursuing dangerous professions." Tun drank the last of his wine. "You have a rescue mission to mount in the morning. I could sit and talk all night, or perhaps we could play stones or drafts. Or chess."

"Gods, anything but chess." Aelis set down her wineglass, which was an alchemy flask sized to hold half a bottle. "About the morning . . ."

40

REVELATIONS

Bardun Jacques was angry, which Aelis expected.

"Only the two of us, de Lenti," the Archmagister sputtered. Aelis had put him on her gray, which was the easier rider of the two. "That's what I planned for . . ."

"Well, you didn't share those plans with me," Aelis said. "Timmuk, Andresh, Darent, and Dashia have every right to be here; they are Maurenia's friends and companions. Besides that, I can't manage our mounts, the pack-horse with all the gear you want to bring, and the pathfinding. So extra hands are necessary. Last, *I'm* the warden here."

Bardun Jacques narrowed his eyes to angry slits but grunted and tried to nudge the horse to move. It ignored him.

Aelis started her own mount on its way and let out a soft whistle. The gray followed.

◆　◆　◆

The weather was agreeable; warm but not too warm, no hint of rain, a soft wind. But the first night out Aelis cursed herself for not having prepared larger doses of Bardun Jacques's medicaments, because at the dosage he now required, she wasn't going to have enough for the trip back.

Well, I've done field-expedient alchemy before. I can do it again.

Still, it was another worry. She spent her watch that night surveying the trees that surrounded them, the waning moons giving her just enough light to see by. When they reach Maurenia's . . . *Rhunival's* . . . hall, Onoma's moon would be rising. She looked forward to that.

There was nothing interesting in the trees. Or at least, nothing that she could see.

Darent and Dashia made efficient scouts; Timmuk and Andresh were indifferent riders on small, shaggy ponies, but for clearing a camp, starting a fire, and getting biscuits or ash-bread and stew cooked they couldn't be beaten. Aelis spent most of her time tending to the packhorse, careful with whatever equipment Bardun Jacques had packed. He refused to answer questions about it, but insisted it was important and had to be treated with the utmost care, so Aelis did.

She also treated him. Travel was not agreeing with his lungs or his heart, and by the end of each day's ride, he was gray faced and tired. No one approached him with camp chores, and though he grumbled about soft treatment, he often fell asleep until dinner was brought to him.

Aelis began to worry about having enough medicine for the trip there.

The ambush came when they were perhaps an hour from Maurenia's vale, as Aelis was beginning to recognize turns of the road and specific trees, but also getting confused by the elusiveness of the track she expected to follow. *Is Maurenia keeping us out?*

The question was answered when a hail of crossbow bolts came whispering out of the trees. Aelis flung up wards, but most of the bolts caught fire in the air and burned to an ash that spread on the wind.

Aelis glanced at Bardun Jacques, who stood with his staff upraised, coruscations of energy swirling around the Eye of Anaerion. Then three bolts of orange-white energy shot out from it. Aelis could feel the heat press against her skin as they flew past, into the treeline, and heard two distinct, liquid screams as they found targets.

More men emerged onto the track ahead of them, crossbows upraised, their fire concentrated on Aelis. She raised a ward centered on her forearm, made her body small beneath it by crouching low to the ground, and felt the impact of three bolts. A hand axe went flying past her up the road, loosed by one of the Dobrusz brothers, found a home in one of the crossbowmen, who was quickly replaced by another.

Then Aelis felt a tremendous wave of power wash over her, and all the yelling and tumult behind them ceased. Still crouched behind her ward, she turned to see Dashia laying her sword against Bardun Jacques's neck, and a voice cried out, "Warden! Drop your sword, put your hands out!"

She turned in the direction of the voice and felt a stab of betrayal at the small green-robed figure that picked delicately clear of the underbrush, another crossbowman by his side, his weapon trained on her.

"Magister," Urizen said, nodding to her. "Archmagister." A nod at Bardun Jacques. He held his wand, a smooth length of rune-carved ebony, delicately in one hand.

Aelis heard footsteps behind her, the whisper of a blade leaving its sheath, and then a sword was laid along her throat. Wisps of air gathered her sword delicately from her hand and her dagger from her belt and tossed them away into the dirt, as the gnome's conjuring orb slipped into his other hand.

"Urizen," Aelis said, hoping her voice didn't sound as plaintive to him as it did to her. "I hoped it wouldn't be you, despite all the evidence."

"Evidence, *Warden* de Lenti?"

"The poison-enchantment given to the censors, and to the necromancer back at the keep. That was you, wasn't it? I should've remembered that you were an alchemist as well as an enchanter . . ."

"Oh, very good! Yes, you figured it all out." Urizen rolled his eyes.

"I'm ashamed to say I didn't, until just now," Aelis said. "Maybe that's because I didn't want to believe it. But when you poisoned Mihil in your office, I should've known."

"Wastrel. Discredit to his race," Urizen spat. "I wish I'd made it a strong enough dose to kill him. But then you might've suspected when there was still time to do something about it."

"Why, Urizen? Why all this?"

"Because the Shadow Congress has too many members as it is," he hissed. "Because I will not be supplanted by a stripling! Because I will not have my achievements overlooked for the hero worship of a mere fire-flinger! Because you have *no idea* what power was gathered up here! It's trying to keep us out, but I'll find a way in. A captured spirit of pure magic? And you thought it was a woodshade. Fool." His eyes gleamed in the light shed by his wand.

Aelis tried to turn, slowly, against the blade; she caught a glimpse of the Dobruszes slumped asleep in the road. She couldn't see Darent behind her, but Dashia's eyes were glazed and empty.

"Dwarves are so hard to compel properly." Urizen sighed. "Humans, now . . . The staff, Jacques. Set it down."

Bardun Jacques lowered his staff but did not drop it. "Are you sure the sword in the hands of your puppet can kill me before I burn you to bone, worm?" The swirl of energy in the Eye of Anaerion began to emit a low hum.

"On the ground, or I'll have him cut your protégée's throat and you can watch *her* bleed to death in front of you."

Without a word, his face fixed in complete calm, Bardun Jacques let his walking stick fall from his hands. The sword against Aelis's neck drew a thin line of blood.

"So, you're going to kill us all to prove yourself to the Shadow Congress?" Aelis spoke very carefully, very slowly, trying not to press her skin against the razor edge of the sword. She was trying to buy time; she assumed that much would be obvious. But she hoped *the why* was a little less so.

"The ritual to take the power from old, useless artifacts is *mine. I* researched it. *I* proved it would work. And Duvhalin shows it to you, gives it away . . . he thinks he knows you, thinks he can control you, but I know you're too young, too foolish to understand why it's the *only way*, and you'll . . . *Why are you smiling?*"

"No reason," she said, pointedly not looking in the direction from which she'd heard the loud, deliberate snap of a branch.

An enormous bear exploded from the treeline onto the track, one razor-tipped paw swiping at the crossbowman standing next to Urizen. The attack sent the man's head flying clear across the road.

Urizen whirled to face this new threat, conjuring air that lifted him bodily in the air and set him down halfway between Aelis and Tun. The sword at her neck wavered and Aelis kicked at Darent's knee, wincing when she felt his leg stiffen and go out from under him.

At the same time, she whipped out one of the daggers hidden in her shoulder belt and threw it at Urizen just as he raised his wand. She was aiming for his chest, but his hand got in the way. The knife thudded hilt first against his knuckles, but the gnome was surprised enough to knock the wand from his hand.

Aelis dove for the ebony length. Her fingers fumbled at it and just missed closing around it as it wafted into the air. It had only just settled back into Urizen's hand when Aelis felt a shadow come in front of her, eclipsing the sun.

Tun, stretched to his full bear's height over the gnome, perhaps twelve feet, let out an ear-splitting roar.

Aelis stood slowly, and the bear came back to all fours to put its snarling snout scant inches from Urizen's face.

Tun let out a growl that made the hair on the back of Aelis's neck stand on end, the fear instincts buried in her brain screaming for her to run in panic. But she only smiled.

"I think he wants you to drop the wand, Urizen."

The dark wood clattered to the ground, the green-lit runes dying out.

◆ ◆ ◆

"Why didn't you tell me you had an orc werebear in your back pocket?" Bardun Jacques asked as they made an impromptu camp to deal with the mess.

"Half-orc," Tun said quietly.

"Because he's not in my pocket," Aelis said. "He's my friend. And because his secret is his to reveal, not mine."

Timmuk and Andresh came back from dragging Urizen's dead hired goons off the road. Timmuk had three crossbows slung over his back and Andresh carried the daggers as well as the mail shirts in a bundle in his arms.

"Waste not, want not," Timmuk said at Aelis's raised eyebrow, and they dumped their spoils into a pile. "Besides, they had no coin on them."

Urizen was flung gagged and hogtied on the back of one of Dashia's remounts.

"What do we do with him?" Dashia asked. She colored as Aelis's eyes swung on her, and looked away, rubbing her temples.

"Dashia . . . there's no shame in being enchanted by an Archmagister of Elisima's Art. He is a very powerful wizard."

"Slit his fucking throat," Bardun Jacques said.

"No," Aelis said. "There have been enough deaths here today. Keep him gagged and on the horse. I'll force catsbane and witsend down his throat until he can't do sums, much less reach for a First Order Enchantment. Dashia and Darent can take him back to Lone Pine from here."

"And then what do we do with him? Send him on from Lone Pine on foot?" That was Bardun Jacques again. "He'll be trouble."

"No. We send him home. With the Dobruszes to administer the doses that will keep him unable to do basic math, much less cast a spell. And to, yes, cut his throat if he tries."

"Gladly," Timmuk said, sliding a knife from his belt and testing its edge against his thumbnail.

"After what he did?" Anger had brought color back to Bardun Jacques's face, but Aelis felt none of it herself. She was sad, betrayed, but most of all, she was tired.

"I want to send him back with a message." Aelis walked over to where Urizen slumped over a saddle. She bent to look him in his angry, bulging eyes.

"I found the book you had removed from the library. Your bagwoman didn't get it out of your office fast enough. I hoped the entire way home that I was wrong . . . and it wasn't until I saw you step out of the trees that I knew I wasn't."

She freed the gag from his mouth and Urizen sputtered with rage and spit.

"I demand my implements be returned—"

"Shut up," Aelis said. "I have had enough demands spat at me by people like you for a lifetime. I'm keeping your wand. As for the orb?" She stood up, pulled the object free from a belt pouch. "Andresh?" The dwarf looked up, and Aelis threw the orb into the air.

Andresh snapped into action, and a throwing axe met the orb on its descent, shattering it into so much useless glass. Aelis put her face close to Urizen's and shoved the gag back into place.

"I want you to understand this, and I want you to tell it to anyone else from the Shadow Congress who wants to come up here and play a game. Are you listening?"

The gnome stared at her, jerking weakly against his bonds.

"You all know where to find me. That's fine. I'm not going anywhere. But know this: I've got bone saws, a calcination oven, and thousands of fucking acres to hide the ashes of the next one who comes for me. Remember that. Tell it to anyone who needs to know. Those words *exactly*. Do you hear me?"

Urizen nodded frantically, and Aelis turned away, disgusted with the entire business.

"Get me my medical kit," she said through gritted teeth. "Time to dose him."

◆   ◆   ◆

Aelis hadn't planned it this way. She hadn't planned anything anyway, now she thought of it. But the day she came to free Maurenia was supposed to be triumphant, and she was supposed to be alone.

Maurenia was waiting at the same tree as the last time Aelis had visited. Her hood was down, and her hair had grown past her shoulders, longer than Aelis had ever seen it.

"Did you bring a fucking circus with you?" Maurenia didn't smile, but Aelis felt reasonably sure the words were meant in jest.

"Not exactly." Aelis wasn't sure how everyone else had decided to let her ride ahead while they all stayed at least fifty yards back, but it had happened, and Aelis felt awkward with the audience behind them.

"Is that the Dobruszes? And Tun. He's hard to miss."

"It's . . . a long story."

"And you can tell it to me immediately after you free me from this fucking prison."

"Let me introduce you to Bardun Jacques." Aelis turned in her saddle and waved the rest of them forward. Maurenia was more than happy to shake the hands of Timmuk and Andresh and Tun, but she and Bardun Jacques stopped and stared at each other.

"Heard a lot about you," Maurenia said. "Not sure you live up to the hype."

"We'll see about that. Somebody give me a hand off this damn horse. No time for tales or kisses or tears," he snapped. "You've got a workshop or an outbuilding I can set up an alchemical lab in, eh? Let's get to it."

Maurenia led them into her compound, the trees making way for the long hall, the sheds, the wood pile. It had all taken on a kind of military appearance. Sagging corners had been shored up. The thatch roof was evenly trimmed. The fire hole in the center had been replaced with a more conventional chimney.

"You've been busy," Aelis noted.

"I have a lot of time on my hands, and I can't abide idleness."

"Go on and get that equipment in there," Bardun Jacques said. "Time's wasting, and I mean to have this done before nightfall! The rest of you, get the horses squared away."

Maurenia and Aelis wrestled Bardun Jacques's crates off the packhorse and carried them into her hall.

"Does he know what he's doing?" Maurenia's words were grunted with the effort of the crate she was carrying.

"Onoma's tits, I hope so," Aelis said. "He swears he has a plan, but he refuses to tell me what it is."

"Well, it had better . . ."

Aelis knew the signs of someone fainting when she saw them—the slurred speech, the eyes rolling up, the sudden boneless fall forward—so she was there to catch Maurenia when she went down. The elfling woman was taller than her and well muscled, so she wasn't a light burden, but Aelis would have died before she let her fall.

"Timmuk!" she yelled, and the dwarf appeared too fast to have been coming at her call.

"Warden, your man out there, well . . . you'd better run," he was saying. When he saw Aelis holding Maurenia up, he darted forward. "I'll take her. Not sure what the seventeen hells he just did, but . . ."

Aelis reluctantly handed the unconscious Maurenia over to Timmuk and ran back out into the last of the sunlight. Andresh was laying Bardun Jacques down onto the dirt, a knife falling from the old man's hand.

Aelis could see, could sense, the blood on it.

You old fool, she thought as she ran toward him, sliding her dagger from its sheath, panic clawing its way into her throat and her limbs.

But when she came to her knees at his side, she saw he was breathing. She Delved; his heart was fine. No one would mistake his lungs for a younger man's, but they seemed to be working easier than they had on the trip up.

Aelis saw the wound on his hand, the bloody knife, and knew what he'd done.

"Please help me get him inside, Andresh. It will be hours before he wakes."

✦   ✦   ✦

She sat up late into the night monitoring both of them, having laid Bardun Jacques in the only bed and made up a pallet for Maurenia out of her blankets and what extra bedding she found about the hall. The rest were sleeping outside in the cool night air, and she let the hearthfire get very low. Onoma's moon was up, and enough light filtered through the thatch for her to see by.

It was three hours past the turn of the day when Maurenia sat bolt upright from her blankets and tossed them all aside. Her eyes were wide and wild.

"You . . ." Aelis rose from her stool, only to see Maurenia take off running, gliding on bootless feet past the sleeping forms of the Dobruszes and Tun. Aelis was in excellent shape, but right then she could not have caught Maurenia if her life depended on it. They ran a mile, Aelis sweating, slowing, an ache starting on her side, while the elfling woman seemed to run even faster.

Then, suddenly, with no warning, Maurenia stopped, and Aelis almost crashed into her back. Aelis watched as Maurenia took a slow, deliberate step forward. Then another. And another.

Maurenia fell to her knees, and Aelis came up cautiously behind her, placing a hand on her shoulder.

She felt it tremble, and Maurenia let out the most unexpected sound Aelis could have ever imagined coming from her throat.

She sobbed. She sobbed, and her shoulders heaved, and Aelis knelt and held her as Maurenia cried, "It's gone. I'm free. It's *gone*."

Aelis wanted to kiss her, wanted to explain, wanted to say a thousand things, but they sat there like that for what seemed like a long time. She feared that one of the others might follow them, see this moment that she knew Maurenia would probably rather no one saw.

They didn't. Slowly, Maurenia came to herself, and wiped the back of her hand across her eyes, focused them on Aelis.

"How?"

"I . . . think I know, but we might have to wait till morning to find out."

"If you tell any of them I cried, I'll . . ."

Aelis leaned forward and pressed her lips to Maurenia's. She found her kiss answered and more.

They were some time getting back.

41

RETIREMENT

Bardun Jacques woke up at the exact moment a ray of sunlight hit the interior of the hall. Aelis knew, because she hadn't slept at all, and was waiting for the moment.

As soon as his eyes snapped open, she was ready with her questions.

"What did you *do?*"

He pushed himself up on his elbows until he could lean against the timber wall. He glanced down at the bandage on his hand, nodded, yawned dramatically.

"I made a bargain. I think the exact words were . . . 'You manky fucking spirit, if you're still out there, take my bargain. Me for her.' Then I cut my palm open and squeezed the blood onto the soil."

He took a deep breath. "Worked, didn't it?"

"Why, Archmagister? There had to be some way to break the . . ."

"There isn't. Not with what we knew. What were the original terms that summoned Rhunival? Who did it?"

"Dalius."

"My first question still stands. Without that, without knowing exactly how he was bound, to what, for how long, it can't be broken. But the bound spirit . . . the gestalt entity of all the spirits of this forest, or whatever Urizen thought it was, or a woodshade . . . can still be bargained with."

"Then why? Why bind yourself?"

"Midarra's *ass*, de Lenti. Why do you think?"

"This cannot be a favor owed to me."

"Stop thinking only of yourself." He swung himself out of bed, reached for his Wychwood leg, and began fastening its braces onto the stump of his thigh. "I have spent fifty years making enemies. Not just wizards, mind. Rebels and nobles and criminals and pirates and tax-collectors and government functionaries and generals and knights . . . enough to fill any *two* entries in *Lives of the Wardens*."

He stood, slowly, and looked down at her. "Now, for however long I've got left, I'll see every single one of the bastards coming."

"And how long have you got left? And if you're bound here, what of your soul? Will you haunt this place?"

"If so, lucky I know a good necromancer." He smiled. "Besides . . . Anaerion has a claim on my soul that long predates whatever bargain I made here."

"What does that mean?"

Bardun Jacques gave her a long, considering look.

"I expect you'll find out some day."

◆ ◆ ◆

"So, he hauled all that gear here as a distraction?"

Maurenia and Aelis were walking in the woods *outside* the bounds of Rhunival's valley, because Maurenia could, and nothing but meals would make her spend one more minute inside the confines of her former prison than she had to.

"No, so he'd have an alchemical lab once he pulled his stunt."

"He's a formidable old bastard, isn't he?"

"More than even I knew, I think."

Maurenia took her hand and held it, squeezing it impulsively. "You kept your promise."

"I would have died before I broke it," Aelis whispered.

"I'm glad you didn't."

"That makes two of us."

Maurenia seized Aelis and kissed her fiercely, then began to whisper against her lips. "I can't stay up here long. I can't. I have to . . . see other parts of the world. I'm not made for a life in one place, Aelis, I'm just not."

"I know," Aelis said, leaning her forehead against Maurenia's neck. "I know. Just . . . one thing at a time. One moment at a time."

"Fair. But I won't stay here, not one more night, I . . ."

"Maurenia," Aelis said, stepping back to focus on those startling blue eyes, "no one is going to trap you here. No one is going to keep you here against your will. If you want to take a horse and some supplies and go, you can. Tun will go with you. I need to see to Bardun Jacques. One day, that's all."

Maurenia shuddered. "I can't. I can't. But I'll wait for you in your tower."

"You had better be there," Aelis said.

"I will." Maurenia smiled, though there was something haunted in it. "I promise."

Just hours later, Maurenia was wearing her studded armor her sword, had her crossbow slung on her saddle horn and her long green cloak. She looked every inch the fierce, wild adventurer who'd ridden out of the wilds and immediately stolen Aelis's attention, and she had it still. They squeezed hands for a moment. Maurenia's eyes narrowed with a promise, and Aelis felt a thrill run down her spine.

Tun and Maurenia set off, Aelis watching them until Bardun Jacques's harsh voice called her back to the hall.

She helped him set up his small alchemical lab, the two of them working in silence.

"If I order more equipment brought up to Lone Pine by the post, will you freight it up here?" She was almost startled to hear his voice.

"Provided I can get it on a packhorse. Have you thought about what you're going to do for food?"

"Looks like your woman put up two years' worth of dried fruit and grains, there's a cellar full of roots, tubers . . . there's mushrooms all over the place, chickens, I'll set nets down in the lake."

"She said she quickly lost her taste for most meat. You should be warned."

"I'll deal with that if it comes."

"You're not much of a planner, are you?" she said glumly.

"Never could stick to one. So eventually I stopped wasting time making more of them than I really needed."

The rest of the day was filled with small tasks as she helped Bardun Jacques put things in the order he preferred, conversing about nothing in particular. Timmuk and Andresh did what they always seemed to do whenever they had a free day—take out all the deadly ironmongery they carried and inspect, clean, polish, and reassemble it. They had a great spread of knives out on one of the tables, the crossbows and knives they'd liberated, even the chain mail shirts they'd taken.

"Go on, Warden, pile your own on there," Timmuk said. So Aelis set down her sword, her dagger, and the two knives that sheathed flush into her shoulder belt.

"Just don't try to take the furniture off the sword or dagger," Aelis said.

"Or what?"

"Or the resulting release of magical energy will probably cook your hands." That was a lie; she didn't know what would happen, but it wouldn't be desirable.

Aelis decided to look for something to drink, eventually digging up an earthenware bottle that smelled like brandy. She dragged a stool out to the front of the hall, propped herself against the wall, and slowly sipped from the bottle till the day passed, till dinner—freshly caught fish, fried with onions— was called, and then she pulled slowly at that bottle till she was tired enough to sleep.

She was afraid she'd dream of trees, of the sea, of something vast and un-knowable, of magisters and assassins come from the south to kill her.

Instead, her sleep was dreamless, and she woke with only a baby hangover—cured with lots of water and the dregs of the bottle—and was saddling her horse before the dwarves were even awake.

"So eager to leave me?" Bardun Jacques snuck up on her as she got the mare and the dwarves' ponies ready.

"I have duties to attend to," Aelis said. *And the most beautiful woman I've ever seen waiting for me, probably in my bed* right now. "A village that needs me."

"A woman who loves you."

Aelis sighed heavily. "I don't know if she does. But I think I love her." She waited. She looked at Bardun Jacques. "Well?"

"Well, what?"

"Aren't I going to get a lecture about not falling in love . . ."

"Teachers have to lie sometimes, you know. I'm not about to lay out my own history . . . it's long ago, far away, profoundly dead. You've chosen a hard life, Aelis, and it suits you. But it doesn't always suit lovers."

Aelis nodded, finished tightening a strap, saw the dwarves shamble out of the hall, yawning.

She came forward and offered her hand to Bardun Jacques. "Thank you, Archmagister. For everything."

"Why do you insist on titles when you know I hate them?"

"A sign of respect."

Bardun Jacques grunted. "Be well, Aelis. Come and visit an old man from time to time. I expect I'll get bored and stir up trouble, if I can."

"If anyone could . . ."

"Aren't we even going to have breakfast?" Timmuk groused.

"Breakfast is in the saddle today, like proper horse soldiers. A family tradition."

"Give us a moment to get dressed and packed."

"I'm starting down the trail. In a quarter of an hour, I'm setting off at a gallop, and I'm taking these ponies with me."

Timmuk stared at her. "You wouldn't."

"Maurenia Angra is waiting for me, dwarf. Don't bet on what I *wouldn't* do."

◆　◆　◆

Aelis set a hard pace on the trail back, though not so hard as to endanger the Dobruszes or their ponies. It was a smooth, trouble-free trip, and yet every single second of it was too long for her. She had nervous energy at every pause, no matter how short or needful, and could not wait to be back in the roan's saddle. The horse sensed her excitement and started meeting it. The mare was restive to get moving each morning, patient only long enough to be saddled and fed, and kept wanting to pull away from the ponies, to run.

She tasted none of the camp food Timmuk and Andresh cooked. She paid almost no attention to the Dwarfish lessons they both tried to give her, till eventually Timmuk said she'd *forgotten* whatever they'd managed to teach her.

"Send me a Dwarfish grammar and the standard teaching texts when you get back to Lascenise, and . . ."

"Warden, a true Dwarfish grammar is etched in stone with gold or silver letters. We don't have a wagon strong enough to carry it."

"Then just . . . send me a printed one?"

"It won't be the same," the dwarf sniffed.

"But it'll do the job."

"No appreciation for *artistry* among your kind."

On the last day of the trip, they'd stopped trying to teach her anything, and when she saw familiar landmarks, the stones and trees that let her know Lone Pine, and her tower, were but a short ride ahead, the mare started pulling at the reins and danced on the track.

"Go on, Aelis. Me and Andresh can find our way from here. Tell Renia we'll see her tonight."

"No, you won't," Aelis shot back. She gave the mare her head and let her run.

And run, she did. For the first time, Aelis let the horse really open herself up and put everything she had into pure speed, and it was exhilarating, and not a little terrifying. She'd ridden since she was a girl but, she was beginning to realize, never on a horse like *this*.

By the time her tower was in sight she had pulled the mare into a slower pace, but she had more in her if Aelis had wanted to let her go.

When she reined up outside the tower, her heart began hammering for other reasons entirely. She saw the gray lightly ground-hitched, as Tun had recommended, and she did the same with the mare and then ran up the ramp and threw open the door.

There was a fire, a small one, in the hearth. Maurenia sat in her reading chair, a book in her lap, wearing only a light robe, her hair loosely pulled to one side of her neck.

"Took you long enough," she said, turning a page, not looking up.

"Should've sent the dwarves with you. Their ponies slowed me down."

"They could've found their own way."

"I don't like to walk away from friends," Aelis said, finally shutting the door. She resisted the urge to throw off her cloak, her sword belt, her clothes. Instead, the cloak went onto a peg in the short entryway, her shoulder belt and weapons on a prominent hook in the wall of the main round living space.

Maurenia hadn't moved, still reading the pages in the book in her lap.

"Think you'll get a chapter in one of these, someday?" She held it up and looked up at Aelis for the first time. *Lives of the Wardens* was embossed down the spine in silver.

"Who even cares," Aelis said.

"You do. You might pretend you don't, but you want to do great things."

"Maybe I do," Aelis said. "But I'll settle for doing *good* if that's the chance I get."

Maurenia stood up slowly, stretching in a way that Aelis thought was likely calculated to drive her a little closer to despair. It worked.

"No, you won't. I know you're going to stick it out here, because I know how you feel about obligations. But . . ."

"Shut up," Aelis said. She covered the distance to Maurenia in two steps and claimed Maurenia's mouth with her own.

After a long interval, Maurenia said, "You know I can't stay forever. Not even long. If I ever see another tree, it'll be too fucking soon."

"I know. But let me repeat myself. Shut. *Up.*"

✦ ✦ ✦

Three days passed in relative ease. Aelis made rounds of the village, looking in on the elderly or the sick, some pregnant women and some who'd delivered while she was gone. Emilie shadowed her for all of that, watching her with shrewd narrowed eyes, but she no longer tried to interrupt. Pips dropped off her dream journal, and one glance told her that the girl had been dreaming of Maurenia's curse and Bardun Jacques—a red stone with flames joining the trees, becoming one of them, not burning them, was how the girl described one of the dreams.

Maurenia read, relaxed, slept, drank wine, went on walks, rode the gray, rode the red, did not do one iota of domestic work. Occasionally she cleaned her sword or crossbow, but seemed ill inclined to practice with either of them, even when Aelis went out in the rising heat of the morning to work on her own sword forms.

It was on that third night that Aelis could no longer ignore how restless the other woman living in her tower truly was.

Whatever comes, face it head on. She took a deep breath as she poured for both of them from the flagon of beer that had been brought up with their dinner.

"I love you, Maurenia. But I know you have to go. I know it has to be soon. Make it the morning if you need to." The words all tumbled out in a rush. "I know you can't stay. I wouldn't ask."

Maurenia bent over her cup, hiding her face with her dark red hair. She mumbled something that *might* have been *I love you, too,* but Aelis wouldn't have sworn to it. Then she stood.

"I'm sorry, Aelis. But if I stay in this place for one day longer . . ."

Aelis set down the flagon and took the half-elf's hand. "I know. Don't apologize. It's who you are. I wish I could go with you, wherever that is, but . . ."

"But you have obligations. That's the difference between us, Aelis, when you get down to it. You live for obligations; I try to avoid them."

"I'm not trying to lay any upon you. So go. In the morning. Take the gray."

Maurenia met her eyes for the first time. "Aelis, that is too great a gift. I . . ."

"Take the horse. I don't need two of them, and the mare suits me better. He'll take you wherever you want or need. If he brings you back here in the next year or two . . . so much the better."

Maurenia smiled. "I will take care of him."

"I ask only one thing: if you cannot take him with you somewhere . . . if you go to sea again, say . . . contact the Urdimonte and offer to sell him back to my sister. They'll handle it."

"I will," Maurenia promised. "Though I don't know where I'm bound. Perhaps the Dobruszes need a hand on their expanding mercantile lines;

maybe I'll buy a wagon and turn it into a mobile armbruster's shop, selling crossbows at every village and crossroad. I just have to move."

"I know," Aelis said. "Now can we stop talking about it?"

She could see Maurenia relax. "Oh, by the Worldsoul, yes. There's nothing worse than . . . talking . . . about . . ." She waved a hand vaguely in the air, indicating "feelings" or "plans" or whatever.

They ate in relative silence, mostly picking at their food. Their plates still half-full, Aelis gave up, took Maurenia's hand, and led her to the bed.

She stayed awake as long as she could that night, willing it not to end. Eventually she fell asleep, just as the sky was turning the faintest gray-blue, only to be awoken by Maurenia, who was dressed, saddlebags in hand.

"Stregon's balls, woman, how do you do that so quietly?" Aelis said sourly, blinking against the light.

"Because I don't want to wake up a beautiful woman only to see her scrunch up her face like that. Also because you needed the sleep . . . and this would all be easier if you weren't getting in my way and trying to drag me back into bed."

The compliment softened the rest of it considerably. Aelis dragged herself up and threw on working clothes. They walked to the door of the tower hand in hand.

"It's not goodbye, Aelis. Just . . ."

"It can be, if it has to be," Aelis said, trying very hard to be the more mature one and hating it tremendously.

"But it isn't. Look, I wish there was some elvish saying I could give you, something about . . . oh, I don't fucking know, branches all leading back to the tree or rivers forking and then meeting again, but I don't know a damn thing about my father's people and I'd just be lying." Maurenia closed her eyes, took a deep breath. "I *do* love you, Aelis. But I have to go."

Aelis had never felt simultaneously the spreading of the warmth that came from hearing these longed-for words and the grief of her heart shattering. She would've preferred a slap in the face, really, but one didn't choose one's obstacles, only the reaction to them.

"This posting won't be permanent. I owe these people, and I will discharge that. Then I will go where the Lyceum and the service send me. I'm very afraid it's going to be somewhere *worse*, after all the enemies I made down there."

"You made a promise to free me. You kept it. Now it's my turn. I will see you again, Aelis Cairistiona de Lenti un Tirraval. I *will*. And I will carry you with me wherever it is I go." Maurenia smiled, and Aelis felt tears threatening her eyes. She hated crying, and she wasn't going to do it in front of Maurenia, no matter what. "I'll send letters with the post. I'll buy and train a raven or a pigeon or whatever to carry them . . . but I will see you again."

She reached up to touch the wet corner of Aelis's eye, but Aelis caught her hand and held it. They kissed, softly, tenderly, and then, with no more words, Maurenia turned down the ramp, mounted the gray gelding, and started him off without looking back.

Aelis wandered back into her tower, considering breakfast and finding herself not hungry, considering coffee but not wanting to take the time to make it. She let her tears fall then, hating every one of them. For how long, she wasn't sure, but long enough for someone to fill the door she'd left open.

"Warden," a young man's voice called tentatively. "We need you . . . Bruce was fixing his thatch and fell off the roof. Might've broke his arm."

Aelis wiped at her face without turning around. She wasn't going to show tears to one of her people. She reached for her shoulder belt, then her small medical kit.

"I'll be right there."

THE END
OF *ADVOCATE*, BOOK III OF THE WARDEN

ACKNOWLEDGMENTS

Like its predecessor, this book has my name on it but many hands made it real.

Thanks to Paul and everyone at J&N.

To Oliver, Jeff, Rima, and everyone else at Tor/Macmillan, thank you for your hard work. To Lindsey for bringing Aelis, and everyone else, to life in audio.

Thanks to the Editor Cats, Rose of Sharon Cassidy who has settled admirably into her job, and Miss Vee, who generally can't focus for more than a few minutes at a time, but whose efforts remain appreciated nonetheless.

If there were magical words, I would say them, but there aren't, so small and inadequate words like "thanks" or "love," for L.

ABOUT THE AUTHOR

Carroll McDorman

DANIEL M. FORD (he/him) is a native of Baltimore. He has an M.A. in
Irish literature from Boston College and an M.F.A. in creative writing from
George Mason University. He lives in Delaware and teaches at a college prep
high school in rural Maryland. When he isn't writing, he's reading, playing
RPGs, lifting weights, or mixing cocktails. His previous work includes *The
Warden*, *Necrobane*, the Paladin Trilogy, and the Jack Dixon novels.

danielmford.com
Twitter: @soundingline